From Hallie McCarthy's Diary:

January 1

A new year generally starts out with me writing a few inspiring lines about how I'm going to lose five pounds—let's be honest, it's ten—and pay off all my credit cards, and other high expectations like that. It's the same every January. But <u>this</u> year's going to be different.

Oh, I still want to lose those extra pounds, more than ever, but for a different reason.

<u>I want a husband. And eventually a family</u>.

And that means I need a plan. Being a goal-oriented person, I start by identifying what I'm after (MARRIAGE!) and then work out a logical procedure for getting it. Which, in this case, includes <u>looking good</u>. (Not that I look bad now, if I do say so myself. But I'm talking <u>really</u> good. Are you listening, thighs?) Because, as I've learned in advertising, <u>packaging counts</u>.

Unlike my friends Cassie and Jamie and Rita, I didn't get married right out of college. Not me. No, I wanted to kick some butt in the business world first. Make a name for myself. And I've done it. I've accomplished a <u>lot</u>, and I won't minimize my achievements, but now I've realized there's more to life than getting the Woman of the Year Award from the chamber of commerce.

So, last week I made <u>the</u> decision: <u>Marriage</u>!

Watch for DEBBIE MACOMBER'S
newest novel from MIRA Books
May 1998

Debbie loves to hear from her readers.
You can reach her at:
P.O. Box 1458, Port Orchard,
Washington 98366.

DEBBIE MACOMBER

This Matter of Marriage

MIRA BOOKS

MIRA

ISBN 1-55166-260-4

THIS MATTER OF MARRIAGE

Printed in U.S.A.

For Paula and Dianne
You know why

ACKNOWLEDGMENTS

I remember watching the Academy Awards and wondering just how long it would take for the award winner to spout off all the names of those who'd helped along the way. The list seemed endless. While I'm not an Academy Award winner—at least, not yet—I have my own list of people to thank, so please bear with me.

Thanks, first and foremost, to my husband, Wayne, who loved and believed in me enough to allow me to follow my dream. To my agent, Irene Goodman, who held my hand all through contract negotiations. To my best friend, Linda Lael Miller, who taught me everything I needed to know about power-shopping. And thanks to Susan Wiggs for our twice-a-month neurotic lunches.

No writer has been blessed with a better support team. Thank you, one and all.

Working with MIRA has been a writer's dream. Everything in life should be this much fun. Thank you, Paula, Dianne, Randall, Candy, KO, Stuart and Brian. I hope it was as good for you as it was for me.

One

Starting Now

January 1

A new year generally starts out with me writing a few inspiring lines about how I'm going to lose ~~five pounds~~—let's be honest, it's ten— and pay off all my credit cards and other high expectations like that. It's the same every January. But <u>this</u> year's going to be different. Oh, I still want to lose those extra pounds, more than ~~ever,~~ but for a different reason.

I want a husband. And eventually a family.

And that means I need a plan. Being a goal-oriented person, I usually begin by identifying what I'm after (MARRIAGE!!) and then I work out a logical procedure for getting it. Which, in this case, includes <u>looking good</u>. (Not that I look bad now, if I do say so myself. But I'm talking <u>really</u> good. Are you listening, thighs?) Because, as I've learned in advertising, <u>packaging counts.</u>

Putting all this into words is something of an eye-opener for me. I've come a long way from those college days when I refused to give in to what I called the "female escape route," like some of my friends. Cassie, Jamie, Rita and Jane all got married within six months of graduation, and as far as I could see, the only reason they did was because they found the real world more of a challenge than they'd anticipated, and used marriage as a cop-out.

Not me. Oh, no, marriage was much too conventional for me. I wanted to kick some butt in the business world first. Make a name for myself with my very own graphic arts firm. And I've done it! Now I feel like I've come full circle. I've accomplished a lot, and I won't minimize my achievements, but this Christmas I realized there's more to life than getting the Woman of the Year award from the Chamber of Commerce.

So, last week I made the decision: Marriage!

It's time to let a man into my life. Until now I've viewed relationships like…dessert. Nice occasionally, but not with every meal. My friends have been tossing potential husbands in my direction for years, and I've frustrated them again and again.

I'm too picky, that's what Rita says. Not true. I have my standards; every woman does. But my work's the reason I haven't married. I've poured my heart into making a success of Artistic License. For the past six years my focus, my talent and all my energy have been with the business. It's filled every waking minute.

Then, this Christmas it hit me. I want more. I suspect this has something to do with losing

Dad last June. Mom's still struggling, but then so are Julie and I. The holidays were really hard without him. Somehow, the celebration seemed empty and sad, and we were all kind of weepy thinking about the Christmas things he used to do—getting the tree every year and making a big deal out of hanging the decorations Julie and I made when we were kids. Reading the Nativity story on Christmas Eve. Putting on his Santa apron to carve the turkey. Things like that.

I'm so sorry Dad missed his granddaughter's first Christmas. I knew Julie's baby would help Mom through the grieving process, but I didn't expect little Ellen to have such a profound effect on me.

I've always thought of myself as the strong independent type. I haven't wanted a man around for fear I might be forced to admit I need someone. I don't know why I'm like this. (Then again, I'm not sure I want to know, either.) The point is, I feel differently now.

It started when Julie gave me the baby to rock. I swear my heart melted when I held her. In that moment I felt something I can only describe as maternal instinct, and I realized this is what I want. This is what's been missing from my life. A husband, a family.

With the right husband, I know I can have it all. Home, family and career. Plenty of women do it, and I can, too. Funny how a little thing like holding a baby can change a person's attitude. I'm ready. Past ready. Starting now, my life's taken an abrupt turn. What was vital a month ago has shifted to the back burner.

So, yes, I admit it.

I want a husband and children. Obviously, what I need first is the man. (I plan to do things in the right order!)

Mom always says that once I make up my mind I don't let anything stand in my way. I've set my goal, made my plans, and I figure I should find a husband in two, three months, tops. This time next year, I expect to be a married woman. (Maybe even a pregnant one!)

Just how difficult can it be?

Sweat rolled down Hallie McCarthy's forehead, dripping in her eyes and momentarily blurring her vision. Using the towel draped around her neck, she wiped her brow. Although she'd promised herself she wouldn't, Hallie glanced at the timer on the treadmill.

One minute left.

Sixty short seconds. She could endure that. With a renewed sense of purpose, she picked up her pace and waited impatiently for the buzzer.

The treadmill had all the bells and whistles, as it should, considering what she'd paid for it (plus the three designer running suits, color-coordinated with the treadmill). At the end of her workout a digital message would flash across the four-inch computer screen, complimenting her on a job well-done.

Donnalee had suggested she join a gym to meet men, and she would, Hallie told herself, once she was at her goal weight. But not now. She wasn't about to go prancing around a gym with thighs that resembled ham hocks. Which, she supposed, was something like cleaning her house before the cleaning lady arrived—but she'd done that, too.

Huffing, her heart feeling ready to explode, Hallie gripped the sides of the treadmill as the timer counted down those final seconds. This last minute was proving to be the longest of her life.

Needing a distraction to take her mind off the physical agony while she raced toward an imaginary finish line, Hallie turned to look out her living-room window at the luxury condominium next door.

Hey, she was getting a new neighbor. A moving van was parked in front and a crew of able-bodied men—*very* able-bodied, she noted appreciatively—unloaded its contents. A big truck that probably required a step stool to climb into was parked behind it. The license-plate frame was one of those customized ones. Squinting, she was able to make out the words: BIG TRUCK. BIG TOOLS. Hallie groaned aloud and rolled her eyes. Men and their egos! Two muscular guys wandered into her line of vision, and she wondered if one of those good-looking hunks might be her neighbor.

Willow Woods, the condominium complex where she'd moved six months earlier, had all but sold out. She'd speculated it wouldn't take long for the place next to hers to sell. Especially since it was a three-bedroom unit, the most spacious design available. Must be a family moving in. She was definitely cheered by the thought of having neighbors.

The timer went off, and the treadmill ground to a halt. Hallie heaved a sigh of relief and rubbed her sweat-drenched face with the towel. Her cheeks felt red and hot and her short curly hair was matted against her temples. Her old gray sweats—she didn't feel com-

fortable sweating in her new color-coordinated ones—
were loose around the waist. A promising sign. The
temptation to run into the bathroom and leap on the
scale was strong, but she'd made that mistake too often
and vowed she'd only weigh herself once a week.
Monday morning, bright and early—that was when
she'd do it.

She'd lost five pounds in twenty-one days. The first
two had fallen away easily, but the last three had been
like chiseling at a concrete block with a tablespoon.
She'd starved herself, exercised faithfully. She'd
counted fat grams, carbohydrates, calories and chocolate chips to little avail.

Her best friend, Donnalee Cooper, claimed Hallie
was putting too much stock in the physical, but Hallie
believed otherwise. It was that packaging thing again.
The men she knew based their reactions to women—
at least their initial reactions—on looks. It didn't matter
if the woman had a brain in her head as long as her
waist was tiny...and her other assets weren't. Of
course, attracting a man wasn't Hallie's *only* incentive
for becoming physically fit. She didn't exercise nearly
enough, had taken to skipping breakfast and was downing fast food on the run. Not a healthy life-style. Donnalee seemed unconvinced when Hallie explained this,
though, pointing out that she hadn't worried about her
health *before.*

Donnalee was single, although she'd had a brief disastrous marriage in her early twenties. To Hallie's
delight, when she'd shared her goal of finding a man
and marrying within the next twelve months, Donnalee
had decided to join forces with her. She said that she'd
never meant to wait this long to remarry, and like Hal-

lie, she wanted children. But Donnalee brought a different strategy to their marriage campaign.

"Just be yourself," she'd advised.

"Being myself hasn't attracted a whole lot of attention so far," Hallie complained. That, at least, shut her friend up. Dating opportunities had dwindled to a trickle in the last few years, but she was determined to improve the situation.

Hallie showered and changed clothes, then phoned her mother who lived across Puget Sound in Bremerton, on the Kitsap Peninsula. Hallie and her father had been close, both in personality and in appearance, but it was from her mother that she'd inherited her artistic talent. Despite her ability, Lucille McCarthy had never worked outside the home. It had always troubled Hallie that a woman so genuinely talented would be content to do little more than keep house. Not until she was an adult living on her own did she recognize her mother's contribution to the family. Over the months since her father's sudden death, Hallie had come to appreciate her mother's quiet strength. At Christmas, she'd encouraged her to take up oil painting, and Lucille had recently begun a class.

The conversation went well, with Lucille cheerfully describing the portrait she'd started to paint of a sleeping Ellen. Afterward, Hallie wrote her weekly grocery list, threw on a jacket and hurried out the door, eager to finish her Saturday-morning chores. It was when she climbed into her car that she saw her new neighbor. At least, she thought he was the one. He was tall and not as brawny as she'd thought at first glance. Solid, she decided. All shoulders, with good upper-body strength. Handsome, too, in an unobtrusive way. In other words, seeing him didn't make her heart beat faster—which was just as well, since he was obviously married with children.

He did have an interesting face, a lived-in face, and seemed the type of person she'd like to know. Not romantically, of course, but maybe as a friend. She turned her attention from him to the two kids at his side. A girl and boy, who were probably about eleven and nine. Great-looking kids. The girl waved, her smile wide and friendly.

Hallie waved back, inserted the key into the ignition and drove off.

The moving van was gone by the time she returned an hour or so later. The two kids were riding their bicycles when she pulled into her driveway.

The girl headed her way, long coltish legs pumping the bicycle pedals.

"Hi," she called. "My dad just moved next door." She stopped abruptly and hopped off the polished chrome bike.

"So I saw," Hallie said, leaning across the front seat and removing her bags of groceries.

"I'm Meagan. That's my brother, Kenny." She nodded toward the younger boy, and as if on cue, Kenny joined his sister.

"You got any kids?" Kenny asked hopefully.

"Sorry, no." She balanced both grocery bags in her arms.

Some of the enthusiasm left the boy's eyes. "Do you know anyone around here who does?"

"Unfortunately, I don't think there are any kids your age on this block." Most of the couples who'd moved into the complex were just starting out. Hallie suspected there'd be any number of children in the neighborhood within a few years, but not now.

"Here," Meagan said, tilting her bike onto the grass. "I can help you carry those in." She took one bag out of Hallie's hands.

"Thanks." Hallie was touched by her thoughtfulness and said so.

The girl beamed at the praise. "Mom says I'm a big help to her now that she and Dad are divorced."

Meagan's expression grew sad when she mentioned the divorce. Hallie's heart immediately went out to her—but she couldn't help musing that her new neighbor was available, after all. It was an automatic reaction, triggered by her newly activated husband-seeking instincts.

Hallie briefly recalled her first impressions of him and decided then and there that she wanted someone with a bit more...finesse. A guy who drove a truck with a license-plate holder advertising his big tools didn't overly impress her. It wasn't only that, either; she'd seen what the movers had carted into his house. Sports equipment. Boxes and boxes of it. There didn't seem to be anything this guy hadn't tried. From mountain climbing to kayaking to scuba diving.

Hallie led the way into the kitchen, where she dumped her sack on the countertop. Meagan carefully put hers beside it. "Thanks again, Meagan."

"Are you married?" the girl asked.

"Not yet." But there were visions of entwined wedding rings dancing around in her head. She had a prospect, too. A man she'd just met yesterday, as a matter of fact.

"Well, gotta go have lunch. See you next weekend," Meagan said, rushing for the front door.

As Hallie started to put the groceries away, she saw that the message light on her answering machine was blinking. Probably her mother again, or her sister, Julie,

calling to report on baby Ellen's latest adorable exploit.
But what if it was *him? Him* being the new loans officer at Keystone Bank. Hallie had gone in on Friday
afternoon to make her deposits and been introduced to
John Franklin.

The minute she'd laid eyes on him she realized he
was everything she sought in a husband. Tall, dark and
handsome. Friendly, polite and clearly intelligent. He
met all the basic criteria, including availability; she'd
noticed the absence of a wedding ring. He was close
to forty, she estimated, but that didn't disturb her. An
eleven-year gap didn't make much difference, not at
her age. She'd be thirty in April, three months from
now. Surely she'd be engaged by then.

Unfortunately the message wasn't from John. It was
from Donnalee, who sounded excited and asked Hallie
to phone the minute she walked in the door.

Hallie rang her back. "You called?"

"I've found the answer," Donnalee blurted.

"What's the question?" Hallie grumbled in response; she hadn't had lunch and was never at her best
on an empty stomach.

"Where do we meet the men of our dreams?"

"Hmm." Her friend certainly had her attention now.
"Where?"

"The answer's a bit complicated, so stay with me."

"Donnalee…"

"All I ask is that you hear me out. All right?"

Hallie muttered a reply. This dating thing had been
much easier in high school and college. Apparently
she'd lost the knack. Oh, there'd been a few romances
in the years since, most of them what you'd call short-
term. One had lasted the better part of six months, until
it, too, fizzled out. The fault, Hallie admitted, had been

her own. Gregg had complained about her long hours and her total commitment to Artistic License, and she'd told him that wasn't likely to change.

"I found an ad in the *Seattle Weekly* for a dating service," Donnalee announced.

Hallie groaned. As far as she was concerned, only people who were desperate resorted to dating services. She didn't even want to *think* about the kind of men who applied to meet women that way. "You're joking, right?"

"You promised you'd hear me out."

Hallie closed her eyes and prayed for patience. "Okay, okay. Tell me all about it and *then* I'll tell you I'm not interested."

"This is different."

"They use videos, right?"

"No," Donnalee said indignantly. "Would you kindly listen?"

"Sorry."

"You and I are successful businesswomen. Most men are intimidated by women like us."

Hallie wasn't convinced *that* was true, but didn't say so.

"In my case, I've been married once and it was a disaster."

"That was over thirteen years ago."

"Soon it'll be fifteen and then twenty, and my whole life will have passed me by. All because I made a stupid mistake when I was barely out of my teens. Hallie, I want a man in my life."

"The whole nine yards," Hallie added.

"Children, the house in the suburbs with a white picket fence. Cat, dog, family vacations. I can't believe

I've put it off this long! I'd probably still be putting it off if you hadn't come up with your plan.''

"You're saying you want me to contact a dating service, too?"

"Would you *listen*, darn it? First you have to apply and if you're accepted, you pay a hefty fee and they'll arrange for you to meet a suitable match. One on the same financial level as you, whose personality fits yours. The woman I talked to claims they're very selective and only take on a certain number of clients. If you're accepted, the company is committed to finding you a match."

"How hefty is the fee?" Hallie had recently forked over fifteen hundred bucks on exercise equipment. So much for paying off her credit cards.

Donnalee hesitated a moment. "Two grand."

"Two thousand dollars!"

"Yup."

"I damn well better get a date with Brad Pitt for that."

Donnalee laughed. "Brad wouldn't date someone as old as either of us."

Her friend's words were of little comfort. "You aren't serious, are you?" For that kind of money Hallie figured she could have liposuction and forget the treadmill and the dieting.

"Yup," Donnalee said with a hint of defiance. "I'm thirty-three. I don't have as much time as you. If this agency can help me find a decent man, then I'd consider the money well spent."

"You *are* serious."

"Just think of it as a shortcut."

Hallie still wasn't sold. "I haven't actually started looking yet." Using a dating service felt like waving a white flag before she'd even stepped onto the battle-field. Surrendering without so much as a token effort.

"What are you going to do, wear a sandwich board that says AVAILABLE in big black letters?" Donnalee asked.

"Don't be ridiculous."

"You've had your entire life to find a husband, and you haven't. What makes you think it's going to be different now?"

"Because I'm ready." This probably wasn't the time to remind her friend that she'd had relationships over the years, the most promising one with Gregg. While it was true that those relationships had grown fewer and fewer, and her social life had become rather dull, she'd barely noticed, working the hours she did. However, since the first of the year, she'd taken measures to correct that, delegating more responsibility to Bonnie Ellis, her assistant.

"And your being ready for marriage changes everything?" Donnalee sounded skeptical. She sounded skeptical a little too often, in Hallie's opinion.

"There's a man I'm interested in right now," Hallie confessed, thinking of John Franklin.

"Really? Who?"

She should've guessed Donnalee would demand details.

"A banker," she answered with some reluctance. "He's the new loans officer at the Kent branch of Keystone Bank. He transferred this week from the downtown Seattle branch. We met Friday, if you must know. I liked him immediately and he liked me. He's really good-looking. Sensitive, too."

"Good-looking and sensitive," Donnalee repeated.

"Single good-looking men are hard to find," Hallie

insisted, wondering at her friend's slightly sarcastic tone.

"That's because the majority of them have boyfriends."

Hallie paused. John? Was it possible? "Do you know John Franklin?" Since Donnalee managed a mortgage company, she was familiar with many bankers in the area.

"I know *of* him."

Hallie's suspicions mounted. "What do you mean?"

"John Franklin's the perfect reason you need the services of Dateline."

"Oh?" Her confidence was shaken.

"You're right," Donnalee continued. "John's sensitive, friendly, personable and handsome as sin. He also happens to be gay."

Hallie's spirits sank to the level of bedrock. John Franklin. Hmm. With some men it was obvious and with others...well, with others, it wasn't.

"So, are you going to join Dateline?" Donnalee asked.

"Two thousand dollars?"

"Consider it cheap since the men are screened."

"If Brad Pitt's out, then for that kind of money they'd better come up with royalty."

"If they do, kid, I've got first dibs," Donnalee said with a laugh.

"I'll look into Dateline, but I'm not making any promises."

"Just call and they'll mail you a brochure. Phone me once you've read it over. Promise?"

"Okay, okay," Hallie mumbled, and wrote down the

number. She replaced the telephone receiver and shook her head. Who'd ever have thought this matter of marriage could be so complicated?

Two

Breaking Up Is Hard To Do

Steve Marris's day wasn't going well. A parts shipment was lost somewhere in the Midwest, his secretary
had quit without notice, and he suspected his ex-wife
was dating again. The parts shipment would eventually
be found and he could hire another secretary, but the
news about Mary Lynn was harder to take.

He poured himself a cup of coffee and noted that
it'd been at least a month since anyone had bothered
to clean the glass pot. He'd make damn sure his next
secretary didn't come with an attitude. This last one
had refused to make coffee, claiming she'd been hired
for her secretarial skills—not that they'd been so impressive. And she'd never understood that in *his* shop,
everybody pitched in. No, he was well rid of her.

He sipped the hot liquid and grimaced. Todd Stafford must have put on this pot. His production manager
made the world's worst coffee. Steve dumped it and
rinsed his mug, then sat down at his desk, sorting
through the papers amassed there until he found the
invoice he needed.

Todd opened the door. "You going to sit in here all
day and fume about Danielle quitting?"

Todd was talking about their recently departed secretary. "Naw, we're better off without her."

Todd came into the office, reached for a coffee mug and filled it. He pulled out Danielle's chair and plopped himself down, propping his feet on the desk. "If it isn't Danielle walking out, then my guess is you're sulking about Mary Lynn."

His friend knew him too well. "I heard she's dating again."

"Heard? Who from?"

"Kenny," Steve admitted reluctantly.

"You're grilling your kids for information about your ex-wife?"

"I know better than that." Steve experienced a twinge of guilt. He hadn't *intentionally* asked his nine-year-old if his mother was dating. Kenny had been talking about joining a softball team in the spring, all excited about playing shortstop. He'd wanted his mother to toss him a few balls, he'd told Steve, but she couldn't because she was getting ready for a date. The kid had Steve's full attention at that point. It hadn't taken much to get Kenny to tell him Mary Lynn was seeing Kip somebody or other.

What the hell kind of name was Kip, anyway? Sounded like a guy who traipsed around in ballet slippers.

"So, what'd you find out?"

Steve ignored the question. He didn't like *thinking* about Mary Lynn dating another man, let alone talking about it. What had happened between them was painful even now, a full year after their divorce. An idea struck him suddenly, and he marveled at the genius of it. "I wonder if Mary Lynn might consider filling in here at the office until I can hire another secretary."

"She hates it here," Todd muttered. He sipped his coffee, seeming to savor every drop. "You know that."

What his friend said was true, but Steve welcomed the opportunity to spend time with her. She might even tell him about Kip. "It couldn't hurt to ask," he returned, sorry now that he'd said anything to Todd.

"You're divorced."

"Thanks, I guess I must've forgotten." Steve glared at him, hoping his sarcasm hit its mark.

"It's time to move on, old buddy. Mary Lynn has."

Steve rose abruptly from his chair. "Shouldn't you get to work?"

"All right, so I touched a raw nerve. No reason to bite my head off." Todd hurried back to the shop, and Steve swallowed his irritation. Damn it, he still loved Mary Lynn. No one had told him how painful this divorce business would be.

They'd been married twelve years and fool that he was, Steve had assumed they were happy. Then, one day out of the blue, Mary Lynn had started crying. When he'd tried to find out what was wrong, she couldn't say—except that she was unhappy. They'd married too young, she'd missed out on all the fun, all the carefree years, and now here she was, stuck with a husband, kids, responsibilities. Steve tried to understand her concerns, but everything he said and did only made matters worse. The thing that really got him was her claim that she'd never had her own bedroom. As it turned out, that was more important than he'd realized, because she asked him to move out of theirs shortly afterward.

Steve had called her bluff, firmly believing it *was* a bluff. He'd voluntarily moved out of the house, thinking that would help her "find herself," something she apparently couldn't do with him there. She needed to make contact with her "inner child," become "empowered" or some other such garbage. Okay, maybe he wasn't the most sensitive man in the world. She became incensed when he suggested she was watching too many of those daytime talk shows. Then, a month or so after he'd left, Mary Lynn shocked him by asking for a divorce. Before he could fully comprehend what was happening, they'd each hired lawyers and were soon standing in front of a judge.

By that time, with attorneys involved, things had gotten heated, and he and Mary Lynn were more at odds than ever. It'd taken over a year to even start repairing the damage the attorneys and courts had done. He was sick of living apart from his family. He wanted his wife back.

Never mind what Todd had said—he *would* ask Mary Lynn to fill in for Danielle. Just until he could hire another secretary. Just until he could convince her that being apart was pure insanity.

Feeling pleased with himself, he reached for the phone. Mary Lynn answered on the third ring. "Hello," she murmured groggily.

She never had been much of a morning person. "Hi. It's Steve."

"Steve. Good grief, what time is it?"

"Nine."

"Already?"

He could hear her rustling the sheets in an effort to sit up. During their marriage, he'd loved waking her, having her cuddle against him all soft and warm and feminine, smelling of some exotic flower. Their best loving had been in the mornings.

"What's wrong?" she asked, and yawned loudly.

"Nothing. Well, my secretary quit."

She went very quiet, and he could almost hear her resentment over the telephone line. "I don't type, Steve, you know that."

After all those years together, Mary Lynn could read him like a book. He took a certain perverse pride in that. "I need someone to fill in for a few days until I can hire a new secretary."

"What about getting a temporary?"

"Sure, I could call an agency and they'd send someone out, but I'd rather give you the money."

"I've got school. It isn't easy for me attending classes all afternoon plus keeping up with the kids and the house, you know."

"I realize that, but it'd help me out considerably if you came in for a couple of days, just in the mornings. That's all I'm asking." Since paying for her education had been part of the settlement, he was well aware of her schedule.

"You always say that!" she snapped.

"What?" This conversation was quickly taking on the same tone as their arguments before the divorce. He'd say or do something that irritated her, and for the life of him, he wouldn't understand what he'd done.

"You *say* you realize how difficult my schedule is. You don't."

"I do, honest."

"If you did, you'd never ask me to pitch in while you take your own sweet time finding a new secretary. I know you, Steve Marris. Two days'll become two weeks and I won't be able to keep up with my classes. That's what you really want, whether you know it or not. You're trying to sabotage my schoolwork."

Steve choked back an argument. "I understand how

important your classes are," he said. And he did. What he failed to understand was why her getting an education precluded being married to him. Not only that, he wondered what she intended to do with a major in art history. Get a job in some museum, he supposed—if there were any jobs to be had. But he certainly couldn't say that to her.

"Do you really, Steve?"

"Yes," he said, still struggling to show his respect for her efforts. "It's just that I thought since your classes don't start until one, you might be willing to help out, but if you can't, you can't."

She hesitated and he closed in for the kill.

"All I need is a couple of hours in the morning. And like I said, if you can't do it, that's fine. No hard feelings."

"Do you realize how much reading I have, how many assignments?"

"You're right, I never should have asked. I guess that's been the problem all along, hasn't it?"

"Yes," she agreed sharply. Then there was a pause. And a sigh. "I guess I could fill in for a couple of days, but no longer. I want to make that perfectly clear. Two days and not a minute longer, understand?"

"Perfectly." Steve wanted to leap up and click his heels in the air. Calling Mary Lynn had been one of his better ideas. He was confident it wouldn't take long to make her forget all about this other guy.

"I hope you don't want me there before eight?"

He let the question slide. "You're wearing the pink nightie, aren't you?"

"Steve!"

"Aren't you?" His voice grew husky despite his attempts to keep it even. Some of their best sex had come after the divorce. It was so crazy. Mary Lynn wanted him out of the house but continued to welcome him in her bed. Not that he was complaining.

"Yes, I'm wearing your favorite nightie," she whispered, her voice low and sexy.

Slowly his eyes drifted shut. "I'm coming over."

"Steve, no. I can't. We can't."

"Why not?"

"Well, because we shouldn't."

Steve was instantly suspicious, convinced her decision had something to do with what Kenny had told him. "Why?"

"We're divorced, remember?"

"It hasn't stopped us before. I could be at the house in fifteen minutes. You want me there, otherwise you'd never have told me about the pink nightie."

Mary Lynn giggled, then altered her tone. "Steve, no, I mean it," she said solemnly. "We've been divorced for a year now. We shouldn't be sleeping together anymore."

His jaw tightened. "When did you make that decision?"

"Since the last time."

He exhaled, his patience fading fast. He did a quick review of their last rendezvous. It'd been late morning, before her classes and while the kids were in school. He'd invented some excuse to stop over. Mary Lynn knew what he wanted, and from the gleam in her eye and the eager way she'd led him into the bedroom, she'd wanted the same thing.

He couldn't imagine what had changed, other than her dating this Kip character. Unfortunately he couldn't ask her about it or let on that he knew. The last thing he wanted was to put his children in the middle, between two squabbling parents, something he'd seen other divorced couples do all too often. The divorce had been hard enough on Meagan and Kenny without complicating the situation. So their private lives, his and Mary Lynn's, would stay that way—private. At least as far as the kids were concerned.

"What happened to change your mind about us sleeping together?" he asked, instead.

Mary Lynn sighed. "Nothing. Everything. We have to break this off. It's over for us, Steve."

Steve didn't say anything. He knew his wife—ex-wife—well enough not to argue. Something else he knew about Mary Lynn—she possessed a healthy sexual appetite. As strong as his own.

"You'll be here in the morning, then?" he said, just to be sure.

"I suppose. But remember I agreed to two days, and two days only."

"Bring along the pink nightie."

"Steve!"

"Sorry," he murmured, but he wasn't.

He hung up the phone a few moments later, his mood greatly improved.

The rest of his day was relatively smooth. The transport company located the lost shipment in Albuquerque. The parts were guaranteed to be delivered within the next forty-eight hours. The majority of his orders came from a major aircraft builder in the area, for whom he supplied engine mounts, but he also did lathe work, blanchard grinding and other steel-fabrication work for a number of customers. His company was growing, taking on larger and larger orders, and he employed almost a dozen people now.

On the drive home that afternoon, Steve's gaze fell

on his hands—clean hands—gripping the steering wheel. He used to have grease under his fingernails, and that had always bothered Mary Lynn. The irony didn't escape him. The last year and a half, he'd spent the majority of his time in the office and rarely dirtied his hands. She'd always wanted him to have a white-collar job; when he was finally able to grant her wish she wanted him out of her life. Damn it all, the machine shop had been good to them—it had bought her house, supported the kids, paid for her education. A little grime around his fingernails seemed a small inconvenience.

The January drizzle grew heavier, and the truck's windshield wipers beat against the glass, slapping the rain from side to side with annoying regularity. He exited the freeway and headed down the west hill toward Kent. He hadn't been keen to buy the condominium. If he'd had a choice, he'd be moving back in with his family, but it was going to take longer than he'd first thought for that to happen.

He probably wouldn't have moved into this complex if he hadn't grown tired of apartment living. A small apartment was no place for kids, and Meagan and Kenny spent almost every weekend with him.

He would have preferred a real house but living on his own, he didn't want the bother that went along with it. The condo was a decent compromise. A friend who sold real estate had convinced him it was a good investment. In addition, the builders were offering an attractive buyer-incentive program. The condo was just as nice as the house Mary Lynn and the kids lived in. Not quite as big, but that was okay. The kids liked it, and they'd managed to make friends with his next-door neighbor in short order too, he mused, as he switched off his windshield wipers. The rain had tapered off to almost nothing.

Steve hadn't met Hallie yet—Meagan had told him her name. From what he'd seen of her, she was an exercise freak. His kitchen window overlooked her living room, and she had a treadmill set up there, alongside one of those stair-stepping machines. Every time he caught a glimpse of her she was working out. She didn't seem to be enjoying herself, either.

Steve turned into the Willow Woods complex and stopped in front of the two rows of mailboxes aligned at the entrance. It wasn't until he climbed out of the truck that he saw her. Hallie stood in front of her mailbox studying a large envelope as if she wasn't sure what to do with it.

"Howdy, neighbor," he greeted her, inserting the key into his mailbox.

Startled, she looked up. "Hello."

"Steve Marris." He thrust out his hand. "I moved in next door this past weekend."

She blinked a couple of times. "You're Meagan and Kenny's dad."

"That's me."

"Hallie McCarthy." She placed her hand in his. "Nice to meet you."

"Same here."

"You've got two terrific kids."

"Thanks," he said, and smiled. He felt that way, too.

With a nervous motion, Hallie glanced down at the envelope she still held, then shoved it into her purse. "Well, uh, Steve, I have to go. I'm sure we'll be seeing each other again."

Steve had caught the logo on the envelope. Dateline.

He'd heard plenty about the pricey exclusive dating service. Shortly after the divorce, a well-meaning friend had tried to talk him into signing up, but he'd recoiled at the idea of paying two thousand bucks for a date. He'd have to be a whole lot more desperate than he was now before he'd even consider it.

Hallie raised her head just then. "I... A friend suggested I write for information," she blurted. Her cheeks had turned a bright shade of pink. "I'd never..." She paused, squared her shoulders and gave him a smile that was decidedly forced. "I want you to know I don't need any help finding a man." Head high, with a dignity Princess Diana would have envied, Hallie McCarthy walked to her car. However, the speed with which she drove off kind of spoiled the effect.

Watching her leave, Steve slowly shook his head. Maybe he should steer the kids away from her. She seemed nice enough, but a little on the weird side.

Three

Seven Down, Three To Go

A rare burst of February sunshine showered Puget Sound, and after weeks of being cooped up inside for her daily exercise routine, Hallie decided to take advantage of this respite from the rain. She donned one of the three coordinated running outfits she'd purchased; it was a lovely teal green with a hot pink racing stripe up the outside of the legs and a geometrical design decorating the zippered jacket. If nothing else, Hallie knew she looked great—and she felt great. Seven of those ten unwanted pounds had vanished. Not without considerable effort, however.

She wasn't entirely confident that those pounds were gone for good. Were they hiding around the corner, waiting for her to lower her guard? One day away from the treadmill or succumbing to the temptation of a chocolate-chip cookie and they'd be back. Which was why she'd been so rigorous about her diet and exercise regimen. Three pounds to go, and she'd weigh the same as she had at her high-school graduation, more years ago than she cared to remember.

Goal weight. What perfectly lovely words they were. She hoped she'd manage to achieve it before Valentine's Day. She'd set the target date back in January, giving herself ample time to reach her physical best. Already she'd let a few select friends—the ones who'd wanted to line her up with their single brothers, unattached male acquaintances and recently divorced colleagues—know she was in the market for a meaningful long-term relationship. She hadn't heard back yet, but it was still early.

She opened the front door and stepped into the welcome sunshine. It didn't take long to realize she wasn't the only one outside enjoying the warmth.

Her next-door neighbor and his son were playing catch in the front yard. She was afraid she'd started off on the wrong foot with Steve Marris, but wasn't sure how to correct that. Of all the rotten luck for him to see the envelope from Dateline! Her mistake had been not keeping her mouth shut. Oh, no, that would have been too easy. *She* had to go and blurt out some stupid, embarrassing remark. She wanted to groan every time she thought of it.

"Hi, Hallie."

Steve's daughter raced over to her. With no other kids around her age, Hallie thought, Meagan must get restless spending weekends with her father.

"Howdy, kiddo. What're you up to?"

"Nothing," she said in a bored voice. "Dad's teaching Kenny how to be a great shortstop. I don't like baseball much."

"Me, neither," Hallie said. It wasn't that she disliked sports; she just didn't understand the big attraction. A bunch of guys racing around a field or across some ice, all chasing a ball or whatever—what was the point?

Hallie raised her hands above her head and slowly

exhaled before bending forward and touching her fingertips to the walkway. She wasn't sure of the reason for this, but she'd seen runners do it before a race, and she supposed they knew what they were doing. Warming up or something.

After a month on the treadmill, averaging two miles a day on a preset course that simulated a run on hilly terrain, Hallie thought she was ready for one real-life mile. From her car speedometer, she knew it was exactly half a mile to the entrance of Willow Woods. She figured she should be able to run there and back without a problem. Actually she hoped she wouldn't work up too much of a sweat, fearing it would leave marks on her new running suit.

"What are you doing now?" Meagan asked, watching her go through a series of bends and stretches.

"Getting ready to run."

"You run?" The kid seemed downright impressed.

"Sure."

"How far?"

"A mile." That was as much as she wanted to tackle her first time out. If it went well, she might consider longer distances later.

"Can I come, too?"

"If it's all right with your dad." Hallie shook her arms, then placed her hands on her hips while she rotated her head.

Meagan quickly ditched her bike on Hallie's lawn and raced toward her brother and father.

Hallie felt almost smug. Watching "Wild World of Sports" with Gregg had taught her something, after all. Or was that "Wide World of Sports"? She heard Meagan hurriedly ask permission and felt Steve's scrutiny before he agreed.

"Dad said I can," Meagan shouted, racing back.

In deference to Meagan, Hallie set a slow rhythmic pace as she started down the road. Meagan picked up the tempo as they rounded the first corner. Within minutes, Hallie became winded. That was understandable, she told herself, since they were running uphill. By the end of the third block, she felt the strain.

"It isn't a race," Hallie gasped when she found the oxygen to speak.

"Oh, am I going too fast for you? Sorry." Meagan immediately slowed down.

An eternity passed before the brick-walled entrance came into view. "I...think I'm...wearing the wrong... kind...of shoes," Hallie panted. She stopped, braced her hands on her knees and greedily sucked in as much air as her aching lungs would allow.

There wasn't a damn thing wrong with her shoes, and Hallie knew it.

"You okay?" Meagan looked worried.

"Fine...I feel great."

"Can you make it back? Do you want me to run and get my dad?"

Hallie wasn't about to let Steve Marris see her like this. She straightened and, with effort, managed to smile and act as if nothing was amiss. The burning sensation in her lungs made it nearly impossible to breathe normally. The good news was that the trek back was downhill. The bad news was that she was half a mile from home with an eleven-year-old kid who could run circles around her.

"I'm sure my dad wouldn't mind. He's real understanding."

Hallie lied through her teeth. "I'll be fine, no problem."

"You're sure?"

"Positive." Leave it to a kid to humiliate her. As for not sweating, that was a lost cause. Perspiration poured out of her, soaking her hair, beading her upper lip and forehead.

She made a respectable showing on the way back, jogging past her neighbor and his son toward her front porch. She collapsed on the top step and tried to look as if she'd been enjoying herself, which was something of a trick considering she felt like a candidate for CPR.

"Aren't you going to cool down?" Meagan asked.

"I thought I'd take a shower."

"Dad says you're supposed to walk after a run and give your body a chance to catch up with itself." Meagan strolled about, and Hallie joined her, soon discovering that, yes, this part of her workout she could handle. A cool breeze refreshed her, and after a couple of minutes her heart settled back into place.

After thanking Meagan for the company, Hallie turned to enter the house and saw a familiar car round the corner. Donnalee. Pleased to see her, Hallie waved. Both women led busy lives, and although they talked on the phone practically every day, they weren't able to get together nearly as often as they would have liked.

Donnalee was tall and svelte, a striking woman with thick shoulder-length auburn hair. She unfolded her long legs from the car and stood, wearing her elegance naturally, as much a part of her as her soft Southern drawl. They'd met through a mutual friend five years earlier and quickly become friends themselves. Their friendship had grown close; Hallie had much more in common with Donnalee—especially when it came to attitudes and values—than with her college friends. Most of them had married, and some were already on second husbands—while Hallie had yet to find a first. And she wanted her husband to be her first *and* last. She wanted a marriage like her parents'.

As professional businesswomen, Donnalee and Hallie shared a great many similar experiences. Over the past couple of years they'd become a support system for each other. If Hallie was having trouble with an employee or a customer or just about anything else, it was Donnalee she talked to. If Donnalee had a problem, it was Hallie she phoned. That they should both feel a need, at the same time, to change the focus of their lives didn't surprise Hallie. Their thoughts often followed the same paths. They read the same books, enjoyed the same movies, had many of the same tastes. In fact, two years earlier they'd gone shopping separately and purchased the same pair of shoes. The only difference was the color.

Hallie was a personable sort, and she'd had a lot of friends from the time she was in kindergarten, but she laughed more with Donnalee than she ever had with anyone. Laughed and cried. Donnalee was that kind of soul friend. That kind of real friend.

"Did you call them?" Donnalee asked.

"You know I did." Hallie opened her front door and led the way into the kitchen. She might have lacked culinary skills—she was the first to admit it—but she compensated for that with her artistic flair. The room was bright and cheery, decorated in yellow and white with ivy stenciled along the top of the walls. Hallie removed a plastic bottle of springwater from the refrigerator and poured herself a glass. Her throat felt parched.

Donnalee pulled out a stool at the kitchen counter and declined Hallie's offer of water with a quick shake of her head. "What'd you think?"

"About the brochure?" Hallie decided to break the news quickly, before Donnalee could talk her into signing up. "I'm not going with Dateline."

Donnalee didn't bother to hide her disappointment. "You haven't talked to them, have you? Because if you had, you'd realize that this is the only practical way to break into the marriage market these days. It isn't like when we were in college, with eligible men in every direction."

"I know that, but I want to try it by myself first." Two thousand bucks wasn't anything to sneeze at, and Hallie figured the least she could do was try to meet someone on her own before resorting to spending big bucks. Besides, Donnalee made more money than she did; she could afford Dateline. Hallie's plan was to give it her best shot and wait to see what happened before maxing out her American Express card.

"I called Rita," Hallie confessed. Rita was the mutual friend who'd introduced Hallie to Donnalee. She had a reputation for being both unpredictable and romantic, and she wasn't above arranging dates for her friends.

Looking mildly worried, Donnalee leaned forward. "You didn't tell her I went to Dateline, did you?"

"No, don't worry. That's our little secret. All I said was that I had sort of an awakening this Christmas and decided it's time I committed myself to a long-term relationship." She smiled at the memory of their colleague's reaction. "Rita has this theory about my sudden desire to meet a man. She thinks it has to do with losing my dad, so she says I might end up in a situation I'll regret." Hallie shrugged comically. "After all these years of her pushing me to date one man or another, I would've figured she'd be pleased to know I was serious about getting married.'' Hallie paused, remembering the conversation. "When I told her I was ready for a family, she suggested I find myself a guy with good genes, get myself pregnant and dump him.''

"Rita said that?''

Hallie nodded. "Awful, huh?'' She liked Rita, made an effort to keep in touch, but they were basically very different kinds of people. For instance, Rita prided herself on saying the most outrageous things.

"I guess that's an idea if all you want is to have a child,'' Donnalee said hesitantly.

"Which I'm not. I'd also like a husband. I'm no fool—I watched my sister with Ellen and I don't know how she managed. A newborn demanded every minute of her time, even with Jason and Mom and me all helping. Fortunately for her, Jason's one of those really involved fathers. I don't know how *any* woman can manage alone. It's more than I want to attempt.''

"Me, too,'' Donnalee agreed, her drawl more noticeable than usual. Donnalee had moved from Georgia when she was thirteen, but had never quite lost the accent. Unexpectedly she grinned. "Can you imagine us as mothers?''

"Yes,'' Hallie said, although it seemed a stretch. She wondered if other women their age went through this. If so, it wasn't a subject her single friends discussed often or frankly. Many were like Donnalee, divorced and gun-shy. Hallie didn't have that excuse.

"Guess what? Dateline called me yesterday,'' Donnalee said, avoiding eye contact. She fiddled with the leather strap of her purse, opening and closing the zipper, a sure sign she was nervous. "They came up with a match for me." She darted a look in Hallie's direction.

"Already?" Hallie hated to say it, but she was impressed.

"They faxed over the pertinent information and asked me to review it and call back. So I did. Then Sanford phoned me an hour later and I'm meeting him for dinner this evening."

"Sanford?"

"I know. The picture of a stuffy conservative type immediately comes to mind, doesn't it, but then we spoke and..."

"And?" Hallie prodded when her friend didn't continue.

"He seems, I don't know, ideal."

"Ideal?" Dateline was beginning to sound better every minute.

"I'm frightened, Hallie. I felt the same way about Larry when I first met him, but what the hell did I know? I was nineteen and away from my family for the first time. I probably would've welcomed attention from a serial killer."

Donnalee didn't mention her ex very often. He'd dumped her for another woman after their first year of marriage. Donnalee's self-esteem had been shattered and her ego left in shreds. It'd taken a decade to regroup, and even then Hallie wasn't sure some of the damage wasn't permanent. She could appreciate her friend's fears and said so.

"But it's different this time," Hallie assured her. "You're not a kid governed by hormones."

"No, I'm thirty-three and governed by hormones."

They both laughed, and then Donnalee took a deep

breath. "Okay. Sanford's thirty-six and an insurance company executive. No priors."

"You mean he doesn't have a police record?" Hallie certainly hoped not!

"Means he's never been married. It's Dateline lingo."

"Oh." So the outfit even had a specialized vocabulary. Interesting. Or maybe not.

"We couldn't stop talking," Donnalee went on. "Sanford felt the way I did. We both signed up for Dateline the same week. He was just as nervous as I was about doing it. We were at work and we talked for more than half an hour. You know, he put me at ease right off and he said I did the same for him. It was as if we'd known each other all our lives. He loves Tex-Mex food, the same as me. He lives on a houseboat, which I've always thought of as wildly romantic. He'll watch anything Emma Thompson's in and reads Steve Martini novels. Can you believe it? I know this is all surface stuff, but it helps to know we're compatible. And at least we have lots of things to discuss." She broke into a radiant smile. "He was just as surprised and pleased after talking to me. We had trouble saying goodbye."

"He lives on a houseboat?" This guy was beginning to appeal to Hallie, too. Maybe if it didn't work out, Donnalee would consider introducing her.

"Now do you see why I'm a nervous wreck?"

Hallie nodded. She wouldn't be any less nervous herself.

"He sounds too good to be true," Donnalee moaned. "The minute I meet him, it'll be over."

"You don't know that." Hallie tried to sound confident, but she shared her friend's fears. There had to be a flaw in this guy somewhere. People weren't always what they seemed, and it was often the small undetectable-to-the-naked-eye character defects that threw her.

"At first I wondered why someone this successful and charming hadn't been married," she continued, as if thinking out loud, "but his letter explains all that." At Hallie's questioning look, she added, "Dateline enclosed a letter he'd written to introduce himself. He's been waiting to marry because he wanted to pay off his college loans. Financial security is important to him. I respect that. Dateline makes it a policy to check their clients' credit records. It's part of the agreement before your application's accepted."

Hallie knew immediately that the minute Dateline got hold of her credit card statements, she was headed for the reject pile.

She was about to say as much when the phone rang. Hallie reached for the receiver and through her kitchen window caught a glimpse of Steve Marris with his son. He was showing Kenny how to hold a softball.

"Hello."

"I hope you appreciate this," Rita said without preamble.

"Appreciate what?"

"I found you a potential husband," Rita announced. "Are you interested in meeting him?"

Four

First There Was Paul, Then George...

Steve glanced at his watch again, although he knew it'd been maybe five minutes since the last time he'd looked. He was wrong. It was three minutes. Almost five o'clock Sunday afternoon and Mary Lynn was late picking up the kids, which could mean only one thing.

She was with this faceless, spineless Kip character.

Steve had gotten his ex-wife to admit she was dating again. That was the reason she'd cut him off physically, although she'd been reluctant to admit it. Probably wouldn't have, if he hadn't cornered her. It left him wondering whether she was sleeping with Kip, but for reasons having to do with his sanity, he didn't pursue the thought. If she was, he didn't want to know.

As for his idea about using Mary Lynn as a replacement secretary, it didn't turn out to be so brilliant, after all. Mary Lynn was ten times worse in the office than Danielle had ever been. He knew she wasn't much good around a computer terminal, but he hadn't realized she didn't know how to answer a phone. Another few days with her and he'd be out of business. She'd filed invoices, instead of mailing them, and managed to insult one of his biggest accounts. It didn't take

Steve long to recognize his mistake. He quickly hired a new secretary, wrote Mary Lynn a generous check for her trouble and took her to lunch. While still in her good graces, he followed her home, thinking—despite her telling him the sex had to stop—that they'd head for the bedroom the way they normally did when he dropped by in the middle of the day.

But she'd meant it when she'd said no sex. And she'd also told him she was seeing Kip.

Once he'd persuaded her to confess she was dating again, he couldn't shut her up. She'd met Kip in a bookstore, she told him, smiling at the memory. Steve knew his ex, and she'd never been a reader, which was probably a detriment when it came to school. He couldn't imagine her buying books for pleasure, something she considered a waste of money. It was clear that her sudden interest in them had nothing to do with enjoyment. Mary Lynn had been looking to meet eligible men. Steve had heard that the singles scene had moved out of the bars and into the bookstores; he supposed this proved it.

Although she'd been more than willing to tell him about meeting the new love of her life, Mary Lynn had kept quiet about what they did together. Curious he might be, but Steve refused to grill his children about their mother's activities. His gaze shifted to the two kids. Meagan and Kenny were curled up in front of the television watching a Disney video. Neither seemed to notice or care that their mother was late.

He stared out his living-room window. His neighbor was outside vacuuming her car, and he smiled, remembering her embarrassment when she realized he knew she'd been talking to Dateline. So Hallie McCarthy was on the prowl. He wished her well. As far as he could see, she shouldn't have much of a problem finding a husband. She was actually kinda cute. Petite with dark brown hair that she wore in short curls. She had a nice face, and she seemed friendly, approachable. Certainly Meagan had taken to her right away. Hallie was just fine in the figure department, too.

He wasn't sure where she worked, but it must be in an office. They'd crossed paths a couple of times in the mornings, and she always maintained a professional appearance. He guessed her to be in her mid to late twenties. Possibly thirty, but he doubted it.

If he had any interest in dating, which he didn't, Steve would be more attracted to her friend. Now *there* was a looker. He'd been outside, horsing around with Kenny, when she'd arrived, and he'd practically dropped the ball. The woman was all legs. They went on and on. Shapely legs with a body to match. But Mary Lynn was beautiful, too. With his thoughts back on his ex-wife, Steve moved away from the window.

"Your mother's late," he said, hoping he sounded casual and unconcerned.

"Kip's taking her to a wine-tasting party," Meagan murmured. Her eyes grew huge, as if she'd said something she shouldn't.

"It's okay. Your mother told me she was dating Kip." Steve didn't want his children worrying about what they did or didn't say.

"She told you about Kip?" This seemed to surprise his daughter.

"Yeah." He sat down between the two kids on the couch and draped his arms around their shoulders. "I bet it's a little weird to have your mother dating again, isn't it?" If he was upset about Kip, then it made sense his kids would be, too. He wanted to reassure them that, no matter what happened, they could always count on him.

"Not really," Kenny said, not taking his eyes from the television screen. "She's gone out lots before."

She has? This was news to Steve.

"First there was Paul, then George."

What about Ringo? Steve scowled.

"None of them lasted very long," Meagan supplied.

"And Kip?" Steve wanted to jerk the words away the moment he uttered them.

"Mom really likes Kip," Kenny said.

"How do *you* feel about him?" Again this was a question that bordered on the forbidden, but Steve couldn't keep himself from asking. This was his wife's—all right, ex-wife's—boyfriend they were talking about, and ultimately that involved his children.

"Kip's okay," Kenny responded with a shrug. "But he doesn't know much about baseball."

That bit of information cheered Steve considerably. Kip had taken Mary Lynn to a wine-tasting party. Steve liked wine, too, but he preferred drinking it to spitting it out—wasn't that what they did at wine-tastings? Not once in their twelve-year marriage had he thought of taking Mary Lynn to something like that. On the other hand, she'd never told him such affairs interested her. One thing was certain, he'd spit wine if it'd help win back his ex-wife.

Steve heard a car door slam and leapt up, racing toward the front door. Mary Lynn was climbing out of her van, and it struck him how happy she looked. Some of that joy faded when she saw him. The words to inform her that she was late died on the tip of his tongue. Mary Lynn could tell time as well as he could. She knew she was late, and reminding her would only serve to widen the rift between them. He wanted to build bridges, not tear them down.

"Did you have a nice afternoon?" he asked, pretending he didn't know she'd been with Kip.

"Wonderful. How about you?"

"Great. Kenny's going to make a helluva short-stop."

Mary Lynn grinned. "Like father, like son." She glanced past him to the condo. Kenny and Meagan were at the door. "You ready, kids?"

"Why don't you come inside?" Steve invited. "You haven't seen the place since I decorated, have you?"

Mary Lynn snickered. "I don't call moving the dirty-clothes hamper out of the living room decorating."

"Hey, I've got a real sofa and chair now. And a dining-room set."

"I heard, and I applaud you for replacing the patio furniture and the card table. That's progress." She motioned for Meagan and Kenny, who trudged past him, carting their overnight bags.

Steve gave them each a quick kiss.

"Bye, Dad."

"Bye, Dad."

Soon his family was inside the van. Steve remained on the sidewalk, waving when they pulled away. He buried his hands in his pants pockets and watched the vehicle disappear.

After a moment he returned to the empty house.

Donnalee was definitely, undeniably nervous. She'd arrived at the restaurant half an hour early for the simple reason that she didn't want to be the one to search out and identify Sanford. This way, she hoped to have a few moments to appraise him without his knowing.

After thirteen years, Donnalee was finally ready to marry again. But that meant meeting men, going through the whole process of acquaintance and courtship—maybe more than once. Apart from some casual and ultimately meaningless dates, she hadn't been involved with a man since her marriage. If she wanted to fall in love again, she had to lower her defenses, make herself vulnerable.

That was the terrifying part. She should have gone into counseling following her divorce. Intensive counseling. Any smart woman would have done that. Well, it'd taken Donnalee far longer to get smart than it should have, but she was there now. Savvy. Worldly. Mature.

Those were the very qualities that appealed to Sanford. He'd told her so during their telephone conversation. She sat at the table, facing the door, eyeing everyone who entered. His picture had shown him to be an attractive dark-haired man with strong classical features—but, as Donnalee knew, studio portraits were often deceiving.

A restaurant was neutral territory. Sanford was the one who'd chosen this upscale Mexican restaurant, located in the heart of downtown Seattle. Judging by the succulent scents drifting from the kitchen, he'd chosen well, although Donnalee wondered how she'd manage to swallow a single bite.

A tall distinguished-looking gentleman entered the restaurant and hesitated. Donnalee quickly lifted a pair of glasses from her lap and slipped them on, then peered toward the door. Like an idiot, she'd lost the last of her disposable contact lenses down the bathroom drain and had to resort to her old glasses. But Sanford had seen her picture, too, and he wouldn't recognize her wearing glasses, so she donned them only when absolutely necessary.

He spoke briefly with the hostess and darted a glance in her direction.

Donnalee lowered the glasses to her lap again and squinted hard. Unbelievable. He even looked good blurred. It was him. It had to be him. If she'd been nervous earlier, it was nothing compared to the way she felt now. As for all her self-talk about being worldly and mature, she felt no evidence of *those* qualities at the moment.

He approached her table. "Donnalee?"

"Sanford?"

His slow easy smile relaxed her. "Your photo doesn't do you justice."

"Yours doesn't either," she murmured, meaning it.

Grinning, he pulled out his chair and sat down.

That was the start of the most fascinating night of her life. Hours later, when she phoned Hallie, Donnalee was still in a dreamy swoon. "He's fabulous. Just fabulous. We talked and talked and talked. We were at the restaurant until midnight. They had to boot us out, so we found someplace else for coffee and talked some more."

"What time is it?" Hallie asked, with a loud yawn.

Donnalee would never have phoned this late if Hallie hadn't left three urgent messages, demanding she call the minute she got home. "Two o'clock."

Hallie gasped. "You mean to say you just got in? But this was just your first date."

"I know." Try as she might, Donnalee couldn't keep the wistful tone out of her voice.

"He's not there with you, is he?" Hallie's voice dropped to a whisper.

"No. Good grief, what kind of woman do you take me for?"

"A woman who's been too long without a man! Was he everything you hoped?"

"More. Hallie, I can't believe it! He's warm and gracious, romantic and so much fun. I could have talked to him all night. We walked along the waterfront and held hands."

"Did he kiss you?"

"Yes...and I even told him about Larry." The subject of her divorce wasn't something Donnalee discussed freely or often, and certainly nothing she'd intended to talk about on her first date. When she'd mentioned it to Sanford, she'd made light of it. The marriage was a mistake, she was too young to know what she was doing, that sort of thing. It amazed her how easily he'd read between the lines. His hand had tightened around hers and he'd stopped. With the breeze off Puget Sound ruffling her hair and the ferry gliding across the dark waters, its lights a glittering contrast to the night, he'd placed his hand under her chin and raised her eyes to his. Then, ever so gently, he'd kissed her.

Donnalee didn't elaborate on the kiss. Hallie was her best friend, but some things you kept private.

"Are you seeing him again?"

"Tomorrow. Today," Donnalee amended. She'd planned to play this cautiously, and she still would but...she *liked* this man, liked him so much it frightened her. It was all happening too soon.

"You're really crazy about him, aren't you?" Hallie sounded almost disappointed. Surprisingly, Donnalee understood. She knew her friend didn't begrudge her happiness; Hallie just hadn't expected her to find the right man this effortlessly. Frankly, neither had Donnalee. So far, Sanford was…perfect. She realized it was too early to say he was the person she should marry— but marriage was a distinct possibility.

"What about you?" Donnalee asked. The last time she'd talked to Hallie, she'd agreed to meet with Rita's husband's friend. The one Rita had declared the ideal match for Hallie. "Did Marv phone?"

"Precisely at seven."

"Isn't that when Rita suggested he call?"

"Yes, and that worries me. He seems to carry this punctuality thing to extremes."

"He's an accountant, so what do you expect? How'd he sound?"

Hallie giggled. "Like an accountant. He couldn't squeeze in a date with me until next Thursday night."

"It's tax season," Donnalee reminded her. "What do you expect?" she said again.

"I don't know. Going out with a guy named Marv doesn't exactly thrill me."

"You might be surprised. I had a preconceived idea about Sanford, remember?"

"Do people actually call him that?"

"Apparently so. He said when he was a kid, his friends called him Sandy, but that just didn't suit him anymore. He said I could call him Sandy if it made me more comfortable. But he doesn't look like a Sandy. Hé looks like a Sanford. It's a perfectly respectable name, and so is Marv."

"Marv," Hallie repeated slowly. "You're right. It's not a bad name."

"Not at all." Neither of them pointed out that Hallie

had gotten a date—without paying two thousand dollars for the privilege.

"How long did you two talk?"

"A minute," Hallie murmured, "two at the most. He's on a schedule."

Donnalee was beginning to understand her friend's qualms. "Don't be too quick to judge him. Who knows, he might turn out to be Mr. Wonderful."

"Why am I having trouble believing that?"

Five

Bachelor #1

February 20

Tonight's the night. I'm meeting Marvin—
Marv. It goes without saying that I shouldn't
count on this blind date, but I can't help myself. Not after the way I've worked to turn myself into a desirable enticing woman, irresisti-
ble to mortal man.

Yes, I'm at goal weight. It would have been
easier if I'd blasted away those ten pounds
with dynamite, but they're gone, which is reason enough for celebrating. Marv's taking me
to the Cliffhanger, a pleasant surprise. The
fact that I actually have a dinner date (with
someone Rita feels is perfect!) excites me. I
have faith in networking. Donnalee is delighted with Dateline, as well she should be
for two thousand bucks, but I prefer to tackle
this dating thing on my own. So far so good,
although I haven't actually <u>met</u> Marvin—Marv.
We've talked a couple of times and he
sounds…interesting.

It isn't like I've spent the last six years in a

vacuum. Dating isn't exactly a new experience. But now, I'm looking at each man as a potential husband and father. Not that I'm going to ask for a sperm count or character references, but there are certain traits I want in a man. Commitment is a biggie to me. I want to do this marriage thing once, and only once, so I plan to do it right.

This date with Marv is the beginning of a journey, though I can't say exactly where this journey will take me. My, oh my, I do get poetic. I'll write tomorrow after I meet Marv. I only hope Rita knows me as well as she thinks.

Hallie was going to annihilate Rita. The instant she opened the door and met Marv, she had her doubts. For starters, he didn't look like she'd expected—or Rita had implied. Not like Sean Connery at all. More like Elmer Fudd. *And* he wore a checkered bow tie.

She wasn't the only one disappointed. Marv seemed dissatisfied, too. So much so that Hallie wondered what Rita had told him about *her*.

"You must be Hallie," Marv said, stepping inside her home. He glanced around like an appraiser, as though tallying the worth of her furniture and personal effects.

He was so short—*that* wasn't his fault, though Rita might've warned her—she was a good two inches taller without wearing her heels. But his brusque unfriendly attitude was another matter. If he'd bothered to greet her with a smile, she would have felt differently. Instead, he scrutinized her the way he had her furnishings, without emotion, without warmth.

"Would you like a glass of wine before we leave?" she asked, hoping her first impressions had been wrong, willing to give the evening a try, if for nothing more than the fact that she'd spent almost a hundred dollars on her dress. Besides, he was taking her to her favorite restaurant, one she could seldom afford on her own. Any man who invited her to dinner at the Cliffhanger was probably redeemable.

He declined her offer of wine, explaining severely, "I'm driving."

"Coffee, then?"

"Decaffeinated, please." He helped himself to a chair while she got their drinks. He pinched his lips in disapproval when she returned with a mug for him and a wineglass for her. If this was how the evening was going to continue, she'd need that wine. Maybe she should bring the bottle with her; a swig now and again was bound to improve her mood—if not his.

"I understand Rita's husband works with you," she said, hoping to cut through the awkwardness and salvage this so-called date.

He nodded. "You're a friend of Rita's, correct?"

"Uh, correct."

"You've known her how long?" he asked, removing a pad and pen from inside his suit jacket.

"Rita?" She frowned, wondering why he felt this information was important enough to warrant documentation. "Oh, for years. Actually we've known each other since college. Nine or ten years, I'd guess."

"I see." He entered the fact on the pad. "You're how old?"

"Twenty-nine." Hallie took a restorative sip of her wine.

"Never been married?"

"No. What about you?" she asked, gritting her teeth. She hadn't agreed to an inquisition, and this was definitely beginning to resemble one.

He ignored her question. "You own a graphic-arts business?"

"That's right." She felt as if she was filling out a credit application. "Look. Is there a reason for all these questions?"

"I prefer to have significant background information on any woman I date."

"I...see." She almost wished he'd asked how much she weighed. For once in her life, she would've been happy to tell someone.

He flipped the book closed and reached for his coffee. "Overall, I rate you at seven and a half."

"You're rating me?" She was furious enough to throttle him, and they hadn't so much as left the house.

"I do every woman I date." He grinned suddenly and the movement of his mouth softened his expression.

"Do that again," Hallie said, waving her finger at him.

He frowned, destroying the effect.

"Smile," she demanded.

He complied, then immediately lowered his gaze, and Hallie realized he was actually shy. He hid behind the questions and his ratings and obnoxious demeanor. Knowing this made her slightly more sympathetic toward him.

He helped her on with her coat and opened the car door for her. Hmm. Good manners were gentlemanly. Things seemed to be improving. They were on the freeway, with Marv driving at a predictably cautious speed, when she first heard the engine rattle.

"What was that?"

Marv scowled and pretended not to hear her or the noise.

"Sounds to me like there's something wrong with your car," Hallie pressed.

He took his eyes off the road long enough to glare at her. "My car is in perfect running order."

Uh-oh, the date was going downhill again. "I'm sure you take good care of your car," she said soothingly. "But I'm telling you I hear something that doesn't sound right." Whatever the problem, it didn't delay them. They arrived five minutes ahead of their reservation time. Hallie figured that if Marv chose to ignore signs of engine trouble, there wasn't anything she could do about it.

The Cliffhanger was perched on the side of a high bluff that overlooked Commencement Bay in Tacoma. Everything about the restaurant was first-class. Hallie smiled with pleasure.

Once they were seated, however, and the waiter had taken their order, Marv removed the pen and pad from his pocket again. He read over his notes, then said, "I have a few more questions for you."

"More?" She didn't bother to disguise her irritation.

"I'll get through the questions as quickly as possible. I hope you don't mind, but it'll help me later when I make my decision."

When he made his decision? Did he think she was applying for the opportunity to marry him? "Decision," she repeated. "*What* decision?"

"Unlike others, I prefer to choose my wife based on facts rather than feelings, which I think are completely unreliable. Since marriage is a long-term contract, I believe it's necessary to gather as much information as

I can. I understand that you, too, are in marriage mode, so this evening can be beneficial to us both." He held her gaze for a moment. "I have to tell you, Hallie, you're getting good marks." The tips of his ears turned red and he cleared his throat before saying, "You're quite...attractive, you know."

The compliment mollified her—although she had to admit she was a little shocked by his blatant approach to this date. *And* to the matter of marriage.

"It doesn't hurt that you're in a financially superior position," he added, ruining any advantage he'd gained.

"Financially superior?" Her? Now that was a joke if ever she'd heard one.

"You own your own business. That puts you several points ahead of the others."

"Exactly how many others are there?"

"That's, uh, privileged information." He smiled lamely, unfolding a computer printout. "We've finished with the preliminaries. Let's get into your family background now."

"I beg your pardon?"

"Medical history, things like that." He sounded impatient. "It's important, Hallie."

"All right, all right," she muttered, resigned to the fact that their dinner was going to be one long interview. Thank goodness their appetizers had just arrived. While she had the waiter's attention, she ordered a glass of wine. Marv frowned and wrote a lengthy note. "What do you want to know?"

They'd discussed heart disease, alcoholism and mental illness by the time their salads were served. Surely the entrées couldn't be far behind! But before she tasted a single bite, he was making inquiries about

STDs, fertility and childhood illnesses. Hallie had finally reached her limit. This guy wasn't shy, nor was he hiding behind a pad and pen. He calculated everything down to the size of her panty hose.

"Any problems with—"

She held up both hands. "Stop!"

"Stop?"

"I'm finished answering your questions. You aren't going to find a wife by interviewing for one. I thought this was a dinner date so we could get to know each another."

"It is," he argued. "I'm getting to know you by asking questions. What's wrong with that?" He made another notation, writing furiously.

"What was that?" she demanded.

"Attitude. I'm beginning to have my doubts about you in that category."

Hallie pushed aside her half-eaten salad. "*You* have your doubts. Listen, buster, I'm not answering another question. This is ridiculous—a woman wants to be wanted for who she is, not what she has to offer in the way of good genes!"

Her outburst appeared to unsettle him. "But you've rated the highest of anyone."

It was a sad commentary on the state of her ego that she was flattered by this. "Thank you, I appreciate that, but I refuse to spend the entire evening talking about my grandmother's arthritis." Now was as good a time as any to break the news. "I'm sorry, Marv, but I don't think this is going to work."

"I wouldn't be so quick to say that. Although your attitude is a bit problematic, I find myself liking you. Once we know each other better, you'll value the effort I went through to gauge our compatibility."

"I believe I've already gauged it. Unfortunately, we aren't the least bit compatible." She tried to be gentle, to tell him in a way that left him with his pride intact. "I have my own test, so to speak, and I can tell that a relationship between us simply isn't going to work."

"You're sure?"

"Yes." For emphasis she nodded.

Marv didn't blink, didn't even put up a token resistance. Instead, he closed his pad, placing it inside his suit jacket, and refolded his printout. "Well, then," he said, "I'm relieved you recognized it this soon. You've saved us both a considerable amount of time and effort."

Hallie congratulated herself for not rolling her eyes.

Neither spoke, and before long Marv reached for his pad again. Now he seemed to be jotting down numbers—but Hallie didn't ask.

Finally he glanced up. "You might be interested in knowing that out of a possible one hundred points, you scored a seventy-six for the opening interview."

"Really?" She'd be sure and let her next date know that.

"But I have to agree—it wouldn't work."

Their dinner arrived, and Hallie savored the silence as much as she did the blackened salmon. Marv seemed equally engrossed in his meal; in a restaurant noted for its steak and seafood, he'd ordered liver and onions.

After declining dessert, Hallie decided to turn the conversational tables on him. "What about *your* family's medical history?'' she asked. It wouldn't surprise her if there was a case or two of mental illness.

''Fit as a fiddle. I have one grandfather who lived to be ninety.''

''Longevity runs in the family, then?''

''On my maternal side. It's difficult to say about the paternal.'' The waiter brought the bill and Marvin grabbed it. ''Unfortunately, very little is known about my father's people.'' He launched into a lengthy dissertation on what he'd managed to learn thus far. Ten minutes into it, Hallie yawned.

Marvin stopped midsentence and pulled out a pocket calculator. ''Did you have three or four of the crab-stuffed mushrooms?''

''I beg your pardon?''

'The appetizer,'' he said, his finger poised above the calculator keypad.

''Three.''

''You're sure?''

''Was I supposed to have counted?''

''Why, yes.'' He appeared surprised that she'd ask.

Hallie stared in shock as he tallied the dinner bill and stated, ''Your half comes to forty-five dollars and thirteen cents, including tip.''

''*My* half?''

''Why should I pay for your dinner?'' he asked. ''You said yourself that we're incompatible.''

''Yes, but...you asked me out.''

''True. Nevertheless, it was with the unspoken agreement that this date was between two people interested in pursuing a relationship. You aren't interested, therefore, your half of the dinner bill comes to…" He appeared to have forgotten and looked down at his calculator.

"Forty-five dollars and thirteen cents," she supplied.

"That includes your portion of the tip."

Disgusted, Hallie picked up her purse. It wouldn't do any good to argue. Luckily she had two twenties and, yes, a five, which she kept hidden for emergencies. The thirteen cents practically wiped her out.

With nothing more to say, they left soon afterward.

Hallie heard the car well before the valet drove it into view. She glanced at Marv, wondering if he'd ignore the clanking sound *this* time. He did.

Rather than point it out again, Hallie climbed inside and steeled herself for a long uncomfortable ride home. She wasn't far from wrong. When they reached the interstate the engine noise had intensified until even Marv couldn't miss it.

"What was that?" he demanded, as if she was somehow responsible for the racket.

"Your car?" She was unable to avoid the sarcasm.

"I *know* it's the car."

"There's no need to worry," she said, parroting his words, "your vehicle's in perfect running order, remember?"

"Correct. Nothing could possibly be wrong." Then he cursed and pulled off to the side of the freeway. Smoke rose from underneath the hood, billowing into the night.

"Oh, dear," Hallie murmured. This didn't look good. The way things were going, he'd probably make her pay for half the tow truck, too.

Marv slammed his fist against the steering wheel. "Now look what you've done."

"Me?" Of all the things he'd said, this was the limit. The final insult. "I have a few questions for you," she snapped. "When was the last time this car had an oil change? A tune-up? Did you bother with antifreeze this winter?"

Marv leapt out of the car and slammed his door.

Hallie got out, too, shutting hers just as hard.

He glared at her over the top of the hood. "I don't find your attempts at humor the least bit amusing."

"The biggest joke of the night was my agreeing to go out with you!" The cold wind whipped past her and she tucked her hands into the pockets of her coat. Unfortunately, she'd worn a flimsy coat, more of a wrap, because its jade green went so well with her new dress. Her wool coat hung in the closet. The only thing she had to keep her warm was her anger—and so far, it was working.

"Until I met you, my vehicle *was* in perfect running order."

"Are you suggesting I put a hex on it?"

"Maybe you did," he growled.

Hallie seethed, crossing her arms. "You're the rudest man I've ever met!"

His eyes narrowed and his mouth thinned. It wasn't until then that she realized how deeply she'd insulted him. Marv obviously prided himself on his manners—opening the door, helping her on with her coat, those gestures so few men observed these days. Well, she'd take a normal man who let her open car doors over Marvin anytime!

"If that's how you feel," he said stiffly, "you can find your own way home."

"Fine, I will." She carelessly tossed out the words, slapped her silk scarf around her neck like Isadora Duncan and started walking, high heels and all.

This wasn't the smart thing to do, Hallie soon realized. She was chilled to the bone, blinded by all the headlights flashing by and, dammit, one of her heels chose that moment to break off.

At least it wasn't raining.

Six

The Loan Ranger

The ringing woke Steve out of a sound sleep. He rolled over, thinking the incessant noise was his alarm. He hit the switch, but it did no good. Then he noticed the time. Eleven-thirty. What the hell?

He sat up and realized the irritating sound wasn't his alarm clock but his doorbell. He grabbed his jeans and pulled them on as he hobbled into the living room. He had no idea who was calling on him so late at night—but the last person he expected was his next-door neighbor.

"I'm sorry to wake you," Hallie said, her eyes desperate in the pale porch light. A scruffy-looking fellow hovered behind her, and a taxi stood parked in her driveway. "Could I borrow twenty dollars?" she pleaded. He stared at her. "Just until tomorrow afternoon," she added.

"Sure," he said, and reached in his hip pocket for his wallet, extracting a bill.

"Thank you," she breathed, then whirled around to give the taxi driver his money. "I told you you'd get paid!" she said fiercely.

"You can't blame a guy for doubting. You wouldn't be the first lady who tried to stiff me."

"Well...thanks for bringing me home."

The cabbie handed her a business card. "Sure, lady. Listen, the next time some guy dumps you on the freeway, give me a call and I'll make sure you get home."

"Thanks," she muttered, sending an embarrassed glance in Steve's direction. She waited until the driver had left before explaining. "Really, it's not as bad as it looks." Nervously she pushed a trembling hand through her tangled hair. "I'll get the twenty dollars to you after work tomorrow afternoon. I...I quit carrying my credit cards and didn't have my ATM card with me," she explained, rushing the words. "It took all my cash to pay for my half of dinner."

"Don't worry about it."

"I promise to have the money back by tomorrow. You have my word on that."

He grinned. "I said not to worry about it."

"At this point, it's a matter of pride." She turned away and limped toward her own condo. It took him a moment to realize the heel on one of her shoes had broken off.

"Hallie?" he called out, curiosity getting the better of him. "Do you want to come in for coffee and tell me what happened?"

She paused, and he knew she was tempted to accept. "If you don't mind, I'll take a rain check on the coffee. I'm fine, really. It was just a date gone bad."

"From Dateline?"

"No. I decided against...I didn't sign up with them. This was a date arranged by a friend. A *former* friend." She filled in a few of the details: the questions, the restaurant bill, the car. He listened sympathetically, nodding now and then, marveling at her ability to laugh at her situation.

"Don't let it get you down," he advised.

"I won't," she said, and although she looked disheveled and pitiful, she managed a weak smile. "It'd take more than a pudgy accountant to do that."

"Good girl." He waited until she was all the way inside her house before he closed his own door. Only then, did he allow himself to laugh. He had to hand it to Hallie McCarthy. The lady had grit.

"What's so funny?" Todd asked Steve the following morning.

"What makes you think anything's funny?" Steve leaned over a pile of metal shavings to avoid meeting his friend's gaze. Todd was right; his mood had greatly improved. It was because of Hallie, he suspected. Every time he thought about her and that jerk accountant, he found himself grinning from ear to ear. No wonder he wasn't eager to get back into the dating scene. It made far more sense to win back his ex-wife. He only hoped Mary Lynn met up with a few of Hallie's rejects. Then maybe she'd realize he wasn't so bad, after all.

"You've been wearing this silly grin all day." Obviously Todd wasn't about to let the subject drop.

"Would you rather I stormed around making unreasonable demands?"

"Nope," Todd admitted. Then he shrugged. "You ready for lunch?"

"Sure." Steve packed his own now, same as he had when he was married—which meant he picked up something at the deli on his way into work. He and Todd headed for the small room adjacent to his office, stopping to let Mrs. Applegate, his new secretary, know he was taking his lunch break. She was working out well. He'd found her through a business college. She was older, described as a displaced homemaker, whatever that meant. But Mrs. Applegate appreciated the job and worked hard.

"Would you care for a cup of coffee with your lunch?" she asked.

"Please."

"That woman's going to spoil you," Todd commented as he sat down across from Steve. He pulled a submarine sandwich from his lunch pail and peeled away the wrapper.

"I'm going to let her, too." In comparison to Danielle and Mary Lynn, Mrs. Applegate was a paragon—organized, efficient, cooperative. He wondered how he'd ever managed without her.

"Now tell me what's so damn funny," Todd said after the coffee had been served. "I could use a good laugh."

"My neighbor." Steve could see no reason not to relay the events of the night before. "Apparently she's on the hunt for a husband."

"What's she look like?"

"Why? You interested?"

Todd took a big bite of his sandwich and chewed vigorously as he considered his response. "I might be."

"You? It wasn't so long ago you told me you wanted nothing to do with women."

"*Some* women. Go on, I want to hear what happened to your neighbor."

"She got me out of bed at eleven-thirty last night and asked to borrow twenty bucks. The guy she'd been with acted obnoxious all evening—even made her pay for her own meal. Plus he had car trouble, blamed it on her, then dumped her on the freeway and told her to find her own way home. Which she did.''

''Good for her.''

''That's what I said.'' He bit into his pastrami-on-rye and found himself smiling again as he recalled Hallie's story. She'd done a hilarious imitation of this Marv guy demanding his forty-something dollars.

''You like this neighbor of yours, don't you?''

''Like? What do you mean?'' Sure he liked Hallie. What wasn't to like? But he had no romantic interest in her, and there was a difference.

''Are you going to ask her out?''

''Naw,'' he answered, dismissing the suggestion. ''She's not my type.''

''Exactly what is your type?'' Todd pressed.

''Damned if I know.'' The only woman he'd ever loved had been Mary Lynn. She was all he'd ever wanted, all he'd ever thought about. That wasn't going to change.

His answer appeared to satisfy Todd, who nodded. ''Same way I feel. I might date again, and I might not. Sure as hell, the minute I start getting serious about a woman I'll run into problems, just like I did last time. So I figure, if I meet someone, fine. Great. But I'm not going out of my way.''

Steve frowned as he listened to Todd. It distressed him that Mary Lynn seemed to be involved with another man, and according to his kids, had been dating for some time.

''You look upset,'' Todd remarked.

Steve set his sandwich aside, his appetite gone. ''Mary Lynn's seeing someone.''

"I know, you told me earlier. You've been divorced a year or better—what did you expect?"

"I expected her to see the light," Steve muttered.

"Well, it's not going to happen. She wanted out of the marriage. And as far as I can see, nothing's changed."

"When did you become an expert on my relationship with my ex-wife?" Steve asked irritably. They'd had this discussion before, and it irked him that his friend saw things differently. More than anyone, Todd knew he hadn't wanted the divorce. More than anyone, Todd knew he loved Mary Lynn as much now as he had the day they'd married.

Todd threw up his hands in disgust. "Let's drop it, all right? I butted in where I didn't belong. You want to moon over Mary Lynn, for the rest of your life, then be my guest."

Seven

Make Mine A Double

"Donnalee Cooper's holding for you on line two," Bonnie said. Hallie stared at the blinking phone. It wouldn't help to put it off any longer. Her friend had a right to know—even to gloat.

"Hi, Donnalee," she said with forced cheerfulness.

"You didn't phone," Donnalee accused. "What happened?"

"You don't want to hear."

"I wouldn't have called if I didn't. I haven't got much time, either. I've got clients due in five minutes, so cut to the chase, will you?"

"Okay, then—gloat. This guy was a jerk. Big time. He wanted to investigate my family genes to make sure I was qualified to bear his children. When I told him I didn't think we clicked, he made me pay for my half of the dinner. Then his car broke down on the freeway and I was stuck finding my own way home. To add insult to injury, I had to get my neighbor out of bed and borrow twenty bucks to pay the cabdriver."

A lengthy pause followed her condensed version of the previous night. Hallie suspected Donnalee had covered the receiver with one hand to hide her laughter.

"Well?" she challenged. "Say something."

"Okay," Donnalee replied slowly. "Are you ready to invest in Dateline yet?"

"No." Hallie was determined to pay off her credit cards, not add another two thousand dollars to the balance. "Besides, I have another date."

"Who?" Donnalee—predictably—sounded skeptical.

"Bonnie's uncle Chad." Bonnie had mentioned him early in January, but Hallie had wanted to be at her best before agreeing to a date with him. "You know that old saying about getting back on the horse after you fall off? Well, I accepted a dinner invitation this very morning."

"When are you seeing him?"

Hallie didn't know what to make of Donnalee's tone. It was a mixture of wonder and patent disapproval. "Soon," Hallie said. "Monday night." Actually she wondered how smart this was herself. Monday was only three days away.

Chad Ellis had sounded nice enough over the phone, and Bonnie had said he was her favorite uncle. Someone related to a member of her trusted staff seemed a safe bet—especially after the disastrous Marv.

"Did you go out with Sanford last night?" The change of subject was deliberate.

"Yes—and it was wonderful. He's a dream come true," Donnalee said with the same wistful note she used whenever his name was introduced into the conversation.

"Have you talked to him today?" Hallie didn't know why she insisted on torturing herself.

"He sent me a dozen red roses this morning."

"Roses?" Hallie was almost swooning with envy.

While Donnalee was being courted and pampered, she'd been grilled for hours and then abandoned on the freeway.

"I'm falling in love with this guy," Donnalee confessed. "Head over heels."

"So am I, and I haven't even met him."

Her friend chuckled. "I wish you'd reconsider Dateline. Chad might be Bonnie's uncle, but how much do you really know about him?"

"Just what Bonnie told me. He's divorced, has been for five years. He sells medical equipment and is on the road quite a bit, but he'll be back in town after the weekend. For a while, anyway." She wasn't sure if that was luck or fate. Their one all-too-brief conversation had taken place that morning. He sounded...interesting. Which, come to think of it, was the same word she'd used following her telephone chat with Marv.

"If you don't call me Tuesday morning, I'll track you down and torture the information out of you," Donnalee warned.

"I'll phone," Hallie promised. No date could possibly be as awful as the one with Marv. Sheer chance assured Hallie that the odds of Chad's being a decent date were good.

At this point she wasn't even looking for Mr. Right. Mr. Almost Right would satisfy her nicely. If she'd learned anything from the experience with Marv—and she *had*—it was that she needed to lower her expectations. No Mr. Knight-in-shining-armor was going to gallop up to *her* front door.

On her way home that evening, Hallie stopped off at the bank for cash. Her ATM card remained in her bottom dresser drawer, along with her credit cards—safe from temptation.

Wanting to put the task of repaying her neighbor behind her, Hallie headed directly for his condo after she parked her car. His lights were on and she assumed he was home, but it was Meagan who answered the door. "Hi, Hallie!"

"Hi, Meagan. Is your dad there?"

"Yeah. He's in the shower. You can wait, can't you?"

"I don't actually need to talk to him." She pulled the twenty-dollar bill out of her purse. "Would you give this to him?"

"Sure."

"Give me what?" Steve strolled barefoot into the hallway, wearing jeans and an unbuttoned plaid shirt. A damp towel was draped around his neck, and his dark hair glistened with water. "Oh, hi, Hallie."

"Hi." She smiled weakly, embarrassed about their last meeting.

"Hey, Dad," Kenny shouted, leaping off the sofa. "Hallie brought you twenty bucks. Let's go out for pizza, okay?"

"Uh…" Steve hesitated.

Meagan's eyes were as bright as her brother's. "Can Hallie come, too?"

"I…can't. Really." Hallie looked over her shoulder at her empty condo, tempted to suggest she had places to go, people to meet. It would have been a lie. "I just wanted to repay the loan and thank you for coming to my rescue. I don't know what I would've done if you hadn't answered the door." Well, she would have managed—she would've retrieved her bank card from the bottom drawer and… But Steve had saved her time and spared her inconvenience. She'd been in no shape to go driving around with a seriously annoyed cabbie, looking for a bank machine.

"*Can* we go out for pizza, Dad?" Kenny asked again, his hands folded in prayerlike fashion. "Please, please, please?"

"I don't see why not," Steve relented, grinning. He turned to Hallie. "You're welcome to come along. Actually, I wish you would. The kids will desert me for the video games the minute we arrive and I'll be stuck sitting there with no one to talk to."

She wavered. Even if she didn't have any plans, she didn't want to intrude.

"Please come!" Meagan urged.

"Sure," Hallie said before she could change her mind. Although it wasn't the thought of her empty condo or equally empty refrigerator that persuaded her. It wasn't even Meagan's invitation. It was the pizza. Pizza, loaded down with cheese, spicy sausage and olives. After nearly two months of exercise, after week upon week of eating lettuce and vegetables, skinless chicken and Dover sole, she deserved pizza. She'd walk an extra mile on her treadmill, but heaven help her, she wanted that pizza.

"I'm glad you decided to come," Meagan told her when they arrived at the local pizza parlor, a five-minute drive away. To Hallie's relief, Steve had taken his car—not his truck, which he'd left at work.

The place was filled with Friday-night family business, the noise roughly equal to that of a rock concert. While Steve stood in line at the counter to order their dinner, Hallie steered the kids toward one of the few empty tables.

Steve returned five minutes later with two soft

drinks, a couple of beers and a pile of quarters. Kenny's eyes lit up like the video games he loved and he reached forward to grab the coins. "Twelve quarters each," Steve said, gazing sternly at his offspring. "And they have to last you all night. Once they're gone, they're gone. Got it?"

"Got it."

The quarters disappeared along with Meagan and Kenny.

Steve sat down across the picnic-style table from Hallie. She spread one of the red-checkered napkins on her lap, aware that it was taking her an inordinately long time to do so.

"It was kind of you to invite me," she finally said, slightly uneasy at being left alone with Steve. To her surprise she found herself revising her earlier estimation of him. He was really quite good-looking. Funny she hadn't realized that earlier. The fact that he'd been willing to help her out only added to the attraction.

"Hey, I appreciate the company. Mary Lynn and I used to bring the kids here once a month. Meagan and Kenny would like to come more often, but I feel stupid sitting by myself."

"What about trying your hand at the videos?"

"Are you kidding? It's an invasion of territory. None of the kids want me there. The one time I tried it I was banished and sentenced to sit out here with the rest of the parents."

Hallie smiled. She'd half expected him to ask her more about her awful date and was grateful he didn't.

They each talked about their jobs, which took all of five minutes. Their discussion of the weather took less than one. A not-uncomfortable silence followed before Steve spoke again.

"Listen, you can tell me to mind my own business, but why was a gal like you going out with a creep like that?"

She sighed. She might as well level with him, seeing that he'd already had her groveling at his front door in the middle of the night, needing a loan. "I guess you've gathered I'm trying to meet a man. I, uh, decided this was the year I'd get married."

His head came up and his eyes narrowed. "Women *decide* this sort of thing?"

"Not all women," she told him. "It's just that I'm turning thirty in April, and—"

"Hey, thirty isn't old."

"I know, but I'm not really sure where my twenties went, if you know what I mean. I was busy, happy, working hard, and then one day I woke up and realized most of my friends were married, some for the second time. My dad recently died, and my younger sister just became a mother." She struggled to explain. "Somehow, things changed for me. My goals. My feelings about what's important in life. For years, I threw all my energy into my work—and now I want…more. I want someone to share it with."

"So you figure marriage is the answer."

"Something like that." Hallie shrugged comically. "I've been dating since I was sixteen, and not once in all that time did I ever meet anyone like Marv. It's appalling how slim the pickings are. You see, Donnalee made it look easy." Maybe Donnalee was right; maybe she *should* reconsider Dateline.

"Is she the friend who stopped by your place a couple of Saturdays ago? The one with the long…the tall one?"

Men rarely had a problem remembering Donnalee.

"That's her. She found Prince Charming after *one* date."

"You mean to say she isn't married?"

"Not yet. She's the person who suggested I sign up with Dateline. She plunked down her money, and first time out she met this fabulous guy. From everything she said, he's wonderful." Hallie couldn't hide the wistful longing in her voice. "It wouldn't surprise me if she was married by summer."

"Slim pickings," Steve repeated, and Hallie wondered if he'd heard anything else she'd said. He became aware of the lull in conversation and cast her an apologetic look. "I was just thinking over what you said about available men. My ex-wife is starting to date and frankly—" he paused, grinning broadly "—it wouldn't hurt my feelings any if she was to meet up with the joker you went out with last night. Maybe she'd be more willing to talk about the two of us getting back together."

"You want to patch things up with your ex?"

Steve nodded, and his eyes held hers sternly, as if he anticipated an argument.

"I'm impressed." In Hallie's opinion, too many families were thrown into chaos by divorce. It did her heart good to know there were men like Steve who considered it important to keep the family intact.

Predictably, Meagan and Kenny arrived within seconds of the pizza. The biggest pizza Hallie had ever seen. Pepperoni, sausage, mushroom and black olive. Her favorite. For a while, there was silence as they all helped themselves to huge slices.

When they'd eaten their fill, Steve and Kenny went to find a cardboard container for leftovers. Meagan smiled at Hallie. "I'm glad you came with us," she said again.

"I'm glad you asked."

"Kenny and I like this place, but we don't come often because Dad gets lonely without Mom here."

It wasn't the first time Hallie had noticed Meagan worrying about her father. Her tenderness toward him was touching, and Hallie squeezed the girl's shoulders. "I hope your parents get back together," she said.

"Kenny and I used to talk about it a lot."

"Your father certainly loves your mother."

"I know."

But Hallie noticed that the girl's eyes dimmed as she spoke, and she wondered what that meant.

"Mom's dating Kip," Meagan said. "Dad knows. Kenny and I weren't going to tell him, but he knows. Mom is...I don't know, but I don't think she wants Dad back. She likes Kip and gets upset if we try to talk to her about Dad. She said that sometimes people fall out of love, and that's what happened with her and Dad."

Hallie was a little uncomfortable with these confidences. "Everything will work out the way it's supposed to," she said, wanting to reassure the girl and afraid she was doing a poor job of it. It was clear that Meagan loved both her parents, and like every child, wanted them together.

"I like that," she said, biting her lower lip. "Everything will work out the way it's supposed to." A smile brightened her pretty face. "I'll remember that, Hallie. Thanks."

Eight

Bachelor #2

It was déjà vu all over again, as a baseball great—often quoted by her father—used to say.

Hallie sat across the linen-covered table from a man she normally would've crossed the street to avoid. "Sleazy" was the word that came to mind. Chad Ellis had hair combed from a low side part to disguise his baldness; it contained enough grease to avert an oil shortage that winter. He wore a suit coat with a bright floral-print shirt unbuttoned practically to his navel and no fewer than fifteen gold chains in various lengths. He looked up from the menu and flashed her a smile that said she was lucky to be with him. Hallie had trouble believing that her own assistant, someone who *knew* her and presumably liked her, could possibly believe she'd be compatible with this clown.

Hallie reviewed the menu selections, keeping an eye on price. If she was going to end up paying for her half of dinner, she wanted to be sure she ordered a meal she could afford.

Chad made his selection and set aside the menu. "How about a little something to loosen our inhibitions?" he suggested. The thought of loosening anything with this character terrified her. "Such as a double martini."

Hallie had ordered a martini once, and the only thing worth remembering was the olive. "Uh, I'd like mineral water."

He jiggled his eyebrows a couple of times. "Liquor is quicker."

A blind person could read the writing on the wall with this one. She chanced a look in Chad's direction and her stomach tightened. This creep was Bonnie's uncle? Did her assistant honestly think she was that desperate?

The waiter arrived and Chad ordered a double martini, while Hallie chose a Perrier. They both ordered their meals—seafood pasta for her, steak for him. "You aren't nervous, are you, cupcake?"

She gritted her teeth. "The name's Hallie."

"Women like pet names."

"Not this woman." Hallie was determined not to get into an argument with him until he'd paid the bill, but she wasn't sure she'd last that long.

"Chad said you're—"

"Chad said?" Then understanding dawned. "If you aren't Chad Ellis, who the hell are you?" She was almost shouting.

"All right, all right. Damn, I should've known I couldn't pull this off. Chad had to leave town unexpectedly and he asked me to fill in for him. My name's Tom Chedders."

"I was supposed to have dinner with Chad Ellis!" Her blood heated to the boiling point. That Chad had lacked the decency to tell her he couldn't meet her and sent a stranger in his stead was all she needed to know about him.

"Don't worry, you'll have a good time with me," Tom told her, glancing around to make sure they weren't attracting attention. "Chad will vouch for me. We've been good buddies for a lot of years. We work for the same company."

"Why didn't you tell me right away who you were?"

"I was afraid you wouldn't have dinner with me if I did," he said. "Like I told you before, I'm an all-right kind of guy. No need to get bent out of shape, now, is there?" He flashed her a toothy grin.

Hallie wasn't sure. "I would've preferred it if you'd been honest with me from the beginning."

He did at least look mildly guilty. "You're right, I should've, only...I didn't want to give you an excuse to cancel. All I'm asking is that you give me a chance."

Hallie sighed deeply. "Let's be honest with each other from now on, okay?"

"Scout's honor."

"You were a scout?"

He shook his head. "Nah, they were a bunch of sissies, far as I was concerned."

"I see," she muttered, and gazed yearningly toward the front door. The evening could prove to be a very long one indeed.

"So you're divorced," Tom said, then thanked the cocktail waitress with a wink and a quarter tip. It took him a moment to turn his attention back to Hallie.

"No, Chad must have misunderstood. I've never been married."

She'd say one thing for Tom. He had the most expressive eyebrows she'd ever seen. Right now, they rose all the way to his hairline. "Never married. What's the matter with you?"

"The matter?"

"There's gotta be a reason a pretty gal like you never married. Well, never mind, I'm going to take good care of you, sweetie pie. You and me are gonna have fun."

Hallie sincerely doubted that. "The name is Hallie," she reminded him, feeling the beginnings of a headache. "Not cupcake or sweetie pie or anything else."

He gulped down his double martini and raised his glass in the direction of the bar to signal for another. "Whatever you say, darlin'."

Hallie ground her teeth in an effort to maintain her composure. "How long have you been selling medical equipment?" she asked, striving to sound interested.

"I don't. Now before you get all upset again, I didn't lie. I work for the same company as Chad, only on the pharmaceutical side. I sell condoms."

A lump of ice went down her throat whole. "Condoms?" she choked.

"Yep. We've got 'em in all kinds of flavors. Our flavor for February is cotton candy. We've got 'em in all colors, too." He stared at her intently, and Hallie shuddered. "White's the top seller, though. Can you believe it? Why would anyone choose white over candy-apple red?"

"I couldn't tell you." Hallie slid a guarded look in both directions, praying no one could hear their conversation. "Do you mind if we discuss something else?"

"Sure," he responded amiably. "I do a brisk business in laxatives, as well. Won the top salesman award two years running." He laughed as if what he'd said was uproariously funny. "Laxatives...running. Get it?"

Ha. Ha. Ha. "No," she said flatly. Hallie's head was starting to pound in earnest now, and she knew she couldn't go through with this. Even if she ended up paying for a meal she didn't eat, she couldn't stand another minute in this man's company. "Tom, listen, I'm really sorry, but this isn't going to work." She set her napkin on the table and reached for her purse.

He assumed a hurt little-boy look. "Not going to work? What do you mean?"

"I was expecting to meet Chad Ellis, not you."

"Gee, I thought we were getting along just great. What's wrong? Tell me what's wrong and I'll fix it."

"In this instance I think it might be best to leave well enough alone."

"But I thought, you know, that you and I would get together later." He did that jiggling thing with his eyebrows again.

"Get together?"

"You know. In bed."

"Bed?" She said it loudly enough to attract the attention of the maître d'. "Let me assure you right now," she hissed, "that I'm not interested in going to bed with you."

"That's not what Chad said."

"What *did* Chad say?" Bonnie was going to hear about this.

"That you were hot for a real man—and, baby, I'm the one for you. I can teach you things you ain't never gonna see in a textbook. I haven't been in the condom business all these years without learning a few tricks of the trade, if you catch my drift."

His drift came straight off a garbage heap, in Hallie's

view. "I don't know what to say, Tom. You've been misinformed. I'm not even mildly lukewarm as far as you're concerned, and I'm not interested in any of your...lessons."

"You mean you were willing to let me wine and dine you—but you weren't gonna give *me* anything? I thought this was a bread-and-bed date."

"What I'll give you is money for my meal." She pulled out her wallet and threw a fifty-dollar bill on the table. Her fingers tightened around her purse strap. "Good night, Tom. I wish you well." She couldn't in good faith tell him it had been a pleasure to meet him. It had been an experience she didn't want to repeat. An experience she wasn't likely to forget. No more blind dates, she swore to herself. It wasn't only discouraging, it was getting too expensive.

"Good riddance. I'll find a real woman, one who knows how to satisfy a man." She noticed that he snatched up the money and shoved it in his pocket.

As Hallie walked out of the restaurant, she felt every eye in the place on her.

"Would you like me to call you a taxi?" the receptionist asked.

Hallie nodded, then with a sinking sensation, she checked to be sure she had enough cash to cover the fare. No, that fifty was all she'd had—and her pride wouldn't allow her to run back to Tom Chedders and demand change. It looked like she was going to need another loan from Steve.

"Your cab will be here in a few minutes," the receptionist told her with a sympathetic smile.

"Thanks." She glanced toward the door, groaning at the thought that Steve might not be home. She'd better phone him first.

Not knowing his phone number, she called directory assistance. The way her luck was going, she was afraid he'd have an unlisted number. But the operator found it and Hallie released a sigh of relief.

Steve answered on the first ring in a lazy I've-been-sitting-here-waiting-for-your-call voice.

"Hi," she said, deciding to ease into the subject of another loan, rather than blurting out the sorry details and throwing herself on his mercy.

"Hi," he responded.

Hallie suspected he didn't recognize her voice. "It's Hallie, from next door."

"Yeah, I know." He chuckled. "Wouldn't it be easier to stick your head out the kitchen window and yell?"

"I'm not at home. I went out on another blind date."

"Not with that same jerk?"

"No—I found an entirely new jerk. I just walked out on him and I don't have enough cash for the cab fare home. Could I take out another loan?" It humiliated her to ask, but she had no option. "This'll be the last time it ever happens, I promise you."

"Where are you?"

"Some restaurant—I don't know where." Dumb. Next time she'd pay attention. Next time she'd bring her own car.

"I'll come and get you."

"No." That was the last thing she wanted. "I appreciate the offer, but I refuse to let you go to that trouble."

"You're sure?"

"Positive."

The taxi arrived and Hallie rattled off her address,

climbed into the back seat and closed her eyes. The urge to give in to tears was almost overwhelming.

Naive and stupid. That was the way men viewed her. Well, no wonder. You'd think she'd have learned something the first time around—but no, all her credit cards and her bank card were still at home. Though who would've guessed this would happen *twice?*

Steve's front door opened the minute the taxi pulled up in front of her place. He loped across the lawn and took out his wallet.

"How much do you need?"

"Eighteen bucks. I'll have it for you tomorrow afternoon."

He paid the driver, who promptly left. "You all right?" Steve asked.

"No," she admitted, "but I will be soon enough. Thanks for the loan. Again."

"Hey, what are neighbors for?" He smiled, patting her gently on the back.

Hallie unlocked her front door and walked into her darkened home. She tossed her purse on the sofa, switched on the lights and headed straight for the phone in her kitchen.

Donnalee answered immediately. "You're right," Hallie said without preamble.

"I love hearing it," Donnalee said, "but I'd like to know what I'm right about."

"Dateline. I'm calling them first thing in the morning."

Her announcement was followed by a short pause. "What happened?"

"You don't want to know and I don't want to tell you. Suffice it to say I'd pay Dateline double their normal fee if they could find me a halfway decent man."

"Oh, Hallie, you poor thing. I'm sure there's someone out there for you."

"I'm sure there is, too, and at this point I'm willing to pay for the privilege of meeting him."

Nine

Bingo!

March 20

They say the third time's the charm. Well, I'm charmed. Dateline took long enough finding me a match, but Mark Freelander was worth the wait. We met last night for the first time. I drove to the restaurant myself—Donnalee advised me to arrive early—only to discover that Mark had, too. We laughed about that.

I was nervous, but Mark put me at ease. I like him. That on its own is a scary thought. I know it's too soon to tell, but I could see myself married to someone like Mark. He's intelligent, well mannered and just plain nice. The kind of guy my mother would approve of. Dad, too, if he were here.

Mark's an engineer, divorced, no kids. The fact that he was willing to invest two thousand dollars to find the right woman tells me he's as serious about this matter of marriage as I am. We're seeing each other again soon.

I can hardly wait.

Hallie rolled her grocery cart over to the display of fresh tomatoes and carefully made her selection. She wanted everything to be perfect for this dinner. She'd been dating Mark for two weeks now, and he'd teased her into agreeing to cook for him. Granted, her expertise in the kitchen was severely limited, but she knew how to grill a decent steak. Her antipasto salad—thick tomato slices, mozzarella cheese, Greek olives, roasted red pepper and salami—was impressive; even her mother said so. Add baked potatoes and steamed asparagus, and she'd come off looking like a younger, slimmer version of Julia Child.

"Hey, Dad, there's Hallie."

Hearing her name, Hallie turned to find Steve shopping with his kids. His cart was filled with frozen pizza, canned spaghetti and a dozen or so frozen entrées.

"Howdy, neighbor," Steve called out.

"Hi, guys," Hallie replied, pleased to see them. "How's it going?"

"Great," Steve said. "I haven't seen you around lately."

"I've been putting in a lot of extra time on a project at work and—" she beamed as she said it "—I'm seeing someone."

"Seeing someone?" Steve prompted.

She looked around and lowered her voice. "I signed up with Dateline. They put me together with Mark."

"Congratulations. I knew you'd eventually land on your feet."

"Thanks. Mark and I've been seeing each other a couple of weeks now, and so far so good." She held up both hands, fingers crossed.

"Hey, Dad, ask Hallie," Meagan urged, pulling on her father's sleeve. "She'd be perfect."

"Yeah, Dad, you can ask Hallie," Kenny said excitedly.

Steve ignored the pleas and would have moved on if Hallie hadn't stopped him.

"Ask me what?"

He shook his head. "It's nothing."

Clearly he was lying. "Steve!"

"All right, all right." He didn't seem too eager to elaborate. "Would you mind if we talked about this over a cup of coffee?" He gestured at the small round tables set up in front of the grocery-store deli, which sold sandwiches, salads and hot drinks.

"Sure." Hallie had to admit to being curious. She followed the Marris family to the deli; while she made sure their carts weren't blocking the aisle, Steve purchased two cups of coffee, plus hot chocolate for the kids.

His son and daughter sat down with them, Meagan waiting patiently for her father to speak. Kenny, less patient, kicked at the legs of his chair.

With a quelling frown at his son, Steve asked Hallie, "Do you bowl?"

"Bowl? As in ball and pins?" Hallie said. "Yeah, I guess, although it's been a few years." She hadn't been all that adept at bowling, but then she'd never been athletically inclined.

"What was your average?"

"Well, I could generally knock down three or four pins. Why?"

"Dad needs a woman who can bowl," Kenny explained.

Steve darted his son another quelling look. "I prefer to do this myself, all right?" He turned back to Hallie. "I'm part of a couples bowling league, and since my marriage breakup my sister's bowled with me. Unfortunately her husband was transferred to Wichita last month and she had to drop out of the league just before the tournament."

"Dad needs a female partner for the tournament," Meagan clarified.

"Oh," Hallie muttered, her heart sinking. She was sure she'd be more of a liability to Steve than a benefit. Heaven knew she owed the guy, but she wasn't sure he'd appreciate the kind of help she could give him.

Steve noted her hesitation. "Don't worry about it, Hallie. It's no big deal. I'll find someone."

"It's just that I don't think I'd do you any good. Like I said, I haven't bowled in years."

"It'd just be one afternoon." Again it was Meagan who spoke. "You could bowl one afternoon, couldn't you?"

"Surely there's someone better qualified than me?" she asked hopefully. Maybe she could rope Bonnie into helping him. Her assistant was due a little penance.

"Nope," Kenny said. "Dad's already asked everyone he knows."

"Kenny, Meagan," Steve said gruffly, "Hallie says she can't do it. Let's leave it at that, shall we?"

"But...but we could teach her," Meagan persisted. "She can't be that bad." So said the girl who'd run circles around her.

"Well..." Hallie felt herself weakening. Twice this man had come to her rescue, and not once in the weeks that followed had he reminded her what a fool she'd made of herself. That in itself demanded her consideration.

"I'd be willing to give it a try," she offered, gesturing vaguely. "The kids are right. All I probably need is a refresher course. And, really, one afternoon isn't going to hurt. It's the least I can do after all the help you've given me."

"So you will?" Steve asked, sounding pleased.

"Like I told you, I'm going to need a little coaching first."

"No problem," Steve replied. "How about Friday night? We'll take the kids bowling and then go out for pizza."

"When's the tournament?"

"The next day—Saturday afternoon."

"Okay." Hallie hoped she didn't live to regret this. "I'll mark my calendar."

"I knew Hallie would do it!" Meagan grinned.

"Glad to help," Hallie said, and swallowed tightly. "What are neighbors for?"

The dinner with Mark went even better than she'd dared hope.

He arrived with a bottle of her favorite wine and a bouquet of spring flowers. He raved about the meal, especially her antipasto salad, and claimed he'd never tasted better. Hallie figured she could get used to having a man tell her how wonderful she was.

They sat in front of the television, sipping the last of the wine from her best crystal goblets. The latest action-movie video played, but neither paid much attention to the actors racing across the screen. Mark relaxed against the sofa, his arm around her shoulder.

"You've been holding out on me," he said in a chiding voice.

Half smiling, she twisted her head to look at him. Not for the first time, she was surprised at how classically handsome he was. Blond, blue-eyed, with a square jaw and perfect masculine features.

"What do you mean?" she asked, linking her fingers with his.

"Not only are you a successful career woman, but you can cook. Do you know how rare that is these days? Most women do whatever they can to keep out of the kitchen."

The last thing Hallie wanted was to mislead him. "Sure, steak and a baked potato. Everything else is a challenge."

He chuckled and kissed the tip of her nose. His eyes grew serious. "Everything feels right with you, Hallie. I can't believe I'm here with you in my arms."

She lowered her gaze, not ready to let Mark know how attractive she found him. "I feel the same way. You're worth every penny I paid for you."

He threw back his head and laughed. "I knew when you arrived at the restaurant a half hour early that we'd get along just fine."

She snuggled closer to him. "I was a nervous wreck."

With deliberate movements, Mark took the wineglass from her fingers and set it aside. Cradling her head between his hands, he slowly lowered his mouth to hers.

Hallie felt the kiss all the way to her toes. She'd been kissed plenty of times before, but not like this. Never like this. His touch, his kiss, reminded her that she was indeed a woman. A desirable woman.

"You taste so damn good," he murmured close to her ear.

"It's the wine."

"It's you," he countered. "You intoxicate me."

She opened her mouth to remind him that they'd shared an entire bottle of wine, which might have explained any intoxication, but he chose that moment to lower his mouth to hers again. The kiss was deep and involved, and when he raised his head they were both breathing hard.

"Oh, my," Hallie whispered, her eyes closed. The taste of his lips lingered on hers.

Mark began to kiss her neck and the underside of her jaw. Hallie leaned her head back as awareness shivered up and down her spine.

"I knew almost from the moment we met that you were the one," Mark whispered.

She'd shared his reaction, his enthusiasm. Meeting Mark had made up for her unhappy experiences with Marv and Tom. He was everything she'd hoped to find in a man—in a husband.

He continued kissing her, and his hands traveled to the front of her sweater, cupping her breasts. "You're so damned beautiful," he whispered.

Hallie bit her lower lip, as he manipulated his thumb over her nipples, which rose instantly to attention.

"Look how responsive they are." His voice was elevated slightly with sexual excitement. "I can't believe how perfect you are."

He slipped his hand under her sweater, his fingers investigating her warm smooth skin. All the effort that had gone into losing those ten pounds had been worth it, Hallie realized. She'd gladly do it all over again just to hear the awe in Mark's voice as his hand stroked her abdomen.

He kissed her once more, his tongue parting her lips, exploring her mouth. His breathing was heavy and labored when the kiss ended. "Hallie, sweet Hallie."

"Oh, Mark…"

"I realize we haven't known each other long."

"Two weeks." It seemed as if he'd been in her life for months.

"Let me spend the night. I know it's soon, but I need you so much."

Her eyes flew open and the warm sensual fog began to clear. She'd known—hoped—that eventually this would happen. She thought of the glorious silk nightgown she'd purchased a couple of months ago with this moment in mind. But it was too early in the relationship.

"I'm crazy about you." He kissed her again, weakening her resolve. The series of kisses that followed left her drowning in a sea of arousal. She searched desperately for a life preserver, a reason, an excuse.

"Hallie, can't you see what you're doing to me?"

"Yes, but…"

"It'll be good, I promise you."

"Mark, I need to think."

"Don't think, Hallie, feel." He removed her bra before she was aware of what he was doing. When she heard her jeans zipper ease open, she pressed her hand over his. Their eyes met in the semi-darkness.

From somewhere deep inside she found the answer. "Not yet."

Disappointment clouded his eyes. "Soon, though, right?"

She smiled and kissed him. "Soon."

Mark accepted her decision with good grace, then helped her adjust her clothes. When her desire had cooled slightly, she went into the kitchen to make a pot of coffee. Mark followed her and agreed they were both in need of something to sober them up.

They sat back down in the living room with their coffee. "I've got a tight travel schedule this week and I'll be gone for a few days," he said regretfully. "I'll call you, though."

She nodded. "I'll be here every night but Friday."

"Friday?" He frowned suddenly and studied her.

Rather than launch into a lengthy explanation, she said, "I'm helping a friend. Saturday afternoon, too, but I'll be home by about four."

"A friend?"

"Yeah." She didn't elaborate.

Again she felt his scrutiny. "Save Saturday night for me."

She smiled, oddly discomfited by his frown and at the same time relieved that he hadn't questioned her further.

Ten

The Lady With The Curve Ball

This wasn't going to work. Steve knew it the moment he saw Hallie grip the bowling ball and step in front of the pins. The first time he watched her throw the ball, he was reminded of an old Fred Flintstone cartoon. It looked, honest to God, as if she'd raced down the alley on tiptoe. And the bowling ball had headed straight for the gutter.

She looked guilty when she turned back. "I don't remember it being this difficult."

"Don't worry. Just relax." He tried to reassure her, a little afraid that if he offered her too much advice she'd change her mind and run.

The bowling ball was returned. Hallie reached for it and approached the line a second time. She made some inexplicable movements with her feet, shuffling a couple of inches to the left, to the right and then back to where she'd started, which was by no means where she should be. Up she went on her toes, glared menacingly at the pins, then raced forward like a ballerina terrorist.

"You might try aiming for the pins," he suggested when her bowling ball slammed into the gutter again. He had to give her credit, though; her ball had gone maybe a foot farther before falling off the lane this time.

"I *am* aiming for the pins," she said righteously. She rotated her arm and shook her hand back and forth, as if all she needed to improve was her wrist action.

"My turn," Meagan said, rushing forward. Both his children had inherited his talent for sports. Meagan walked up the alley like a pro, released the ball just the way he'd shown her, and effortlessly knocked down eight pins.

Steve placed two fingers in his mouth and whistled loudly in appreciation. Meagan had missed the spare. but she hadn't had a chance to warm up yet.

Kenny was next. Steve got a real kick out of watching his son bowl. What he lacked in strength and finesse, Kenny made up for with instinctive skill. He carried the bowling ball up to the foul line, studied the pins, then bent forward and gently let the ball go. It moved as if in slow motion and when it reached the pins, they fell almost gracefully. He knocked down six and then three.

Now it was his turn. Steve threw a strike, his ball exploding against the pins. He was good and had the trophies to prove it.

Hallie waited for the rack to reset the pins. She re trieved her ball, walked up to the starting point, shuf fled to either side, then turned back and looked at Mea gan.

His daughter shook her head and motioned with her hand for Hallie to move to the left. Hallie did as Mea gan advised, but when she released the ball, Steve could see that she was standing in the wrong place Again. The bowling ball headed straight for the right hand gutter, just as it had earlier.

Steve closed his eyes. Maybe it wasn't too late to back out of the tournament. He opened his eyes in time to see Hallie's bowling ball balancing precariously on the outer edge of the lane, then unexpectedly taking a sharp turn toward the headpin. It missed that and struck two pins to the left. *The left.* The bizarre thing was that her ball had been slanting toward the right-hand gutter two seconds earlier.

All in all, Hallie managed to strike down six pins. Steve had seen plenty of curve balls in his day, but this was something else. She missed the spare, but returned to her seat, looking pleased with herself. Steve congratulated her.

"It just took me a while to remember what I was supposed to do," she informed him. "This isn't difficult, you know."

"Right."

They bowled three games and Hallie improved with each one. She never did get a strike, but came close a number of times. If for no other reason, her handicap would help him in the tournament, and he'd save face. It'd look bad if he couldn't find a replacement for his *sister*. It was bad enough having Shirley bowl with him, but to show up without a partner on Saturday would be a blow to his image. Hallie would have to do. He realized that seemed grudging; actually, he was grateful she'd agreed to help.

He wondered if anyone tomorrow would mistake Hallie for his girlfriend. Not that it really mattered. At the very least, it might convince his league buddies and their wives to lay off the matchmaking.

Plenty of people knew he was divorced, and more than a few had tried to set him up with women. He'd resisted their attempts for the simple reason that he wasn't interested in dating again. He preferred to keep trying with Mary Lynn, despite the fact that she was still dating that Kip character. They talked frequently, which Steve considered a promising sign, and Mary Lynn had him over for a family dinner every now and again. Less in the past couple of months than he would've liked, but he wasn't complaining.

Mary Lynn's birthday was coming up next week, and he'd ordered her a dozen red roses, plus two white ones. She loved roses, and he wondered if she'd figure out the significance of the two white ones. They'd been married twelve years and apart two. Those two years had been the most confused, difficult, painful years of his life. Damn it all, he wanted to be a full-time family man again. And he wanted Mary Lynn back—not the manipulative woman she'd become, but the loving passionate wife she'd once been. They both had to make some changes; he understood that. He was certainly willing to work on it, but he couldn't do it alone.

"Are you guys ready for pizza?" he asked the kids when they returned from handing in their bowling shoes.

"You bet."

"How many quarters do we get this time?" Kenny demanded.

Steve hid a smile. "Who said anything about quarters?"

"Aw, Dad."

"Don't worry, you'll get quarters." He ruffled Kenny's hair.

Although it was almost nine, the pizza parlor was as busy as it had been their previous visit. There weren't any families at this hour; the place seemed to be inhabited by teenagers. Hallie and the kids located a table while he ordered the pizza and bought a pitcher of root beer for the kids and glasses of dark ale for Hallie and him.

Once he'd brought over the drinks and relinquished the quarters into his children's hot little hands, he sat down with Hallie. "I really appreciate your doing this for me," he said. As for helping *her* out, that had cost him no money and little effort. She'd conscientiously repaid him each time. If anything, she'd added comic relief to his life when he needed it most.

"I'm glad I can return the favor."

She really did have lovely brown eyes, Steve realized. Eye color wasn't something he particularly noticed in a woman and he probably wouldn't have this time if she hadn't looked so happy. Her irises were an unusual color. Sort of like the ale they were drinking. Deep, dark. Striking.

"Do I have a frosty mustache?" she asked, and raised her fingertips to her upper lip. When he shook his head, she said, "I don't? Then why are you staring at me?"

"I was just thinking how happy you look."

The skin around the eyes he'd been studying a moment earlier crinkled with silent laughter. "I *am* happy and for a very good reason. Remember I told you I met a wonderful man through Dateline? Well, I think I'm falling in love with him."

"Really?" Steve didn't mean to sound skeptical, but he thought it all seemed awfully quick. He'd seen the guy who'd come by her house a couple of times. Steve hadn't thought much of him; he wasn't sure why. But he just didn't see this guy as Hallie's type, although if she was to ask him to define her type, he wouldn't be able to do it. But then, what did he know about love and romance? Apparently not much, seeing that his own marriage had been such a failure.

"Uh, I haven't seen him around lately, have I?" Steve added. It'd been a week or so since he'd last caught sight of the guy. The same day, in fact, that he and Hallie had met in the grocery store.

"He's been out of town. The last few days have felt like forever. We've talked long-distance for an hour every night. I hate to think what his telephone bill's going to be."

Steve didn't know what two people could talk about for an entire hour. He'd never been one to chitchat comfortably over the phone. Even face-to-face was something of a strain. He and his good buddy Alex Rochester used to fish for hours without saying so much as a word. Steve always figured they didn't need to talk to communicate. Pretty good basis for friendship, he thought. Well, that and the fishing.

Alex had moved to Texas three years earlier, and Steve still missed him. Come summer, he planned to take a couple of weeks and drive down to visit Alex. But then he'd been saying that every summer since Alex moved. Maybe this year.

"I'm happy for you, Hallie," Steve said, and he meant it. He didn't know his neighbor all that well, but he liked her. Finding a husband had seemed important to her, and he wished her and this Mark fellow the best.

"Thanks." Her hands circled the chilled mug. "Mark's everything I want in a husband. He's friendly and outgoing, smart, responsible, kind. I haven't met too many men like that. He's tender, caring, romantic..."

She had the dreamy look women get when they're crazy about some guy. His former secretary, Danielle, had fallen in and out of love half-a-dozen times in the three years she'd worked for him, so he was familiar with that faraway expression.

It wasn't until they'd all piled into the car for the ride home that Steve realized he'd actually enjoyed himself. He had the other time, too, when Hallie'd gone out with him and the kids. He was *comfortable* with her. He supposed that was because they weren't romantically involved. They could be themselves without worrying about impressing each other or meeting inflated expectations.

"Can you be ready at eleven-thirty tomorrow?" he asked as they drove through the brick entrance to Willow Woods and onto the well-lit streets.

"Sure, no problem."

"Great."

Hallie inhaled sharply. "That looks like Mark's car!" she exclaimed, excitement raising her voice. "He must've been able to get away sooner than he expected."

Steve pulled into his driveway.

"Have you got a moment to meet him?" she asked.

"Sure," Steve answered, feigning enthusiasm.

Hallie climbed out of the car and waved. "Mark!" she called. "You're back early."

As Steve retrieved his bowling ball from the trunk, he heard Mark say, "Is this the *friend* you were helping out?"

Steve detected the nasty sarcasm in the man's voice, even if Hallie didn't. The kids caught it, too, and they exchanged startled glances.

Steve introduced himself, then stuck out his hand. Mark ignored it.

"You and I need to talk," Mark said to Hallie, his one glacial.

He didn't look at Steve at all.

Eleven

Disappointments

Donnalee should have known. Sanford was too perfect. Too wonderful.

And this evening, she found that out.

He'd cooked her a fabulous dinner aboard his houseboat on Lake Union. The Seattle skyline and the snow-capped Olympic Mountains had served as a romantic backdrop. Afterward, when the sun had set and they'd finished their meal, they sat in front of the fireplace, cuddling. She leaned against the solid strength of his chest and he wrapped his arms about her. Every now and again, he'd bend forward to kiss her neck, taste her, tell her how beautiful she was. How desirable.

But now she understood why he'd never responded whenever she made comments about children or talked about family. Why he'd seemed distant.

He didn't want children. She loved him, yet they wanted different things.

"Surely this doesn't come as a surprise," he prodded gently.

That he would even ask told her how little he knew her. "It does, Sanford. It comes as a shock."

"But if I'd wanted a family I would have married

years ago. When I contacted Dateline I was specific about the type of woman I wanted. One who's as career-oriented as I am. One without children.''

"But *I* want a family. That's the reason I decided to go ahead with the dating service. I've always wanted children.''

Sanford released his breath slowly and leaned forward to rest his forehead on her shoulder. She felt his frustration as keenly as she did her own.

"Oh, Donnalee, I never dreamed this would be a problem."

"I don't know what to say." A heavy sadness weighed on her heart. There could be no compromise for them.

"I've never seen myself as a father," Sanford insisted. "I have no desire to bring children into this world.''

"Perhaps in time?''

"No." His voice was adamant, final. "I'm afraid this isn't something I'm willing or able to negotiate. I feel very strongly about it, always have. That's the reason I went ahead and had a vasectomy a few years back.''

Donnalee felt as though her heart had gone into a spiraling free fall. A vasectomy. He'd felt so certain about not having children that he'd had a vasectomy?

"I'm crazy about you, Donnalee," he whispered into her hair. "I don't want to lose you.''

All these years she'd waited for a man like Sanford. He was everything she'd ever dreamed of finding. It excited her that he seemed to care for her just as deeply. He was a considerate lover, gentle and eager. He'd be a perfect husband.

But not as perfect as she'd once thought.

"Say something," he urged, sounding anxious. His grip on her shoulders tightened. "It worries me when you're this quiet."

"I've...always wanted a family." She knew she was repeating herself, but it was the only thing she could say.

"We won't need children. We'll invest all the energy a family would require in each other. We'll build our dreams around each other and enjoy the freedom other couples our age will never know." He spoke softly, persuasively of the future, painting a glittering picture of what their lives would be.

Donnalee closed her eyes and tried to let his fantasy carry her away. Tried to make herself accept his vision of the future. She tried, she honestly did. But what he described sounded shallow and empty to her.

They'd never argued before, never found themselves in opposing camps. So this, she realized, was a true test of how they would settle their differences.

"What if I said I couldn't continue to see you if you didn't agree to having the vasectomy reversed?"

He stiffened momentarily. "I don't want to think about that."

"I don't, either," she whispered. Then, because she was afraid, she twisted around to face him. "Kiss me, Sanford. Hurry, please, show me how much you love me."

He answered her urgent demand with a hunger of his own, sliding her body down onto the thick carpet and lowering his mouth to hers. Soon they were panting and needy, eager to bridge whatever kept them apart. There had to be a solution. She'd find one, Donnalee vowed, rather than lose Sanford.

They never did make it to the bedroom. Their lovemaking was wild and abandoned, right there on the living-room carpet, with the log fire spitting and hissing beside them. Tears glistened in her eyes when they were finished, but she didn't let Sanford see.

It was in those moments of passion that Donnalee had finally grasped what was wrong. She loved Sanford and he loved her, but he held back a part of himself. While he gave her his body, he held back his heart—his deepest feelings. While his body filled and satisfied hers, he kept her at arm's length emotionally.

Now she knew why. Only when she relinquished her dreams would he commit himself wholly to her.

If then. If ever.

She understood that their relationship would have to be on his terms. Either she accepted them or broke this off now, before it went any further.

Donnalee closed her eyes and breathed in the warm musky scent of the man she loved. Children weren't everything, she told herself. She could pamper and lavish attention on her sister's brood, and eventually Hallie would marry and start a family. She'd love her sister's children and those of her friends; she'd make do. Sanford was right. They didn't need anyone but each other.

"You're quiet again," Sanford whispered, then kissed her gently, stirring the fires he'd so recently quenched. "Tell me what you're thinking?"

"I'm not sure I can."

"I need to know, Donnalee." He took hold of her hands, interlocking their fingers, and pressed them against the carpet. Slowly he positioned himself above her. Their eyes met in the firelight.

"I love you, Sanford."

"I love you."

The urgency in his voice thrilled her. "If you don't want a family, then I have to accept that," she finally whispered.

She saw the relief in his eyes, the gratitude.

"I'll make it up to you," he promised, kissing her over and over. He rolled onto his back, taking her with him. "We don't need children, we never will, not when we have each other."

"Yes," she whispered.

He made love to her again, and this time he gave her everything she wanted—unreservedly gave her all that was in his heart.

Donnalee recognized this.

But she still felt empty inside.

Twelve

Bachelor #3

"**M**ark?" Hallie had never seen him like this. He was a stranger.

Now he grabbed her arm and steered her toward the condo.

"Tell me what's wrong," she demanded.

She felt his hand tighten, as though he resented her questioning his order. "We'll discuss it inside," he snarled.

Hallie tossed Steve an apologetic glance, not knowing what to say. He stood next to his car, his face hard. Was he waiting for her to ask him to intercede? One look at his clenched fists told her he was more than ready to do so. Meagan and Kenny hovered beside him, Kenny clutching his father's bowling bag with both hands. The kids seemed stunned, their eyes wide with shock.

Too numb even to think, Hallie unlocked the front door. Her hand trembled as Mark urged her to hurry, then followed her inside. "I notice you didn't mention that the *friend* you were helping was male."

"Does it matter?" She didn't like his attitude or the way he'd embarrassed her in front of her friends. Mark was behaving like a jealous idiot, but it would do no good for her to get angry, too. One of them had to remain calm. Surely there was an explanation for his behavior.

"Damn right it matters." He punctuated his words by repeatedly stabbing his index finger at her. "I'm not going to have any woman of mine—"

"I'm *your* woman?" This was news to Hallie.

"I paid two thousand dollars to meet you, bitch," he shouted. "You damn well better consider yourself my woman."

Hallie was so outraged she couldn't find the words to speak.

"Let's get something straight right now," he went on. "You don't go out with another man when you're with me. Understood?"

It took her all of two seconds to recover. She met his look, her own anger spilling over. "For your information, I'm not your woman, not your bitch and not your friend. As of here and now, it's over. We're finished. Now leave!" In case he needed help finding the door, she pointed it out to him.

"I'm staying until you get this straight," Mark insisted.

"Oh, no, you're not. You're going to walk out that door and never darken it again."

"The hell I am!"

She planted her hands on her hips. "No man calls me a bitch. You and I are through. Now get out."

"Just a minute here—"

"What part of 'get out' don't you understand?"

The doorbell chimed and they both ignored it, too intent on staring each other down.

"Hallie?" Steve shouted from the other side. "Answer the door, damn it. Are you all right?"

Mark switched his attention from her to the front door and the sound of Steve's voice. "I suppose you're sleeping with him. That's why you turned me down, isn't it?"

His idea was so ridiculous she almost laughed. "I suggest you leave now before this gets any uglier," she said without emotion. While she might have appeared outwardly calm, her heart raced, thundering wildly in her ears.

"We're going to settle this," Mark said, his voice ominous.

Hallie wanted nothing more to do with him. She walked across the room and threw open the front door. "Leave. Now."

Steve was now pounding on the patio door off the kitchen. "What's going on in there?" he demanded.

"Mark was just about to go, isn't that right?" She waited for him to walk out, but he surprised her by holding his ground.

"Okay, okay," Mark said, sounding calmer, more in control. He raised his hands apologetically. "Okay, so maybe I overreacted."

"Perhaps you didn't hear me," Hallie said, her voice equally calm. "I want you to go. Now."

Mark blinked, just as Steve raced around the house to the front lawn. "I believe the lady asked you to leave," he said. His hands flexed several times, as if he was itching to help Mark out the door.

"All right," Mark growled, pushing past Hallie. "If that's the way you want it, fine."

"Don't come back, either," she said. She stood on the top step, her arms wrapped around her middle as she struggled to ward off the embarrassment and bitter disappointment. She was beginning to doubt herself and her own judgment. Mark had seemed so perfect—until tonight. She shook with fury every time she thought about the way he'd claimed she was "his woman" and the ugly word he'd called her. She would never have guessed he was capable of saying such things.

Steve met Mark on the grass, apparently ready to escort him to his vehicle. With military-style precision Mark walked toward his parked car; halfway there he paused and turned around. "I still think we should talk this out," he said, directing the comment to her and ignoring Steve.

Meagan and Kenny stood on the lawn a few feet away.

"I've heard everything I need to hear," Hallie replied. "You aren't half the man Dateline led me to believe. Goodbye, Mark."

From under the glow of her porch light, Hallie saw his eyes narrow.

"You do have something going with this caveman, don't you?" he accused. "I knew it the minute I saw you with him."

"Get a life," Hallie shouted, wondering what she'd ever seen in him. To think that only a few days earlier they'd been kissing on her couch and she'd actually been tempted to go to bed with him. It made her sick to her stomach, knowing she'd allowed herself to be deceived this badly.

"You aren't any prize yourself, Hallie," he yelled back. "Take a look in the mirror if you don't believe me. No wonder you have to pay a dating service to find a man."

"Belt him, Dad," Kenny shrieked, punching the air a couple of times with his fist.

"Yeah, Dad, teach that creep a lesson," Meagan joined in.

Mark hurriedly climbed into his car, slamming the door loudly. He revved the engine and took off with the tires squealing.

Hallie sank down on the step and closed her eyes, barely able to believe what had happened. Mark had shown up at her place tonight to *spy* on her, see who her friend was. Then when he saw her with Steve and his kids, he'd exploded into a jealous rage.

"You okay?" Steve asked with a gentleness that nearly brought tears to her eyes.

"Fine," she said. "Hunky-dory." But she was shaken to the core.

Kenny flew to her side. "Was that your *boyfriend?*" he wanted to know, sounding incredulous that anyone with half a brain would date a guy like that. Hallie didn't blame him.

"Not anymore," she told him, and managed a frail smile.

"Good thing, 'cause that guy's a real jerk."

Mark had succeeded in fooling her. From the beginning, there'd been signs of his possessiveness, his proprietary attitude, but she'd lacked the ability to interpret them. No, she'd refused to see them. While he was out of town this past week, he'd called her at the oddest hours, wanting to know where she'd been and who with. She hated to admit it, but his phone calls weren't because he'd missed her. He was simply checking up on her.

Hallie recognized now that because she so badly wanted a man in her life, she'd answered all his questions, spent hours reassuring him. She was ashamed to acknowledge that it wasn't only her desire for a husband that had blinded her to Mark's character flaws, it was also the money she'd invested in Dateline. Seeing that she'd paid top dollar to meet Mark, she'd been determined to make the relationship work, convinced that it should. After all, Donnalee's experience with the dating service had gone so well....

In retrospect, she told herself, if Mark thought *he'd* been shortchanged, it couldn't compare with how cheated *she* felt.

"She doesn't look so good," Kenny whispered to his dad.

Hallie opened her eyes to discover Steve and both his children staring at her as if she were about to shatter and break into a million pieces. She was afraid she already had.

"Hallie?" Steve asked.

Hallie realized she was incapable of pulling this off. She'd put on a brave front, but now that Mark was gone, reaction had set in. She started to tremble visibly.

"Come inside. You need to sit down." Steve carefully took Hallie by the arm, then led her back into the house. Meagan and Kenny followed.

Racing ahead, Meagan grabbed the pillow off the sofa and fluffed it up. Kenny got her a glass of cold water.

"Who was the jerk, anyway?" Meagan asked.

"Yeah. He's lucky my dad didn't kick his butt."

"Kenny!"

"You wanted to, Dad."

Steve didn't bother to contradict his children. "Maybe it would be a good idea if you two waited for me at home," he suggested.

Both kids seemed reluctant to leave. "You sure?" Meagan asked in a soft voice.

Steve nodded. "I won't be long."

Rarely had Hallie been more embarrassed. Her face burned. "I can't tell you how sorry I am, Steve," she said when they were alone.

"You? What did you do that was wrong?"

"Dated Mark Freelander." She shuddered as she said his name.

"You didn't know."

Hallie just shook her head. What a fool she'd been. Marrying Mark would have been the biggest mistake of her life—and had his behavior tonight not forcibly opened her eyes, she might have done it.

"*You* didn't do anything wrong," Steve repeated.

"I wore blinders," she said, unable to forgive her own stupidity. "You know what it was, don't you?" She paused, but he didn't respond. "The money. I figured if I paid two thousand dollars to meet him, he had to be okay. I figured if there was anything wrong, the fault must be with me."

"Don't you think you're being a little too hard on yourself?"

"No!" she countered sharply. Sitting still was nearly impossible. She stood and started pacing the living room. "Apparently I'm not the judge of character I thought I was."

"Hallie, there's no need to blame yourself for this."

"Why not? It's what I deserve."

Steve sat down, reached for the glass of water Kenny had fetched for her earlier and drank it himself.

"Look at me, Steve. Really look." She stood up straight, squaring her shoulders. Her gaze pinned his. She could trust him to tell her the truth; she didn't doubt that for a second. "Answer me this and don't spare my feelings. Is there something wrong with me?"

"Wrong?"

"Am I repugnant? Ugly?"

"Good grief, no."

"Do I look naive or stupid?"

"No." But this he said with less conviction.

"Then what is it about me that attracts major jerks?"

"Hallie, be fair. The first two were blind dates."

"Yes, but Rita's a good friend and she knows me, and she hooked me up with Marv."

"He's the one who made you pay for your dinner and dumped you on the freeway?"

Hallie didn't appreciate being reminded of the details, but nodded.

"The second creep was a colleague of your blind date's, sort of a blind date once removed, right?"

Again she nodded.

"You can't blame yourself for Mark, either. An agency trained in personality assessment set you up with him. He buffaloed them, too."

"It doesn't matter," she muttered miserably. "I'm finished." She waved her arms dramatically, wishing she could obliterate the last three months of her life— except those ten pounds. She didn't want those back.

"Finished?" Steve echoed.

"With men." She had a sudden craving for double-fudge macadamia-nut ice cream. It'd been Christmas since she'd last eaten anything cold and sweet, and if she searched her freezer, she'd be willing to venture she'd find a carton there.

"Don't you think that's a bit drastic?"

"Eating double-fudge macadamia-nut ice cream?"

"No," he said, confused, "cutting yourself out of the dating scene."

"At this point, no." She hurried into her kitchen and opened the freezer door. Standing on her toes, she peered into the deepest recesses. She shoved aside her Weight Watcher frozen entrées and thrust her arm in, feeling around for an ice-cream container. There was none.

She rested her forehead against a stack of vegetarian lasagna. "No. No. No." Oh, the unfairness of life, without even the consolation of ice cream. When she looked up, Steve was standing next to her.

"Maybe I should call a friend for you. I think it's a woman you need just now."

Steve was right. On her way over, Donnalee could stop off at Baskin-Robbins.

Thirteen

Bring On The Ice Cream

As it happened, Hallie didn't have a chance to talk face-to-face with Donnalee until Sunday afternoon, and by that time she'd managed to collect herself. Mark Freelander had taught her a valuable lesson.

"I can't believe a guy would *do* something like that," Donnalee murmured, for the third time, her expression stunned as Hallie relayed the sordid details.

Hallie sat cross-legged on the sofa. She tilted her bowl and scooped up the last of the melted double-fudge macadamia-nut ice cream, then licked the back of her spoon. "Believe it. I don't think I've ever been angrier."

"Did you lose your cool? I can't blame you, but you're usually so calm in a crisis. I've always admired that about you."

"I barely raised my voice," Hallie said. "It wasn't until later that I completely lost it."

"How do you mean?"

"Check out my freezer," Hallie said, motioning with her head to the kitchen.

"Your freezer?" Donnalee's eyes widened.

"Peek inside and you'll know what I mean."

Donnalee went into the other room and opened the upper half of Hallie's refrigerator. A moment later Hallie heard her friend laugh. She knew it was because the entire front was stacked with ice-cream containers, one on top of the other, four across. "What did you do, buy out the store?" Donnalee said, returning to the living room.

"That's exactly what I did. The five-gallon container wouldn't fit in my freezer, so I bought Baskin-Robbins's entire supply of double-fudge macadamia-nut in one-quart containers. And that isn't all." She gestured at the fireplace mantel. "Did you happen to notice my trophy?"

"As a matter of fact, I did. When did you take up bowling?"

"I haven't, but I filled in for Steve's sister, and we took third place in a tournament yesterday."

"You and Steve took third place! That's wonderful!" The admiration was back in Donnalee's voice— or was it amazement? Well, Hallie had to admit she was pretty amazed herself. "I didn't know you bowled that well," Donnalee added.

"I didn't, either," Hallie said, and smiled to herself. Steve had been no less surprised. Friday night when they'd gone out to practice, she hadn't scored more than a hundred points in any of the three games they'd played. But during the tournament she'd averaged more than 160 points a game. If she had to credit anyone with this sudden turnaround, it was Mark Freelander.

Her anger had carried over to the following day, and it seemed as if she couldn't do anything wrong on the alley. She was much more focused than she'd been in her few previous attempts at sports. Maybe it came from imagining Mark's face on every one of those pins.

She suspected Steve wasn't pleased with the amount of attention she'd attracted from his friends and competitors, but he didn't say anything. He'd been thrilled, however, when they took third place and was kind enough to let her keep the trophy.

"What's with you and your neighbor?" Donnalee asked, settling down on the big overstuffed chair.

"With us? Nothing. We're friends." Hallie dismissed the question, hard-pressed to put into words her relationship with Steve. "He's a great guy, you know, but he's hung up on his ex-wife."

"You've had a steadier relationship with him in the last couple of months than you have with anyone. And he *is* single."

It was true. She'd gone out with him and his children more consistently than anyone, except maybe Mark. But she wasn't romantically interested in Steve. Knowing how obsessed he was with his ex-wife, Hallie had never really considered her neighbor "available." He was exactly what she'd told Donnalee—a friend.

"Ever thought about getting together with him?" Donnalee suggested in a way that implied the idea should have been obvious. "Friends are supposed to make the best lovers."

"Nope," Hallie answered. "I like Steve, don't get me wrong, but he's not my type."

"Do you have a type?"

"Sure," Hallie answered casually. "Don't we all?"

Donnalee lowered her eyes. "I suppose. Tell me, what's your type?"

Hallie had given this a good deal of thought, mulled over the perfect man in her mind. "Well," she began, "I'm not necessarily looking for someone tall, dark and handsome—although I wouldn't rule him out if he was.

As long as he met my other qualifications." She dropped her bare feet to the floor and rubbed her hand down her jeans. "Looks are nice, but frankly, I've discovered they're not all that important."

"I agree," Donnalee murmured.

"I want a man who'll love me, who'll appreciate me for the woman I am," Hallie said thoughtfully. "Someone generous and honest. A man of integrity, who values family and commitment. I suppose I'd want him to be a risk-taker, but not foolish enough to jeopardize what's important."

"Hmm."

"Hmm?" Hallie repeated. "What's that mean?"

Donnalee wore the skeptical look of a banker when the numbers don't add up. "Does such a man really exist?"

"Of course. There are men like that. Lots of them." Hallie *had* to believe that, or she'd give up hope of ever getting married. She stood, taking the empty ice-cream bowl to the kitchen. "It was easy for you," she said as she returned.

"Easy?"

"To find the perfect man. You met Sanford, and that was that." She tucked her hands into her back pockets. "I can't help being a little envious." At one time, she'd assumed it would be that easy for her, too. It sounded a bit conceited in light of her recent failures, but she'd viewed herself as, well, something of a prize. She still did—despite Mark's parting insult.... She was creative, outgoing, intelligent. She had her own business, was fairly attractive, financially solvent. No emotional baggage from a previous marriage, either.

Donnalee had gone strangely quiet. "How are things with you two, anyway?" Hallie asked.

"Great. We've decided to shop for an engagement ring next weekend."

Hallie couldn't believe Donnalee hadn't said something sooner—but then, she hadn't given her friend much of a chance. The moment Donnalee arrived, Hallie had launched into her sad and sorry tale of Mark Freelander.

"That's wonderful! Congratulations."

Donnalee smiled, but Hallie noticed that the joy that should have shone in her eyes was missing. Did Donnalee feel nervous about making this commitment, or what?

"You *are* happy, aren't you?" Hallie asked.

"Of course. Who wouldn't be?"

"Oh, Donnalee, you're going to be married." Hallie felt almost giddy. "I'm thrilled for you. Sanford's wonderful. I like him a lot." They'd met briefly a few weeks earlier, and she'd definitely been impressed. With good reason. Just looking at him made the backs of her knees sweat. The guy was gorgeous. A hunk. And he obviously adored Donnalee.

Hallie's mood changed swiftly and she flopped down on the sofa. "I'm taking a reprieve from this whole dating thing," she announced solemnly.

"But, Hallie, it's too early to throw in the towel."

"I'm not quitting, exactly. I feel like I need to step back and analyze what I'm doing. Adjust my attitude. Regroup. Maybe I've been going about this the wrong way."

"Don't give up on Dateline," Donnalee said. "And what about having Steve set you up with a friend of his?" she suggested. "Really, it makes sense."

Hallie gave that a moment's thought, then shook her head. It was just too demeaning to ask Steve to scrounge up a date for her. If he'd *offered* to introduce her to a friend, that would be different. But he hadn't, and she wasn't going to ask.

Besides, after meeting Rita's "perfect" man, Hallie had serious reservations about letting her friends arrange blind dates for her. You never knew what type of person they might consider suitable dating material. Although, granted, Rita had been shocked by Marv's behavior and apologized profusely.

"Personally," Donnalee said, "I think you and Steve would make a good couple. You like him, and you're always talking about his kids."

"Forget it," Hallie said, rejecting the idea with a wave of her hand. "It would be like hanging out with my brother. If I had a brother. I can't even *imagine* kissing him. No romance."

"You're sure about that?"

"Pretty sure." Steve's longing for Mary Lynn was unmistakable. Hallie had never seen a guy so much in love with the woman who'd divorced him. "Anyway," she added, "I told you how he feels about his ex."

Donnalee nodded slowly. "Okay, but the least you can do is make him your ally. Steve could be an excellent resource for you, give you a few hints, maybe teach you a little bit about men, what they're looking for and so on."

Now that was good thinking—the kind of thinking that made Donnalee so successful in business. Evaluate the circumstances, identify resources, then use them. Yes. Hallie wondered why it had never occurred to *her*.

She smiled, and Donnalee's eyes brightened. "Great. Talk to him tomorrow—and quit being so hard on yourself."

* * *

Hallie wanted insider information from Steve Marris, and she'd come to get it.

After work Monday night she'd given him plenty of time to shower and have his dinner before she'd walked across their connecting yards and rung his doorbell.

He looked mildly surprised to see her. "Come on in," he said, gesturing toward his living room. Hallie had never been in his place before; one glance told her he hadn't put a lot of effort into decorating. The walls were practically bare, although the fireplace mantel was crowded with sports trophies. Not a look she favored.

She noticed the photograph of his wife and kids prominently displayed on the big-screen television. Noticed? She could hardly miss it. The TV was the visual focus of the room, and his furniture, the little she saw, was plain. Utilitarian. Sofa, chair, coffee table, lamp. He seemed to view living here as a temporary thing.

"I need your help," she said, figuring he'd appreciate it if she came right to the point of her visit.

"Another loan?" he asked, smirking. He sat on the chair across from her, one ankle resting on the opposite knee.

"No." She didn't find the question humorous, even if he did. "As you know, I'm hoping to find a husband, settle in suburbia, have a couple of kids. Live happily ever after."

"You haven't exactly made a secret of that."

"Right. Well, after my recent failures—Mark Freelander, most notably—I've been forced to give serious consideration to my...approach."

"And?" He looked wary, suspicious, as if he feared she was going to propose something he wasn't going to like.

"And I realize I've made a fundamental mistake. All

along I've looked at a potential husband for what *he* could bring to a partnership. Is he intelligent, kind, financially solvent, a man of integrity—those sorts of things.''

''That's wrong?''

''No, not wrong. But in retrospect I see that, as well as looking at what a man can give *me*, I should examine what *I* have to offer a relationship.''

''Oh.'' He settled against the back of the chair. ''Like what?''

''Basically the same things. Intelligence, integrity, et cetera. What I need to know is how to present myself in the best light.''

''You think being who you are isn't enough?'' He frowned.

''I need an edge.''

''An edge?''

''You know, a gimmick.''

The frown deepened. ''This is where I come in?''

''Exactly.'' She was glad she didn't have to spell it out. ''Actually Donnalee was the one who had this idea, and she's right. If I'm going to be open enough to admit I'm looking for a committed relationship, then I need an edge. Something that'll attract the attention of the kind of man I want to meet.''

Steve didn't respond.

''Something that'll give me an advantage—that'll tell him who I am and what I want without scaring him off. Men don't like the idea of commitment. It terrifies them.'' She shook her head. ''Fifty-three million men in the world, and only twelve of them are serious about a permanent relationship.''

''I hate to admit it, but you're right.''

''I feel I have to be up-front because I can't afford

to waste time in a dead-end situation with some guy who'd rather play house. I want it all and I want it yesterday.''

"What am I supposed to do?" Steve asked.

"It's simple." She noticed that his shoulders relaxed when she said this. "All I need you to do is tell me what a man *really* wants in a woman he intends to marry. The first thing he's going to look for.''

"What a man wants in a woman he intends to marry," he repeated slowly.

Hallie could almost see his mind working. "Think about it. There's no need to rush. You don't have to come up with an answer right away." The question was complicated, and she wanted him to give it his full consideration before responding.

"I don't have to think about it. I already know."

Hallie's heart started to pump with excitement. "You don't mind telling me?"

He grinned. "No problem."

Hallie waited.

"Let's start with the physical."

She should've known that would get top priority. "All right."

Steve studied her as if to gauge how honest he could be. "I don't know a man who isn't attracted to a woman with big, uh, boobs—'' he glanced at her quickly "—and long legs."

He paused, waiting for her reaction. Hallie refused to give him one, although she had to bite the inside of her mouth to keep quiet.

"It doesn't hurt if she can cook, either," he added, "and these days that's something of a plus. The fact is, I'd marry a woman who could make a roast chicken dinner as good as my grandmother's."

Unable to contain herself any longer, Hallie leapt to her feet. "You mean to say that for a man everything comes down to the physical? And if she can cook? That's disgusting! I'm serious here."

"Hey." He raised both hands in a conciliatory gesture. "So am I. Most men check out the equipment first. You wanted the truth and I'm giving it to you. Don't blame me."

"This isn't a joke?" She stared at him hard, her outrage simmering just below the surface.

"No way."

He might have looked sincere, but she still wasn't sure if she should believe him. "What about integrity and commitment? What about loyalty and honesty?"

"What about 'em?" he asked.

"Don't any of those qualities matter?"

"Well, sure, but that was understood. I thought you wanted something to give you an edge. Well, I'm telling you what it is."

"You mean men really are that superficial?"

"Well...yeah."

Hallie rolled her eyes. As far as she could see, she was a lost cause. She was short, had small breasts, and other than steak and salad, she couldn't cook worth a damn.

Fourteen

Does He Wear Panty Hose?

April 16

Something's wrong with Donnalee. She should be happier than Cinderella, since she's marrying Prince Charming. The woman's sporting the Rock of Gibraltar on her ring finger, yet it seems to be an effort to even smile. Sanford is a dream come true, but every time Donnalee and I chat, I'm left with the feeling that something's wrong. I've tried to talk to her about it, but she keeps dodging me. Says I'm imagining things. But I know Donnalee too well to be fooled. Something <u>is</u> wrong, and come hell or high water, I'm going to find out what it is.

It's been a couple of weeks since my big blowup with Mark Freelander. I couldn't believe it when he phoned the other day as if nothing had happened. The man's got nerve—and little else. I told him not to call me again, and I doubt he will. Dateline called, too, with the name of another man and asked if I was interested in meeting him. Right away the adrenaline started flowing and my imagination kicked in and I saw myself standing behind a colonial house with a white picket fence. I could picture two toddlers and a puppy frolicking on the lawn. The man beside me in this idyllic scene was kind of shadowy, though. That made me realize the odds of being disappointed again were way too high—which says a lot about my state of mind. Like I told Steve and Donnalee, I still need time to regroup, think things over and analyze what's happened. With regret, I told Dateline I'd pass, but to keep me in mind.

My problem is I need a break from all this. I've thought about Steve's so-called advice and I'm still annoyed. But I guess men do like well-endowed women. It's a fact of life; girly magazines prove that much. It makes me feel sort of disgusted, sort of amused—and a teeny bit envious of women like Rita. (And Donnalee!)

Plus, that cliché about the way to a man's heart being through his stomach obviously has some basis in fact. So I could have saved myself the embarrassment of asking Steve, since he had nothing new—or useful—to tell me.

Speaking of Steve, Mary Lynn has taken to dropping off Meagan and Kenny on Friday afternoons before Steve gets home. I've talked to her a few times, and frankly, I find her shallow. A real airhead, in my opinion. I'm probably prejudiced because I like Steve, but it seems crazy for a woman with a decent husband and two beautiful children to destroy her marriage in order to "find herself." She's easy enough to like, though, and I wish her well. Steve, too, of course.

Meagan has a key to Steve's place and the kids are perfectly capable of staying on their own for an hour or so, but they've been coming over to my house, instead. Actually, I enjoy their company. They're great.

As for dating, I've decided to stop for a while. I'll try again as soon as I've repaired my confidence. That shouldn't take too long. I've got too much invested in this project to quit now. Whenever I'm tempted to give up, I sit down and read through my goal planner.

This is possible. I can do this. I <u>will</u> do this.

The knot in Donnalee's stomach hadn't gone away from the moment Sanford had slipped the two-carat diamond engagement ring on her finger. She'd tried to ignore her discomfort, tried to pretend she was happy and, to her surprise, fooled everyone except Hallie. So far Donnalee had been able to put her off, but she didn't know how much longer her stall tactics would work.

Sanford joined her on the park bench. They'd been selecting china patterns at a downtown department store and had taken a long-overdue break to walk along the Seattle waterfront. Donnalee tried to absorb her surroundings, tried to shut out her thoughts. April winds whistled down the wooden piers, whipping the canvas awnings, and the American flag outside the fire station snapped to attention. The scent of seaweed and deep-fried fish blended with the tang of salt water.

Sanford wrapped his arm around her shoulders. "You've been so quiet lately," he murmured.

Donnalee looked out over the water, and for no reason she could explain, her eyes filled with tears.

"Donnalee?"

She couldn't do it.

Right then and there, she realized she couldn't go through with the wedding, with pretending it didn't matter that this man she loved wanted a different future than she did. He'd made the idea of life without children sound wonderful and exciting—with exotic travel and expensive cars and sophisticated pursuits. She'd tried to believe it. But when she was alone, she found herself thinking that what he'd *really* described was a self-absorbed life-style—empty and devoid of everything that was important to her. Not having a family was the right choice for some people; Donnalee wasn't one of them.

She stood slowly, her legs weak and trembling. "I'm sorry," she said, her words breaking as she struggled to speak.

"Sorry?" Sanford looked confused and Donnalee sympathized. Her friends would call her a fool for letting Sanford go. He was a good man, a loving person, and she loved him, but this one thing came between them. He didn't want children.

For days she'd walked around attempting to convince herself that she'd made the right decision in agreeing to marry him. But no matter how adamantly or how often she said it, she couldn't make herself believe it.

Unable to speak, Donnalee removed the diamond from her finger and handed it to Sanford.

He shook his head in puzzlement. "I don't understand. Don't you like the ring?"

"Very much. It's just that... Oh, I feel so awful about this." She bit her lower lip hard enough to taste blood. "I've decided it would be a mistake for us to marry."

He paled. "You don't mean that."

"I'd give just about anything if it wasn't true. I've tried to tell myself it didn't matter, us not having a family..."

"So that's what this is all about." His face tightened, and she knew he was closing himself off from her.

"I'm not judging you for that," she went on. "It's not right to bring children into the world if they aren't loved and wanted. You recognize that, which says a great deal about the kind of man you are—honest, mature..."

"Then what's the problem?"

"I'm the problem," she whispered, fighting to hold back tears. "Me, not you. Please don't think I blame you in any way."

"You're going to have to explain this a little more clearly, Donnalee."

She wasn't sure she could. "I married when I was young and for all the wrong reasons. I was in love, or so I thought. I had this dream of raising a houseful of happy children, being an at-home mom while they were young, continuing with my own education after they started school. I had this warm wonderful fantasy—and I had a husband who'd married *me* for all the wrong reasons." She took a deep breath. "I thought my dream had died with the divorce. But you woke that dream in me again. You allowed me to believe in the possibility of it. Your love restored what my ex-husband stole from me.

"I do love you, Sanford. But I want children. More than I ever realized. And you don't. It would be wrong to marry you under these circumstances."

He didn't say anything for a long moment. "You're sure of this?"

"Yes," she whispered, her voice cracking under the strain of her anguish.

"Then that says it all, doesn't it?"

"Yes..."

"I hope you get what you want, Donnalee."

"You, too." She saw regret in his eyes, even some pain. But without another word, he pocketed the diamond and walked away. In her heart of hearts, she knew she'd never see him again.

Somehow Donnalee made it home. She didn't remember getting into her car, driving, entering her house—nothing. She sat in her living room, arms wrapped protectively around herself, feeling a numbness that was very like what she'd experienced after her divorce.

Eventually she phoned Hallie. She needed a shoulder to cry on. Someone to talk to. A friend.

Hallie was on her doorstep within the hour.

"I *knew* something was wrong," Hallie said forcefully when Donnalee answered the door.

"I broke off the engagement," Donnalee whispered, sobbing and shaking.

Hallie said nothing. Taking Donnalee by the hand, she led the way into the kitchen and pushed her gently into a chair. Hallie moved about as if it was her own home, opening and closing drawers, putting a kettle of water on to brew tea. "My mother always said nothing's quite as bad over a pot of tea."

Donnalee was content to let her friend do as she pleased.

"All right," Hallie said, carrying two steaming china cups and saucers to the table. "Tell me why."

"You'll call me a fool," Donnalee said, and blew her nose into a crumpled tissue. "Everyone will."

Hallie frowned. "I doubt that. What did Sanford do—wear panty hose to bed?"

Donnalee laughed and wept at the same time. "Hardly." The picture was ludicrous. Sanford in panty hose.

"Are there problems with the family? His mother refused to allow another woman in her son's life, right?"

"No." Again, laughing and crying, Donnalee shook her head. She grabbed a fresh tissue, inhaled deeply, then announced, "Sanford doesn't want children."

Hallie slowly lowered her teacup. "No children?"

"He doesn't like children. He doesn't want them in his life."

"Not even his own?"

Donnalee wearily closed her eyes. "No. He's very certain of how he feels—so certain he's had a vasectomy. It'd be foolish to get married, hoping that in time he'd change his mind. And even if he did, there's no guarantee the procedure could be reversed." She wiped her eyes. "Getting married would be unfair to both of us. Unfair and wrong."

"I agree." Hallie gripped Donnalee's hand and squeezed her fingers.

"I tried to believe we could be happy, just him and

me—but, Hallie, I want a family. Every time I see a young mother I find myself longing for the day I'll have a child of my own. I want to feel a baby growing inside me.''

"It was holding my sister's baby that woke me up, remember?'' Hallie reminded her in a soft voice.

Donnalee smiled tremulously. Her friend had recently framed a photograph of herself and the baby. In it, Hallie sat in a rocking chair cradling Ellen, gazing at her with a raptness and a wide-eyed concentration that revealed the intensity of her desire.

"I know plenty of women are single mothers by choice,'' Donnalee said, sipping the hot tea, feeling it begin to revive her. "But I want it all. Husband, traditional family, the whole thing. Am I being selfish?''

"No,'' Hallie said, her voice rising with the strength of her conviction.

They sat in silence for a while. "How did Sanford take it?'' Hallie asked at last.

"He didn't argue with me. I know he was hurt, but then so am I. I should never have accepted the engagement ring, but I'd convinced myself I could live with his decision. Not until later did I realize I...just couldn't.''

"Oh, Donnalee, I'm so sorry.''

"I am, too. I thought I'd be content lavishing love and attention on my sister's two children. But then, a couple of Saturdays ago, I had my niece and nephew over—so Sanford could meet them. In the back of my mind, I was thinking, hoping really, that he'd be so enthralled with them he'd be willing to reconsider.''

"Didn't work, huh?''

"Hardly.'' She raised her eyes to the ceiling. "It was a disaster. Katie and Ben are six and eight, and it didn't take them two minutes to pick up on his attitude. Sanford and the kids did an admirable job of ignoring each other. After we dropped them off at the house, he asked how often I'd be seeing them and—" it was painful to say the words "—he hoped I didn't mind, but in the future, if I wanted them around, he'd prefer that he wasn't."

"Oh, my."

"I understand his feelings. He's never spent any time with children. He's an only child and he feels awkward around kids."

"There'll be someone else for you," Hallie said with such confidence Donnalee was tempted to believe her.

"Yeah, but is it going to take me another thirteen years to find him?"

"I doubt it." She ran the tip of her finger along the edge of the china cup. "Do what I'm doing and take a breather. Give yourself time to get over this, then try again. There's someone else waiting and wondering if the right woman is out there for him. I comfort myself with that whenever I think about giving all this up. Next time you'll find someone who wants the same things you want. I'm sure of it."

"You know what I'm going to do?" Donnalee said, feeling better already.

"Tell me."

"I've got two weeks' vacation scheduled, and I'm going to take one of them, call my mom and book us a trip to Hawaii. I've never been there and we could both use a break."

"That sounds like a great idea." Hallie stood and refilled their cups. "I know how difficult this is for you. I want you to know how much I respect you for refusing to compromise your dreams. You *will* find the right man.''

Donnalee wanted with all her heart to believe that. In the beginning Sanford had seemed to be that man. But now... She looked at Hallie, grateful for the friendship they shared.

A good friendship—like this one with Hallie—endured. It sustained you during times of crisis. It was there for you during the good times and the bad.

The same thing, Donnalee reflected, couldn't always be said of romance.

Fifteen

What Friends Are For

"Hey, Dad, do you know what tomorrow is?" Meagan asked Steve as he led the way from the soccer field to the parking lot. He'd played on an adult league for a couple of years, and both kids participated in the children's fall league. Steve enjoyed helping them hone their skills. It was good for killing a Sunday afternoon, like today, when the kids were restless and ready to go back to their mother and their friends. Their weekday lives. It hurt to know they were sometimes eager to leave him, but he swallowed that pain along with everything else the divorce had brought.

"Dad, I asked if you know what tomorrow is," Meagan said impatiently.

Other than the fact that tomorrow was the twenty-eighth of April, Steve had no idea. He'd never been much good at remembering important dates. Valentine's Day had come and gone, St. Patrick's Day, as well as April Fools' Day. Mary Lynn's birthday...no, that couldn't be it. That was last month and he'd actually remembered it. What the hell was so important about April?

"Hallie's birthday," Meagan announced. "She's

turning thirty. Her friend sent her flowers, and when I asked her, she said they were for her birthday. She said it was the big three-O.''

"Really?'' Steve hadn't seen much of his neighbor lately. He got a kick out of her reaction to his husband-hunting advice—he'd heard from the kids that she'd signed up for cooking classes. He knew he'd offended her by mentioning a woman's bustline, but what he'd said was the truth. He wasn't talking about himself, of course. He didn't spend a lot of time looking at a woman's chest. Oh hell, he'd own up to it. He did look now and then. What man didn't?

"She isn't dating anyone,'' Kenny added, climbing into the car behind his sister. The kids preferred him to take his car rather than his work truck. More room.

"How come?'' he asked. His kids saw far more of Hallie than he did.

"She's regrouping,'' Meagan explained.

"Yeah, she's baking cookies and stuff.'' Kenny bounced the soccer ball on his knee. "When I asked her why, do you know what she said? She said men needed help knowing they wanted to get married. Is that true, Dad?''

"Ah...I guess so.''

"Do you like Hallie?'' The question came from his daughter.

"Like her? Sure.''

"I mean *like* her.''

"You mean romantically?'' Steve knew that was exactly what Meagan meant. He could tell by his daughter's tone that his answer was important to her. Wouldn't his kids be more interested in seeing him back with their mother? Most children were. Maybe they knew something he didn't.

"Hallie's a wonderful person," Steve answered carefully. "I like her a lot, but she isn't the woman for me." It didn't seem necessary to remind his children that the only woman he'd ever loved was their mother.

"Why isn't she the woman for you?" Kenny asked.

"Well, because...she just isn't. Don't get me wrong, Hallie's great, but—"

"She isn't Mom," Meagan finished for him, and he thought he heard a note of sadness in her voice.

"Yeah," he said. "She isn't your mother."

"But Mom's dating Kip," Kenny threw in.

The sound of the man's name made Steve clench his teeth. He didn't know where Mary Lynn was going with this relationship or how serious it was. Every time he asked her she got defensive.

"So she's still seeing the ol' Kiperroo," Steve joked, trying to disguise his concern.

"A lot." Kenny sighed deeply.

This was the last thing Steve wanted to hear, but he'd rather know the truth so he could deal with it. Clearly it was time to change tactics if he wanted to win back his ex-wife. This hands-off wait-and-see-what-happens-with-Kip approach hadn't worked. He'd call Mary Lynn, he decided, and talk to her again. Soon.

"I think you should ask Hallie out," Meagan said, studying him intently.

"Hallie and me on a date?" Steve tried to keep it light. "No way."

"But she's a lot of fun, Dad," Kenny insisted. "And her chocolate-chip cookies are real good. She let me take some to the guys last week and everyone liked 'em." He paused. "She's funny, too. She bakes all these cookies and then gives them away. I asked her why she doesn't eat some, and she said it's because she's come to hate her treadmill."

Steve grinned.

"Will you think about going out with Hallie sometime?" Meagan asked.

He should have known his daughter wouldn't let this drop. "I'll think about it," he promised.

"Which means no," Meagan muttered.

Steve felt he had to justify his hesitation. "Not so," he argued. "I will think about it." The last thing he wanted was to disappoint his kids, but he couldn't allow them to dictate his love life.

Steve didn't give his conversation with Meagan and Kenny another thought until the following evening. He'd never been keen on yard work, but the lawn badly needed to be mowed. Monday afternoon he returned home from work and decided he couldn't delay that chore any longer. If he did, the condo association might come pounding on his door.

At least the weather was beautiful, unseasonably warm and summer-bright. Perfect for outdoor tasks.

Steve made sure he had a couple of bottles of cold beer in the refrigerator before he started. It took three tugs to get the old mower going, but it finally kicked in.

Being a generous kind-hearted soul, or so he told himself, he tossed aside his shirt and mowed Hallie's half of the shared yard when he'd finished his own. She'd done more than one favor for him, and he appreciated knowing that Meagan and Kenny could stay at her place if he was late on Friday afternoons.

It was when he turned off the lawn mower that he heard the music. A blues number. The wail of a solitary saxophone that seemed to speak of sadness and trouble. He thought the music was coming from Hallie's place.

He stood quietly, listening to be sure. When he glanced through her sliding glass door, he caught a glimpse of her lying on the living-room carpet, arms spread out. Her eyes were closed and she wore the woeful look of a woman done wrong. He paused and wondered what *that* was all about. Then he remembered what Meagan had told him.

This was the day Hallie turned thirty.

Steve had spent his last two birthdays alone. He'd tried to tell himself he didn't care, that birthday celebrations were for kids. But he remembered the empty feeling in the pit of his stomach when he'd climbed into bed those nights, regretting that there hadn't been anyone around to make a fuss over him.

Was anyone making a fuss over Hallie? Like him, she'd probably heard from her family and a few friends—one of them had sent her flowers. But she was alone now and obviously miserable. Poor thing. His heart went out to her.

Steve showered and changed clothes, but couldn't forget how depressed and lonely Hallie had looked. Hell, he'd been there himself.

Before he could change his mind he stuck a candle in a snack cake, grabbed the two bottles of beer and knocked on her front door.

He listened as the mournful music abruptly ended. A moment later he heard the lock turn as she opened the front door.

"Happy birthday to you," he sang, and handed her the chocolate-flavored cupcake.

"Who told you?" she asked, wide-eyed with surprise and what he hoped was delight.

"The kids. Hey, it isn't every day you celebrate your thirtieth birthday."

"Come on in," she said, leading the way into her living room. "Although I don't know that I'm fit company."

"Because you've turned the dreaded three-O?" He'd heard some women saw thirty as the end of their youth, which struck him as ridiculous. Besides, if the kids hadn't told him, he wouldn't have guessed Hallie was a day over twenty-five. All right, twenty-eight.

"Thirty," she muttered, collapsing onto the sofa, "and not a marriage prospect in sight."

Steve uncapped one of the beers and passed it to her. "Tell Uncle Stevie all about it."

"*Uncle* Stevie?"

"Hey, I'm five years your senior. I've spit in the eye of middle age—spreading middle, weak knees, failing eyesight and everything."

A smile twitched at the corners of her mouth.

"Thirty's not so bad," he assured her, "once you get used to it."

"That isn't all. I have other reasons for being depressed."

"You owe the IRS?" Since they both owned their own businesses, he knew what a killer tax time could be.

"Yes," she said with a groan, as if he'd reminded her of something *else* to be depressed about. "But that's the bad news with the good. I made more money than I did last year, so I can't really complain too much." She tipped back the bottle and took a respectable swig of beer.

Some women sipped beer like they were tasting fine

single-malt Scotch. Not Hallie, and he liked her the better for it.

"I gained back five of the ten pounds I lost," she said plaintively. "I suffered to lose those five pounds. One little slip with the double-fudge macadamia-nut ice cream and they're back."

As far as he could see, those few pounds hadn't hurt her any. He didn't think she had any cause for concern. Despite having reached the big three-O, she looked just fine.

"I don't know what made me decide to step on the scale this morning. I told myself I wouldn't, seeing that it's my birthday and all." She downed another swallow of beer. "And there they were." She fell back against the sofa cushion and closed her eyes. "It wasn't supposed to happen like that." Suddenly she gave him a stricken look. "I can't believe I'm telling you this. Usually I only discuss this kind of stuff with Donnalee. You must be a better friend than I thought."

"Uh, maybe there's something wrong with your scale," he said, trying to be helpful.

"I'm not talking about that," she muttered, although she was touched by his attempt to shift the blame for those five pounds to her scale. "The thing is, according to my goal planner, I should have met him by now."

She opened one eye and stared at him. He suspected she was asking him to inquire further, which he obligingly did. "Him?"

"My husband-to-be," she said, enunciating just a little too clearly.

"Oh, yeah. Him."

"This beer tastes really good." She finished off the bottle and set it aside.

Steve had barely tasted his. "Have you had dinner yet?"

Her head lolled against the back of the sofa, both eyes tightly shut. She seemed to find the question amusing and smiled broadly. "Not breakfast or lunch, either. Too much work."

That explained why the beer had gone to her head so fast.

"Then listen, this is your lucky day because I was about to order Chinese. There's a new place off Meeker that delivers. It's on me."

"Happy birthday to me, happy birthday to me."

"Exactly." He walked over to her phone, removed the business card from his wallet and ordered enough to feed them both for two or three meals.

"Donnalee's in Hawaii," Hallie said.

He had no idea why she felt the need to tell him that.

"She had flowers delivered."

"That was nice of her."

"Very nice," Hallie agreed.

He noticed that she perked up after the food arrived. The scent of sizzling pepper beef and almond fried chicken wafted enticingly through the compact kitchen. "This is one of the sweetest things anyone's ever done for me," she said, arranging two plates on the table and putting water on to boil for tea.

Steve was impressed that she used chopsticks. He did, too, pleased that she was willing to eat in the traditional Chinese way. Mary Lynn had refused to even try and lost patience with him when he insisted on doing so.

Because they were both hungry, they ate in silence. It no longer surprised him how comfortable he felt with

Hallie. As he'd explained to his children, he wasn't romantically interested in her, but he considered her a friend. He'd come to believe that in many ways friendship was of greater value.

"I feel so much better," she said when she'd finished. She pushed her plate aside, placed her hands on her stomach and slowly exhaled. "Both physically and emotionally. Thank you, Steve."

"No problem." He didn't want her getting all sentimental over a little thing like a bottle of beer and some take-out dinner. "You've been a real help to me with the kids on Friday nights. This was the least I could do for your birthday."

"My thirtieth birthday," she said.

Afterward Steve wasn't sure when he'd made the decision to kiss her. It was an impulse, he rationalized later, no doubt prompted by Meagan and Kenny's questions from the day before.

It happened as he was leaving.

"I'm glad you're my neighbor," Hallie said, walking him to the front door.

"I am, too." He opened the door, then turned and gently held her shoulders.

He saw the surprise in her eyes and wondered if it was a reflection of his own. "Happy birthday, Hallie," he whispered before lowering his mouth to hers.

As kisses went, it was good. Unexpectedly good. Her lips were soft and pliable, molding easily to his. She smelled and tasted great. Her mouth parted slightly and he found himself deepening the kiss. The ol' adrenaline started to flow about then, and he drew back abruptly, not wanting things to get out of hand.

She buried her face in his shoulder. He ran his fingers through her hair and kissed the top of her head.

"There's someone special just waiting to meet you, Hallie," he whispered, and her hair tickled his nose. "Don't worry, he's out there, wondering why it's taking so long."

"That's funny," she murmured.

"How's that?"

"I recently told Donnalee the same thing. It sounded much more convincing when I was saying it, though."

Steve chuckled. "You'll be just fine."

She broke away with obvious reluctance. "Thanks again, Steve. For everything."

He wondered if she was including the kiss.

Sixteen

Not My Type

"Did you have a nice birthday?" Kenny asked, leaning against Hallie's kitchen counter.

"Very nice," she answered, lifting cookies hot from the oven off the baking sheet. She'd mastered chocolate-chip and was moving on to oatmeal-raisin. She intended to create a repertoire of baked goods to entice the most discriminating connoisseur. Kenny was an enthusiastic admirer of her baking, but hardly discriminating. Right now, he waited impatiently for the cookies to cool. "Your dad bought me dinner."

"Dad did?" This bit of news evidently piqued Meagan's interest. She slid off the sofa where she'd been reading and hurried into the kitchen, joining her brother at the counter.

"It was a kind gesture," Hallie said. She'd thought about it a lot since Monday night—thought about the kiss too, more than she should. It was a kiss between friends, nothing more, yet she found herself remembering it at the oddest moments. Like this one. But maybe that was good, because Meagan and Kenny were a reminder of how much Steve hoped to reconcile with Mary Lynn.

Unable to wait any longer, Kenny reached for a cookie and burned his hand. "Ouch," he yelped, sucking on his fingertips.

"Hallie told you they were hot," Meagan chided. "Where did Dad take you?"

"He ordered in Chinese." She didn't tell the kids she'd been so depressed she'd lain on the carpet listening to the saddest blues CD she could find. She'd stacked an entire music menu on her player, including bagpipes, funeral dirges and mournful ballads. Sad troubled music for a sad troubled day.

"Do you like my dad?" Kenny asked, tossing the hot cookie from hand to hand.

"Sure." Hallie absently scooped dough onto the sheet for a new batch of cookies.

"Enough to marry him?"

"Marry him?" Hallie gave her full attention to Steve's kids. Both were studying her with dark unblinking eyes. She remembered the kiss again. Although it had been a *satisfying* kiss, it wasn't a kiss between lovers or even potential lovers. She could embellish it in her mind as much as she wanted, but she knew very well that Steve wasn't interested in a more complex relationship. They were friends and neighbors, and that was all.

"You said you liked him," Kenny said.

Hallie placed the cookie sheet in the oven while she considered how to respond. Something told her the answer was important and she needed to choose her words carefully, a task made more difficult by not knowing the status of Steve's relationship with Mary Lynn or the likelihood of reconciliation.

"I think your dad's great. He works hard and loves you kids. I've been impressed with what a good father he is." She paused, wondering how much she should say. Meagan and Kenny continued to study her as if waiting for more. "I like his sense of humor." Kenny smiled encouragingly. Recalling how Steve had twice lent her money to pay taxi drivers, she added, "He's generous and caring." He hadn't pressured her into the bowling tournament, either. "He's a friend, a good one, but—"

"That's great," Kenny interrupted her, "but do you like him enough to marry him?"

"Don't rush her," Meagan barked, glaring at her younger brother.

Kenny ignored his sister. "You'd make a cool step-mom."

"You would," Meagan agreed, nodding.

They were still watching her so intently. Hallie felt a bit unnerved. "I'm glad you think so," she said slowly, frowning as she glanced from one to the other. "But..."

"But?" Kenny cried. "I hate it when Dad says 'but' because it always means no." His shoulders sagged and he propped his chin on the kitchen counter. "Go on," he said in a resigned voice, as if he already knew what she intended to say.

"I'm just not the right woman for him." Honesty was the best policy, Hallie had determined, even if it disappointed her young friends. "Your dad's a great guy, but he isn't for me. I hope you don't mind too much."

Kenny helped himself to a cooled cookie. "Not too much. That was what I figured you were going to say."

Hallie was relieved.

"Besides, when we asked Dad, he said almost the same thing."

Goose bumps rose on the back of Hallie's neck. "You asked your father about marrying me?"

"Sort of," Meagan answered.

"And what *exactly* did he say?"

"That you have a neat personality and everything," Kenny explained, "but then, like I told you he said almost the same thing you did. You aren't his type, either."

"Not his type!" Hallie couldn't believe her ears. "Well, if that doesn't beat all," she muttered under her breath, not wanting the kids to hear.

The timer rang and she grabbed the last tray of cookies from the oven rack with more force than necessary. "Not his type," she muttered again, her back to the kids. The man's attitude rankled—never mind whether or not *she* was being rational.

She clumsily scraped the cookies off the sheet, mangling more than one. Why, Steve Marris would be the luckiest man in the world to marry a woman like her. Of all the nerve!

"Hallie, are you mad about something?" Meagan asked.

"Mad?" she asked, her voice squeaking. "What do I have to be mad about?" She'd wring Steve's neck, that was what she'd do. How dared he tell his kids he liked her "personality." That was the kind of thing men said about the women eager mothers pushed on unwilling sons. It was the kind of thing men said about women they found sexually unattractive. But then, what did she expect from a man who'd suggested the way to find a husband was to enhance her bust size?

The phone rang and Hallie whipped the receiver off the wall. "Hello," she snapped, suspecting it was

Steve. *Hoping* it was, so she could set him straight about a few things.

"Hallie?" Donnalee asked uncertainly. "Is something wrong?"

"Donnalee!" she cried. "You're back! How was Hawaii?"

"Wonderful. I'm relaxed, tanned and feeling more like myself. Have you got plans for tonight?"

Hallie's mood lifted instantly. "I suppose you brought me one of those windup hula dolls?"

"Yes," Donnalee teased, and they both laughed.

Her friend had been gone eight days and it felt like a month to Hallie. "Come on over any time." Friday night, sitting around with a girlfriend—that pretty well summarized the sorry state of her love life, she thought, smothering a giggle.

"I'll be there in an hour," Donnalee promised.

As it happened, Hallie didn't get a chance to talk to Steve, which was just as well all round. Kenny was looking out the window when Steve pulled up. "Dad's home," he yelled, leaping off the sofa. He grabbed his backpack and headed toward the front door.

"Don't be upset with my dad," Meagan said, staying behind a moment. "He didn't mean anything by what he said."

"I'm not upset," Hallie assured her. Well, she had been at first, sort of, but as the kids had pointed out, she'd said the same thing about him. It was her ego talking, not her reason. In fact, she felt a little embarrassed over the way she'd reacted—like a woman scorned.

Still Meagan lingered.

"You wanted to ask me something?" Hallie asked.

Generally Meagan was as eager to see her father on Friday nights as Kenny.

"Next week is Take Your Daughter to Work day," she announced, speaking quickly as though the words were bursting to get out. "Mom's not working 'cause she's in school, so I asked Dad about it, and he said I could go to the office with him, but I don't want to be a machinist. I'm kind of interested in art, though, and I'd like to see what you do, Hallie. Can I spend the day with you?"

The idea appealed to Hallie right away. She recalled herself at Meagan's age, how she would have given anything to see a commercial artist at work. "That would be wonderful. Are you sure your dad won't mind?"

Meagan beamed her a wide carefree smile. "He'll be glad. He'd take me if I really wanted, but it'd be much more fun going with you. Thanks, Hallie." Meagan gave her a quick shy hug and raced outside.

Hallie walked to the door and watched as Meagan excitedly told her father that Hallie had agreed to take her to Artistic License. Steve looked over to find her standing in the doorway. Hallie waved.

"You're sure Meagan won't be a bother?" he called.

"Positive."

Even from this distance, Hallie could see his relief. He pointed his finger in her direction. "I owe you one, neighbor."

Hallie shook her head, laughing. "Don't worry about it. We'll have a good time."

True to her word, Donnalee arrived about half an hour later. She hadn't exaggerated about her tan; she looked bronzed and beautiful. Rested and obviously at peace with herself and her decision.

They hugged and Donnalee presented her with a box of chocolate-covered macadamia nuts. "It's an emergency supply in case you don't have any ice cream handy when the next tragedy strikes," she joked.

Unable to resist, Hallie opened the box, sampled one, gave one to her friend and then promptly stuck them in the freezer and away from temptation.

"Something's different," Donnalee observed, studying her.

"Different?"

"Physically," Donnalee said. "You haven't done anything to your hair, have you? Something's up."

Feeling smug, Hallie threw herself onto the sofa. "That's an interesting turn of phrase, my friend. What's up, quite literally, is my bosom."

"Hallie, you didn't!"

"I did. I succumbed and got myself one of those enhancer bras." She was unwilling to admit that Steve had been the catalyst.

"I can't believe you'd do that," Donnalee said with more than a hint of indignation. "It's ridiculous to think that a push-up bra is going to make you a better person—or even help you meet a man."

"True," Hallie agreed, feeling a little silly. "But it's given me a psychological boost, which, after more failures than I care to admit, is one I badly needed."

"It's sexist. Those bras take the women's movement back ten years. It's degrading." Donnalee sounded stern and unrelenting. She paused, dragged in a deep breath, then asked, "How much did it cost and where can I buy one?"

Both dissolved into giggles. It felt good to laugh again.

"No, seriously," Hallie said. "I thought about this.

I don't see it as sexist. It's no different from makeup or hair spray or anything else women use to enhance their appearance. It's fun and it makes me feel good, and if it happens to be attractive to men...well, all the better.''

"I know, I know," Donnalee said. "Hey, do I smell cookies?" She wrinkled her nose and sniffed loudly.

"I've been taking cooking classes," Hallie admitted with some reluctance, wondering if her friend was going to comment on that, too.

"The old 'way to a man's heart is through his stomach' routine?"

"Yup." No point in denying it.

"Good thinking," Donnalee said with a grin. "Why not go for the tried and true? Then, once you've lured him and fed him, you can dazzle him with your *real* personality."

In that moment Hallie noticed the sadness in her friend's gaze. She reached for Donnalee's hand. "Second thoughts about Sanford?"

"Every day," she admitted. "I really loved him. It's difficult to turn off my heart. Forgetting him isn't easy."

"He hasn't called or contacted you in any way?"

"No, but then I didn't expect he would. And I really don't want him to." She brushed the hair from her face and inhaled sharply as if struggling to hold back tears. "Hawaii helped. Mom and I had a wonderful time. We slept in every day, lazed on the beach, visited all the tourist places and shopped till we dropped. It was exactly what I needed."

"And now you're home," Hallie said, watching her friend.

"And alone once more. Only..."

"Only now you feel even *more* alone," Hallie finished, certain she knew what Donnalee was experiencing.

"Yes," she murmured.

"Are you going back to Dateline?" Hallie asked. She was preparing to leap back into the dating world herself, with hesitation but resolve. After several weeks' sabbatical, she was ready to try again.

"I'm going to give it a bit of time first," Donnalee said thoughtfully. "Some time for myself. The way you suggested. I'm feeling kind of battered."

"It's a good idea," Hallie said. "Step back, evaluate and then move forward from there."

Donnalee grew quiet. "I remind myself on a daily basis that there's a man out there for me. Someone who'll share my dreams."

"I know there is." Of this Hallie was confident. For her friend. Although she still had some doubts concerning her own prospects.

"What about you?" Donnalee asked, apparently reading Hallie's mind. "Are you ready to go back to Dateline?"

"Yes. Actually I already have." She reviewed the name of the applicant she'd been paired up with this time. Larry McDonald. She'd received the information on him the day before. "They sent me another bio this week."

Donnalee sat up excitedly. "Let me see."

Hallie brought it out, and while Donnalee read over the page of information, Hallie studied her reactions. Nothing. Donnalee didn't reveal so much as a flicker of emotion—which described her own feelings, too. She'd read the file numerous times, and each time she felt completely…untouched, completely dispassionate about the details of this man's life. He seemed nice enough—a science professor was sure to impress her family—but unfortunately he also seemed dull.

"Larry." Donnalee said the name slowly, as if the sound of it would help her decipher his personality.

"It's unfair to judge him without meeting him first, don't you think?"

"Absolutely," Donnalee agreed. "Have you set up a time?"

Hallie nodded. "We're meeting in a bookstore. It's not very original, but we both like to read and, well, it seemed a good idea at the time."

"When?"

"Sunday afternoon."

"You'll call me afterward?"

Hallie agreed, but frankly, she didn't hold out any great hope for Larry McDonald.

But then, she reminded herself, she was certainly willing to be surprised.

"What are you doing?" Meagan asked. The eleven-year-old stood behind Hallie at the drafting table in the large workroom at Artistic License. The front office was staffed by two employees, Liz and Evie, who handled walk-in traffic, took orders and answered the phone. Four copy machines of various sizes hummed, while the largest of the printing presses droned like a snoring troll in the room next door to Hallie.

"You're done helping Bonnie?" Hallie asked. It had taken her a moment to break her concentration.

"Yup. It was fun, too." Meagan maintained a respectful distance from Hallie's drafting table.

"I'm working on a logo design," Hallie told her. She'd been playing with a number of ideas for the better part of an hour. This was often the most difficult aspect of her job. The client had approached her with several ideas, but unfortunately translating those concepts into a viable image was proving difficult.

"Bonnie let me move things around on the computer screen."

Because Hallie was working to deadline with this logo project, she'd had Meagan work with her assistant on the production of a brochure they were creating for the local school district.

"Did you enjoy that?" Hallie asked.

Meagan's eyes lit up. "It was great. I learned a lot."

"She did a good job, too," Bonnie called out from the other side of the room. "Hallie, I've got to go over the layout for the Bergman Hardware ad. The newspaper needs it before three."

"No problem. I'll have Meagan work with me."

Hallie glanced at her watch. It was another hour until lunch, and she'd hoped to have a couple of designs ready for the Prudhommes by that afternoon. "Pull up a chair, kiddo, and I'll explain what I'm doing—after I talk to Hank about one of our print jobs."

Hank Davis took care of all the print orders, which had steadily increased every month since the first of the year. She jumped up to discuss a question of priorities with him, then stayed a minute to chat about their expanding workload. If her business continued to grow at this rate, she'd need new equipment, more staff and either another building or an addition to the existing place. The prospect delighted her. Her reputation for quality had been earned, one customer at a time.

She rejoined Meagan, who'd dragged a chair next to Hallie's. "I don't draw very good," Meagan said, sounding worried, "but I'll try if you want."

"What I'm looking for now are ideas to advertise a French bakery," Hallie told her. "The logo will be printed on the front window, takeout boxes, napkins, letterhead and so on. The logo is an important promotional tool for any business."

"It's going to be on everything then?"

"Just about. Mr. and Mrs. Prudhomme have specific ideas about the kind of image they want—something clever and cute. They serve coffee and pastries, but their specialty is petit fours."

"What're those?"

"Small frosted cakes a little larger than chocolates." Hallie's mind refused to stop spinning and she deftly sketched a picture of the Eiffel Tower. Next she drew a van with the name of the bakery on the side, to show that the Prudhommes also welcomed catering opportunities.

Meagan sat by her side and watched silently.

"Do you want to try?" Hallie asked. She was fresh out of ideas herself. While she understood what the Prudhommes wanted, she hadn't managed to translate it onto paper.

Meagan picked up the pad and sucked on the end of her pencil the same way Hallie did. Hallie smiled, sliding her arm around Meagan's shoulders. The girl smiled back. "Being a graphic artist is fun, isn't it?" Meagan asked.

"Sometimes." Also frustrating, challenging and a few other choice adjectives, Hallie mused.

"It's a lot different than I thought it would be."

"What do you mean?" Hallie asked as she scribbled away at a new concept. She didn't want to lose the idea.

Meagan glanced over her shoulder, drew a deep

breath and gestured around her. "It's so big. Dad's going to be surprised when he picks me up this afternoon. When I asked him what your shop was like, he said he wasn't sure, but he thought you sat around and drew pictures all day."

"Really?" That amused Hallie. Poor Steve hadn't a clue how involved or complicated her business was. She did everything from letterheads, designs and printing to commercial photography. The list was endless. But then, she didn't know all that much about machine shops, either. Hallie suspected if she was to visit *his* workplace, she'd have her eyes opened, too.

"You know what I thought when you said petit fours?" Meagan asked. "I thought of really short numbers." She laughed softly to herself.

"Short 4s?" Hallie asked.

Meagan nodded.

Hallie nimbly drew a series of elongated numbers, each with a face and personality. Their only apparel was a French beret, rakishly tilted. A row of short 4s stood in front of their much taller cousins.

Meagan looked at the drawing and giggled.

Hallie laughed, too. It wasn't bad, although the other numbers distracted from the overall effect. She set the 4s dressed in their berets on top of a linen-covered table. The steam from two smiling cups of coffee circled a base with a single red rosebud. Clever and eyecatching, just the effect Hallie had been trying to capture. She needed to work with it, develop the idea further, but she was on to something. Thanks to Meagan.

Hallie took Meagan to lunch at Lindo's, her favorite neighborhood restaurant, although it'd been at least a month since she'd gone there. Because she was so often working to deadline, she'd gotten into the habit of ordering her lunch to go and having someone stop by for it. She'd designed and printed the menus for the owner, Mrs. Guillermo, several years earlier and had recently updated them.

When Hallie arrived nearly a full hour before the heavy lunchtime rush, Mrs. Guillermo welcomed her enthusiastically. "I don't see you for too long," she said in her heavily accented English.

Hallie introduced Meagan, and Mrs. Guillermo's expressive face broke into a wide smile.

"Today is Take Your Daughter To Work day," Hallie explained.

The older woman nodded. "I read this is special day in newspaper. My granddaughter is here."

"That's wonderful."

"Your daughter is as beautiful as you," she said, and before Hallie could explain that she wasn't Meagan's mother, Mrs. Guillermo handed the menus to a girl about the same age. "Rosita will see you to your table," she said proudly.

Meagan didn't say anything until after they were seated. "I'm glad you didn't tell her I'm not really your daughter," she said, then shook her head sadly. "Sometimes I can't help wishing you *were* Dad's type."

Seventeen

She Bakes

June 2

Larry and I have been seeing each other steadily for a month now. Steadily, but not often. Once a week at the most, which, to be honest, is fine with me. Everything was so intense with Mark. He had to know where I was and who I was with every minute of the day. It felt like we were constantly together.

Larry's on the quiet side, and that makes me all the more talkative. I don't know why I feel this need to fill the silences, but I do. Anyway, I suppose you could say he's your basic nice guy. Once we're more comfortable with each other, I'll be able to judge my feelings more accurately. Right now, our relationship is still a bit awkward.

So far, we've gone to a number of museums. These are all places I've wanted to see, but have never taken the time to visit. If we aren't touring museums, we're in bookstores. The most exciting date so far has been to a Moroccan restaurant. Larry's a mathematics professor, and I don't think he has a lot of discretionary income, but then, I'm not interested in a man for his money. He was serious enough about finding a wife to plunk down the two thousand bucks, which is all I need to know.

He kissed me for the first time last week—on our third date. It was all right. It's come as something of a shock to realize how wildly romantic I am. I want a man panting with desire for me, one who won't be able to remove that silk nightgown fast enough. The nightgown that's lying untouched in my bottom drawer. For reasons I have yet to understand, I can't imagine Larry panting with desire for anything.

Speaking of that nightgown, I take it out occasionally and wonder how long it'll be before I don this masterpiece of silk and lace. Will it be for Larry? Try as I might, it's difficult to think of Larry getting excited about anything. Nor can I picture him nude. I wonder if he'd wear his glasses to bed.

Mom always said still waters run deep. If that's the case, Larry's deep all right, so deep I wonder if I'll ever touch bottom.

On a brighter note—all isn't wasted. Larry likes my cookies.

It was well past closing time, but Steve had to finish this paperwork. He left as much of the bookkeeping as he could to his secretary and the accountant, but there were some things he had to handle personally.

Todd stuck his head in the door. "You staying late again tonight?"

"I won't be much longer," Steve replied without looking up from his desk. He wondered if it was true. "Go ahead, I'll lock up."

"How about a cold beer? I don't mind waiting. Fact is, I've got some stuff I need to clean up, anyway."

A cold beer sounded good. It'd been a long day, and with a stack of paperwork looming in front of him, it was going to be longer still. "Sure. That'd be great."

Tackling the pile with renewed enthusiasm, Steve finished within an hour. He found Todd and they drove to a local bar, taking their own vehicles. Although Steve considered Todd one of his best friends, they didn't often socialize. No need to, really, since they saw each other five days a week. Todd had been a good confidant during the divorce proceedings and the days that had followed. If Steve had ever needed a friend it was then.

He hadn't heard much from Mary Lynn in a while, and that worried him. Kenny hadn't said anything about Kip lately, but that didn't mean Mary Lynn wasn't seeing the guy—who, he'd recently learned, was a car salesman.

They arrived at the Sure Shooter separately and parked out front. "It's been ages since we were here," Todd said when the waitress, dressed in Western garb, delivered a pitcher of beer and two frosty mugs. Country music blared from the jukebox. A twanging female voice belted out the tale of a man who'd done his woman wrong—and paid the price. A cry-in-your-beer kind of song about a truck-driving, gun-toting, whiskey-guzzling son of a bitch.

Steve filled the mugs and realized that Todd was

right; it'd been damn near seven or eight months since they'd sat across from each other in a tavern. It sometimes shocked Steve to notice how fast the time flew by. Without much trouble he could remember changing Meagan's diaper. Now, before he knew it, she'd be a teenager.

Thinking about babies and diapers brought Hallie to mind. He'd gotten a panic call from her the other day. Apparently her six-month-old niece would be in her care for the weekend, and Hallie wanted to make sure Meagan would be around to lend a hand if she needed one. Steve couldn't even begin to imagine the trouble Hallie could get into with an infant. He planned on sticking around himself, just for the hell of it.

A few years back Steve had tried to talk Mary Lynn into having another child. She wasn't interested. It'd been a disappointment at the time, but considering what had happened with them, he was grateful she'd refused.

"So," Todd said, gazing at his beer, "how's it going?"

"Great," Steve replied automatically. "What about you?"

"Good. Damn good. I've been spending most weekends at the lake, working on the cabin, remodeling it You ought to stop by with the kids one weekend. You'd be surprised at the changes."

"I will." Todd had inherited the summer home from his grandparents. If Steve remembered correctly, it was out near Key Center on Carr Inlet. Every now and again Todd brought him some fresh oysters. Steve had never tasted any finer.

"Everything's going well, then," Todd said.

"Great. Say, did I tell you Meagan wants to take art classes? She spent a day at work with my neighbor a few weeks back and has since decided she wants to be a commercial artist.''

''Really?''

''Yeah. Apparently she came up with an idea that Hallie used, and now Meagan's convinced she's found her career path.'' He grinned every time he thought about it. Not that he didn't believe Meagan could do it. What surprised him was the effect that one day of working with Hallie had had on his daughter. He was genuinely thankful for Hallie's encouragement.

Hallie. He smiled just thinking about her. They'd had a confrontation of sorts a couple of weeks back. He'd been minding his own business, washing his car late one Sunday afternoon, when she'd come out of the house, looking dejected and miserable. It'd taken him a while to ferret out the reason. He'd been sure it had to do with the latest character she was dating, but no, that wasn't it. Seemed she'd stepped on the scale that morning and discovered she'd gained two pounds. Furthermore, she said *he* was to blame, since he was the one who'd talked her into baking all those cookies.

Steve told this story to Todd, then laughed until his throat felt raw. Two pounds, and she'd made it sound like fifty.

''Are you sure you aren't more than friends?'' Todd asked.

The question caught Steve unawares. ''Of course. What makes you ask something like that when you know how I feel about Mary Lynn?''

''Well...'' Todd folded his hands around his mug. ''Your eyes light up when you talk about Hallie.''

Steve digested that and shrugged. His eyes? Todd must have been watching ''Oprah'' a few too many times. ''Hallie makes me laugh,'' he said simply. He'd never been friends with a woman the way he was with Hallie.

"She's bright and funny," he continued, "and the thing is, she doesn't realize how funny she is. She paid this agency two thousand bucks to find her a husband, and I'll tell you, she's dated some real screwballs."

"You sure you're not interested in her yourself?"

Steve shook his head. "No way. You should meet this guy she's dating now. He's got 'nerd' written all over him. He comes complete with a slide rule and thick glasses. Hallie tells me he teaches math at Green River Community College. Now I'm sure he's a perfectly okay guy, but him and Hallie? That matchmaking service has got oatmeal for brains if they think Hallie'd be happy with this joker."

Grinning, Todd leaned back and listened.

"My kids love her, and with good reason. She spends more time with them than Mary Lynn ever did. Plus, I've never eaten better since she started those baking classes."

"You mean she bakes more than just cookies?"

"Yeah, homemade bread and cinnamon rolls, for starters. She brought over a huge plate of maple bars last weekend. The kids and I stuffed 'em down before lunch. They were the best I've ever tasted."

"I can't remember the last time I tasted homemade anything," Todd muttered, and it was easy to tell he envied Steve a neighbor who baked. "A man could marry a woman for that alone."

Steve straightened and laughed outright. "That's exactly what I said."

"You offered to marry her?" Todd studied him as if he wasn't sure if this was a joke.

"Don't be silly." The question was ridiculous.

"Hallie isn't interested in me, and vice versa. But she *is* looking for a husband, and I helped."

"She got advice from *you?*"

Steve decided not to take offense. "Some time ago Hallie asked my opinion on what a man wants in the woman he marries, and I told her."

"You told her?" Todd sounded even more incredulous.

"Damn straight," Steve announced proudly, although he refrained from repeating his comment about a woman's physical attributes. "I was honest, and Hallie was smart enough to take my advice seriously." She wasn't the only one who'd put on a few pounds since then, either. Steve knew from the way his clothes fit that he'd gained four or five pounds himself, although in his case it didn't really matter. He'd lost at least that much in two and a half years of making his own dinners.

Todd reached for the pitcher and refilled their mugs. "The kids are fine? They've adjusted to the divorce?"

"As far as I can tell. Meagan's turning into quite the young woman. Kenny's sprouting faster than a weed. They spend most weekends with me—I wish it could be more. I miss having them around all the time."

Todd bent forward, resting his elbows on the wooden table. "You haven't mentioned Mary Lynn in quite a while. You two still seeing each other?"

"Sure we see each other," Steve said, knowing he sounded defensive. "Every week when she drops off the kids. She calls once in a while, too." Generally when she was low on cash and needed a loan until the next support check. She'd never mentioned the roses he'd sent on her birthday. When he'd brought up the subject, she'd smiled and thanked him, but her heart wasn't in it. He'd almost felt as if she'd resented his sending her flowers. He'd been disappointed by her reaction and tried not to think about his lack of progress in the past few months.

"I saw her the other day," Todd said casually. Too casually.

His tone instantly sparked suspicions in Steve. He decided to make it easy on his friend. "I suppose she was with some guy."

From the abrupt way Todd inhaled, Steve could tell he'd taken him by surprise.

"As a matter of fact she was."

"Probably Kip," Steve told him, shrugging it off, although it gave him no pleasure to confront what he'd been ignoring for months. Mary Lynn was still involved with this sleazy salesman.

"Is this the same guy she was dating right after the first of the year?" Todd wanted to know.

"Yeah, I guess it is," Steve admitted reluctantly. He'd been waiting for her infatuation with this jerk to run its course; so far it hadn't happened. "What's he look like?" It was the kind of question he couldn't ask his children. One thing he knew for sure: Kip didn't get grease under his fingernails.

"Hell, I don't know," Todd answered. "Polished-looking. He was wearing a suit."

"Like a talk-show host?" That was the way Steve pictured the other man—slick, debonair, just the type of guy who fit Mary Lynn's new taste in men.

"Yeah," Todd said, with a sharp nod. "That pretty much describes him."

"Where were they?" he asked, his lips tightening despite his effort to hide his feelings.

"At Southcenter. I had to run into Sears to replace a wrench, and I happened to catch sight of Mary Lynn. Looked like they'd been there for some time, too. Kip's arms were full of packages."

Steve snorted softly. "So she finally found a man who likes to shop. More power to him. I last ten, fifteen minutes tops in any mall. I don't care how many discount stores there are. You take that SuperMall in Auburn. The kids were after me for weeks to take them there. It was a madhouse. I'd rather tear apart and rebuild a car engine anytime." He hoped the change in subject wasn't too obvious. He didn't want to talk about Mary Lynn, and he sure wasn't interested in hearing about Kip.

Apparently his effort to change the subject wasn't obvious enough, because Todd said, "You seem to have dealt with Mary Lynn dating again."

Steve sighed. "The hell I have." Continuing with this charade was turning out to be more than he could handle. Every time he thought about his ex-wife with another man, he had to grit his teeth. When he'd learned she was dating Kip, he hadn't pressured her, suspecting that if he did, he'd drive her straight into the other man's arms. So he'd bided his time, confident that it wouldn't take her long to lose interest. Clearly he'd made a tactical error. Well, he could still reverse his strategy. Starting now.

Steve stood and slapped a ten-dollar bill on the table.

Frowning slightly, Todd looked up. "You're leaving?"

"Yeah." He reached for and drained his mug.

"Where you headed?"

"Where else? To talk to Mary Lynn." As he turned away, he thought he heard Todd groan. He left the tavern to the accompaniment of Garth Brooks belting out something about friends in low places. Kind of fit Mary Lynn's image of him, he told himself sourly.

The tires on his truck churned up gravel as he sped out of the parking lot. He drove around for an hour or so, clearing his head. Then he stopped for some take-out food and spent a while figuring out exactly what he wanted to say to Mary Lynn. But he waited until he knew the kids would be down for the night before he approached the house. No need to involve them.

He never could get used to knocking on the door of the place he'd bought and paid for himself. Legally it was Mary Lynn's house now, but still...

Mary Lynn answered the door, obviously surprised to see him. "Steve. What are you doing here?"

"Have you got a few minutes?" he asked. He was struck again by her beauty, her delicate features and dark glossy hair. He'd missed her in so many ways; perhaps what he missed most of all, what he most wanted to recover, was the companionship of their early years together. He'd made a lot of mistakes in his marriage, but then so had she. It was time for them to admit that and try again. He couldn't understand why Mary Lynn seemed so unwilling to agree.

She hesitated, then joined him on the porch, quietly closing the door behind her. They used to sit on this very porch and gaze at the stars, but that had been years ago. The porch light was off and the stars smiled down from the heavens, the same way they had back then, on fine summer nights. To Steve it was a good sign. He needed one.

Mary Lynn sat on the top step, and he sat beside her. He was glad he'd followed his instincts, instead of waiting until Mary Lynn came to her senses. This conversation was already long overdue.

"What's on your mind?" she asked.

"Everything's okay with the kids, isn't it? They aren't having any problems in school, right?"

"No, of course not. What makes you ask?"

"Nothing," he assured her. "You're doing a good job with them, Mary Lynn."

"Thanks, but I'm sure you didn't come all this way to compliment me."

He hesitated. "You did a fine job being my wife, too."

She lowered her head so she wouldn't have to look at him. "That was a long time ago."

"Not that long ago. I remember everything about us, especially how good you felt in my arms and how we used to—"

"Steve," she said abruptly, cutting him off. "Don't say any more."

"Why not?" He'd thought very seriously about what he wanted to tell her. He'd planned to remind her of good times in the past, talk about how the kids needed an intact family, promise to be the kind of husband she wanted. She had to know he'd do damn near anything to get his family back.

"It's over, Steve. It has been for years."

"Not for me it hasn't."

"Then maybe it's time you faced facts." She stood and he reached for her wrist, stopping her.

"Don't go," he asked gently, and because this was important, he added, "Please."

Sighing, she sat back down on the step. He placed his arm around her shoulders. She held herself stiff and unyielding against him, but gradually she relaxed as he nuzzled her neck, stroked her hair. "Remember how we used to sit out here and watch the stars?"

"That was years ago."

"You sure? Seems like yesterday." She smelled so good it was all he could do to keep from burying his face in her hair and inhaling her sweet perfumed scent. He planted soft moist kisses along the side of her neck, working his way toward her ear. He felt some of her resistance melt away when he caught her lobe gently between his teeth.

It'd been so damn long since they'd last made love that he was already hard. His hands fumbled with the opening of her blouse.

"I don't think this is a good idea," she whispered, but he noticed she wasn't actually stopping him.

"On the contrary I think it's one of the best ideas I've had in months."

Her hand closed tightly over his. "Don't."

He dropped his hand, but continued kissing her neck, knowing if she allowed this, his chances of getting her in bed would increase a hundredfold. That was where he wanted her, soft and pliant beneath him, reaching up to him with her arms, drawing him down. Loving him, taking away the ache of his loneliness. Afterward they would talk....

"Let me kiss you," he said, his voice husky with

need. He wasn't someone who pleaded often, but he did now, feeling like a man who was about to let something of great value slip out of his grasp. He loved Mary Lynn. Needed her and their family.

"I...have to get back inside."

"We'll both go in," he whispered. Taking her face between his hands, he directed her mouth to his. Her resistance was weak, a token effort, and that gave him hope. She might not say it, but she damn well wanted him as much as he wanted her.

The kiss was almost brutal with sexual energy. Soon he had his tongue entwined with hers and she was crawling all over him. The only reason they ended the kiss was to breathe, and even then it was with reluctance.

"Don't you remember how good it is with us?" Steve whispered. "Let's go inside," he urged with a groan.

Mary Lynn buried her face in his shoulder, breathing hard.

Steve got to his feet, pulling her with him. He was halfway to the door when she stopped him.

"We can't go in there."

"Why not?" If the kids were awake, they'd hurry them off to bed and then head in that direction themselves.

Mary Lynn didn't answer.

Steve advanced another step.

"No," she cried, breaking away from him.

"Why not?"

She squared her shoulders and whispered, "Kip's here. He fell asleep in front of the television. I had him over for dinner."

Steve couldn't believe his ears. Mary Lynn had sat on the porch making love with him while another man waited for her inside the house?

"You shouldn't have come," she whispered angrily. "Don't do it again, Steve. We're divorced. I wish to God you'd remember that."

Eighteen

Aunt Hallie

She was insane, Hallie told herself. Because only an insane woman would have agreed to look after a six-month-old infant for two days while her sister and brother-in-law spent the weekend camping on the Oregon coast. Lucille McCarthy had originally agreed to watch Ellen, but she'd come down with a bad cold she was afraid of passing on to the baby.

Julie had phoned Hallie in tears, distraught because she'd have to cancel this long-awaited retreat with Jason. Caught off guard, Hallie had offered to take Ellen for the weekend. Just how much trouble could a six-month-old baby be? she asked herself with bravado. Infants that age slept twenty hours out of twenty-four. Didn't they?

Hallie's first doubts had surfaced the moment she'd hung up the phone. Though she loved kids, she hadn't done much baby-sitting as a teenager. Well, maybe as an adult she'd do all right. And this time with Ellen would be a bonding experience. Two minutes later she called Steve to make sure Meagan was going to be around.

The next day, when Julie arrived with enough paraphernalia to fill a moving van—including a portable crib, a mammoth diaper bag, a miniature plastic bathtub, and more—Hallie was once again gripped by the anxiety of those who know they're in way, way over their heads.

"Ellen's a good baby," Julie assured her. "You've got nothing to worry about."

"All right." Besides, her mother lived little more than an hour away. Not so far that Hallie couldn't leap in the car and drive to the Kitsap Peninsula if she got desperate. "And," she told her sister cheerfully, "there's always Mom. She must be getting over her cold by now."

Julie and Jason glanced at each other as if silently debating which one should tell her.

"Mom's gone away for the weekend," Julie finally said.

"Away?" Hallie said, her throat closing up on her.

"She felt a lot better yesterday, and then this morning a friend invited her to Vegas for the weekend. Jason and I told her she should go."

Jeez, no one had asked *her,* Hallie thought. And her mother's defection left her without parental support—her ace in the hole, if things went wrong. Now that Lucille was hanging out with Wayne Newton and Hallie had no way of contacting Julie and Jason—except through Smokey the Bear—she was on her own. With maybe a bit of help from next door.

Hallie's fears exploded to life even before the fumes from Jason's car had disappeared.

Ten minutes later Ellen woke up.

The kid, even at six months, was no fool. She knew immediately that the woman holding her wasn't her mother or grandmother. She took one look at Hallie and let out a scream a horror-movie starlet might envy.

Hallie cuddled the baby. "It's Auntie Hallie," she said, a little desperately. "Remember me?" Apparently not, but really, who could blame Ellen? She'd only seen Hallie a handful of times, and then it had been at family gatherings when she was surrounded by familiar faces. Now there were only the two of them, and Ellen didn't like it.

"Hey, McCarthy, you said you wanted to be a mother." Hallie tried again, this time with a bit of self-talk. If she couldn't comfort Ellen, she'd work on re-assuring herself. "This is where the rubber meets the road."

Motherhood wouldn't be all baby powder and gurgles. What she was experiencing was the real nitty-gritty of being a parent. This was what she wanted for herself, so she might as well practice now.

Hallie continued to hold and rock Ellen until the screams gradually eased to pitiful sobs.

When Meagan appeared at the kitchen door, Hallie could have kissed her.

"This is your niece?" Meagan asked.

"She isn't all that familiar with me yet." Hallie felt she had to explain Ellen's discontent.

"Is her diaper wet?"

Her diaper. Hallie hadn't given it a thought. "Poor, poor baby," she cooed, reaching for the diaper bag Julie had left behind. The *big* diaper bag. Hallie extracted baby food jars, bottles, blankets, rattles, teething rings, a squeezable yellow duck, a pacifier, comb, brush, socks, three different pairs of shoes. But no diapers.

"I think they might be in the side," Meagan said.

Sure enough, there was the storehouse of disposable diapers. Plenty of those, along with wipes, powder, diaper-rash ointment and a furry blue bear. No instruction manual, though.

Ready to prove she was capable of such an undertaking, Hallie spread a flannel blanket on the carpet and placed a squirming Ellen in the center. She smiled proudly over at Meagan. "This isn't so bad."

She promptly revised her opinion when it became apparent Ellen wasn't going to make this easy. The only other diapers Hallie could remember changing had been on childhood dolls. The ones she'd owned had talked and cried and wet their pants. But none had kicked and fussed, twisted and turned, making the task damn near impossible.

By the time she'd finished, Hallie was exhausted.

"You did great," Meagan congratulated her.

A glance at her watch showed that Julie and Jason had been gone less than an hour. Only thirty-five more to go. Piece of cake, Hallie mumbled under her breath.

"Dad's taking Kenny to softball practice, but I can stay and help you, if you want."

If you want... Hallie all but grabbed the girl's shoulders and hugged her, she was that grateful.

With Meagan's help, Hallie made it through the rest of the morning and well into the afternoon. When Ellen went down for a nap, Hallie did, too. No one had bothered to tell her about the energy required to entertain a six-month-old.

The afternoon passed quickly, and at suppertime she said goodbye to Meagan, feeling confident now that she could manage. It seemed that Ellen had become accustomed to her. Hallie felt ecstatic; she wasn't as inadequate at this motherhood business as she'd feared. Yes! She could do this.

She changed her mind shortly after midnight. Ellen woke her out of a sound sleep, screaming so loudly that Hallie hurled herself out of bed and stubbed her toe while madly searching for the light switch. She'd completely forgotten about the lamp on her nightstand.

If Ellen had felt comfortable with Hallie earlier, she wanted nothing to do with her now. In fact, the infant had taken a sudden and apparently irreversible dislike to her aunt.

Babe in arms, Hallie walked until one of her slippers formed a blister on her big toe. It did no good; Ellen was in no mood to be comforted. Even a rerun of "The Andy Griffith Show" didn't interest the kid.

"You're a hard sell," she muttered.

After two hours, Hallie was at her wits' end. She'd done everything she could think of. Ellen's forehead was warm to the touch, but Hallie couldn't be sure if that was due to hours of nonstop screaming or a raging fever.

Maybe Ellen was seriously ill and needed a doctor. Maybe she'd eaten or swallowed something while Hallie wasn't looking. Maybe Hallie had done something wrong.

Just as the thought of calling 911 entered her mind, she happened to notice a light on in Steve's kitchen. Hallie raced to the phone.

"What's wrong?" Steve asked groggily.

"If I knew that, I wouldn't be phoning you," Hallie snapped. "What are you doing up at this time of night, anyway?" Whatever the reason, Hallie felt only gratitude. Steve was a father; he'd been through all this and survived. He'd know what to do.

He made all the practical suggestions.

"Do you take me for an idiot?" Hallie cried, close to breaking into sobs herself. "Of course I changed her diaper! Ten times or more."

"How long has she been crying?"

"Three lifetimes," Hallie said. "Listen, big boy, I'll give you a thousand dollars if you can get her back to sleep."

That shut him up. "You're kidding."

"Do I sound like this is a joke?" She was forced to yell as Ellen increased the volume of her cries.

"Give me five minutes."

It took him three. "Come on," he said, standing in the doorway, dressed in wrinkled gray sweats.

"We're going somewhere?" So he felt Ellen needed to go to the emergency room, too. Relieved, Hallie reached for a thigh-length sweater and slipped it over her pajamas.

While she wrapped Ellen in an extra blanket, Steve carried the car seat out to his truck, positioning it in the middle of the seat. At the last minute Hallie remembered her purse and grabbed that, locking the front door on her way out to Steve's monster truck.

He skillfully took the baby out of her arms and placed Ellen in the car seat, then helped Hallie climb inside. "What hospital are we going to?" she asked, locking her seat belt. Luckily Julie had given her a signed permission slip before she left, in the event of something like this.

"We aren't." He had to speak loudly to be heard over Ellen's fevered cries. Hallie had to give the kid credit; Ellen had one fine pair of lungs.

They hadn't gone more than two blocks before silence reigned. At first, Hallie waited, tense, expecting the noise to start again any second. Gradually she relaxed as the silence continued. She'd never heard anything more blissful in her life.

"My guess is she's teething," Steve said.

"So soon?" Hallie assumed kids didn't get teeth until much later. Not that she'd really thought about it.

"Sure." He glanced over at her and nodded for emphasis.

Well, Steve should know.

"My kids fell asleep the minute I turned the engine on. My car's in the shop so I've got the truck tonight, but I figured it'd work just as well. Based on experience, I'd say that if there's nothing seriously wrong, Ellen should fall asleep within six blocks. How're you holding up, Aunt Hallie?"

"Good," she said, lying through her teeth.

He drove along the Green River where there were few streetlights, and the rumble of the engine and the twisting road lulled Ellen into a deep slumber. But it wasn't only Ellen who fell asleep. Hallie discovered her own eyes drifting shut, and she struggled to stay awake.

She must have dozed off because the next thing she knew they were parked outside her condo. She jerked her head up and discovered Steve lifting Ellen, car seat and all, out of the truck. "Sorry to wake you, Sleeping Beauty," he whispered.

Hallie opened the passenger door and climbed awkwardly out of the truck. Turning around, she slid off the seat on her stomach, inching her feet toward the ground.

Her house was dark and still when she unlatched the dead bolt.

Gently Steve removed Ellen from the car seat and

placed her in her little crib. They both waited, fearing the worst. After a few minutes it became apparent that Ellen wasn't going to stir, and they tiptoed out of the room.

"Thank you," she whispered.

"Think nothing of it," Steve returned. "Just don't forget you owe me a thousand bucks."

Hallie opened her mouth, then closed it with a groan. She'd forgotten their ridiculous bargain.

Steve grinned. "Hey, not to worry. I take VISA." Having said that, he kissed her on the forehead and let himself out.

Hallie had decided long ago that shopping was therapeutic, and the weekend after playing the role of Aunt Hallie she decided to treat herself. Donnalee agreed to come with her. They were both in need of a little self-indulgence, and the solution was a shopping spree. Not the normal half-off sale in some local department store, either. Oh, no, Donnalee declared that their current depressed state called for a full-fledged bout of conspicuous consumption. Something that included a passport, a facial and cheesecake.

"I'll have you know I emptied my entire Christmas savings account for this," Hallie grumbled as they neared the Canadian border.

"Not to worry," Donnalee said as she eased her vehicle into the long line of cars waiting to clear customs. "By Christmas you'll be married and your rich husband will foot the bills."

Husband. So many of her thoughts and plans in the past few months had focused on that word. *Husband. Marriage. Family.* Recently Hallie had come to a deeper understanding of what had brought her to this stage in her life.

"Hey," Donnalee said, taking her eyes from the road long enough to glance at Hallie. "You look awfully serious all of a sudden."

Hallie forced a smile, then decided that if she couldn't tell Donnalee about the emotional crisis she'd endured all week, she'd never be able to tell anyone.

"What's up?" Donnalee prodded gently.

"It's been a year now since my dad died, and I don't think I've ever missed him more." Her voice broke and tears filled her eyes, embarrassing her. She ran the back of her hand under her nose and, with tears streaming down her cheeks, she laughed. "I apologize. I didn't realize I was going to do this."

"Hallie, it's me—Donnalee, your best friend—remember?"

Hallie reached for her purse and rooted around for a tissue. "Besides Dad, I've been thinking about Gregg. I should have married him. In the back of my mind I knew it then, but I was too…stubborn to realize that I *wanted* what he was offering."

"Gregg Honeycutt? But I thought the two of you broke up years ago."

"We did. He wanted to get married and I didn't." She paused long enough to blow her nose. "Quite a switch, isn't it? The guy being the one who wants to marry. I'd taken out a huge loan to get Artistic License up and operating, and I refused to allow my personal life to get in the way of business."

"You think you should've married Gregg?" Donnalee asked, sounding skeptical.

"Oh, I don't know." Hallie sighed deeply. "My hindsight isn't as clear as I'd like it to be. He was so wonderful and I loved him, I really did." She paused and added, "But apparently not enough."

"What makes you think about Gregg now?"

Hallie wasn't sure. At Christmas she'd received a photo card of Gregg, his wife and their two small children. He looked happy, really happy, and so did his wife. After her weekend with Ellen, Hallie's feelings about wanting a family of her own had grown even stronger and more certain. It was because of this, she supposed, that Gregg's family photo had come to mind. She'd even mentally replaced his wife's image with her own—but only for a moment.

"It's like this huge hole opened up inside me," she confessed, twisting the damp tissue around her index finger. "I first noticed it after my dad died, and that hole has gotten bigger and bigger ever since."

"Is that why you decided to marry?"

The tissue around her finger grew tighter and tighter. "Yes. Last weekend with Ellen was crazy, but you know what? I loved it. By the time Julie and Jason arrived, I was hooked on motherhood and I didn't want to let her go."

"You didn't?"

"Oh, I made it sound like it was one disaster after another, but it wasn't. On Sunday Steve brought over some ointment to numb her gums, and after that, Ellen was a jewel. I know now that I could deal with the sleepless nights and hard times—because I know it's worth it." She drew a shaky breath. "Rita's been telling me for a long time that when it comes to finding a husband I'm too picky. I laughed her off, but you know what? I'm beginning to think she's right."

This appeared to surprise Donnalee.

"Not that I wouldn't still be discriminating. I mean,

a few years back I might have married someone like Mark. I wouldn't have had the maturity to know otherwise. But I do now." Drawing another shaky breath, she added, "And now there's Larry. I really don't know how I feel about him. He's sweet, but...oh, I can't imagine being married to him."

"Come on, Hallie, stop fretting and let's enjoy our weekend."

"You're right." Hallie said, determined to take Donnalee's advice. While she was plagued with doubts about the status of her relationship with Larry, it didn't compare to what Donnalee was going through.

Word had gotten back to her that Sanford was dating again. Some so-called friend had taken delight in filling her in on the particulars. Shortly afterward, Hallie and Donnalee had arranged this getaway, and Hallie figured Donnalee needed it even more than she did.

Hallie had been a bit concerned about the cost, but on reflection realized she had very little to worry about. Her taxes were paid, her head was above water, she had plenty of work coming in. If she had to shop at Wal-Mart for Christmas, her family would understand.

The hotel deserved every one of those tiny stars listed in the tourist guide. It came complete with little chocolates on the pillow at night, plush bathrobes, perfumed lotion, plus a sauna and exercise room. Not that either one of them needed exercise after three hours of shopping.

Hallie's shoulders ached from hauling packages around, but they soon found a cure for that—the hotel masseuse. Never having experienced the delights of a massage, Hallie was apprehensive, but the woman put her at ease immediately. An hour later Hallie felt as relaxed as a wet noodle, not sure whether she wanted to crawl into bed or bound out to face the world. A facial followed, and then a manicure.

They dressed for dinner in short skirts with dark hose and ate in the revolving restaurant atop the hotel. Anything they'd saved shopping with a thirty-five percent discount, thanks to the Canadian dollar, they splurged on a bottle of Dom Pérignon—certainly the most expensive champagne Hallie'd ever had.

The night was lovely. Vancouver spread out before them, a panoply of twinkling lights. Hallie didn't know if it was the beauty of their surroundings or the shopping or the effect of having her body deliciously pummeled, but she felt rejuvenated—and surprisingly happy.

"It's like we're celebrating," she said. Although there was little evidence that she was any closer to achieving her goal now than when she'd started, she felt a sense of anticipation, of renewed energy.

"We *are* celebrating," Donnalee said, holding up the crystal flute. "To us. And to our future husbands, whoever they may be."

"To our future husbands," Hallie returned as they touched glasses. Husband. It meant a man who would be her lover, her partner, her friend. Her companion in life.

"I feel good," Donnalee said, leaning back in her chair. "Not just physically, either."

"I do, too," Hallie said.

"Funny—losing Sanford doesn't hurt as much as it did this morning." She smiled. "I guess that's what a day of total self-indulgence will do." Donnalee gazed at the view below them for a minute. "I knew it would be painful when I broke the engagement, but I wasn't prepared for how...lonely I'd feel afterward. How empty.''

Hallie admired her friend for being unwilling to accept less than her dream in such an important matter as family. For trusting that eventually there would be someone else, a man who shared her goals and who wanted children as much as she did. A man worth waiting for.

They slept late the next morning, ate breakfast at the hotel and with reluctance began the drive back to Seattle early in the afternoon. This weekend had been an escape from their real lives, and now they were returning to those lives, refreshed and optimistic. Hallie was determined to hang on to her positive feelings.

It started to rain shortly after they crossed the border, but she tried not to read any significance into that.

"You're the one who told me there'd be another man for me after Sanford," Donnalee said. She smiled softly. "I feel ready to look for him now."

"That's great." Hallie pressed her head against the seat, pleased with Donnalee's decision. "Then you're going back to Dateline?"

Donnalee took a long time to respond. "I don't think so."

"Why not?" Donnalee couldn't have surprised her more had she announced that she'd already met the man she planned to marry.

"I can't give you a logical explanation. But I have the feeling I won't meet him through any dating service."

It was on the tip of her tongue to remind Donnalee that *she* was the person who'd convinced her to sign up with the service. She supposed she had no real reason to complain, though; Dateline had already sent her a number of potential dates. Two of them she'd dated extensively. Mark and Larry. But Mark had been a serious—even frightening—disappointment. And Larry…well, Larry was probably as indifferent to her as she was to him.

Hallie was mulling all this over when she noticed that Donnalee had exited the freeway. She was only minutes away from home. Once they arrived, she felt a rush of pleasure and satisfaction; her condo, with its neatly planted shrubs, its hanging basket of ferns, its bright door and attractive curtains, looked so welcoming, so dear and familiar. She unloaded her suitcase and all her accumulated treasures from the trunk of Donnalee's car, then waved a fond farewell as Donnalee drove off.

When she was inside out of the rain, Hallie glanced at her phone. She should call Larry and let him know she was home safe and sound. Hesitating, she wondered if Larry really cared—and knew the answer.

Before she could talk herself out of it, she walked to her wall phone and lifted the receiver. Her purse was still draped over her shoulder. Her suitcase and assorted packages sat in the middle of the living room.

"Hello," Larry answered without enthusiasm, as if he resented the phone's intrusion on his day.

"It's Hallie."

"How was Canada?" he continued in the same dry tone, devoid of any hint of enthusiasm or energy. Hallie often wondered how his students were able to sit through his lectures and not fall asleep.

"Canada," she repeated when she realized he was waiting for her answer. "Spectacular. Wonderful."

"Good."

Silence.

"Larry...this time away has given me an opportunity to do some thinking." She was a coward, Hallie decided, to be doing this over the phone. A living breathing coward. "I haven't made any secret of how much I admire you," she said, focusing her eyes on the ceiling, praying God would forgive her for this lie. She wanted to spare his feelings as she delivered the message that she no longer wished to date him.

"I imagine that a man of my education and background is impressive to someone like you."

She took exception to the "someone like you" and under normal circumstances would have questioned him. Doing so now would only prolong the inevitable.

"This time apart has been good for us both," she began. "It's given me the opportunity to, uh, clear my head."

"A person needs that occasionally. Eliminate the frivolous and concentrate on what's important."

"Exactly." Now all she had to do was find a way of explaining that she no longer considered *him* important. Unsure how to accomplish that, she asked, "Did you miss me while I was away?"

"Miss you?" He sounded surprised. "I suppose I did...but you weren't away more than thirty-two hours. We haven't known each other long, Hallie, and it's really not a question of missing you. The significance of someone's absence is relative to the amount of time two people have been exposed to each other, which in our case has only been a matter of weeks."

"Six," she muttered, cursing herself for doing such a miserable job of this.

"My point exactly."

"If you don't know how you feel about me now..."

"Feel about you," Larry said. "I hardly know you!

Are you pressuring me to propose, Hallie? Because if so, I think you should know that I refuse to bend to pressure.''

Propose. He thought she wanted him to propose!

"I wasn't expecting a marriage proposal," she told him, wondering how their conversation could have gone so far off course. "Actually I was looking for a diplomatic way to say that I think it would be best for us both to move on and date others." In case there was room for misunderstanding, she added, "Not each other."

Her announcement was followed by a stiff silence. ' You mean to say you want to break up with me?'' He sounded aghast. Shocked.

"Yes," she replied meekly, then hurried to say, "I don't want to hurt your feelings. I'm sure there's someone perfectly wonderful waiting to meet you."

"That's what the last woman told me," he said gruffly.

"I'm sorry, but there just isn't any...spark between us."

The line grew quiet. Then, "If you're looking for sparks, I suggest you snuggle up with an electric fence." With that, he hung up on her.

Hallie allowed herself a little sarcasm. "Goodbye, Larry. I wish you well, too." Shaking her head, she replaced the receiver.

Nineteen

Take It Like A Man

Meagan glanced guardedly over her shoulders, as if she expected her brother or father to show up at any second. She'd appeared at the kitchen door minutes after Hallie—or rather, Larry—ended the phone call.

"What's wrong?" Hallie asked, anxious to know what was troubling the girl. She'd rarely seen Meagan agitated or upset—unless it was at her younger brother. For the most part, Hallie found Steve's daughter to be good-natured, congenial and easygoing.

Meagan's nervous gaze returned to her father's house. "Can I come in?"

"Of course."

She helped Hallie pick up her packages from the living-room floor and carry them into the bedroom. Then, as if she'd been holding them in all weekend, Meagan's words came out in a rush. "Oh, Hallie, I'm real worried about my dad."

Hallie frowned; surely Steve wasn't sick or injured? "What's wrong with him?"

The half-wild look was back in the girl's eyes, and it seemed Steve wasn't the only distressed one. "Mom's decided to marry Kip."

Hallie felt her heart sink. It went without saying that the news would devastate Steve. "I take it your father doesn't know?"

"Not yet," Meagan said. "Mom said she was going to tell him tonight when she comes to get Kenny and me."

"Oh, boy," Hallie whispered, dropping onto her bed. Steve had always made clear that he was working hard toward a reconciliation. He'd based his entire future on their remarrying.

"My dad still loves my mom," Meagan said, her voice slowly fading. Hallie watched as the girl's eyes filled with tears. Like any kid, Meagan wanted her parents together. Even when Meagan and Kenny had asked her if she'd be willing to marry their dad, Hallie hadn't taken them seriously. She suspected that all along they'd been more aware of Mary Lynn's intentions than Steve had, but now that their mother was actually getting married, they weren't ready to face this new reality. Steve's children, like Steve himself, wanted a reconciliation.

Hallie held out her arms and Meagan walked into them, hiding her face in Hallie's sweater. "Will you talk to my dad?" she asked after a moment.

Hallie's gut instinct was to stay out of it, and she would have, if it wasn't for two things. Steve had been there for her. He'd seen her through the heartache of celebrating her thirtieth birthday alone. And only last weekend, he'd saved her sanity by helping her with Ellen. In many ways he was as good a friend as Donna-lee.

"I'll do what I can," Hallie promised, but she didn't know what she could say, or if Steve would want to hear it. She stroked Meagan's hair, murmuring, "Don't worry, honey, your dad's an adult. He can handle this."

It wasn't as if the news would come as any great shock. Steve knew his ex-wife was dating again, although he'd chosen to ignore what that meant.

Meagan lifted her tear-streaked face to Hallie's. "I've been waiting for you all weekend."

"Oh, honey, I'm sorry I wasn't here when you needed to talk."

Meagan shrugged. "That's all right. It's more important that you be here for my dad. He's going to need a friend and he won't call Todd."

"Todd?"

"His best friend. You haven't met Todd?"

"Not yet." Other than the bowling tournament and a few pizzas with him and the kids, Hallie hadn't socialized with Steve. Come to think of it, he'd never formally met Donnalee, either.

Hallie heard a car pull up out front.

"I gotta go. It sounds like Mom's here." Meagan wiped her face with her sleeve and slid off the bed. "Bye!"

Because she knew what was coming, Hallie stood and watched out her living-room window, hidden behind her drapes so Steve and his family wouldn't be able to see her. She felt like a voyeur but told herself she'd now become part of this scenario; if she was going to be any comfort to Steve, she needed to understand his reaction. Looking dejected, Meagan and Kenny climbed into their mother's car, dragging their overnight cases. Both slumped in the back seat, heads lowered.

Steve followed the kids across the lawn to the car. Mary Lynn waited outside the vehicle, with the open door on the driver's side between her and Steve. As a barrier, it couldn't have been more obvious.

Hallie watched as Meagan put on earphones, as if she needed to drown out the conversation between her parents. Steve's ex-wife had her back to Hallie, and Steve was smiling at the woman. Hallie knew he looked forward to these Sunday afternoons when Mary Lynn stopped by for the kids.

After a few moments Hallie noted that his mood changed dramatically. He repeatedly shook his head, in denial, and he made a confused helpless motion with his hand. Next his face tightened and he slammed his fist against the hood of the car.

Hallie grimaced, sure he must have injured his hand. He and Mary Lynn were now exchanging comments—insults?—in low voices. Unable to watch any longer, Hallie turned away, angry with herself for intruding on what should have been private. She felt sick to her stomach at what she'd seen.

Knowing that Steve was probably in no mood for company, Hallie waited an hour. Daylight filtered weakly through a dark and threatening sky—but she managed to see into Steve's condo. It took her a moment to realize he was lying on the carpet, listening to the stereo at full blast. Hallie didn't know whether to laugh or cry; it was exactly what she'd been doing that night in April. Her birthday. She had to listen carefully before she recognized the song: "Send in the Clowns."

She searched the back of her cupboard until she found the bottle of rich Tennessee bourbon a grateful client had given her last Christmas. She didn't often drink hard liquor, but if ever an occasion called for booze, this was it. She scrounged up a shot glass, souvenir of a trip to Las Vegas for her twenty-first birthday, and headed for Steve's.

Standing in the rain at his front door, she repeatedly rang the bell, but to no avail. Wasn't he going to answer?

"Steve," she shouted, pounding on the door. "Would you open up before I drown?"

He threw open the door a moment later—having turned down the music—and didn't look any too pleased to see her. "What are you doing here?"

She held up the bottle and the shot glass. "I thought you might need medication."

He frowned in puzzlement. "You know?"

"Meagan told me."

He stepped aside and let her in. "I can't believe it." He looked like a man walking around in a daze, like an accident victim left to deal with the aftermath of tragedy. He collapsed onto the sofa and leaned forward, wiping a hand down his face.

Hallie made her way into the kitchen and found a couple of clean glasses. She filled them both with ice and poured him a double with no mixer. Her own, she watered down considerably.

He glanced up and offered her a feeble smile when she handed him the drink. He held on to it for several minutes, gazing blankly ahead of him, until Hallie suspected he'd forgotten she was there. She figured if he wanted to talk he would; she had no intention of pushing him.

Sitting down in the chair across from him, she tentatively tasted the drink and blinked rapidly as it seared a path down her throat. Her eyes filled with tears and she pounded her chest in an effort to keep from coughing.

"You all right?" Steve asked.

She nodded, blinking furiously, wondering what her reaction would have been had she taken the bourbon straight.

Their eyes met, and Hallie could barely look at the misery in his. "I'm so sorry, Steve. I know how much you wanted to get back together with Mary Lynn."

His shoulders heaved in a deep sigh. "She's actually going to marry that creep."

This didn't seem the time to point out that Steve didn't know Kip well enough to judge his character. All he cared about was that this other man was stepping in, taking *his* place within the family. He didn't need to say it for Hallie to know what he was thinking.

"We met in high school," Steve said after a while.

"You and Mary Lynn?" she asked, not sure she wanted to hear him talk about the other woman or how much he loved her. She was tempted to ask him to stop, to say that stirring up the memories would only hurt him, but she didn't have the heart. If he wanted to vent his pain with her, the least she could do was listen. She owed him that much.

"Mary Lynn was new that year and so damn pretty my heart would stop every time I saw her. She used to come by every day to watch the football team practice...."

"I imagine you were the star player." Athletic as he was, Hallie couldn't imagine Steve being anything else.

"Quarterback. How'd you know?"

"Lucky guess," she returned with a grin.

Steve downed the undiluted drink in one giant swallow. He closed his eyes and shook his head like a dog stepping out of a lake. He cursed under his breath, then set the glass aside. "Damn, but that's good bourbon."

"Only the best for my friends."

Steve leaned back against the sofa cushion. The music continued to play softly in the background and Hallie recognized Paul Simon singing "Still Crazy After All These Years."

"I loved her from the moment I saw her," Steve said. "That's never changed, not once in all that time."

Hallie remembered her own high-school sweetheart and the intensity of their relationship. They'd broken up during her senior year and he'd taken someone else to the prom. Hallie had ended up attending the dance with her best friend's out-of-town cousin, whom she'd met the summer before. He was a nice guy, but he wasn't Les.

It'd killed her to watch Les dance with another girl, but for pride's sake, she'd been forced to pretend she didn't care.

Steve laughed once, sharply. "I asked her to marry me on our first date." Steve let his head fall back against the sofa and closed his eyes. "I knew the first time I kissed her that I was going to love her. Later, my dad told me the same thing happened to him when he met my mother. He asked her to dance at a USO party. One spin around the floor was all it took."

How romantic. Hallie wished it could be so easy for her. Instead, she was stuck dating a cast of misfits, one after another, in her search for a man to love. She almost giggled as the CD player picked Tina Turner next, singing "What's Love Got to Do with It?" Then she sighed. Here was Steve, her friend and neighbor, and he'd found the woman he loved when he was a teenager. Now Mary Lynn didn't want him. A broken marriage, a betrayed love, might be an everyday tragedy, but it was a tragedy nonetheless.

"I gave her a ring the very next week," Steve said, his voice low and mellow, presumably from the bourbon. "Naturally we didn't tell anyone it was an engagement ring. Our parents would've hit the roof if we'd been talking about marriage on such short acquaintance."

Hallie would never have guessed that Steve possessed such a romantic soul. This was the kind of thing women dreamed about, this consuming once-in-a-lifetime love. And Mary Lynn had thrown it all away. It was so terribly sad. Her throat tightened; the kind of love Steve felt was exactly what she'd hoped would happen to her. But no man had ever loved her like that, or wanted her so much.

"I married her in my heart the night of our first date. That was when we found each other. That was when our hearts connected and I knew I wanted to spend the rest of my life loving Mary Lynn."

The lump in Hallie's throat thickened painfully, and she tried unsuccessfully to stifle a sob.

Steve's eyes fluttered open. "Hallie?"

She bit her lower lip and searched in her pocket for a tissue. "It's nothing."

"You're crying?"

"I'm not." The lie was ludicrous since it was patently obvious that she was.

Steve disappeared and returned with a box of tissues. He studied her as if he didn't know what to say.

"Thanks," she said, reaching for a tissue. This was more than a little embarrassing. She blew her nose and tucked the tissue in her pocket. Steve sat down next to her.

"I'm sorry," she wailed, and reached for a fresh

tissue. She clutched it tightly, trying to ignore Eric Clapton's plaintive "Tears in Heaven."

"Sorry for what?" Steve asked gently.

It didn't look as if she was going to be able to stop crying. Her shoulders trembled and she grabbed a handful of tissues, jerking them out of the box two and three at a time. "I'm supposed to be the one—" she sobbed openly "—comforting you."

He placed his arm around her shoulders, and she pressed her head against his, soaking up the solace, even though *she'd* intended to be the one offering it. She couldn't begin to explain the tears.

"I never understood why Mary Lynn wanted the divorce," Steve whispered.

"I don't know why, either," she said, sniffing hard in an effort to stop crying.

It'd been the grief, the pain and absolute desolation in Steve's eyes, she decided. He was about to lose the family he cherished, and his life would never be the same. He'd lost the woman he loved.

Steve had gone to the kitchen. Just as she thought she should leave, he was back. "Here," he said, handing her a fresh drink.

"Alcohol creates more problems than it solves," she said, forgetting that she was the one who'd hand-delivered the bottle.

"Trust me, I know. The day the judge declared the divorce final, I got rip-roaring drunk. It was the sorriest day of my life, and the night didn't improve. Next morning, I had the mother of all hangovers. I haven't gotten drunk since and don't plan to."

"I'm glad to hear it," she said, then gulped down the drink. Choked, gasped and had trouble breathing.

Steve patted her on the back. "You're a good friend, Hallie McCarthy," he said.

"You, too, Steve Marris."

His arm came around her and they hugged for a long time. It amazed her how good it felt to be in Steve's arms. To feel his heart pounding against hers, his breath against her neck. Peaceful. Friendly.

His kiss didn't come as a surprise. He lifted his head, and she gazed into his eyes before he lowered his mouth to hers. His lips were undemanding and tender, restrained. It was a kiss like the one they'd exchanged on her birthday. A kiss free of promises, free of claims. A kiss between friends.

He pulled away and asked, "Want me to walk you home?"

"No. I can make it across the lawn just fine." She swiped at the moisture on her cheeks. "Are you going to be all right now?" she asked.

"Sure."

Although he sounded confident, Hallie didn't know if she should believe him. Mary Lynn's announcement had come as a blow. But he'd taken it like a man.

Dionne Warwick's "I'll Never Love This Way Again" followed Hallie out the door.

Twenty

Chicken Soup For The Heart

Steve stepped up to home plate and swung the bat around a couple of times to loosen the stiffness in his shoulders. He assumed the batter's stance and waited for the pitcher's first throw. A fastball zoomed toward him. It wasn't a baseball Steve saw, but Kip Logan's face.

The unmistakable cracking sound as the bat slammed against the ball and shattered echoed across the field. Steve dropped the piece he still held on the ground and raced toward first base. He kept his eye on the ball and was satisfied to see it fly over the fence. Another home run.

He was out of breath when he returned to the dugout. His fellow team members slapped him jovially on the back and congratulated him.

"What's with you tonight?" Todd asked, shifting seats to sit next to him. "This is your third home run."

"Really?" Steve said, pretending he hadn't noticed. He leaned forward on the hardwood bench and braced his elbows on his knees. "I'm having a good night, is all."

"True, but this is the second bat you've busted all to hell. Something's eating you."

"You're imagining things." Steve's gaze didn't waver from the field. The problem with friends like Todd was that it was difficult to hide things. Removing his hat, Steve slapped it against his thigh, aware of Todd's scrutiny. He supposed he might as well let Todd know. "Mary Lynn's decided to remarry," he said with forced nonchalance. Billy Roth stole second base and Steve leapt to his feet and cheered wildly.

Todd remained seated. "When did you find out about this?"

Steve sat back down, keeping his attention on the game. "Sunday night."

"I wish you'd said something sooner." Todd sounded as if the news about Mary Lynn affected him personally.

Steve told himself he should have taken drastic steps as soon as he'd learned she was dating again. Instead, he'd assumed her relationship with that vulture of a car salesman would die on its own, without any help from him. What he'd hoped for was that Mary Lynn would date some of Hallie's rejects. Or similar losers. He was convinced that once his ex had gotten a look at some of the weirdos out there she'd come running back to him.

Steve had spent hours daydreaming about her asking him to move back in with the family. Welcoming him back into her bed. The bubble of his fantasy world had burst on Sunday afternoon, when Mary Lynn broke the news about her engagement.

"Are you okay with this?" Todd asked next.

"Yeah, I'm jumping up and down for joy," Steve said dryly.

Todd shook his head. "I was afraid something like this would happen."

The comment earned a glare from Steve. What he didn't need was his best friend saying he'd told him so.

Todd took immediate offense. "I told you I saw her shopping with Kip, remember?"

Steve wished Todd would quit while he was ahead. Every time he opened his mouth, he only made it worse.

"I could tell then that she was serious about this guy," Todd continued, undeterred. "It isn't the kind of news you want to tell a friend. I said what I could and hoped you'd read between the lines."

Unfortunately, Steve hadn't seen what in retrospect should have been obvious. He had no one to blame but himself. Kenny had hit him with the news that his mother had a boyfriend shortly after the first of the year. Meagan, too, had dropped a number of hints. He should have recognized that something was going on when Mary Lynn cut him off physically. But then, Steve figured he always did have trouble seeing the obvious; it was what had led to the divorce in the first place.

"You're up to bat next," Steve said, grateful Todd was leaving the dugout. He didn't want to talk about Mary Lynn. Didn't want to think about her, either. Every time he did, his head pounded and his gut twisted. He had to let go of her, of their lives together. A dozen people had said the same thing: it was time to move on. That was also what the relationship experts recommended—and he should know, because he often listened to talk radio. He'd learned their jargon, about "taking ownership" of his past and his problems, and "affirming his validity" and "forgiving" himself and Mary Lynn for the failure of their marriage. He'd even started to believe this stuff. Recently he'd happened upon a program with a phone-in psychologist, and he'd actually sat in his car and listened until the program was over. It'd helped.

Dr. Brenda wasn't the only one who'd come to his emotional rescue. Hallie had been there for him, as well. In a week filled with pain and sadness, thinking about Hallie made everything seem more bearable. She'd come to him, bottle of bourbon in hand, offering comfort—and ended up blubbering her way through an entire box of tissues.

In some strange way her crying had been a release for *him*. When she'd first arrived, he'd wanted to send her back to her own place. He'd been in no mood for company. What man would be? His heart felt like it had been ripped from his chest...and yet Hallie had managed to bring a smile to his face.

Steve felt fortunate to have a neighbor like Hallie McCarthy. When he counted his blessings, she was among them. He sure hoped she found a man worthy of her.

Todd struck out at bat. He'd been in a hitting slump during their recent practice sessions, and now he returned to the dugout muttering curses.

"Don't worry about it," Steve said. "This is only the first game of the season."

Todd looked as if he wanted to say something, but instead, he found himself a quiet corner and sat there scowling. If it had been one of his kids, Steve would have called it pouting.

After the game several of the team members, including Todd, decided to stop off at the local watering hole for a few cold beers. Steve declined, not wanting to answer uncomfortable questions about Mary Lynn. He'd said everything there was to say and didn't care to elaborate.

It was still daylight when he arrived home. He noted that Hallie's car had been parked in the same spot for the past two days. It wasn't the kind of thing he normally paid much attention to, but she was just shy of being ticketed for parking too close to a fire hydrant.

He glanced at her condo as he started walking toward his own. It probably wouldn't hurt to check on her, he decided. Yeah, that was the neighborly thing to do.

She responded to his knock by calling faintly for him to come inside. Steve opened the front door to discover her sprawled on the sofa amid a conglomeration of pillows and blankets. Dressed in an old robe, she lay facedown, her arm dangling over the edge, knuckles brushing the carpet. A variety of medicines lined the coffee table, along with three or four dirty cups, a box of tissues and a thermometer. An empty wash bucket was positioned close by.

"You look like hell," he said. "Are you sick or something?"

"You don't miss much, do you?" She didn't lift her head.

"My, my, are we a little testy? And what, by the way, is your front door doing open? This isn't 'Little House on the Prairie,' you know."

"Don't come any closer," she called, raising her arm to stop him. "Believe me, you don't want whatever brand of flu I've got." She frowned. "Oh, the door. Donnalee's supposed to come over later, and I wasn't sure I'd have the energy to get up and let her in.''

"Have you seen a doctor?" he asked.

"I'm too sick to see a doctor. Do I look like I'm in any condition to drive?" she returned crankily.

"No," Steve admitted. "Do you need someone to take you?"

She appeared to consider his question. "Thanks, but no thanks. The worst of it's passed." Then she added, "I appreciate the offer, though."

He walked into her kitchen, which was, to put it mildly, a mess. Used mugs and glasses littered every surface. An empty orange-juice container had toppled and the last dregs of juice had dried on the counter. A package of soda crackers lay open, crumbs scattered about.

"When was the last time you ate?" he asked, poking his head around the living-room corner.

"Please," she whispered miserably, "don't talk about food. I haven't been able to keep anything down for two days."

"I hope you're drinking plenty of liquids."

"I must be, otherwise there wouldn't be anything to vomit."

She had his sympathy there; he knew what it was like to be sick and alone. He stuck the dirty dishes in the dishwasher and wiped off the counter.

"Thank you," she said when he brought her a cup of tea.

"Anything else I can do for you?"

"Would you mind helping me into the bathroom?" she asked weakly. "I tried to get up earlier, but I felt light-headed."

"Of course."

She sat up, and he saw that her skin was pale, her hair on one side had gone completely flat, and the upholstery of her sofa had left a floral imprint on her cheek. She wrapped the housecoat around her and tied the sash.

She swayed when she stood upright, and he slid his arm around her waist to steady her. Once he was confident that she could maintain her balance, he guided her down the hallway. He turned on the bathroom light.

"Would you move the scale away from the wall for me?" she asked in the same weak voice.

"The scale?" he asked incredulously.

"I want to weigh myself."

Steve was certain he'd misunderstood. "Why in the name of heaven would you want to do that?"

She gave him a look that suggested the answer couldn't be more obvious. "To see how much weight I've lost," she explained, enunciating each word with painstaking clarity. "I haven't had anything but juice and crackers for two days."

It made no sense to him, but Steve knew better than to argue. He crouched down to pull the scale away from the wall.

"There," he said, patiently waiting for her to step forward.

She hesitated. "You can't look."

"I beg your pardon?"

"Turn around."

"For the love of..." But Steve did as she requested and turned his back. He heard Hallie step on the scale, and then a pathetically feeble cry of triumph.

"I take it you've lost?"

"Yes," she answered in a whisper. "Isn't that wonderful?"

"If you say so." He'd never understood why Hallie was so obsessed about her weight. He thought she looked just fine. Yet the entire time he'd known her, she'd analyzed everything she put in her mouth. Well, other than that one episode with the double-fudge macadamia-nut ice cream.

He helped her back to the living room and fluffed up the pillows. "Where's Nerdman when you need him?" It seemed to Steve that professor friend of hers should be the one checking up on her.

"We decided not to see each other anymore," she replied. Steve couldn't detect any deep regret.

"Oh."

"I couldn't imagine him naked."

Steve did a poor job of hiding a grin. "Do you do that often? Imagine men naked?" He made a show of clutching the neck of his uniform in a false display of modesty.

"Hardly. Just some men. You don't qualify."

"Glad to hear it."

"The only thing I ever saw him get excited about was a program on the public channel about mold."

If there was a hidden message in that statement, Steve wasn't sure he wanted to dig for it. "So you called it quits?"

"I'm back to square one—again."

"There's a man for you out there, Hallie. Don't lose heart."

"That's what Donnalee keeps saying. I don't understand it. I thrive on challenges. I write out my goals and plan to succeed, and so far all I've done is fall flat on my face."

"Don't be so hard on yourself."

Hallie sighed dramatically. "I never thought I'd be this thin and without a man in my life."

Steve didn't know how to respond to that.

"Thanks for coming by."

"No problem. You sure I can't get you anything else?"

"I'm fine now. Thanks for asking."

Steve left, and as he crossed the lawn to his own condo he realized he was smiling. He did that a lot when he thought about Hallie. She seemed to find the humor in life; at any rate, *he* tended to find it when he was with her.

He showered, changed clothes and checked out the contents of his kitchen cupboards. He found a can of chicken-noodle soup and heated it. Pouring it into two bowls, he left one on the table for himself and brought the other to Hallie.

She looked surprised to see him again.

"Here," he said, setting it down on the coffee table for her and grabbing the soda crackers from the kitchen. "Eat this and you'll feel better."

"You're so thoughtful," she told him, her dark eyes wide with gratitude.

"That's what friends are for," he said, and leaning over, kissed the top of her head.

Twenty-One

Back In The Saddle Again

June 22

Well, Larry's out of my life, not that I'm gnashing my teeth or anything. But I do admit to being disappointed. It seems I take one step forward, stumble back and fall into a ravine. Tom Chedders and Mark Freelander disgusted me, but Larry McDonald discouraged me. Is he the best I can do? How depressing.

On a brighter note. Donnalee accepted a date with a real-estate broker she's known for a number of years. It'd be a hoot if Donnalee ended up marrying someone she's known and worked with for years. But even if she doesn't, I don't imagine it'll take her long to find the right man. She's smart, attractive and, according to Steve, she's got what it takes. Physically, for sure. <u>And</u> she's a wonderful, loving, compassionate person. If she wasn't my best friend, I might even hate her!

Speaking of Steve, he's been really great, dropping by when I was sick, cleaning up for me—even moving my car. I sometimes toy with the idea of the two of us, but I'm afraid he's still hooked on his ex-wife. He claims otherwise, but I can't help wondering.

I talked to the people at Dateline and they're reviewing their files. The woman I spoke to said they'd have another name for me by the end of the week. I told them to take their time. I'm in no hurry to meet someone new just yet. I want to take a week or two to revive my enthusiasm. Maybe I should do what Donnalee's doing (and what I started out doing!) and be willing to date someone I haven't met through the agency. The new man from the office-supply store is cute. I wonder how old he is, or if he's married.

I'm feeling ambitious now that I'm over the flu and bought myself some Martha Washington geraniums, lovely deep red ones. I'm going to plant them this afternoon.

Steve was washing his company truck when Hallie went outside to plant the geraniums. She'd never known a man who took having a clean truck so seriously. He was wielding the long green garden hose, which snaked across the lawn, but he paused when he saw her.

"You seem a lot better," he said.

He looked darn good, Hallie noted, with his shirt unbuttoned all the way down, revealing a strong muscular chest. The bronze sheen of his skin invited investigation—not hers of course, she was quick to add. After living next door to him all these months, she found herself oddly *surprised* to realize how physically attractive Steve was.

"I'm feeling much better," she told him. She adjusted her large straw hat and wished she'd applied sunscreen to her bare arms. Kneeling on the soft moist grass, she cleared a space between the tulips and daffodils that had bloomed earlier in the spring.

"What are you planting now?" he asked.

She replied in far more detail than he'd wanted to know, Hallie suspected; she'd even explained about leaving the stalk and leaves of her tulips and daffodils so the bulbs could absorb the nutrients. She'd seen his eyes glaze over, but he'd listened politely. Hallie wasn't sure why she was being so talkative. It probably had to do with the weather, which was glorious, and the fact that she'd spent the week cooped up inside, sick as a dog. Then, too, it might have to do with his open shirt.

When she'd finished transplanting the geraniums from the plastic containers to the flower bed, she strung her hose across the yard.

"I've never understood what a woman sees in flowers," Steve said. "If it was up to me, I'd stick a couple of plastic tulips in the ground and let it go at that."

Hallie rolled her eyes. "Well, it's men and their he-man trucks that get me."

"Women and their romance novels."

Hallie wasn't going to stand still for that. "Men and their remote controls."

Later Hallie couldn't remember if she'd *intentionally* doused Steve. She'd laughed while holding the hose, which had jerked and splashed water on the legs of his jeans.

When it happened, Steve's eyes slowly met hers. She

opened her mouth to apologize, but then realized she wasn't sorry. Not at all. He was so smug and self-righteous.

"Do you have anything to say for yourself?" he asked, advancing toward her, a menacing look on his face.

Hallie retreated one small step for each giant step he took. The water dribbling out of her hose was no match for the power sprayer he'd been using on the truck.

"I stand by my convictions," she announced with melodramatic fervor.

"Do you, now?" He sprayed the legs of her jeans the same way she'd sprayed his, only the water pressure in his hose was much stronger and she was soaked to her knees.

"I'd like to remind you that I've been ill. I probably shouldn't be outside at all." She feigned a cough.

"You should've thought about that before you started this water war."

"Water war?" she repeated. "You wouldn't, would you? Seeing that I've been so terribly ill." She coughed again for effect.

He turned away as if the guilt factor had worked, giving her ample time to cross to the outdoor faucet and increase the water pressure. If she'd stopped to think about what she was initiating, Hallie might have resisted—but the temptation was too strong. Without giving him any warning, she liberally sprayed his backside.

Steve's reaction was quick as lightning. Soon an all-out water fight had erupted, complete with threats and shouts of retribution. In seconds they were both drenched to the skin. Wet tendrils of hair dripped onto

Hallie's neck and shoulders. Her hat had long since disappeared, and her blouse was plastered to her front.

"You're a wicked, wicked man," she declared after being forced to plead for mercy.

"And you're not to be trusted," he returned.

She laughed, enjoying their exchange. "I just lost control," she said—which was true enough. His attitude had certainly inflamed her, not to mention his open shirt...well, no man had the right to look that sexy.

"You better get inside and change clothes before you catch your death of cold," he said.

"You, too." He might not be as wet as she was, but Hallie had done womanhood proud. Water dripped from Steve—just not as much of it.

"Do you have any plans for later?" he called unexpectedly just as she was about to enter the house.

"Apart from remaining dry? No, not really."

He smiled. "I thought I'd ride my bike along the Green River. Want to join me?"

Hallie smiled back. The idea was appealing; she'd seen lots of folks on the trail and had always thought it seemed a great way to enjoy a sunny afternoon, biking along the paved road. Exercising, but with scenery. Minus the boredom.

"I'd love to, but I can't," she said regretfully. "I don't have a bike." She didn't mention that it'd been at least ten years since she'd ridden one.

"You could use Meagan's. I'm sure she wouldn't mind."

Hallie's spirits lifted. She knew Steve was at loose ends this weekend. Meagan and Kenny were at their mother's parents for some family function. He didn't seem to know what to do with himself without the kids there.

"This shouldn't be such a difficult decision, Hallie."

"I...don't know if I remember how to ride a bike," she admitted, a little embarrassed.

"Sure you do." He sounded very definite. "Haven't you heard the expression 'It's like riding a bike'? Once you learn, you never forget. It's like sex."

She tossed him a perturbed look. "Very funny, Marris."

"I'll give you a refresher course. On the bike-riding, I mean." He grinned. "It'll take you ten minutes, I promise."

She didn't hesitate. "You've got yourself a deal. I'll change clothes and be right out."

She changed in short order and met Steve in front of his garage.

"I'll probably need to raise the seat a bit," he said, looking at her legs and then the bike pedals. "Here, climb on and I'll see how much I should adjust it."

"But..."

"Don't worry, I'll hold on to the bike. You aren't going to fall."

Doing as she was instructed, Hallie perched on the seat and placed her feet on the pedals. Since Meagan was considerably shorter than she was, her knees thrust up toward her face. Conscious of making a comical sight, she glanced at Steve to discover that his attention had left her and was riveted on a car down the street.

Hallie's gaze followed his to the dark blue vehicle.

"It's Mary Lynn," he said. His voice had a breathless quality that spoke of surprise and delight. His ex-wife pulled to a stop and parked.

Completely forgetting about Hallie, Steve released

the handlebars and started walking toward Mary Lynn. Before Hallie could free her feet from the pedals, the bicycle toppled sideways onto the grass.

Steve didn't notice. Hallie lay sprawled on the wet grass, and for all intents and purposes she might have been invisible. Her backside was completely drenched before Steve looked back at her. He might not have even then if Mary Lynn hadn't said something.

"Are you all right?" Mary Lynn asked when Hallie awkwardly lifted the bike away from her and stood. They'd met briefly a few times, including the day Meagan had gone to work with Hallie. The conversations had always been a bit awkward. They'd waved to each other a couple of times since, when Mary Lynn was either dropping the kids off or picking them up.

Hallie brushed the grass from her pants and noticed a trickle of blood on her elbow, where her arm had struck the concrete. She twisted her arm around to evaluate the damage. It wasn't much, just a little scraped skin, but it fired her anger.

She stared at Steve who was gazing longingly at Mary Lynn. It was pathetically obvious that he was hoping his ex-wife had come to announce she'd had a change of heart and wanted him back.

"Can we talk for a moment?" Mary Lynn asked Steve in a voice that couldn't have been sweeter.

"Of course." He nearly fell all over himself leading the way into the house.

Mary Lynn had the grace to glance guiltily toward Hallie. "If now's convenient?"

"Why wouldn't it be?" Steve asked.

When Mary Lynn continued to look at Hallie, Steve finally seemed to realize she was there. "Hallie, sorry. You okay?"

"Just peachy."

Either he missed the sarcasm or he chose to ignore it. "We'll go cycling another time, all right?" He didn't wait for a response.

Apparently she was of such little consequence, he could leave her without a thought. How dared he treat her like this, dismiss her with no regard for her feelings—as if she was nothing.

She stood in the driveway, hands on her hips. Steve Marris wasn't any different from the other losers she'd met. He was rude, inconsiderate and thoughtless. Good thing she had no romantic illusions about him!

Angry, Hallie returned to the house and doctored the cut. The small scrape didn't really require a bandage, but she applied the largest one she could find. She'd actually been looking forward to cycling with Steve, but there'd be frost in the tropics before she'd consent to do anything with that man again.

Twenty minutes later the doorbell chimed. It was Steve.

"I can't believe it," he muttered in disgust.

"Neither can I," she said coolly.

Apparently he didn't notice her remark. "Wait'll you hear what Mary Lynn wanted."

Hallie supposed he was going to tell her whether she was interested or not. She crossed her arms and blocked the doorway.

"She left the big family get-together to come and ask me in person if I'd be willing to take the kids for two weeks while she's on her honeymoon with Lard Butt."

He seemed to be waiting for her to respond. Hallie didn't.

"Doesn't that beat all?" He shook his head as if this was the most unreasonable thing he'd ever heard.

Hallie would wager a month's income that he'd agreed to do it, too. Anything for his precious Mary Lynn.

"Are you going to?"

"Well, yeah, but that's beside the point."

"Uh-huh. That's what I thought."

He squinted at her. "Is something wrong?"

"Should there be?" she replied, wondering how long it would take him to realize how badly he'd insulted her.

He stepped off her porch as if to get a better view of her. "Mary Lynn used to do that," he said, wagging his index finger. "If you've got a beef with me, spell it out. Don't expect me to play guessing games."

"Beef?" she repeated, highly amused by the term. "What you did to me just now was…" She couldn't find a word bad enough. "Despicable," she decided, spitting it out. "Mary Lynn drives up and not only do you completely forget I exist, you let me fall off that stupid bike right in front of her. I was mortified."

"Oh, come on, Hallie…"

"You embarrassed me. You discounted me. All so you could jump through hoops to satisfy your ex-wife." Hallie had wanted to remain calm and disdainful; instead, her voice shook with anger.

His eyes widened with surprise.

"Friends don't treat each other that way," she explained pointedly, forcing herself to calm down.

He waited a moment after she'd finished. "Okay, I apologize, but frankly, I don't think it was that big a deal."

"It was to me."

He briefly closed his eyes, as if to suggest she'd stretched the incident out of all proportion. "Get over it and let's go bike-riding."

"*Get over it?*" she gasped. "You left me to fall flat on my face! I told you—friends don't do that to friends. Now you want me to get over it, pretend it didn't happen?" Her hands tightened into fists. "Well, I don't need friends like you."

"Fine," he returned. "I don't need any grief from you, either. I get all I can handle from one woman. I don't need another one messing with my life." He turned and stalked toward his house.

"It'd help if you accepted the fact that your marriage is over," she shouted after him, too angry to censor her words. "In case you haven't noticed, Mary Lynn's engaged to someone else."

Steve whirled around, his eyes hard and cold as they raked her. "I suggest you mind your own damn business," he flared. "You can offer me all the marital advice you want once you've found yourself a husband."

His words felt like a slap in the face. She held her breath against the unexpected stab of pain and retreated into her house.

Twenty-Two

The Girl Next Door

Damn, but he missed Hallie. He'd really blown it with her. He'd recognized his mistake the moment his eyes met hers and she'd escaped into her house. He'd seen neither hide nor hair of her since, which was quite a feat considering how often they ran into each other most of the time. They usually met at the mailboxes at the end of the day or walking out to their vehicles in the morning. Hallie must be avoiding him, and Steve found that thought damned depressing.

Even the kids had noticed. "Is something wrong between you and Hallie?" Meagan asked the weekend before Mary Lynn's wedding.

"Wrong? What makes you ask that?" He pretended ignorance rather than admit he'd insulted Hallie. It didn't help that she'd attacked him just after he'd been sucker-punched by his ex-wife.

Mary Lynn had come to him just the way he'd dreamed she would. Only that was as far as his romantic scenario matched what had actually happened. She'd come begging, all right, but not to ask him back into her life. She'd needed a favor, a rather large one as it turned out. Instead of rejoining his family, he would act as guardian while his ex-wife honeymooned with her new husband. He adored his kids; it wasn't that. His feelings had nothing to do with them and everything to do with Mary Lynn. Her remarriage was real to him now, and it meant that hope was truly over. He'd become just a convenience to his ex-wife.

Hallie's lecture afterward had felt like a kick when he was already down. Nevertheless, he shouldn't have said what he did. It was all too easy to recall the hurt and disappointment in her expressive brown eyes.

"Dad?" Meagan waved a hand in front of his face. "I was talking to you about Hallie."

No use trying to hide it any longer. "We had a, uh, minor falling-out."

"That's what Hallie said."

Steve brightened. "Hallie mentioned it?"

Meagan shrugged. "Not really. I asked her if she wanted to come to Kenny's baseball game. It's boring there without someone to talk to, and I thought maybe Hallie could come. I think she might've too, if it wasn't for what you said."

"She told you that?"

"No." Meagan shook her head emphatically. "Just that you were angry with each other."

Kenny walked into the house and slammed the front door. He threw his baseball mitt on the floor. "It's raining," he said, sounding thoroughly disgusted. "How am I supposed to play ball when the weather's like this?" He fell onto the sofa, not bothering to pull off his muddy shoes.

Steve sat down next to his son. Everyone had been short-tempered this weekend, and he suspected it had little to do with the weather.

"We need to talk," he announced. "You, too, Meagan."

"Yeah, Meagan," Kenny taunted.

"About what?" She ignored her brother and sat in the chair crossing her arms defensively, just the way Hallie had the last time they talked.

"We've all been in a bad mood," he began. "And—"

"Not me," Meagan insisted.

To be fair, she'd been the most even-tempered of anyone, including him.

"You think you're perfect." Kenny glared at his sister and probably would have stuck out his tongue if Steve hadn't been watching.

The corners of Meagan's mouth edged upward. "That's because I *am* perfect."

"I think I know what's wrong," Steve said, unwilling to wade into an argument between his children.

"It's the rain," Kenny said. "It rained last week during the game and I played terrible."

"You *are* terrible," Meagan muttered.

"I'm a lot better than you!"

"Kids, please," Steve said, waving his arms in referee fashion. "I think all this has to do with your mother marrying Kip." He dove into the conversation headfirst. At least he had the children's attention.

"I know how you feel," Steve told them, putting his arm around Kenny's shoulders. "But I want you both to know that nothing's going to change with the three of us. It doesn't matter who your mother marries. I'll always be your dad."

"I don't like Kip," Kenny said sullenly. "He doesn't know how to throw a ball and he can't catch worth beans."

A perverse part of Steve was thrilled to hear it. "But he was willing to try, and that's all that counts, isn't it?"

Kenny lowered his eyes rather than answer.

"How can you say nice things about Kip?" Meagan cried, and to his shock, his daughter's eyes filled with tears. "Mom's marrying him when she should still be married to you."

That more or less summed up what Steve felt, but he couldn't say as much. Mary Lynn had her own life to live and she'd chosen to live it without him.

"Your mother has a mind of her own and she's in love with Kip, so much in love that she's decided to marry him. Now it's up to the three of us to accept her decision and be happy for her."

The words stuck in his craw, but he managed to say them with enough conviction to sound as if he meant it.

"But I don't *like* Kip," Kenny said for the second time.

"Give him a chance," Steve urged. His children had to live with Mary Lynn's new husband, and it would behoove them to make their peace with him. "I'm sure he isn't so bad once you get to know him," Steve added.

"He isn't you," Meagan said, getting to the heart of the matter.

It hurt to let go of the dream of getting back together with Mary Lynn. It hurt like hell. That was one thing, but having Kip step into the role of stepfather to his kids was another.

"I love you both," Steve whispered and held out his arms. Meagan and Kenny crowded next to him on the sofa. He wrapped an arm around each one, loving them with an intensity that made his heart ache.

"Nothing's going to change between us," he promised, struggling to find the words to reassure them. "I'm still your dad. I'll always be here for you, no matter what happens."

"I wish Mom—"

"Shh," Steve said, and pressed Kenny's head against his shoulder.

"You'll always be my dad, no matter what?" Kenny repeated. "Do you promise?"

"You can count on it, son."

"Even if *you* get married again?"

Steve couldn't see the likelihood of that happening. "Even if I get married again," he vowed. Nothing on earth was strong enough to keep him from his children.

"Feel better now?" he asked after a few moments.

"I do," Meagan confessed.

"Me, too," Kenny said.

Mary Lynn stopped by to pick up the kids an hour later. Steve didn't walk outside to chat with her the way he did most Sundays. Frankly, he couldn't see the point of it. Why torture himself?

School was out for the summer, and the kids were at the stage where they weren't sure what to do with themselves yet. He'd make a point of seeing more of them and concentrating on being a good father. Actually he was looking forward to having his children with him the two weeks Mary Lynn and Kip were away. It might help ease the loneliness—his, anyway.

The silence that followed their leaving seemed to echo in Steve's mind. He turned on the television, hoping to fill the place with noise, but that depressed him even more than the quiet had.

He decided what he needed was a workout, so he donned his running shoes and sweats. Every once in a while the urge to jog hit him. And right now, pounding out his frustrations on the pavement suited his mood perfectly.

He left the house just as a car pulled up in front of Hallie's—one of those new BMWs he'd admired from afar. The Z3, the one from that James Bond movie.

It took Steve a couple of minutes to realize that the well-dressed man who'd stepped out was Hallie's date. Steve did a number of warm-up exercises, which were little more than an excuse to stick around long enough to get a good look at the guy she was dating this time.

He had to admit this character was better-looking than the others had been. Successful, too, judging by the car he drove.

Steve hoped things worked out for Hallie. And he hoped he and Hallie could be friends again. He missed the laughter she brought to his life and the companionable hours she'd spent with him and his kids.

Yeah, he should've kept his damn mouth shut. He wished he knew how to repair the damage, but he was at a distinct loss when it came to letting a woman know he was sorry. His marriage was a good example of that.

He set off on his run, getting his heart rate up to aerobic level in a few minutes. He soon discovered that his mind was filled with thoughts of Hallie. Not Mary Lynn. Hallie.

He wasn't sure if he should be grateful or infuriated.

On impulse, Steve left a one-word note on her windshield the next morning.

SORRY.

Nothing happened. He was convinced she hadn't noticed. And then, the following morning, he found a piece of paper tucked under his windshield wiper. He unfolded it.

YOU'RE FORGIVEN.

Smiling, Steve stuck it in his pants pocket and headed for work. Todd noticed his improved mood right away.

"You're in good spirits this morning," he commented.

Steve poured himself a cup of coffee. "What do you think is appropriate for a man to give a woman when he wants to apologize. Flowers or candy?"

"What woman?"

"Never mind. Flowers or candy?" Steve repeated.

Todd frowned. "Does this have something to do with that neighbor of yours? Sally? Hattie? No, Hallie, that's it. Hallie."

"How'd you know?"

"Come on, Steve, you talk about her practically every conversation we have. She must be a comedian because you're constantly going on about something funny she's done. I expect to hear you two are hot and heavy under the covers any time now."

"Me and Hallie?"

"Yeah, you and Hallie."

Lovers? The two of them? He thought about it a moment, then shook his head. "Nah. It wouldn't work." It was kind of unfortunate, because he liked her. And because he knew instinctively that they were well matched in ways that mattered.

"Why not?"

"Well..." A long list of excuses crowded his mind. So many that he found it difficult to sort through them all and spit out just one. "Mainly because she's seriously looking for a husband."

"So?"

"Been there, done that, bought a T-shirt," Steve returned flippantly. "I like her as a friend, but I don't want to complicate our relationship with anything physical."

"That sounds like a pretty weak excuse if you want my opinion."

"I don't," Steve said. Then he shook his head. "You see, I don't know if the friendship would hold up if we mixed the two." Why ruin a good thing with sex?

"That's not the way I see it," Todd said. "Friends often make the best lovers. The sexual aspect of the relationship is enhanced by familiarity."

"Maybe." Steve was willing to concede that much. "You never did answer my question. Flowers or candy?" He wanted to divert Todd from the subject of sex, which only served to remind him how long he'd gone without it. Months. Many months. Longer than any other period in his adult life.

"Flowers," Todd said, adding a tablespoon of sugar to his coffee mug. "Definitely flowers."

Steve was leaning toward candy, thinking Hallie would want to share. He'd had a craving for chocolate truffles lately. Todd was right, though; flowers would be for Hallie, but he would've been the one eating the candy.

On his way home from work Steve stopped at an upscale grocery store and bought a single red rose, a small box of chocolates and, to be on the safe side, a bottle of chilled white wine. That way he'd covered all the bases.

He showered, changed clothes and waited until he was certain Hallie was home. Grabbing the wine and chocolates and placing the long-stemmed rose between his teeth, he rang her doorbell.

Hallie answered, took one look at him and laughed. Her smile was like sunshine, and Steve basked in its warmth. "Friends?" he asked.

"Friends," she answered softly, and let him inside. Even though they'd only been on the outs a week, it felt like a month. He was lighthearted with relief now that the friendship had been rescued. But a rose between his teeth was one thing; a heartfelt apology another.

"What I said about getting yourself a husband before offering me marital advice," he started, then cleared his throat. "I regretted it as soon as the words left my mouth. I'm sorry, Hallie."

It seemed to him that her bottom lip quivered ever so slightly, but he might have been wrong.

"What you said was true," she told him, her voice impassive. "I spoke out of turn."

"Not really. Besides, letting you fall off the bike when Mary Lynn arrived wasn't one of my finer moments. You had every right to be upset."

"Let's put it behind us."

"Fair enough." He handed her the wine, the chocolates and the rose.

"Thank you," she said, and stepped forward to kiss his lips. It was a feathery kiss, a light kiss, a kiss without passion.

It was just like the other times they'd kissed.

Which made the heat soaring through his blood difficult to explain. He resisted the urge to reach for her shoulders and pull her back into his arms. Resisted the urge to kiss her again. He longed to feel the pressure of her mouth on his, and the soft and feminine imprint of her body.

Something was definitely very wrong.

Steve could feel his pulse pounding in his temple and was grateful when she suggested they drink the wine on her patio. The evening was lovely, with a cloudless blue sky and the gentlest of breezes.

Hallie sat back on her folding chair gazing up at the sky, her legs stretched out in front of her.

Steve relaxed, too. "You dating Bill Gates these days?" he asked, thinking about the man with the fancy car.

"Bill Gates is married."

Clearly she wasn't going to be forthcoming with the information he wanted. "Who drives the Z3, then?"

"Oh, you mean Arnold. Arnold Vance, Dateline's latest offering." She glanced at him. "You two met?"

"No, I went out for a jog a couple of nights ago and saw him parked outside your house." He hated to reveal how curious he'd been, but there wasn't much point in hiding it now. "He looked like the perfect candidate for a husband."

"You think so?" She sounded surprised. "Arnold's polite and sensitive, a very nineties kind of man, but I didn't feel we hit it off the way we should have."

"Are you seeing him again?"

She nodded but without a lot of enthusiasm. "Next Wednesday. You know what irritates me? This guy is everything a woman could ask for, and all I can manage is token interest. He leaves me yawning."

Steve put a concerned expression on his face, but inside he was grinning widely. So, the car didn't make the man.

"Donnalee's experiencing the same thing," Hallie

was saying. "She's dating this real-estate broker she's known for years. A catch with a capital *C*, and for the life of her she can't dredge up any excitement."

"Why?" Steve asked.

"If I knew that, I wouldn't be sitting here drinking wine with you." He smiled, remembering a similar smart-ass remark the night she'd looked after her baby niece.

This felt good, sitting out on a warm summer evening with his friend. "So," he said, "did you miss me?"

"I did," she said without elaborating. "It surprised me, too. You worked hard at avoiding me all week, I noticed."

"I didn't. I thought you were avoiding me."

"No, but my schedule was crazy," she said. "I left early and got home late." The smile was back in place, and Steve noticed, not for the first time, how pretty she was when she smiled. "In case you're interested, I not only missed you, I felt miserable and guilty. I hope you're satisfied."

"So did I," he said, figuring that if she was willing to be open and honest, he wouldn't be anything less.

They sat in companionable silence for a few minutes, then chatted about this and that—the kids, the neighborhood, movies they'd seen. Eventually the subject of vacations arose.

"I'll be gone a couple of days at the beginning of next week," she told him. "Would it be too much trouble for you to pick up my mail?"

"I'd be happy to." He'd get her mail, water her plants and miss her, too. Sipping his wine, Steve found himself studying Hallie with fresh eyes. He remembered what Todd had said earlier in the day.

Lovers? He and Hallie?

She *was* attractive. Tonight she wore shorts and a blouse with a V neckline. By lifting his head just a bit, he could see the swell of her breasts. His gaze lingered there far longer than it should have. He caught himself thinking about her breasts and how he'd like to see them and—

For heaven's sake, this was Hallie! Steve frowned as he reminded himself. His friend and neighbor. He resisted the impulse to shake his head to clear it.

She continued chatting, and Steve listened with half an ear while she told him about the short business trip she'd planned—to attend a trade fair in San Francisco. He noticed small things about her that he hadn't paid attention to in the past.

Her mouth was incredible; her lips were perhaps the most perfectly shaped he'd ever seen. He studied them as she spoke, noticing the way she moistened them with the tip of her tongue. It was a purely innocent movement, not intended to be seductive at all. Furthermore, he'd seen her do it a thousand times and it'd never affected him like this.

"Mary Lynn's getting married this weekend." Steve wasn't sure what prompted his sudden statement.

"You okay?" she asked with a gentleness that was like salve to his battered soul.

He shrugged. "I don't have any choice but to accept it."

"What about the kids?"

"They aren't happy, but they're young and they'll adjust. I told them to give Lard Butt a chance to prove himself."

"Steve!"

"What?"

"You didn't actually call Kip Lard Butt, did you?"
He chuckled. "Not out loud."

"I should hope not." She threw him a schoolmarm's disapproving glare.

He sighed and gazed up at the heavens. "So Mary Lynn's getting married." He said it again. "Can you imagine her and Lard Butt in the sack together?"

"Steve!"

"I hate to tell you how long I've been without sex," he muttered, downing the last of his wine in one gulp.

Hallie glanced his way. "I'd hate to tell you how long it's been for me."

"Really?" That surprised him, seeing that she'd been dating a long line of men practically from the moment he'd met her.

"Don't act so shocked."

"What about Mark and Larry and the others?"

She pressed her lips together in annoyance, and Steve decided she'd missed her calling. Hallie really should've been in a class room; she had looks some teachers couldn't imitate.

"I don't sleep with every man I date."

"Don't get all bent out of shape. How was I supposed to know that? A lot of women do."

"That's the most ridiculous thing you've ever said to me, Steve Marris."

"Sorry," he said, meaning it. He reached for the wine bottle and replenished their glasses. "I certainly didn't want to offend you."

"I'm not offended...just, I don't know. You sometimes say stupid things."

The wine was affecting her, he observed. Her cheeks were flushed with color and a sheen of perspiration had moistened her brow. He could see the outline of her breasts and her nipples, pearl-hard, through her thin cotton blouse. She probably wasn't wearing a bra, which was a thought he'd rather not entertain in his present deprived—or was that depraved?—state of mind.

"Well, how about this?" He paused, grinning. "Are you interested?" Hell, it didn't do any harm to ask, and she might surprise him.

"Interested in what?"

"Sex, the two of us," he suggested nonchalantly. Maybe it was time to test Todd's theory about friends making the best lovers.

"You're joking!"

"Am I?" His brows rose.

If her face was flushed earlier, it bloomed a deep shade of scarlet now.

He gave a lazy indulgent sigh. "Hey, I didn't think it'd do any harm to ask."

"That's not exactly a turn-on, you know." She wrinkled her face and gave him a goofy look. "'Duh, come on, baby, let's do it'? No wonder you haven't had sex since God knows when."

Since he'd only been joking, Steve didn't take offense. "How else does a guy ask a woman to go to bed?"

"Not like that!"

"If I got down on one knee and said pretty please, would you reconsider?"

"No!"

He laughed. "Yeah," he said. "That's what I thought."

Twenty-Three

Back In The Game

Steve Marris hadn't the foggiest idea how to seduce a woman, Hallie decided, sitting at her desk. Furthermore he had no interest in making love to her. His invitation, if one could use that term for something so crude, was based wholly on his insecurities. His ex-wife had remarried, and Steve was feeling needy and unloved. He longed for a warm body beside him to ease the ache in his heart. Any warm body would do.

Hallie tore the pages—for Monday and Tuesday—off her calendar, since she'd been in San Francisco attending the trade fair those two days. She was about to toss them in the garbage when she paused. Mary Lynn was married to Kip now and Steve would have his hands full with the kids for the next two weeks. Maybe she—

That thought was interrupted by her phone ringing. It was Arnold Vance, calling to break tonight's date. He was going out of town on business. Hallie couldn't scrape up any feelings of regret. On paper Arnold was a perfect match; she should be thrilled to be dating him.

Only she wasn't.

She couldn't even claim he was dull. Arnold was

thoughtful, successful and generous, with one prior marriage and no kids. Like her, he was looking for someone special to settle down with and raise a family. Yet they didn't *click,* and she was sick to death of analyzing why he bored her and, she thought fatalistically, why *she* seemed to bore him. What distressed her most was the feeling that she was the one at fault.

By the time Hallie arrived home from work, she was tired and irritable. Her mood lightened when she saw Steve with his kids on the patio. Apparently he'd decided to barbecue hamburgers. Kenny wore a chef's apron that hung to the tops of his tennis shoes. The sliding glass door off the kitchen was open, and Meagan was traipsing back and forth, carting their dinner out to the small picnic table set up on the grass.

"Care to join us?" Steve called out when he saw her. "Kenny's cooking."

"Kenny?" Hallie tried to sound delighted.

The nine-year-old grinned from ear to ear and held up a spatula with an extra-long handle.

"I wouldn't be so eager if I were you," Meagan warned. "Kenny doesn't know how to cook meat any way but well-done. *Real* well-done."

"Meagan made the salad," Steve boasted, patting his daughter on the head. "It looks fabulous."

Meagan shrugged one shoulder as if to say it wasn't any big deal, but Hallie could see she was pleased by her father's praise.

"I'll just get changed and come right over," Hallie promised. Actually she was glad Arnold had canceled their dinner date. She'd much rather spend time with Steve and the kids than in some fancy restaurant making small talk. An evening with Arnold would be spent trying to dredge up enthusiasm for a perfectly acceptable marriage candidate, and wondering why she couldn't.

Meagan followed her into the house. "Mom's married to Kip now," she announced as Hallie sorted through her mail and tossed the majority of it in the garbage.

"So I understand."

The girl lounged on the end of Hallie's bed while Hallie changed into a comfortable pair of jeans and a red-checkered sleeveless blouse.

"The wedding was nice. Lots of people came."

Steve had mysteriously disappeared over the weekend. Hallie had later learned that he'd made a trek to the mountains and gone camping with a good friend from work. It was just as well he hadn't been home. He'd have moped around and been miserable the entire weekend.

"Mom and Kip are in Hawaii," Meagan continued. "She hasn't phoned, not even once."

Hallie heard the hurt in the girl's voice. "That doesn't mean she isn't thinking of you, sweetheart. You're with your father, and there's really nothing for her to worry about, is there?"

Meagan shook her head. "I guess not."

Hallie placed an arm around the girl's shoulders, and they went out to join Steve and Kenny. It soon became obvious that the two males were desperately in need of help. One burger had fallen into the fire, and a frazzled Kenny was trying to lift it out with the spatula, dumping the remaining hamburgers directly into the fire. In his attempt to help, Steve burned two fingers. While Meagan got ice for Steve, Hallie rescued the burgers.

They laughed at the incident as they ate; in fact, the entire meal was spent laughing, teasing and talking.

Hallie realized again that this was much more fun than any dinner date with Arnold would have been.

"Will you come to my baseball game tonight?" Kenny asked when they'd finished their food, which surprisingly had been delicious, charred burgers and all.

"Please, please come," Meagan added, folding her hands prayerlike.

Steve's gaze caught hers. "You're welcome if you don't have other plans."

"Arnold canceled."

"Then come. You'll be surprised how much fun it is."

"Don't believe him," Meagan muttered.

Kids' baseball couldn't possibly be more entertaining than watching Steve and his son barbecue, but she left that unsaid.

Cleanup following dinner was a snap. Paper plates went into the garbage and leftovers were stuffed in Steve's refrigerator. While Hallie and Meagan wiped down the counters and Steve cleaned the grill, Kenny changed into his team uniform.

"You're coming, aren't you, Hallie?" Meagan asked again, her eyes expectant, hopeful.

"I sure am."

"Yippee!"

The Little League baseball field was across the street from Kent Commons, the community center where Hallie had taken her cooking classes. They parked there and crossed the busy intersection to the enormous grassy field. Eight baseball diamonds were located on several acres, all with portable bleachers.

Steve seemed to be assisting the coach, because he promptly positioned himself at home plate and hit fly balls to the boys. Meagan and Hallie were left to their own devices.

"Your dad's a coach?" Hallie asked, watching Steve interact with the youngsters and admiring his knack with them. She could tell that Kenny's friends liked Steve.

"Not officially, but Dad always attends Kenny's games and started helping out. Now Coach Hawley relies on him," Meagan explained.

Hallie got the impression that her presence had generated a number of curious stares. In the beginning she'd assumed it was because she was an unfamiliar face, but then she realized that the people staring at her were whispering back and forth.

Meagan gestured surreptitiously at one of them. "That's Mrs. Larson," she whispered. "She's got the hots for Dad."

"The lady in the short pink pants?"

"Yup. She introduced herself as divorced and available."

One look assured Hallie that Mrs. Larson more than fulfilled Steve's criteria for the perfect woman. Her breasts threatened to spill out of her top, and she wore tight shorts and high heels. Hallie couldn't help wondering if Mrs. Larson had managed to pique Steve's interest—but somehow she couldn't imagine Steve interested in someone so...obvious.

It didn't take long for the bleachers to fill up with family and friends. A couple of women quizzed Meagan about her mother's wedding; while she answered their questions, the women studied Hallie.

"I'm Steve's next-door neighbor," she told them. "Kenny asked me along to watch him play."

"How nice of you to come," one woman cooed.

"Pleased to meet you," Mrs. Larson said, sounding anything but. The woman had daggers for eyes and they were aimed directly at Hallie, shamelessly assessing her and finding her lacking. Hallie wished she'd thought to wear her enhancer bra.

"This is the first time Dad's brought anyone with him to Kenny's games," Meagan whispered now. "Everyone must think you're dating."

"Oh, so *that's* it." Hallie pretended to be enlightened.

The game started and Steve joined them in the bleachers. Soon everyone's attention—even Mrs. Larson's—was riveted on the playing field.

When it was Kenny's turn at bat, Hallie bit her lip tensely, wanting him to do well. He swung at the first pitch, connected and raced headlong toward first base. The player on second base tried to throw him out, but the umpire raised both arms, declaring him safe. Only then did Kenny glance at the bleachers; Steve who was watching closely, gave his son a thumbs-up.

Hallie whistled and cheered and, in her excitement, stumbled and nearly fell off the bleachers. Would have, in fact, if Steve hadn't caught her. His laughing eyes met hers, and he slipped an arm around her waist. For protection, Hallie told herself. To keep her from losing her balance again.

The next time Kenny was up at bat, Hallie persuaded Meagan and Steve to form their own family cheering wave. In rapid succession they took turns standing with their arms above their heads, moving them slowly back and forth to create the effect of a cresting wave. Soon the entire section was involved in the cheer.

Kenny's team won the game, with a final score of six to three. He raced off the field, beaming. "We're in first place now," he shouted, holding his index finger high above his head.

"Congratulations, sport," Steve said, grabbing the bill of Kenny's cap and pulling it down over the boy's face. He momentarily left them to congratulate the coach and help assemble the equipment.

Another team member strolled over to Kenny's side. "Is this your dad's girlfriend?" the boy asked, looking at Hallie with unabashed curiosity.

"Sort of," Kenny answered. "But I don't think he's going to marry her."

Hallie noticed how the Larson woman's eyes lit up at this tidbit of news.

"You played a good game, Ronnie," Steve said, mussing the other boy's hair when he returned.

"Thanks, Mr. Marris." Ronnie grinned, then glanced over his shoulder at his mother, who'd moved back toward the bleachers. "My mom wants to know about your lady friend. Kenny said you aren't going to marry her."

"Ronnie." His name was faintly heard from the other side of the bleachers. "It's time to go."

"Does Ronnie belong to Mrs. Hot and Pink?" Hallie asked Meagan under her breath.

"You got it."

"Tell your mother, Ronnie, that Hallie and I are very *close* friends." Steve sidled over to Hallie and wrapped his arm around her shoulders, squeezing hard. He gazed down at her, looking lovelorn and deeply infatuated.

"Steve," she hissed, and elbowed him in the ribs.

Steve's infatuated gaze didn't waver. "I'm crazy about this woman."

"You're overdoing it, Marris," she muttered. But

she smiled benignly and went along with his stunt. What troubled her, though, was the excited way her body reacted to having Steve this close.

"Head over heels crazy," he elaborated.

If he didn't cut it out soon, Hallie was going to do him physical harm.

Ronnie took off running and Steve dropped his arm.

"What was that all about?" Hallie demanded.

"Loretta Larson," he admitted. "She always considered me fair game, but now that Mary Lynn's remarried, it's open season. Frankly, I'm not interested."

Now that Mary Lynn's remarried. Of course! She didn't know why she hadn't realized it earlier. She had an idea, one that made perfect sense. With his ex-wife out of the picture, Steve had no choice but to move forward in his life. Date again, possibly even marry. That meant meeting someone new—and Hallie thought she knew just the right woman.

"We need to talk," she said as the four of them walked toward the parking lot. "Privately."

"We do?" They stood at the curb waiting for the light to change. "About what?"

"Dad, are we going for ice cream?" Kenny interrupted, tugging at his father's sleeve.

"You bet, sport."

"Great." Kenny tucked his mitt under his arm and, when the light changed, raced across the intersection toward the car.

"You can't say what you want with the kids around?"

"I'd rather not."

"All right, all right." But he didn't sound too happy.

It was dark by the time they arrived home. While the kids flopped down in front of the television, Hallie and Steve sat in her patio chairs and gazed up at the stars. "What's so important you have to drag me out in the middle of the night?"

"Donnalee!" Hallie said excitedly.

"What about her?"

"She's my best friend and I want you to meet her."

"Why?" he asked, sounding suspicious.

"Why?" she repeated. "Isn't it obvious?"

"No."

The man was dense, but then she had been, too. "I can't believe I didn't think of this earlier."

"Of what?" he asked impatiently.

"You and Donnalee. She's perfect for you."

"Me?"

"It's time you started dating again," she said. "Otherwise women like Loretta Larson are going to drive you crazy."

"Since when did you become my social secretary?"

"Since tonight. Now don't argue with me, because it won't do any good. I'm going to arrange a date for you and my best friend."

Steve was silent for a moment. "There's always Todd."

"Who's Todd?" She couldn't understand why he was throwing a stranger's name at her.

"*My* best friend. He's perfect for you."

"Really?" Funny, he hadn't mentioned Todd earlier.

"Friday night," he said, "the four of us. Agreed?" He held out his hand.

Hallie placed her palm in his. "Agreed."

Twenty-Four

Four Blind Mice

"**Y**ou didn't *tell* Steve, did you?" Donnalee cried, furious with Hallie. "You didn't tell him I don't want to do this...this date thing." She sighed; it was difficult to remain angry with your best friend for long. Still, after everything Hallie had been through with blind dates, you'd think she wouldn't be inclined to arrange them for others.

"I didn't have the heart to disappoint him," Hallie said solemnly, as if breaking this ridiculous dinner date would send him over the edge. "You don't know how much he's looking forward to meeting you."

"Yeah, I'll bet," Donnalee muttered. Hallie had just announced yesterday morning that they were going out on this double blind date. Despite Donnalee's loud protests—she wasn't interested in Steve Marris, or any other man at the moment—her friend had apparently gone full steam ahead.

"Come on, one date with Steve Marris."

"No, Hallie. No, no, no." But Donnalee should have known Hallie wouldn't give up so easily. She'd listed her neighbor's virtues—kind, considerate, responsible, blah, blah, blah. According to Hallie, the guy was too good to be true, which in Donnalee's limited experience generally proved to be exactly right.

"Just one date," Hallie pleaded. "That's all I'm asking."

"No," Donnalee insisted. "Hallie, I'm not interested."

Refusing to be deterred, Hallie glared at her friend. "You two are so right for each other!"

"I don't see it that way." Donnalee refused to budge. Really this was useless and a waste of time. For a whole bunch of good reasons: she couldn't handle another disappointment, he was probably still in love with his ex, she had her doubts about getting involved with the friend of a friend. Besides, she wasn't the one for Steve. Hallie was. Steve was the topic of every conversation—Steve said this, Steve did that. If Hallie wasn't talking about him, it was his kids, whom she adored. Donnalee had trouble understanding how a smart, perceptive woman could be so obtuse. Anyone who listened to Hallie would know she was close to falling in love with Steve. If she hadn't already. Donnalee had seen it weeks ago.

"But he's wonderful with kids. He's patient and good-hearted and more fun than just about anyone. I can't understand why you won't go out with him. Come on, Donnalee, what would it hurt?"

"I can't."

"You can't or you won't?" Hallie's mouth fell open. "Don't you realize how embarrassing this is going to be? Steve's going to arrive in a couple of hours with Todd, just the way we planned, and you won't be anywhere in sight."

Donnalee paraded out her first major objection. "You told me he's divorced and—"

"So are you."

"True," Donnalee concurred, "but from everything you've said, he's still in love with his ex-wife."

"She's remarried now," Hallie argued, "and you're going to make him forget all about Mary Lynn."

Donnalee nibbled on her lower lip. If anyone was going to make Steve Marris forget his ex-wife, it would be Hallie, not her. "Let me ask you something. Why aren't you dating Steve yourself?"

That brought Hallie up short. "Well, because..." she faltered.

"It's a fair question," Donnalee pressed, hoping her friend would stop long enough to examine what was really happening.

"Well, Steve and I are friends. Neighbors. And even if I was interested in him, I'm not the sort of woman he needs right now. There's nothing romantic or mysterious about me. Not like you. I'm just plain old Hallie McCarthy from next door. We do stuff with his kids and go out for a pizza now and then, and..."

As Hallie prattled on, Donnalee felt her resolve cracking. One date. One lousy dinner date wouldn't be so terrible. Perhaps she should reconsider; after all, Hallie was her best friend, and she'd be going along tonight, as the unknown Todd's date.

"If you don't come, the whole evening'll be ruined," Hallie wailed. "I was looking forward to meeting Todd, too." She sounded almost convinced, but Donnalee remained skeptical. Hallie wasn't interested in Todd any more than Donnalee was in Steve. To Hallie's credit, though, she actually seemed to believe she was doing them all a great favor.

"I knew a Todd once," Donnalee said slowly. She'd moved to the Pacific Northwest from Georgia while in junior high. Because of her soft drawl, she'd stood out and been teased unmercifully. She still remembered the interminable Scarlett O'Hara jokes with a shudder. By the time she was in high school, she'd grown quiet and introspective. Much too shy to let a good-looking boy know how she felt about him.

"I've known two or three myself," Hallie said. "Big deal. Now are you going to make me look like a fool, or will you do this one small thing?"

"All right, all right," Donnalee groaned. "Why not?"

"Thank God." Hallie closed her eyes and threw back her head in exaggerated relief.

"But in the future," Donnalee said sternly, "I expect you to confer with me before you commit me to a date."

Hallie folded her hands as if making a vow. "I will. I promise I will."

"Good." Donnalee hoped Steve liked what she was wearing, because she wasn't about to change. What he saw was what he got. "I thought you said his kids were with him this week?"

"They are, but his parents are taking them for tonight." Hallie grinned suddenly. "It's going to be perfect. I don't know what I would've *done* if you'd refused."

"It'd serve you right, best friend!" Hallie was going to be paying her back a long time for this one.

"They're picking us up at eight." Hallie studied her watch. "Which gives us plenty of time to get ready."

"No, thanks," Donnalee said. "This'll have to do." She was wearing black leggings and a long jersey top, black and sprinkled with gold stars. Hallie looked her over appraisingly, then nodded and ran off to her bedroom to change. Not pushing her luck, Donnalee figured.

She settled down to wait for her friend. Hallie had succeeded in wearing down her defenses, not only because she was persistent and persuasive, but for another reason. Sanford was engaged.

He'd had the courtesy to call her himself. The news had come as a shock, so soon after their breakup, but it wasn't unexpected—or especially painful. He'd found the right woman, and Donnalee was pleased for him. It wasn't regret that she suffered, not anymore. Just... She was afraid of not finding someone to love, not living the life she wanted. Not having a family of her own.

Hallie's doorbell chimed precisely at eight. Donnalee'd say one thing for Steve: the man was prompt. Hallie tossed her a look of encouragement mingled with hope as she answered the door. Donnalee recognized Steve Marris from glimpses she'd caught of him during visits to Hallie's place. He entered the condo with a tall attractive man at his side. She could tell by the other man's stance that he wasn't any keener about this double blind date than she was. It was when she saw his face that her heart stopped. Todd Stafford. The Todd from high school.

Somehow Donnalee managed to smile politely while Hallie introduced her to Steve, but she had trouble taking her eyes off Todd. He didn't seem to recognize her, and she wasn't sure she should say anything.

"Hallie, this is Todd Stafford." He shook hands with Hallie, but his gaze returned to her. "Donnalee Norman?" His question was more breath than voice.

"It's Cooper now. I married when I was young."

She realized she couldn't leave it there. "Unfortunately, it didn't last."

"Me, too." With apparent reluctance, Todd dragged his eyes from Donnalee and turned his attention to Hallie.

"You two know each other?" Hallie asked, looking from one to the other.

"We attended the same high school," Todd answered for them.

Hallie's gaze questioned Donnalee, as if to ask whether this was the Todd she'd mentioned earlier. Donnalee nodded. Talk about a fluke. Talk about fate. Talk about coincidence. It was just as it had been all those years ago—he was with someone else. *Hallie.* Her very best friend. All she could do was smile and pretend it didn't matter.

The years had been good to him, Donnalee noted. He looked exactly as she remembered...only better. There was an unmistakable maturity about him that had been lacking at eighteen. The lines on his face revealed depth and character, and his lanky boyish body had matured into hard-muscled masculinity.

"I thought we'd take my car," Steve said, interrupting her reverie.

"Sure." Donnalee had to make an effort to stop staring at Todd. It was even more of an effort to remember that Steve was her date, and Hallie—judging by her expression—was trying to remind her.

Soon they were outside and in the car. Donnalee sat in front with Steve, and Hallie and Todd were in the back. No one seemed inclined to speak. It could have been her imagination, but Donnalee was sure she felt Todd's gaze on her. The way her thoughts were on him.

Steve did try to engage her in conversation, but Donnalee doubted that her one-word replies made sense. She'd assumed she'd outgrown her shyness, but her tongue felt as if it were glued to her teeth, and all because a boy she once knew was in the back seat with her best friend. One thing was certain, she thought with a silent laugh, she needn't worry about Steve wanting to date her after tonight. He'd be glad to be rid of her.

Involuntarily she remembered the Todd of years past. The closest she'd ever come to actually speaking to him had been in the cafeteria a few weeks before he graduated. They stood next to one another in the food line, and afterward, hating herself for being too shy to murmur so much as a greeting, Donnalee had left a note on his car.

It read: *I think you're wonderful.* She hadn't been brave enough to sign her name, something she'd always regretted.

And then there was no more time for memories; they'd arrived at the waterfront Mexican restaurant. The place was filled with wonderful exotic scents— cilantro and chilies—and festive mariachi music played in the background. Donnalee and Todd sat side by side, opposite their "dates." Donnalee noticed that Steve and Hallie did most of the talking. When the waitress came to take their drink order, everyone asked for margaritas.

Donnalee focused her attention on the menu. Hallie and Steve helped themselves to salsa and chips, but Donnalee restrained herself, preferring her tortillas whole and warm from the grill, not deep-fried.

"Could I have an order of soft tortillas?" Todd asked their waitress when she returned with their drinks.

"Me, too," she found herself adding.

Todd glanced at her and smiled, his gaze lingering. She felt indescribably foolish, blushing as if she were sixteen all over again.

When the friendly waitress returned for their order, Donnalee chose one of the specials—two cheese enchiladas and a chili relleno. Todd's choice echoed her own.

"Did you two plan this?" Hallie joked.

"No," Donnalee whispered. It was only a similarity in food preferences, she told herself. *Don't make too much of it.* But she knew, she *knew* that something special was beginning.

Steve asked Hallie a question, and soon the two were deep in conversation. The space between Donnalee and Todd seemed to evaporate. She kept her gaze straight ahead, not knowing what to say, almost frightened by the way her heart behaved at seeing him again. There was so much she wanted to ask him, but she couldn't find the courage. The shy teenager she'd once been had returned to possess her.

Todd seemed equally uneasy. Finally he said, "You won't believe who I ran into recently. Mrs. O'Leary from senior English. Did you ever have her?"

She'd been Donnalee's favorite teacher back then— and she was a safe topic of conversation right now. "Yes! How is she? I haven't heard about her in years."

"She's the same. I don't think time will ever change her. Oh, her hair's a little grayer, but her eyes still twinkle when she talks. I was happy to see her," he said simply. "I always wanted her to know she was my favorite teacher."

"Me, too." Donnalee nodded vigorously. "She was so passionate about literature. She turned Shakespeare's plays into experiences that I lived and breathed." Donnalee's thinking was coherent once again, and she warmed to the topic. "And Jane Austen... Mrs. O'Leary taught me how to look at her books and see not only the past she described, but the way her comments about men and women are still relevant. I reread *Pride and Prejudice* every few years." She paused. "I'll always be grateful to Mrs. O."

"So will I."

By now they were both relaxed, laughing and reminiscing. Soon Donnalee noticed that Hallie and Steve had stopped talking and were watching them with renewed interest. Her best friend seemed none too pleased with her. Hallie pulled her chair in, closer to Todd.

Steve pulled his closer to Donnalee.

Donnalee got the hint. Steve was *her* date and Hallie was Todd's. Donnalee didn't blame her; it must be disconcerting to find your friend being so friendly with your date!

Steve appeared to be having much the same thought about Todd, because he was frowning darkly.

All of a sudden this wasn't going well, and Donnalee didn't know how to improve the situation.

Somehow she made it through dinner, although she didn't remember tasting a single bite. When the waitress came for her plate, she was surprised to see that half her meal was missing and could only assume she'd eaten it.

Steve suggested a walk along the waterfront and everyone seemed agreeable, but as they left the restaurant, Donnalee saw Todd pulling Steve aside. They conducted a low-voiced conversation, with frequent glances at the two women.

Donnalee could guess what they were discussing, but her immediate reaction was gratitude for the opportunity to speak privately to Hallie.

"Don't hate me," she whispered, not knowing how to explain what was happening between her and Todd.

"You mean because you've stolen my date?"

Donnalee had rarely felt so wretched. She couldn't spit out an apology fast enough, but Hallie stopped her before she uttered a word. The irritation in her eyes was replaced with a gentle chagrined look.

"Don't worry about it. I could see the lay of the land the minute you two recognized each other."

"I was crazy about him, Hallie." Donnalee reflected that it hadn't taken long for those feelings to rekindle. Being with Todd was like peeling back the years and uncovering that vulnerable, yearning girl again. What terrified her, though, was the knowledge that she could easily fall in love with him—really in love. Not an adolescent infatuation this time but adult emotions with all their power and complexity.

A minute later she watched as Todd made his way to her side. "I squared it with Steve," he said, and reached for her hand, his fingers closing tightly around hers.

"Do you mind if we go our own way, just the two of us?" he added.

Her heart pounded hard. "What about Hallie?"

"Steve's talking to her now."

Donnalee looked over her shoulder in time to see Hallie grin and wave. "Have fun, you two," she called out cheerfully. Then Steve and Hallie turned and walked in the opposite direction.

She swung back and found herself staring into Todd's unbelievably intense eyes.

"This is the way it should've been from the first," he said, almost daring her to contradict him with what surely would have been a lie. "Hallie and Steve should be the ones dating. Not you and Steve or me and Hallie."

"I think she's half in love with him already," she said.

"Steve's already in love with her."

Donnalee wanted to believe that. "But I thought Steve was in love with his ex-wife."

Todd hesitated before he answered, as if carefully weighing his response. "Yeah, I guess he is. I've never understood it. Mary Lynn's selfish and self-centered. I won't say any more because it isn't fair for me to judge someone else's actions or motives."

Donnalee smiled to herself. "I always admired that about you."

Todd glanced at her. "Admired what?"

"How fair you are. And how generous."

Her answer left him suspiciously quiet. "I saw you leave the note on my car."

Donnalee felt the color explode in her cheeks, and yet she didn't fear the truth. "I meant what I said then and I mean it now."

"I was always sorry I didn't talk to you in the cafeteria that day," he said quietly. "I always had a difficult time talking to girls. Still do," he admitted on a sheepish note. "I wanted you to know that I thought you were nice. The other sophomore girls seemed immature, but not you."

"You were my first crush," she whispered. "I dreamed about you every night that entire year."

They stopped outside the ferry terminal, the cooler

evening wind dancing around them. "I dreamed of you, too, Donnalee."

Unexplained tears crowded her eyes. She wasn't a woman prone to open displays of emotion; mortified, she turned away, not wanting him to witness the effect of his words.

"Donnalee." Todd placed his hand on her shoulder. "I said the wrong thing, didn't I?"

She shook her head. "No, it's not you. I'm...I'm sorry." Fumbling for a tissue in her purse, she blotted her eyes. "Something...strange is happening."

He repositioned himself so that he stood directly in front of her. With one finger he raised her chin so their eyes could meet. "You're trembling."

"It must be a chill from the wind." She offered the first sane excuse that presented itself.

His tattered breath struck her face, as if he'd been unconsciously holding it inside and released it all at once. "You're right. Something very strange is happening. I feel it, too, and damn it all, it frightens me."

"I was married and...the divorce nearly killed me," she said.

"My marriage didn't last a year. I vowed I'd never get involved again. I don't think I could take the pain if something went wrong."

"And now?" she dared to ask.

"And now..." His expression seemed to say he was as shocked, as wary, as she was, and his breathing was ragged.

"I have a cabin," he said, his eyes burning into hers. "Come with me tomorrow—we'll spend the rest of the weekend there."

It didn't take Donnalee two seconds to decide. "Yes."

Twenty-Five

When Todd Met Donnalee

"Doesn't that beat all," Hallie said wonderingly. She walked down the waterfront at a good clip, easily outpacing Steve. "I wouldn't have believed it if I hadn't seen it with my own eyes." She paused and waited for him to catch up. "What is this, *When Harry Met Sally?*"

"When who met who?" Steve asked, pretending to be out of breath.

"That movie—it was out a few years back. Two people arrange dates for each other with their best friends and then the *friends* fall in love and marry."

Steve feigned a look of shock. "Are you saying Todd's going to marry Donnalee? On such short acquaintance?"

"Don't get cute with me, Steve Marris. All I know is that my best friend just stole my blind date."

"In case you hadn't noticed, you aren't exactly building up my self-esteem here," Steve remarked pointedly. "First, I lost *my* blind date to my best friend and then *you* complain about getting stuck with me."

"I'm not complaining." Steve was taking this all wrong.

"Well, you don't look happy."

She slid her arm through his and pressed her head to his shoulder. "Oh, you aren't so bad."

Steve snorted. "Your enthusiasm is underwhelming."

"It's just that I'm disappointed."

"Rubbing salt in the wound?"

Hallie giggled. "I'm disappointed for *you.* I was so sure you and Donnalee would hit it off. She's exactly the type of woman you need, and you're perfect for her. Who would've guessed she'd known Todd in another life?"

"What makes you say Donnalee's perfect for me?"

Hallie sighed loudly. Like every other man she'd ever known, Steve needed help seeing the obvious. "For starters, Donnalee's beautiful *and* intelligent. Plus, she's been through a painful divorce, so she understands what you've been through with Mary Lynn. Donnalee's great with kids, too. I'm sure Meagan and Kenny would like her once they met her. Of course, she's also got what you said a man's looking for."

"What I said?"

"You know—her physical...endowments."

"I hadn't noticed."

Hallie'd just bet! "And your personalities complement each other." She gave another dramatic sigh, this time of regret. "Now it's too late."

"Too late?"

"For you and Donnalee. Because of Todd. I've never seen a man fluster Donnalee that way. Not even Sanford, and he was one in a million." It occurred to Hallie, not for the first time, that she wouldn't have minded dating Sanford herself. Except for his unwillingness to have children, he was every woman's dream.

A dream Donnalee had walked away from, refusing to sacrifice something as important to her as family. She hadn't done it lightly. Hallie wasn't sure what she herself would have done in similar circumstances and was grateful she didn't have to make the decision.

They paused near the waterfront fire station and the large bronze statue honoring Ivar Haglund, a local restaurateur and philanthropist. Suddenly tired, Hallie slumped down on a park bench, as if waiting for a bus.

She looked over at the waterfront concessions. "I wonder if any of them sell double-fudge macadamia-nut ice cream." It was that kind of evening.

"Wouldn't vanilla do just as well?" Steve asked.

"I guess. In a pinch."

"Be right back." He disappeared and returned a couple of minutes later with two hand-dipped chocolate-and-nut-covered ice-cream bars. "It was the best I could do."

Hallie gladly accepted the treat. "I've underestimated you, Marris."

"Hey, I've been telling you that for weeks."

"You don't seem very upset about all this." He wasn't revealing the slightest regret, while her own ego was scraping bedrock. Hard not to feel that way when your date abandons you without a backward glance— although she certainly didn't begrudge Donnalee any happiness.

"Todd going off with Donnalee works for the best as far as I'm concerned," he muttered, unwrapping his ice-cream bar.

"Your best friend walks off with your date and you don't care?"

Steve shrugged. "Nothing would've come of it, anyway."

"How can you be so sure?"

"Easy. Donnalee's looking for a husband, and frankly, I'm not interested. I tried to tell you that earlier. I've been married, and believe me, once was enough."

"In other words, the entire evening was a waste of…of my matchmaking efforts." Irritated, Hallie bit into the ice-cream bar, the cold almost painful against her teeth. Apparently Steve intended to spend the rest of his life mooning after his first and only love. It made Hallie so angry she took another bite of ice cream. A big tooth-chilling bite.

"Why is it we can never have a conversation without talking about Mary Lynn?" she asked, once her teeth had recovered from the shock.

"Mary Lynn? Who's talking about her?" He tossed his half-eaten ice-cream bar into a nearby garbage container.

Hallie sighed. "Look. If you're never going to get married again, why'd you let me set you up with Donnalee?"

His expression was the picture of self-sacrifice. "I did it for you."

Yeah, right.

He must have read the skepticism in her eyes. "I thought you and Todd might hit it off. Todd's a good guy and I wanted to steer you toward somebody decent, instead of those losers you've been dating."

He sounded sincere, and Hallie felt contrite. Then he said, "If things do work out between her and Todd— great. He needs someone."

Hallie couldn't stop the thought of poor Steve, all alone for the rest of his life. "Are you telling me you plan to live like a hermit?" she asked bluntly.

"Hardly. The way I figure it, Mary Lynn's married now and it isn't likely we'll get back together. I can accept that. So I don't see why I can't start dating again. I may not be interested in marriage, but I do want a...social life."

Social life. Uh-huh. The truth was out—his actions hadn't been entirely altruistic. "Then that's the real reason you let me set you up with Donnalee?"

He chuckled. "Bull's-eye."

"Are there any other potential dates lurking close by?" she asked, mildly curious. All right, very curious. She remembered Mrs. Hot and Pink from Kenny's softball game, and suspected there were others. After all, Steve was a virile, handsome guy. Successful, good-natured, in the prime of life.

"A couple."

This came as no surprise. "Who?" Mrs. Hot and Pink and probably someone from the bowling alley, Hallie guessed.

"A friend from bowling."

She nearly laughed out loud. She was right. Too bad his friend, whoever she was, hadn't been around when he needed a partner for the tournament last spring. It would have saved Hallie a lot of grief. Well, not grief; she'd had a good time, reluctant though she was to admit it.

"As it happens," he said, "we're stuck with each other's company for tonight, and you know what? I'm glad."

Hallie sat up a bit taller. "Thanks, I needed that." Was he going to say anything else and ruin the compliment? She braced herself for the insult she was sure would follow. None came. "But..." she prodded, gesturing with her hand for him to finish the thought.

He cast her an amused glance. "No buts. I meant it."

Hallie ate the rest of the ice cream, taking small careful bites. She and Steve were quiet for a while, watching the steady stream of tourists and local visitors. The smells of fresh seafood, the colorful souvenir shops, the trolley cars and street merchants hawking their wares made for a carnival atmosphere.

"Feel like riding the ferry?" Steve asked. The *Walla Walla*, a three-deck car and passenger ferry was docked at the terminal.

"Where to?" It sounded like a good idea, especially if the ferry would take her someplace exotic and wonderful. Like maybe Alaska, which had lots of eligible men and a shortage of women. Or so she'd heard.

"Bainbridge Island. It's only a half-hour crossing. We can walk off, have a cup of coffee and walk back on again."

It wasn't Alaska, but what the heck. "Let's do it." She placed her hand in his and they walked toward the terminal.

Steve purchased the tickets, then led the way onto the ferry. As they stood on the outside deck looking out at the water, they listened to the distinctive sound of car after car crossing the metal gangplanks.

Steve draped one arm casually around her shoulders. Hallie felt comforted; although she'd put on a brave front, she was feeling low. All these months, and she was nowhere near her goal.

She turned to face Steve, prepared to thank him for his company and cry on his shoulder, but instead, found herself incapable of speaking. The words stopped abruptly in her throat as she realized that Donnalee was the one who'd missed out. Steve was a wonderful man.

For some reason she found herself remembering the day she'd seen him washing his truck with his shirt unbuttoned—and the almost unwilling attraction she'd felt. She'd been assailed by a host of contradictory feelings, many of which still confused her. She hadn't wanted to consider him as anything but her friend, her neighbor. And yet...

"Yes?" he asked, gazing down at her.

There could be no denying that she enjoyed the warmth of his body close to hers, the sensation of his arm against her back, his hand on her shoulder. "I was...just thinking."

"It's that difficult?"

"Sometimes." All at once it was impossible to swallow. She turned to face the water, but was blind to the beauty spread before her.

She felt the ferry pull away from the dock and heard the horn blast that followed.

"Excuse me," Steve said, pounding his fist against his chest as if the sound had come from him.

She laughed at his childish joke and shook her head. It was best to leave their relationship as it was. Friends. She could laugh at his jokes, freely tease him. They would continue to help each other. He'd start her lawn mower and she'd watch his kids. It was a fair exchange, she'd always thought. Neighborly. Everything would change if they became lovers. The terms of their relationship would shift and they might risk losing what they had now—an uncomplicated, mutually supportive friendship. Not only that, a romantic and even sexual involvement with Steve wouldn't lead to marriage, given his feelings for Mary Lynn. And marriage was what Hallie wanted.

With the wind beating against her upturned face, she

forced herself to think of Arnold. Dear, sweet, perfect Arnold. No. She couldn't do it. She'd rather swallow cod-liver oil. Hmm, maybe *that* was what she needed. Medicine.

What made being with Steve different from being with any of the men she'd recently dated was a lack of tension, Hallie reflected. An ability to find pleasure in each other's company, regardless of the circumstances. She'd discovered that she and Steve didn't need to talk in order to have fun together. Right now seemed to be one of those easy, silent times. They stood side by side, gazing out at the beautiful green waters of Puget Sound.

When the ferry docked at Winslow, they walked off and found an outdoor café, where Hallie ordered an espresso and Steve a latte.

"Did Todd remember that you drove?" It occurred to Hallie that Todd and Donnalee were stuck downtown without a car.

"He remembered."

"Then how's he going to get home?"

"I gave him the keys to my car."

"You what?"

"We can take the bus easily enough."

"The bus."

"If you're worried abut it, I'll get us a taxi."

"Are you nuts, Steve? First you let Todd steal your date and then you give him your car." She shook her head in mock disgust. Really, though, she was impressed—once again—by Steve's generosity.

It was dark by the time they boarded the ferry for the return trip to Seattle. The city lights blazed in the distance, and the stars shone in the clear night sky above. The sight was breathtakingly lovely, and just as she had earlier, Hallie made her way to the front of the ferry, with Steve following. The wind, chillier now, buffeted her.

Closing her eyes, she gripped the boat's railing, her hands wide apart. Steve moved behind her and stretched his arms out on either side of hers. His warmth seeped through her clothes and deeper, much deeper. A small tremor ran through her.

"You're cold." He folded his arms around her middle. Resting her head against his shoulder, she could feel Steve's heart beating in rhythm with hers. Their chests rose and fell as if each drew the same breath. How long had it been like this, she wondered, this closeness they shared?

They might have remained just as they were forever. Despite the wind, Hallie had no inclination to move, and apparently Steve didn't, either. She was utterly content to stand there, staring at the approaching harbor, wrapped in the protective warmth of his embrace.

All too soon the ferry had docked and they were filing out. Hallie felt a little awkward and wondered if Steve did, too. Their intimate companionable mood had vanished.

"I had a wonderful time," she confessed as they strolled toward the bus tunnel.

"Even if you were stuck with me for the evening."

"That's just fine, since Todd dumped *me* on you."

"You aren't so bad, McCarthy." He reached for her hand, intertwining their fingers.

"Neither are you, Marris. Neither are you."

Twenty-Six

Second Chance At Love

Donnalee awoke to the scent of sizzling bacon. A slow easy smile crossed her face as she rolled onto her back, stretching her arms high above her head.

A glance at the clock told her it was after ten. That couldn't be right. Tossing aside the covers, she climbed out of the narrow bed, reached for her robe and looked over the balcony of the A-frame loft.

Todd stood in front of the stove, humming softly while he turned the bacon, looking masculine and wonderful. Her heart swelled at the sight of him. They'd spent Saturday trout-fishing from the canoe. He'd insisted on cooking dinner, treating her like company. She'd never known fish could taste so good. Later they'd sat under the stars, talking, and there was no subject they didn't discuss. Donnalee had never spent a day she'd enjoyed more. She'd loved every single second.

"Good morning," she called down to him now.

Todd looked up and grinned. "I wondered when you were going to get up."

From the look of him, he'd been awake for hours. "Is it really ten?" she asked, tying the sash of her robe.

"Yup. Hungry?"

"Starved. I'll be down in two shakes." Her overnight bag sat next to the bed, and she quickly found a fresh T-shirt. Pulling on her jeans, she raced down the stairs barefoot.

She arrived just as Todd was dishing up the fried eggs. "I can't remember when I've slept better," she told him, smiling.

"There's something about the country air," he said, his gaze approving as she sat down at the table. "I sleep like the dead out here at the cabin. It's one of the great mysteries of the universe."

He carried two glasses of orange juice to the table, and Donnalee found herself watching him. Watching him and loving him. The realization caught her unawares. *Love.* She was falling in love.

As a teenager she'd been infatuated with him. When they'd met again over dinner on Friday, the flame had sparked back to life. But spending all day Saturday together had set it ablaze.

"My grandparents always talked about how coming here restored them," Todd said, looking at her. "They were the ones who bought this place nearly fifty years ago. It was their private getaway. When the pressures of job and family became too much, they stole away for a weekend."

"It's kind of romantic, isn't it?"

He seemed not to have heard her. "After my divorce, Gramps sent me here and said I should stay a week. I stayed two months. The first month I worked on the place and was up until all hours of the night. I did hard physical work, anything that would keep me from thinking."

"And the second month?"

"I read and slept and healed as much as I could. When I returned to my family, I'd made some basic decisions about my life. First and foremost, I announced I wasn't returning to college—which really disappointed my father."

"You're good with your hands. It makes perfect sense for you to work with them."

"I'm content, but to my parents, having a son choose a blue-collar trade was a step backward. They had big dreams for me as an attorney. It's taken them a long time to accept that I love what I do and I'm good at it."

"It was a wise choice for you."

"I believe so." He stared down at his food. "For the first time in fifteen years I'm questioning the second decision I made that summer," he said. "After the failure of my marriage I decided I'd never love any woman again. I know it sounds pretty melodramatic, but I meant it, and not once in all the years since have I been tempted to change my mind." He paused, his eyes on her. "Until now."

The words were spoken without any telltale inflection, as if he were discussing something as mundane as television listings or the weather.

Donnalee hadn't taken even one bite of her breakfast and realized she couldn't eat to save her life. Emotion clogged her throat. She set the fork aside and pushed herself away from the table, then walked outside. She stood on the porch, head bent, staring at the cedar planks.

"Donnalee." He'd followed her out. His voice was rough, almost sorrowful. "I apologize. I should never have said that."

"Did you mean it?" she asked, her own voice barely above a whisper.

"Yes."

They'd spent an entire day together and he hadn't so much as kissed her. When they'd headed into the house for bed, he'd escorted her to the loft, wished her good-night and promptly left.

"Does that bother you?" he asked. "What I said?"

"No. It makes my heart...glad."

Todd slid his arms around her and brought her close. For the longest time they did nothing but stand in the sun, locked in each other's embrace. Then Donnalee kissed him.

That first kiss was soft, tentative, yet full of raw hungry need. Her whole body began to tremble. She gripped his collar, crushing the material, holding on to it as if this was all that kept her from being swept away in a raging storm. Her moan was wanton. She hardly recognized the sound of her own voice.

Todd bunched the material of her T-shirt at the small of her back. "Do you know what you're starting?" he asked. Then, not giving her time to respond, he asked another question. "Are you sure this is what you want?" She felt his muscles tense with restraint.

"Yes...I know. I'm sure."

His tongue stroked her lips before dipping into her mouth, creating an electricity that arced through her, heating her blood. When he did fully claim her lips, she nearly fainted.

One kiss, one deep kiss, and she was hot and restless. So very restless.

She wasn't alone. Donnalee could feel his need. It shuddered through his body and hers. This urgency was far too potent so early in their relationship. Things were

moving too fast. She'd never been a woman who leapt
from bed to bed. She'd watched others, friends, moving
from one partner to another, from one desperate relationship to the next, without thought, without regret.
Without their hearts ever being involved.

Well, if anyone's heart was involved, it was hers.

They kissed until Donnalee felt she'd die if he didn't
make love to her. When he wrenched his mouth from
hers, she whimpered, begging him without words to go
on.

"Either we stop now," he whispered, his voice
heavy with need, "or...or we continue."

She pulled back until her eyes found his. What he
was really asking was permission to make love to her.
He could have carried her into his bedroom, her head
clouded with passion, and taken her right then and
there. Instead, he'd stopped, giving her the opportunity
to end their passion now if she had any hesitations.
Making sure she wanted him as badly as he wanted
her.

She smiled and kissed him softly and slowly. Thoroughly. "Don't stop. I want you. So very much..."

That was apparently all the reassurance he needed.
He swung her into his arms, carried her into the house
and made straight for his bedroom, where he gently
placed her on the mattress.

They spent the day there. All day. When they
weren't making love, they napped or shared desultory
conversation. Donnalee woke late in the afternoon and
knew it was time to return to the city. She had to be
at her office early Monday morning to meet with clients. For two glorious days, she'd escaped from her
world into one that was simpler. Happier. And incredibly sensual.

Todd lay on his back, his hands behind his head. "Now that I think about it, I'll bet this is how my grandparents spent their time here."

"Making love?"

"I wouldn't put it past Gramps. They were married more than sixty years, and to the best of my memory, I never heard them say a cross word to each other."

"What a wonderful legacy."

"My divorce was the first in the family," he said.

Even now, years later, Donnalee could hear his guilt. She pressed her head to his shoulder and slipped her arm around his neck. "I don't want to leave," she whispered. She feared that once they were back in the city, everything they'd discovered this weekend would be lost. Todd would return to his life; she'd return to hers. She was afraid these brief hours shared in each other's arms would be forgotten, reduced to a pleasant interlude without any further meaning.

Silently they dressed and loaded his car. On the long drive back to Seattle, they exchanged snippets of conversation, but no subject held their attention long.

By the time Todd pulled up in front of her house, Donnalee was convinced he'd experienced a change of heart and regretted everything he'd said and done—the confidences, the lovemaking, the implied promises.

"I had a wonderful weekend," she said, unable to meet his gaze. "I can't thank you enough."

Todd carried in her suitcase and left shortly afterward. He didn't even kiss her before he walked out the door.

Hardly aware of what she was doing, Donnalee unpacked, then sat on the sofa and started to sob. Soon she was crying so hard she could barely breathe. When she'd managed to control her breathing enough to speak, she reached for the phone and punched in her best friend's number.

"Hello," Hallie said cheerfully.

"I did something so stupid!" Donnalee wailed.

"Donnalee? Is that you? What's wrong? Do you need me to come over?"

This was what Donnalee loved about Hallie. Close friend and staunch ally, she was always ready to drop whatever she was doing and rush to her aid. "No. I'll be fine in a little bit." Another lifetime was more accurate, but there was no reason to alarm her friend.

"What happened?"

"Nothing," Donnalee said. Then, with a sob, she added, "Everything."

Hallie was suspiciously quiet. "What do you mean, everything? You went away for the weekend with Todd to his family's summer cabin and..." She hesitated. "You didn't...?"

"We did."

Donnalee could hear Hallie's soft gasp. "You and Todd slept together?"

"We went to bed, but let me assure you, there was very little sleeping."

Hallie gave a snort of disgust. "If you're calling for sympathy, you're plumb out of luck. I'm so jealous I could scream. Why is everyone in the world having sex but me?"

"It was so beautiful," Donnalee whispered, and started crying again. She'd practically emptied the box of tissues, and still the tears showed no sign of letting up.

"Why in the name of heaven are you crying?"

Hallie's question was perfectly logical, but Donnalee didn't have an answer. "I don't know. Because it was good—more than good. Oh, Hallie, I can't even *begin* to tell you how good it was."

"My sympathy level is sinking fast."

Donnalee laughed and wept at the same time. "It's just that I'm so afraid."

"Of what?"

She took a deep shuddering breath. "I love him. Don't laugh, Hallie, please. I couldn't bear it if my best friend told me what a fool I am."

"I wouldn't laugh at you, Donnalee."

"I guess I knew that." She didn't say anything for a moment; Hallie didn't speak, either. "I love him," she said again. "It makes no sense that I'd be so sure of it when we've spent hardly any time together—but I am. Now I think I've ruined everything."

"By sleeping with him?"

"Yes. I've never done anything like this before, and I'm afraid I'm going to lose him."

"Why would you think that?"

"He hardly spoke to me on the drive back." They'd both made an effort to avoid the one subject they should have discussed—how they felt about each other. Donnalee had no idea where their relationship would go from this point. If it was going anywhere at all. Thinking about it terrified her.

'You've got absolutely no reason to worry," Hallie said.

"How can you say that?" Donnalee challenged. She wanted to believe it so badly but didn't dare.

"I saw the way he looked at you during dinner," Hallie muttered. "Him being *my* date and all."

"Oh, Hallie, I'm so sorry."

"Don't be. I was joking—I'm not interested in

Todd. Just calm down. Things have a way of working out for the best.''

"You sound so sure."

"I am sure."

"Now I know why I didn't marry Sanford..." Donnalee said, clenching the damp tissue in her fist. The pain of that separation crept into her consciousness like a bad dream, one she struggled to forget.

Hallie completed the thought for her. "You didn't marry Sanford because of Todd. Your heart must have known there was someone else for you. Someone who wants the same things you do. And what's even better," Hallie went on excitedly, "it was someone you already knew!"

"That's what I want to think, but I can't be sure—especially now." Donnalee could only imagine what Todd thought of her, falling into bed with him like that. Until Todd, she never would've believed herself capable of such a thing.

"Well, my friend, marriage and family are about to be yours." Hallie sounded downright gleeful. "One look at Todd, and I could tell he's got a high sperm count."

"Hallie!"

"You want children, don't you?" Hallie's voice had become serious again.

"Yes, but—"

"Oh, Donnalee, don't worry. Everything's going to be fine."

Donnalee found herself smiling for the first time since she'd arrived home. She did feel better. They chatted for a few more minutes and then rang off.

Keeping busy would help, Donnalee felt certain. If she just kept moving, kept doing routine tasks, sooner or later everything would fall back into place and she could get on with living. She put a load of clothes in the wash. She reorganized her refrigerator. She was plugging in the vacuum when she looked out the window—and her heart stopped. Todd's car was parked in front of her condo. Paralyzed, she watched as he climbed out, walked halfway to her front door, paused and then turned back.

The paralysis snapped. She rushed to the door and threw it open to find him standing on her doorstep, hand raised to knock.

Speechless they stared at each other.

Todd shoved his hands in his back pockets and refused to meet her eyes.

It was over, Donnalee told herself bleakly. He'd come to tell her he didn't want to see her again. A darkness had descended on her when her marriage ended, and it had taken her years to fight her way back into the light. Donnalee thought it might kill her if Todd walked away from her now.

"Walk away from you?" he said.

Good heavens, she'd said it aloud! Mortified to the very marrow of her bones, Donnalee wanted to bury her face in her hands.

"I didn't come back to tell you I don't want to see you again," he said. "I was trying to figure out a way to ask if you'd be willing to see *me* again after what happened this weekend. I didn't mean for things to get so intense so quickly. I was afraid I'd rushed you and ruined any chance I had with you."

"You didn't ruin your chances with me. If anything... Oh, Todd, I'm so glad you're here!" She leapt off the step and into his embrace.

Todd locked his arms around her. She didn't let him

speak, but spread kisses, one after another, all over his face. "I want to see you again. I need to see you again and again and again."

"I'm not sure I'm any real bargain," Todd murmured between kisses.

"*I'm* sure." She directed his mouth to hers and kissed him with a thoroughness that left them both breathless.

"The first thing you'll need to learn is that it's useless to argue with me," she told him, knowing he could see the happiness radiating from her eyes.

"But maybe it's too soon..." He continued to hold her, continued to stroke her hair.

"As far as I'm concerned, it's about fourteen years too late."

"Oh, Donnalee, this is all so crazy." He released her and took two steps away from her, as if he wanted to turn tail and run.

"But it's a wonderful kind of crazy! I found you again and I'm not about to let you go. Let's both accept that we were meant to be together and leave it at that." She reached for his hand and led him into her home. Without pausing she closed the door and pushed him down on the sofa, then promptly sat on his lap and wrapped her arms around his neck. "It looks like you need to be convinced. How long do you think it'll take?" she asked.

Todd grinned. "How about forty or fifty years?"

Twenty-Seven

Large Women Wearing Helmets With Horns

Steve was astonished how quiet the house was after the kids returned to Mary Lynn. He'd moped around yesterday—Sunday—fighting off a sense of loneliness, but that passed soon enough.

He loved his children to distraction, and he'd enjoyed the two weeks they'd spent with him, yet in the past year he'd learned to appreciate solitude, too. He was comfortable with silence now. In the early days of his separation, it had damn near driven him crazy. But over time he'd managed to accept the traumatic changes in his life; he'd adjusted to strange new schedules, such as seeing his kids only on weekends.

He was grateful Meagan and Kenny had adapted so well to their new circumstances, and grateful that he and Mary Lynn had been able to maintain civility in their dealings.

If he was making a list of things to be grateful for, Steve figured he should include Hallie. She'd come to his aid more times than he could count, especially during the past couple of weeks. Thinking back, he realized that Meagan and Kenny had spent nearly as much time at her place as they had at his.

The blind dinner date they'd arranged for each other hadn't gone as planned, but these things happened, and he didn't take it personally. Hallie had seemed a little upset in the beginning, but she'd been a good sport about it since. And she seemed genuinely pleased that the date had worked out so well for her friend.

Standing in front of his refrigerator, Steve surveyed the contents, wondering what he could rustle up for dinner. Cooking for one didn't excite him. Briefly he wondered what Hallie was eating. More often than not these past two weeks she'd either cooked or joined him and the kids for dinner, and he'd come to rely on her suggestions.

Steve glanced out the window to see if she was home. He strained to catch a glimpse of her car, and his spirits lifted when he saw it. So far, so good. Then, feeling a bit like a Peeping Tom, he focused on her kitchen window. Ah, yes, there she was, talking on the phone. She had the cord wrapped about her wrist, and from the way she leaned against the wall, he could tell she was annoyed about something. After a moment she hung up, then immediately reached for the phone again.

His own phone rang and he jerked around. "Hello, Hallie," he answered, thinking himself rather clever.

"Guess what?" she said furiously. "Arnold just called to break our date tonight. That's the third time he's canceled out on me at the last minute, the low-down dirty rat."

Steve didn't understand why Hallie continued to see the guy. She'd never been keen on him, yet she insisted on beating the relationship to death. Although Steve had never been introduced to Arnold, he could tell it was a lost cause just from the few glimpses he'd caught

when he was out jogging or—*let's be honest, Marris*—
watching him through the window.

"I bought theater tickets through the Chamber of
Commerce for this wonderful production I'd been looking forward to seeing." Hallie sounded exasperated
and angry. "Arnold had agreed to come and now..."
She sighed. "The thing is, I've got two perfectly good
tickets, which I refuse to waste."

"Maybe you can exchange the tickets for another
night and go with Arnold then."

"I don't ever plan to see Arnold again. I told him
so, and what annoyed me even more than being stood
up is his attitude. He *expected* me to break it off, and
he even seemed relieved when I told him." She paused
long enough to catch her breath. "Anyway, I can't
exchange them and I don't want to waste them."

He didn't bother to suggest she go by herself. If
she'd considered that an option, she wouldn't have
called. He was afraid she planned to ask him and
groaned inwardly at the thought. Frankly, it'd been a
long hard day and he wasn't interested in sitting
through a play, no matter how good it was reported to
be. "What about Donnalee and Todd?" he tried.

"Donnalee and Todd? You're joking, right?"

"I guess I am." Well, Hallie was right. Those two
were in their own little world. Every morning of the
past week, Todd had arrived at the office wearing a
silly grin. Silly, perhaps, but also...satisfied. Steve had
never seen a man so much in love.

"Can you go with me?" Hallie pleaded. "Oh, shoot.
Monday's your bowling night, isn't it?"

"No," he was sorry to report. "The league takes a
break during the summer."

"Then please, please come with me."

It was one of the rare times she'd requested anything of him. In that moment Steve realized he didn't have the heart to refuse her.

"How formal is it?"

She hesitated, a sure sign he wasn't going to like her response. "You'll need to wear a suit," she informed him. "Dark, if you have one."

He cursed silently. "I do."

He hated that suit. Hated it more every time he was forced to wear it. He kept the thing around primarily for weddings and funerals, so he hadn't worn it in some time, since most of his friends were married and no one he knew had died recently. What he particularly loathed was wearing a tie, which felt like a noose around his neck.

"Does that mean you'll go?"

Steve paused and reminded himself of all the times Hallie had come to his rescue. "I guess," he muttered.

"A little enthusiasm would go a long way, Marris," she muttered back.

Steve grinned. "I'm beginning to think Arnold might have had the right idea."

"I think not. These tickets were fifty bucks. Each."

A hundred bucks was nothing to sneeze at. "What time do you need me to be ready?"

"Seven-thirty." He could hear the relief in her voice and was pleased that he was the one responsible for it.

"Are you throwing in dinner with this invitation?" If he was going to strangle himself with a suit and tie, he might as well get as much out of it as he could.

"You expect me to buy you dinner, too?"

She had a point there, but the kids had cleaned out his checking account. "I'll bring a can of chili," he said.

"I've got..." He turned to the window and watched as she stretched the phone cord as far as her refrigerator door and bent over while she sorted through its contents. Actually, he appreciated the view of her cute little butt. "There's a head of lettuce here and some cheddar cheese. We could make a taco salad. Do you have any chips?"

"If Kenny didn't find them, I do."

"Okay, you're on."

It was a pleasant surprise to discover what culinary magic Hallie could make with a can of chili and a few leaves of lettuce. And he had to admit dinner was a lot more enjoyable with her company.

For fear of dribbling salad dressing on his one tie, knotted for him years ago by Todd, Steve changed into his suit after dinner. He suddenly recalled the last time he'd worn it—the day he stood before the judge when his divorce was finalized. He discovered his attorney's business card in the jacket pocket and quickly tossed it in the garbage.

As he looped the tie over his head and tightened it, he reflected on that devastating day. He'd been divorced more than a year and a half now, separated even longer. It didn't seem possible. The familiar pain threatened to darken his mood, but he managed to ignore its pull. Mary Lynn had remarried and life had gone on. Not the way he'd wanted, but he'd survived. He was even experiencing some of his old pleasures again and finding new ones.

When he arrived to pick up Hallie, he did a double take. The deep blue dress, slinky, silky and body-hugging, did incredible things for her figure. This was Hallie? Damn, he'd never noticed how well proportioned she was. Everything was right where it was supposed to be. And how.

His first thought when he saw her—other than how good she looked—was to wonder if a dress like that required a bra. Not that it was any of his business, but he couldn't help being curious. The sleeveless gown stretched tightly across her chest and hooked behind the neck. Yup, he was almost certain she was braless.

He released a low whistle.

"You like it?" Hallie held her hands stiffly out at her sides—a bit like a penguin, she thought—as she turned in a slow circle to give him the full effect.

"Wow." He'd have whistled a second time if he'd found the breath to do so, but she'd stolen it. Telling her she looked good was an understatement. A gross understatement. Arnold was more of a fool than Steve had realized.

"You look..." All descriptive words and phrases deserted him.

"Fat," she supplied. She pouched out her stomach, what there was of it, which to his mind wasn't much.

"No!" He'd never been a flatterer, and he'd always struggled with compliments. It was a talent, Steve decided, and unfortunately one he lacked. Hallie waited expectantly. It was the same look Mary Lynn used to get when she needed him to say just the right thing to reassure her. The pressure was building and he was afraid he'd fail Hallie the same way he'd too often failed Mary Lynn.

"You look wonderful." It was the best he could do. He paused and waited for some sign of reaction.

She closed her eyes and exhaled.

"Really wonderful," he added, hoping that would help.

"Thank you." She smiled softly. "I won't tell you what this dress cost, but I fell in love with it the minute I tried it on. Let me just say that I'll be packing my own lunch for the next ten years."

"Whatever the price, it was worth it."

"You can be a real charmer when you want to be, Marris."

Him? A charmer? Not likely, but if Hallie wanted to think so, he wasn't going to correct her.

The play was at the Fifth Avenue Theater in downtown Seattle. Their aisle seats were in the first row of the balcony. Steve stopped counting the number of times he had to stand in order to allow other ticket holders into their seats.

Hallie acknowledged several people. A number of names were tossed his way, and he soon quit trying to remember them all. He was a member of the local Chamber of Commerce himself, but he did little more than pay his dues. He'd only attended two meetings in all the years he'd owned his business. From the looks of it, Hallie was an outgoing and popular member, which didn't surprise him.

The theater darkened and the play began. It didn't take Steve long to realize it wasn't a play at all. It was an opera. All the lines were sung. He opened his program and read it for the first time. He didn't recognize the opera's title, but it was clearly German.

While he was no aficionado, Steve liked classical music as much as the next guy, but this was no Mozart. The composer wasn't one he knew or cared to.

Hallie's rapt attention was focused on the stage. As far as Steve could figure, the opera was some tragedy that had people running back and forth across the stage.

There were frequent deaths, too—but not frequent enough.

By the end of the first scene, Steve's attention began wandering. He studied the lovely crystal light fixtures suspended from the ceiling, craning his head back as far as possible to get a better view. The theater had recently been renovated and he was impressed with the improvements.

"Steve?" Hallie was frowning at him. "Is something wrong?"

"Nah, just checking out the new fixtures," he whispered loudly. "I wonder if they're real crystal. You wouldn't happen to know, would you?"

"I wouldn't know."

"The seats are new, too."

"Uh-huh."

He rotated his shoulders, testing out the cushions for comfort and gave a thumbs-up.

Hallie rolled her eyes and reverted her attention to the stage.

Quickly bored, Steve asked her for a pen.

Hallie leaned forward for her handbag, and Steve was given a momentary peek at her front. He'd been right. No bra.

Once she'd retrieved her pen, she placed it in his hand with just a hint of impatience. Steve doodled geometric designs across the front page of the program and then found himself drawing what resembled—he hated to admit it—a series of female breasts. Actually, he was surprised by how good he was.

Years earlier he'd visited an art museum, where he'd seen a painting by one of the century's more revered artists. The painting was on loan, part of a highly touted exhibit, and Steve had studied it for several minutes. All he'd seen was a clothes hanger with two misshapen boobs. The breasts weren't even properly aligned, and yet the artist had made millions.

Steve toyed with the idea of sending his doodles to the artist's agent. Perhaps this was his life's calling and he'd make a fortune drawing breasts. He kind of liked the idea. Hiring women to pose for him, that sort of thing.

With that thought in mind he sketched a couple of ideas. He drew a torso and gave the woman four breasts with multiple nipples. He was just warming to his subject when Hallie glanced over at what he was doing, gasped and grabbed the program away from him. Giving him a pinched-lip look, she promptly crumpled it up.

Okay, okay, he got the hint. Steve tried to pay attention to the actors, he really did, but he'd rarely seen anything this boring. Opera had never appealed to him. Large women who wore helmets with horns and stormed across a stage holding spears and pretending to be warriors were of questionable sexual persuasion as far as he was concerned.

After a while, sure that Hallie was absorbed in the acting, he stole her program and folded it into a paper airplane. He had no intention of flying it, but apparently Hallie assumed otherwise. Her expression would have cracked concrete.

"What?" he asked under his breath.

"You have to ask?" she hissed.

Hands lightly folded in his lap, he focused his attention on the stage again, determined to be a model member of the audience. His eyes drifted closed and he found himself falling asleep, only to jerk awake a second or two later. He yawned loudly, twice. Then swallowed a third yawn when Hallie glared at him. His cheeks puffed out with the effort.

Next he checked the time and attempted to calculate just how much more of this he'd have to endure. Another hour he could take, but two hours was out of the question.

The curtain fell and the lights went up. Intermission. Free at last, he all but leapt out of his seat. "I'll get us something to drink," he said, and was halfway into the aisle when Hallie thrust out an arm and stopped him.

"What's the matter with you?" she demanded.

He knew he was in trouble because she spoke through clenched teeth. "Nothing," he insisted brightly.

"This work is masterful, brilliant..."

"Boring," he said.

"For you, perhaps, but not everyone agrees. Kenny would do a better job of paying attention. You're worse than a five-year-old. Furthermore, what was that you were drawing?"

Steve was convinced she didn't really want to know. He buried his hands in his pockets and shrugged. "I don't know. I was doodling. I do that sometimes. It doesn't mean anything."

"Have you ever shown your doodles to a psychiatrist?"

"I'll be better the second half. I promise."

"Never mind, let's go."

"Go?" His heart raced at the thought of escape. Surely she wouldn't tease about something like that. "Where do you want to go?"

"Home." She didn't elaborate.

His heart filled with gratitude. But once they'd

walked down the large curved stairway and outside into the cool evening, he realized this reprieve might well have come at a price.

"You aren't angry, are you?" he asked. Hallie was a good friend, and if keeping the peace meant enduring the rest of this opera, then he'd do it.

"I'm not angry," she replied, but the way she said it suggested she wasn't pleased with him, either.

"We can stay," he offered, all the while praying she wouldn't change her mind.

Not until they reached the parking garage did Steve recognize the truth. Hallie had been as bored as he was, only she was too polite to let it show.

"You didn't like that opera, either." His step lightened and he cast her a smug look.

"That's not true. The music was—"

"Don't lie, Hallie, or your nose will start to grow."

He watched as a smile quivered at the corners of her mouth, struggling to break free.

"Be honest."

She was suspiciously quiet for a moment, then took one glance at him and burst out laughing. The mirth virtually exploded from her. She wrapped her arms around her middle and bent nearly double. Still laughing, she positioned herself in front of him on the sidewalk, strolling backward as she spoke. "I wish you could've seen yourself!"

"Glad I'm such a source of amusement." A smile threatened to overtake him, too. He took her hand, gripping it firmly in his own. It felt *right* to be walking hand in hand with Hallie.

Both of them thought it seemed a shame to head back home immediately, so Steve suggested coffee. They were a bit overdressed for an all-night diner, but

that was where they ended up. Although they attracted
plenty of curious stares, neither paid much attention.

When their coffee was served, Hallie doctored hers
with cream and sugar, then stared at him as if she was
shocked by what she'd done. "I only add cream when
I'm depressed," she told him, her shoulders sagging.
"I bet this has something to do with Donnalee."

Steve had trouble following her thought process—
cream in her coffee, depression and Donnalee. Apparently there was a connection. Whatever it was would
take him a while to work out.

"It wouldn't surprise me if those two got married,"
Hallie said next.

"It wouldn't surprise me to learn they're already living together," Steve muttered. He'd never seen Todd
like this. Todd, his closest friend. The guy he worked
with every day. The guy who'd shared the secret password to reach level ten of the video game King Kong.
He'd fished with Todd, camped with him, even taken
a weekend trip to Vegas with Todd.

Yet in all the years they'd been friends, he'd never
seen Todd in love. It was almost frightening what love
could do to a levelheaded man. He told Hallie exactly
that.

"I agree with you completely!" she declared, leaning closer to him. Her hands cupped the coffee mug.
"If you think Todd's acting strange, you should see
Donnalee. It's...nauseating." Barely pausing, she
added, "I'm so jealous I could scream. Can you tell?"

Jealous, Steve repeated mentally, and wondered if
that was his problem with Todd. His friend arrived
promptly for work, accomplished each task satisfactorily and left at the end of the day. Steve had no right
to ask more of him, yet he found himself tallying a list

of complaints at the end of the day. Trivial stuff. He *was* jealous. Damn it all, he really was.

"Donnalee has had more sex in the past week than I've had in my entire life," Hallie said, glancing down at her coffee. "That explains it."

"Explains what?"

"Why I'm putting cream in my coffee."

"Oh." Well, okay, he supposed that made some sense, now that he understood the connection. "Same with Todd," he grumbled. "It's like he's walking around in this bubble, breathing in happy gas."

"Exactly," Hallie moaned. "Nothing can burst their bubble. It's...it's disgusting." She raised the mug to her lips, paused halfway there and set it down on the table with a loud clatter. "Are we being petty?"

"No way." He dismissed the question without thought, then reconsidered. "On the other hand, I don't know if I'd be complaining nearly as loud if it was me."

"That's my point," Hallie said, gesturing with both hands.

"What gets me is that I practically had to bribe Todd into going out on this blind date in the first place. He wasn't interested in meeting you. Not even when I mentioned how attractive you are and how much the kids like you."

Hallie glared at him. "If you're telling me all this to make me feel better, I suggest you stop."

Steve grinned. "From what you said, Donnalee wasn't any more interested in meeting me."

She sighed expressively. "True."

"So Todd and Donnalee found great sex together. You had your chance, McCarthy. You turned down the best offer you're likely to get," Steve reminded her. "I was willing to take you to bed, remember?"

"Right!" She rolled her eyes. "How could I refuse a romantic invitation like 'Wanna do it?'"

Steve chuckled, amused as he often was by Hallie. He'd lacked finesse on that particular occasion, he'd admit it. He'd been feeling low at the time. What he'd really needed was someone to listen, and Hallie had provided a sympathetic ear, for which he'd been grateful.

"They're going to wear themselves out," Hallie said. "They'll end up dying of exhaustion."

Steve could only assume she'd returned to the subject of Donnalee and Todd. "Yeah, but what a way to go."

The gleam of pure unadulterated envy was back in her eyes. "If it's like this before the wedding, can you imagine what it'll be like afterward?"

"Yeah," Steve said, then frowned. "My advice to Todd is to get it while he can."

"Steve!"

"You think I'm joking?"

Hallie stared at him as if to ask exactly what kind of wife Mary Lynn had been. But he didn't want to talk about his ex, especially now that she was married to another man. Sleeping with another man. He couldn't dwell on that, otherwise he'd go crazy. So he avoided the subject entirely.

"Seriously, I think Todd and Donnalee will do fine," Hallie said.

"Yeah, I'm sure you're right."

She reached for the small cream pitcher and added more to her coffee, stirring it slowly around and around.

"There's someone for you, Hallie."

She raised her eyes sadly to his. "But when am I ever going to meet him?"

Steve didn't have the answer to that any more than she did.

Twenty-Eight

The Movies

Hallie arrived home late that Friday afternoon, after a long tiring workweek. Meagan and Kenny raced toward her the moment she'd parked.

"Dad's taking us to the drive-in!" Kenny said excitedly.

This was a perfect night for it, Hallie mused. August and the weather was flawless, as it can be in only Puget Sound.

"Wanna come?" Meagan asked.

"I don't think so, sweetheart. Thanks, anyway." It'd been one of those frustrating weeks when little had gone right. It had started with one of her key staff members suddenly up and leaving because her husband had been transferred to the East Coast. And it ended this afternoon with a canceled order, followed by a visit from Donnalee. She'd arrived at Artistic License unannounced wearing a lovely diamond engagement ring. Hallie had hugged and congratulated her, thrilled for her friend. But she was also aware that Donnalee had managed to acquire *two* engagement rings this year, while she hadn't even scrounged up a piece of Cracker Jack jewelry. It wasn't the rings, of course, it was the thought that two men had fallen in love with Donnalee. *Two* men. And during the same period, Hallie had met a selection of losers, cheapskates and creeps.

No wonder she felt depressed.

"Please, please, please, come," said a voice from behind.

She swung around to find Steve gazing at her with an exaggerated expression of woe.

"I'm exhausted," she said. It was a legitimate excuse and true. She was looking forward to a half-hour soak in a bubble bath, and then a lengthy vegetation in front of the television watching reruns of "Mary Tyler Moore." It seemed that she, like Mary Richards, was destined to live the single life.

"I'm tired, too," Steve told her. "But I promised the kids last week that I'd take them, and they invited ten or fifteen of their closest friends along."

"Two," Meagan corrected, rolling her eyes. "We each invited one friend."

"I've got it all figured out," Steve said, squeezing Hallie's shoulders. "We can take both cars and park next to each other. The kids can stay in my car and I'll come over and join you in yours. Does that sound like a plan or what?"

He had obviously given some thought to this, and it was easy to see what would happen to his escape strategy if she refused. He'd be trapped in a vehicle filled with four shrieking kids.

Still, she *might* have refused him if not for one thing. Steve had agreed to accompany her to that ridiculous operatic extravaganza. Not willingly, maybe, but he *had* gone.

"Oh, all right," she mumbled.

"A little enthusiasm will go a long way, McCarthy,'' he said, echoing the remark she'd made herself earlier in the week.

She grumbled under her breath, but if the truth be known, she wasn't all that opposed. Yes, she felt exhausted, but being with Steve and his children had a way of reviving her. If she didn't go, she was likely to drown her sorrows in a bowl of double-fudge macadamia-nut ice cream—something to be avoided at all costs.

Besides, Steve had kissed her when he'd walked her to her door on Monday night. A quick, friendly kiss, very much like the others they'd exchanged. Warm and comforting. But for the first time Hallie had felt *more* than comfort and friendship. She'd felt that kiss all the way to her toes. A nice friendly good-night between neighbors shouldn't curl a woman's toes.

So she agreed to this drive-in idea of his for the elementary reason that she wanted him to kiss her again. Just to check things out.

''Dad's going to make popcorn,'' Kenny said breathlessly, as if that qualified his father for some major cooking award, ''and not use the microwave.'' There was real awe in the boy's voice. ''Dad explained that when he was a kid you used a *stove*.''

Hallie remembered making popcorn that way, too. She felt about a hundred years old. ''That should be interesting.''

''He said we could watch.''

''I don't suppose you'd care to help?'' This from Steve, who didn't even attempt to disguise his plea for assistance.

''Oh, all right.'' Although she made it sound like a sacrifice, Hallie found herself grinning. ''I'll change out of my work clothes and be right over.''

Meagan followed her into the house and helped her choose a pair of shorts and a summer top. "I'm glad you're coming," she said, hopping onto the end of Hallie's bed.

Hallie noticed that the girl looked unhappy, but didn't want to pry. From experience she knew that if something was troubling Meagan, she'd tell Hallie in her own way and her own time.

"I'm glad I'm coming, too."

"Dad let me invite Angie. She's my best friend. Everyone needs a best friend." She paused. "I think you're Dad's."

Hallie was touched. "Your dad's one of my best friends, too."

The girl was quiet for several moments while Hallie changed out of her business garb and donned what she thought of as real-people clothes. She removed her jewelry and makeup and tossed her panty hose and heels aside for canvas slip-ons.

"I don't think Mom and Kip are happy."

The softly spoken statement came out of the blue. Hallie paused, wondering how or if she should comment. "Sometimes when people first marry they have difficulty adjusting to each other. Give them time, Meagan."

"I don't think time's gonna help. Mom found out that Kip's been married before. Twice. She only knew about one ex-wife."

"Oh, dear." Hallie immediately sympathized with Steve's ex.

"He's paying child support to two children, and my mom only knew about the one."

If Kip had misled Mary Lynn in a matter of this

importance, Hallie had to wonder if he was trustworthy in other areas.

"Dad doesn't know," Meagan added.

"Don't worry, sweetheart, I won't tell him."

"I don't really like Kip. I don't know why Mom married him. He tells Kenny and me that we're going to do something fun and we get all excited. But when the time comes he has all these excuses why he can't do it."

"Some people are like that," Hallie said, and sat down next to Meagan. "I had a friend like that once. It got so I never put much faith in what she said. It wasn't that she was a bad person. She just couldn't possibly do all the things she planned or keep all the promises she made. I'm sure Kip's intentions are good, but not everything he promises will happen. Try not to be disappointed when it doesn't, and pleasantly surprised when it does."

"Are a lot of people like Kip?" Meagan asked.

"I don't know, but I don't think so."

"I hope not," the girl said, then she smiled. "You know what? I'm glad you're my friend, too."

"So am I, Meagan." The girl gave her a fierce hug.

As soon as Hallie and Meagan walked into Steve's kitchen, father and son mysteriously disappeared, leaving the women to the serious work of popping the corn in an old kettle. Hallie quickly assembled "goodie bags" for everyone. And she had a great time, laughing and teasing with Meagan.

Because Meagan and Kenny's friends lived in other neighborhoods, they left an hour early, stopping at a McDonald's for take-out burgers and drinks. Meagan and her friend rode with Hallie, while Steve led the way with the two boys. As planned, they parked at the drive-in theater side by side.

Hallie hadn't been to a drive-in since she was a child. She remembered her mother and father sitting close together in the front, she and Julie, wearing pajamas, in the back. It had been an occasional summer-night treat. She couldn't recall any movies they'd watched—just that wonderful childhood feeling of being loved and protected.

The first feature scheduled tonight was an action thriller with Bruce Willis. The kind that was sure to be an edge-of-the-seat fast-paced movie. The second feature was more or less the same kind of show, but without the big-name star.

Once the cars were situated and the radios fine-tuned, Steve left his vehicle and climbed into the front seat of Hallie's. It looked like a perfect plan—until Kenny and his friend started fighting with the girls.

Meagan rolled down her window and shouted, "Kenny ate all his popcorn and he's trying to steal mine."

"And mine," Angie chimed in furiously.

In an effort to keep the peace, Steve sent the boys off to the refreshment stand. "I can't believe I allowed the kids to talk me into this. I asked them how much it would cost me to buy my way out, but they wouldn't hear of it."

Steve, Hallie thought, had no idea how crucial it was to his kids that he follow through on his promises. It told them far more than he'd ever know. "I'm proud of you," she said without thinking.

"Proud?"

"You kept your word."

"I didn't have a choice," he said, protesting her

compliment. He leaned back in the passenger seat and closed his eyes. "It isn't just the drive-in movie, either," Steve grumbled. "Tomorrow is Kenny's Cub Scout camp-out. I can't believe I actually volunteered to spend the night in the woods with ten nine-year-old boys."

"Better you than me," Hallie told him.

The movie started just as Kenny and his friend made it back to the car. They climbed in and all was blissfully quiet as they gazed at the huge screen.

"What I'd really like to know," Steve said in a conversational tone, "is how I got talked into this slumber-party business. Meagan asked if Angie could come to the drive-in, then the next thing I know, Kenny's got a friend and they're both spending the night."

"Don't look at me," Hallie said, eating her popcorn. "I'm an innocent bystander."

He chuckled and helped himself to a handful from her bag. With the console between them, it was difficult to get too cozy—not that the Bruce Willis movie encouraged coziness in any form. Although Hallie had already seen it, she covered her face during a couple of the more gruesome scenes.

"You talked to Todd recently?" she asked as the credits scrolled down the screen.

"Yeah. He told me he asked Donnalee to marry him, but I have to say it didn't come as any surprise."

"Donnalee's hoping to get pregnant right away," Hallie said wistfully. At the rate things were progressing, Donnalee would be a grandmother before Hallie even found herself a husband.

"I figure it'll be a miracle if she isn't already pregnant. Todd's so tired he can barely stay awake. What's Donnalee do—keep him up all night?"

"My guess is they're keeping each other up."

"It's downright sickening, that's what it is," Steve muttered.

"Couldn't agree with you more." Hallie put down her popcorn, her appetite gone. "You know what? We're both so damn jealous we can barely stand it."

"Amen," Steve said. They glanced at each other and broke into peals of laughter. When they looked at the screen again, the second movie had started.

Hallie's seat was as far back as it would go. She was enjoying herself—and it had very little to do with the movies. Reviewing her conversation with his daughter, she felt good that Meagan had described her as Steve's best friend. It was refreshing, she told herself solemnly, when a man and woman could be friends.

She turned to Steve. "Thank you for being my friend," she whispered.

"Thank you for being mine." And then he leaned over and kissed her. His mouth grazed hers and lingered. Hallie kissed him back, increasing the pressure.

She felt the sexual energy of the kiss immediately and so, apparently, did Steve. He bolted upright and looked at her long and hard. She studied him, too. It was as if all the oxygen in the car was suddenly gone.

Neither seemed capable of breathing, let alone talking. The only illumination came from the screen and a solitary light by the refreshment stand, but it was enough for Hallie to see Steve's face. His eyes were wary, as if to say he wasn't sure about any of this. For that matter, Hallie wasn't sure how *she* felt, either.

At last he spoke. "Hallie?"

"Yes." She suspected she didn't sound like herself at all. Her voice seemed distant.

"What just happened?"

"You're asking me?" She tried to make a joke of it and found she couldn't. "We kissed and—"

"And, hell, it was good. Damn good." As if he needed to test this new discovery, he placed his hands on the curve of her shoulders and leaned forward to press his mouth to hers. Hallie closed her eyes, but her mind and her heart were wide open, eagerly anticipating a repeat performance.

At first he was gentle, almost tentative. Her lips parted, welcoming him. The nature of the kiss shifted almost immediately. His mouth grew fierce, demanding. He angled his lips over hers, urgently dragging her as close as the confines of the car would allow.

Her hip was being bruised by the console, but Hallie didn't care. She wanted—no, needed—his kiss. She forgot who she was, where she was. Nothing mattered but Steve. She could feel the beat of his heart throbbing beneath her palm.

She slid her hands from his chest and clenched his shirt collar in a feeble attempt to anchor herself against the oncoming sensual storm. His tongue deepened the level of intimacy.

She whimpered at the erotic play as he sought out every part of her mouth. Her own tongue responded to his, curling and coiling in a passionate game that left them both panting and breathless.

He moaned.

She whimpered.

Abruptly he broke it off and braced his forehead against hers. His breath hissed raggedly through his teeth.

Hallie's breath fled entirely.

When he kissed her again, it was slow and gentle, the way their first experimental kisses had been months earlier. Mmm. A series of nibbling kisses followed that. He tasted of buttered popcorn. He tasted incredible. Long, deep, slow kisses came next.

When he stopped, breathing hard, Hallie fell against the back of the seat, her eyes closed. "Tell me this isn't real."

"It's real."

"Tell me we're all wrong for each other."

"You know better."

She tried again. "Tell me this is just our reaction to what's happening between Donnalee and Todd."

"It isn't. This is real, Hallie. You and me—as real as it's likely to get."

"How can we have been so blind?" This was fantastic. Steve. Steve Marris! For months she'd been conducting this fruitless search to find a man, and Steve had been there all along. Right next door.

It was crazy. No, *she* was. She wanted to kick herself.

Throwing her arms around his neck, she whispered, "I might be a slow learner, but I'm ready to make up for lost time."

He laughed. Then he kissed her cheek, her nose, nuzzled her neck, explored the scented hollow of her neck with his tongue, moistening her skin as he slowly, methodically, worked his way back to her lips. By the time he caught her lower lip between his teeth, Hallie was whimpering anew. She'd waited and waited for the right man. What a fool she'd been not to realize all along that he lived next door.

"I can't believe this is happening," she said in a low voice.

"Believe it, Hallie, believe it." He eased his hand

under her top, cupping her breast. It filled his palm, overfilled it.

She bit her lip as he traced his finger around the outline of her erect nipple.

"Uh-oh," Steve murmured, his voice weighted with frustration. He slipped his hand downward, past the smooth skin of her abdomen. "I'm afraid we have an audience."

"What?"

He tipped his head toward the car with the kids. Hallie casually glanced in that direction and found four pairs of eyes staring at them out the side windows. Apparently she and Steve were putting on a much better show than the one on the screen. When Kenny saw that he had their attention, he waved. Hallie and Steve waved back. She could feel the heat rise in her cheeks.

Steve lowered the window, which had steamed up considerably, something for which Hallie was grateful. "Are you kids ready to go home?"

This question was followed by a long chorus of nos.

"Then you'd better watch the movie."

"Dad, were you kissing Hallie?" Kenny sounded genuinely distressed. "On the *lips?*" He cringed as if he couldn't imagine anything more revolting.

"She's not so bad," Steve said casually.

Hallie elbowed him in the ribs; he greatly exaggerated his reaction, and everyone, including Hallie, laughed. Once they were sure the kids had returned their attention to the movie, Steve raised the window.

He gripped her hand tightly in his, lacing their fingers. He stared straight ahead, but she knew he wasn't watching the screen. "Okay, tell me, where do we go from here?"

She knew exactly what he was asking. "Where?"

she repeated, giving herself time to think. "Are you asking me to go to bed with you, Steve?"

"Yes."

She swallowed. "We need a dose of what Donnalee and Todd have been experiencing, right?"

"No!" She was taken aback by the vehemence of his response. "This has nothing to do with Donnalee and Todd, and everything to do with you and me. I knew something was happening between us long ago—at least I suspected it—and it scared the living daylights out of me."

"I'm scared, too."

He looked at her, and as their eyes met, Hallie saw the hunger in his, realizing it was a reflection of her own. She wanted him. Needed him. Steve lowered his mouth to hers and kissed her with unconcealed desire.

"Does that tell you anything?" he asked.

"Yes." Her heart refused to slow down. She felt she was about to dissolve into hysterical tears—or laughter. She didn't know which. The pendulum could swing either way.

Steve stroked the side of her face, his eyes full of wonder. "I love you, Hallie."

Tears. The pendulum swung to tears. They instantly filled her eyes and spilled down her cheeks. "Oh, Steve, I love you, too," she sobbed, her shoulders shaking with emotion.

"Then why are you crying?"

"Because it took me so long to see the truth. Because I'm so happy. Because...I don't know. No wonder I found Arnold such a dud. I was in love with *you*."

He raised her hand to his lips and kissed her palm. "Like you said earlier, we're going to make up for lost time. Tonight, Hallie. I'm not waiting a moment longer."

"Tonight?"

"As soon as this movie's over, we'll drive home. I'll get everyone to bed and the minute they're asleep, I'll sneak over to your house."

"This is beginning to sound better and better."

"You have no idea how good it's going to be."

Hallie closed her eyes and sighed deeply. "Promises, promises."

"Even though Meagan and Kenny have friends over, it shouldn't take them long to crash." He sounded so eager, just as eager as she was. Her heart pounded with anticipation.

"Last January I bought myself a sexy silk night-gown," she whispered. "I never dreamed I'd be wearing it for you."

Steve groaned as she described the outfit. "Hallie, if you want me to make love to you right here and now, just go on. Otherwise, kindly be quiet."

"I don't think I *can* be quiet. I'm too excited."

He kissed her again and again, and she knew he would have continued if not for the carload of kids parked next to them.

The movie seemed to last forever. The instant the credits began Steve kissed her and leapt out of her car and into his own. He broke the speed limit all the way home. It was a minor miracle neither one of them got a ticket.

When they arrived, Steve ushered the kids into the house. "What's the hurry, Dad?" Meagan complained.

He didn't answer her. "Don't take time to clean out the car now," he ordered. "We'll do that in the morning."

"But you always say we shouldn't put something off we can do now," Kenny whined.

"I lied," Steve said, propelling his son forward by the shoulders. "To bed, everyone. It's late and we've got a big day tomorrow."

Once he'd herded the kids into the house, he raced outside where Hallie was waiting. "Give me twenty minutes, half an hour tops, all right?"

"Half an hour?" It sounded like an eternity.

"I'll sing them lullabies, read them stories. The second their eyes are closed, I'm out of there." He kissed her, then rushed back into the house.

If she had that much time, Hallie was determined to make use of every minute. She'd been waiting months for this; she'd planned it out, detail by exquisite detail.

First she filled the bathtub with hot water and poured in an exotic mixture of scented oils. Then she stripped out of her clothes and sank neck-deep into the water. Closing her eyes, she dreamed of Steve.

Steve. She loved him, really loved him. It astonished her that she hadn't recognized it earlier. All at once everything that had happened in the past few months added up, and the sum total made perfect sense. She loved Steve with an intensity that made her heart ache.

Drying herself with a thick soft towel, she pulled on the slinky silk nightgown, then checked her reflection in the mirror. She liked what she saw—and knew Steve would, too. Tonight she was a beautiful alluring woman. Tonight she would give Steve her body, as well as her heart.

Time to set the scene. First she bundled all the bed linens into her laundry hamper, remaking the bed with fresh sheets and her best quilt. Next she liberally squirted her favorite cologne around the bedroom, then spread her arms and walked gracefully through the aromatic droplets as they fell. Finally she scattered dried rose petals on the antique white quilt. She envisioned Steve carrying her into the bedroom and gently placing her on the bed before he made wild passionate love to her.

Glancing at the digital clock on her nightstand, she realized he'd arrive any minute. Once she'd settled herself on the bed, she decided to pose for him like a tigress on the prowl, the way she'd seen women pictured on calendars. She attempted a number of positions, but felt most comfortable with her hands and one leg outstretched, balancing her weight on one knee. She made a small growling noise deep in her throat.

She held that position for all of three minutes before her knee gave out. Thirty-five minutes had passed. She was ready. More than ready, but Steve had yet to arrive.

She paced.

She stewed.

She peeked.

One look at his place showed that the lights were still on. Hallie thought she saw Kenny race out of the kitchen, and she definitely heard Steve yell after him.

So he'd take a few extra minutes; that was all right by her. Their first time together would be perfect. Steve wanted it as much as she did. She yawned and decided to lie down on the sofa to wait for him. When she heard him opening the door, she'd leap up and race into the bedroom, assume the role of tigress and let him find her on the bed, hungry for her mate.

Sleepy, she leaned her head against the back of the sofa. It'd been such a long day. Soon her eyes were drifting shut. She struggled to keep them open, but to no avail.

She'd hear Steve, she told herself, and if she did fall asleep, he'd wake her.

He didn't.

Hallie woke at first light shivering, still on the sofa, with a decorator pillow bunched under her head.

Steve Marris had stood her up.

Twenty-Nine

Love Is Better Than Chocolate

August 17

If I wasn't so damn much in love with Steve Marris, I'd be furious. But I'm not. Oh, I was in the beginning. It isn't every day a woman's left waiting, wearing a silk nightgown—but I found the sweetest note taped to my front door this morning. Poor Steve. If I was frustrated and disappointed, he was—possibly—even more so. The kids outlasted him. What's really killing him is that he promised to go on Kenny's camp-out. The fact that he'd keep his word makes me love him even more.

I'm in love!! Really, truly in love. I can't believe it's with Steve Marris. I'm shocked that it took me this long to recognize what should have been obvious. It was practically staring me in the face!

I never expected love to feel like this. I get teary-eyed just thinking about Steve, and at the same time I want to throw out my arms and sing, sort of like Julie Andrews in the opening scene from "The Sound of Music."

How easy it is to envision myself spending the rest of my life with him! He's fun and witty and irreverent—and <u>exactly</u> the kind of man I've always dreamed I'd marry. (How come I didn't see it sooner??) Heaven knows, I've dated my share of potential husbands (read: mostly losers) this year. I've run the gauntlet, paid my dues and—finally—found the man of my dreams.

I've decided that since Steve won't be back from the camping trip until Sunday afternoon, I'll cook a veritable feast for him. I'll serve it wearing my enhancer bra and a low-cut blouse—let matters develop from there. I know exactly where they'll lead, too. Ah, well, I still have enough scented rose petals to leave a trail into the bedroom, although if his note was anything to go by, he isn't going to need any help finding the way.

I hope he enjoys spending time with Kenny and the other boys out in the woods, but I pray he isn't too tired to enjoy what's waiting for him right here at home.

Steve lifted his son's sleeping bag out of the trunk of his car, which stood at the curb outside Mary Lynn's. His back hurt, he'd gotten a grand total of maybe three hours' sleep the entire night and he was half-starved. Not only that, he was so damn eager to get back to Hallie he almost hopped back in the car and drove off without saying goodbye to Kenny.

Glancing at the house, he saw Meagan waving through her upstairs bedroom window, telephone receiver attached to her ear. She'd spent the weekend with Mary Lynn—and had probably been on the phone most of that time. He waved back, then turned to his son.

Kenny hugged him close, his skinny arms squeezing Steve about the neck. "Thanks, Dad. I had a great time."

"I did, too, partner." Not so great he'd leap up and volunteer the next time, but good enough to help him forget how miserable he'd been.

"Hello, Steve." Mary Lynn stood on the front porch, looking oddly lost. Her arms were folded protectively around her middle and her mouth was drawn down. He recognized the look. It was the one that usually said she was out of money and needed a small loan to see her through until the first of the month. Well, she had another husband now and she could go to Kip for money. He strengthened his resolve, refusing to allow her to manipulate him.

"Hello, Mary Lynn." He stood next to his car and slid his hands into the hip pockets of his jeans.

Kenny raced toward his mother. "We had a great time! We stayed up real late telling ghost stories and then we all crowded into one tent. In the middle of the night Jimmy McPherson had to pee, but he was too afraid of ghosts to go outside and so he peed in the tent on Johnny Adams's sleeping bag."

Mary Lynn glanced at Steve to verify the story. "It's true," he said. "It'll probably take poor Jimmy McPherson thirty years to live it down. Johnny Adams wasn't too pleased about it, either." Although Steve was anxious to leave, he'd treasured this time with his son—especially now that he had only weekends to build memories with his children.

"I'm glad you two enjoyed yourselves." Even from this distance, Steve could see that Mary Lynn's smile was forced.

"Well, I'm off," he said, as Kenny carried his camping gear into the house.

"Can't you come in for a few minutes?" Mary Lynn asked. "You look like you could use a cup of coffee."

He toyed with the idea of accepting but didn't want to take the time. Instead, he tightened his jaw and reached in his back pocket for his checkbook. "How much?" He'd rather pay her and be done with it than be forced to listen to a long litany of reasons she had to have the child-support check early.

She cast him a hurt look as if he'd deeply insulted her. "I'm not asking for money."

"Fine." He started back toward the car. He needed a shower, shave and Hallie, in that order. Damn, but he was crazy about her. His stomach growled and he amended his list. Shower, shave, food and *then* Hallie.

"You always do this to me," Mary Lynn accused, stopping him dead in his tracks. The woman knew which buttons to push and didn't hesitate to push them, either.

"Do what?" he asked out of sheer habit.

"That. I have something I need to talk to you about. Something I consider important, but you brush me off without a thought and go running to some stupid ball game or bowling or something else that takes you away from your family."

"All right, Mary Lynn," he said, his patience on a short string. "What do you want this time?"

"I hate it when you use that tone of voice with me."

He closed his eyes in an effort to compose himself. "If there's a problem, perhaps we should schedule a time to discuss it." Not now, in other words. Definitely not now.

"Do you have to stand all the way over there? It's ridiculous for us to shout at each other with half the neighborhood listening in."

Steve knew that the minute he stepped into the house he'd be trapped for hours. Mary Lynn always did that to him—and at one time he'd actually welcomed it— but he wasn't up to her games and schemes this afternoon.

He walked across the lawn and noticed that it was long overdue to be mowed. If Kip was going to be living in "his" house, then Lard Butt had damn well better keep up the yard.

He paused at the bottom step. "Better?" he asked.

"Not really."

"Listen, Mary Lynn, I don't have a lot of time. Just say what it is you want."

"You're using that tone with me again."

He felt like he was talking to his aunt Hester. "Is this important or isn't it?" he demanded.

"I already said it was, but it's clear that you're not willing to help either me or your children. I never thought I'd say this about you, Steve Marris, but you've got a cold unfeeling heart." With those words she burst into tears and stormed into the house.

Any other time, Steve would have raced after her. Not now. Mary Lynn had a husband to deal with her moods. He wasn't responsible anymore. His obligation was to his children and to them alone.

Keeping that in mind, he returned to the car and drove off. But despite his intentions, despite his decision about her place in his life, he couldn't stop thinking about Mary Lynn. Must be habit, he thought, or residual guilt. He shook his head, determined to put it behind him. He had another life now, one that excluded Mary Lynn. One that included Hallie.

What he'd told Hallie about loving her was true. Even truer than he'd realized when he said it. He felt like he was seventeen all over again. He wondered at what precise moment he'd fallen for her. Or had their love developed. more gradually, based as it was on friendship? It didn't matter, he decided. It had happened and he was head over heels crazy about her.

For the first time since Mary Lynn had asked him to move out, he felt alive and happy. The kind of happy that went clear through him and didn't get bogged down in regrets and what-ifs. The kind of happy that caused a man to smile from his heart outward. A happiness that wouldn't easily be taken away.

His mind raced as he neared home. He parked the car and headed directly for Hallie's, pounding on her front door. He smelled of camp-fire smoke, sweat, Jimmy McPherson's pee and God knew what else, but he didn't care. He needed to kiss her. Tell her he was home. Hold her, if only for a moment.

At last she swung open the door.

"Am I forgiven?" he asked, barely giving her time to let the fact that he was standing there register.

The screen door was still between them. "That depends."

"On what?"

"On how long it takes you to kiss me, you fool."

He almost tore the screen door off its hinges in his haste. Hallie gave a soft cry of welcome and threw herself into his embrace. He locked both arms around her waist and hauled her against him, savoring her warmth, breathing in her feminine scent.

He'd dreamed of this moment, anticipated it every second he'd been tramping through the woods with ten Cub Scouts. Generally he liked the outdoors, but this time his mind and heart had been with Hallie.

Their kiss was long and slow, filled with the wonder of their newly discovered love. He wanted her to know the depth of his frustration, his profound need for her. His blood quickly fired to life, and it demanded every ounce of restraint he possessed not to make love to her right then and there.

He buried his face in the curve of her shoulder, thinking her love was the closest thing to heaven he was likely to find. Already it was healing him; already he'd felt its effects. Her love was a gift he wouldn't abuse or accept lightly.

"I cooked you dinner. Roast chicken." She said this as if it had some significance.

"I'm hungry enough to eat it, too," he said, and kissed the tip of her nose.

"Hey, I'll have you know I've taken cooking classes."

"Then feed me, woman."

They kissed again with an intensity that all but consumed them. When they drew apart, Steve noticed that his beard had chafed her face. "I'll be right back," he promised, setting her on her feet.

"That's what you said the last time."

"Not to worry. Nothing's going to keep me away again."

"I'm glad to hear it." She smiled, a smile he could get lost in. Maybe it wasn't such a good idea to come here first, because leaving her even for ten or fifteen minutes was proving damned difficult.

He was halfway between their houses when she

called out, "In case you've forgotten, you told me you'd marry a woman who could cook you a decent roast chicken dinner."

He froze. "Marry you?"

She planted her hands on her hips and narrowed her eyes. "You're going to marry me, Steve Marris, if I have to hog-tie you and drag you down the aisle myself."

He forced a short laugh and hurried into the house, his heart in his throat. Hallie wanted a husband; he'd always known it. And now she wanted *him* for a husband. Marriage. He shouldn't be shocked, but he was.

Marriage was serious stuff. *Real* serious. He'd been through it once, fathered two children. The next thing he knew, Hallie would be talking about having kids of her own. The financial responsibility for Meagan and Kenny already weighed heavily on him, and the thought of taking on that kind of obligation for more children—well, it scared him.

He walked into the bathroom, stripped off his clothes and stepped into the shower. The minute the warm spray hit his skin he felt worlds better. They had a lot to discuss, he and Hallie. He loved her, that much he knew, but their entire relationship didn't need to be defined within the next thirty minutes. Not every decision had to be made right now.

Out of the shower, he stood in front of the bathroom mirror with a towel around his waist and shaved a two-day growth of beard from his face. He cut himself once thinking about Hallie, which made him smile. What he should've been doing was paying attention to the blade.

Now that he thought about it, he *had* mentioned roast chicken to Hallie. He remembered their conversation— how his grandmother used to roast a chicken for the family every Sunday, after church. They'd been memorable, those chicken dinners. In all the years he'd been married to Mary Lynn she'd never attempted it. He loved Hallie's willingness to please him.

He slapped some cologne on his face, dressed, grabbed a bottle of white wine from the fridge and hurried back to her house. He entered without knocking.

Hallie stood by the table, smiling when he walked inside. She glowed with happiness, and he felt it as keenly as he did the warmth of the sun.

"Welcome back," she said, sounding almost shy. Damn, but she looked good. She wore a scoop-necked full-length summer dress and sandals. Her dark curly hair was pinned back from her face with two daisy pins.

It was plain to see she'd gone to a lot of trouble with this dinner. A floral centerpiece sat in the middle of the table; there were crystal wineglasses and linen napkins. It was a nice feeling, knowing she'd done all this for him.

Steve frowned, however, when he looked into the kitchen. The chaos was daunting. Judging by the stack of pots and pans, she'd used every cooking dish she owned.

"There's dessert, too," she promised in a low sexy voice that made his blood percolate in his veins.

"I have a feeling it isn't apple pie."

"Time will tell, won't it?" she teased.

As he opened the wine, he noticed a trail of rose petals leading out of the dining room and down the hallway. "What's that?" he asked, pointing.

"Dessert," she answered, smiling coyly.

He followed the fragrant dried flowers as far as her

bedroom. Pausing in the doorway, he saw that the top of her bed was covered with a whole slew of petals. Smack-dab in the middle was the sexiest cream-colored silk nightgown he'd ever laid eyes on.

"Do you actually think you're going to have time to put that on?"

"No, but I wanted you to at least see it."

He brought her into his arms and debated making love to her right then. But considering the effort involved in preparing this dinner, he didn't want anything to spoil it. "You aren't going to need that gown or anything else, Hallie," he whispered before he kissed her. "I want you so damn much now that I'm about to bust out of these jeans."

"You might not be one of the most romantic men I've ever met, but you sure know how to get a girl's heart pounding."

He left the bedroom reluctantly, glancing over his shoulder more than once as he walked down the hallway. Hoping to speed matters along, he tried to help her get dinner on the table, but she wouldn't let him. She took a green salad out of the refrigerator, tossing it with oil and vinegar, then removed the chicken and baked potatoes from the oven. The scent of rosemary and sage bread dressing drifted through the house.

He replaced the handful of cookies he'd stolen from the cookie jar.

"Weren't you the one who told me the old saying's true—that the way to a man's heart is through his stomach?" she asked.

"You already have my heart, Hallie." Surely she knew that.

She held out her hand, inviting him to her table. "Come and sit down."

As if in a trance, he walked over to where she stood. He poured the wine and remembered to pull out her chair before he seated himself. Hallie served him, complimented him on his choice of wine and then spread the napkin across her lap.

She waited for him to take the first bite, watching him carefully. It seemed to Steve that she was holding her breath. He saw her teeth worry her lower lip. As far as he was concerned, the food could taste like monkey vomit and he wouldn't care.

It didn't. The chicken was every bit as good as those his grandmother used to make. For effect, he closed his eyes and kissed his fingertips. "Perfect," he said. "The best I've ever tasted."

"You're sure? It isn't too crisp?"

"No. Taste for yourself."

She did, sampling a tiny cautious bite. Her eyes met his. "It *is* good," she said, sounding bewildered. "It's really good."

Steve took another bite and then another.

"You'll notice this tastes nothing like the chicken from those fast-food places," she said. "I did everything myself, including the stuffing. I had to phone my mother three times for help, but I managed."

"I'm proud of you." And he was.

He ate two huge servings, then helped her clear the table. Try as he might, he couldn't keep his hands off her while she attempted to pour them each a cup of coffee. She stood with her back to him, facing the kitchen counter.

He moved directly behind her, his hands cupping her breasts while he nuzzled her neck. She smelled faintly of roses and a variety of herbs and spices. The mixture wasn't one he'd find at a perfume counter, but it had an immediate effect on him. He rubbed against her, leaving her in no doubt about his state of arousal.

"Steve!"

"I can't help myself. I'm crazy about you."

"Crazy to go to bed with me, you mean."

He couldn't see any need to deny it. "Guilty. Are you sure we need this coffee?"

She hesitated. "It's a special blend..." She hesitated, then turned around to face him. "No, I don't need this coffee. All I need is you."

A frenzy of deep kisses followed, mingled with moans, whimpers and a sense of breathless wonder. Steve was about to lift her into his arms and carry her into the bedroom when the phone rang.

They stopped and stared at each other.

"Don't answer it," he said.

"It's my mother," Hallie whispered, pressing her forehead against his shoulder. "She wants to know how the chicken turned out. If I don't answer it now, she'll phone back later. Like in ten minutes."

Steve wasn't sure how he knew that phone call meant trouble, but he did. The instant she reached for the telephone, he had to bite back the urge to beg her—again—to let it ring.

"Hello." Hallie's eyes zeroed in on his. "It's Meagan," she said, handing him the phone. "She needs to talk to you right away."

Steve took the receiver. "Meagan, is something wrong?"

"I'm sorry to bother you, Dad, but there wasn't any answer at your place, and I thought Hallie might know where you were."

"It's all right, honey, just tell me what's wrong." He turned away so he wouldn't have to face Hallie.

"It's Mom."

Steve heard the worry and fear in his daughter's voice. "What's the matter with her?"

"I don't know, she won't tell me, but she can't seem to stop crying. I don't know what to do anymore—she said she won't talk to anyone but you."

Steve swallowed a groan.

"Dad, what should I do?"

"Nothing, honey. I'll be right over."

Thirty

Mr. Nice Guy

"What do you mean you're leaving?" Hallie couldn't believe her ears. For the second time in as many days, Steve was walking out on her. Her chest tightened with a growing sense of frustration and anger.

"Hallie, it isn't like I *want* to go." It helped to hear the regret in his voice. But not enough.

"Why? What is it this time?" Although she'd heard his half of the conversation, it hadn't told her much. Hallie guessed this supposed crisis had something to do with his ex-wife. Steve had made his feelings for her no secret, and it seemed he'd be forever at the woman's beck and call.

"There's trouble at Mary Lynn's," he explained.

"With one of the kids?"

He hesitated, and in that instant she knew. Whatever the problem, it did indeed involve Mary Lynn. Her knees felt as if they were about to buckle, and she lowered herself onto a kitchen chair. "It's Mary Lynn, isn't it?"

He paused and with reluctance answered, "Yes."

At least she should be grateful he hadn't lied. "I see."

"Hallie, trust me, walking out on you now is the last thing I want."

"Then don't go." Her voice was high-pitched and mildly hysterical.

"I have to. Meagan sounded near panic. It isn't like this is a common occurrence. In fact, it's never happened before." He knelt in front of her and gripped her hands tightly in his. "I'll be back, I promise, and then we can talk. Just remember it's you I love."

Hallie desperately wanted to believe him, but she'd been a fool before and was determined not to repeat the same mistakes. "I don't want to argue about this. If…you feel it's necessary to go, then you should."

His relief was evident.

Steve started to get up, started to walk away, but before he left she had to ask him one last thing. Hastily she got to her feet. "Steve."

He turned to look at her.

It wasn't the time to ask him this. Wasn't even fair, but right now, that didn't matter to her. She'd seen his expression when she'd brought up the subject earlier. Viewed the stricken look in his eyes and laughed it off. She wasn't laughing now. She had to know where they stood before he went to Mary Lynn. "Are you going to ask me to marry you?" she said.

He couldn't disguise the dread in his eyes. "Do we have to discuss this now?"

How odd that she'd smile just then. Perhaps it was because she'd guessed his response long before he spoke. His eagerness to delay the discussion was an answer in itself. "No," she said, putting on a brave ront, "we can talk about that later—that and everyhing else."

"I'll be back before you know I'm gone."

That wasn't possible. She felt his absence immediately, felt it like a knife in her gut. Caught on a gust of wind, the door closed hard. Hallie sat down again after he'd left and shut her eyes. Breathing in deeply, she was surprised to discover she was trembling.

Steve was furious by the time he arrived at Mary Lynn's. He had to hand it to his ex-wife; her timing was incredible. The very last thing he'd wanted to do was walk out on Hallie just then. She'd gone to so much trouble, cooking dinner, preparing a homecoming for him. She'd been trying to prove how much she loved him, and his response had been to walk out on her.

He slammed the car door and marched up the front walk, taking the steps two at a time. He almost walked in without ringing the doorbell—something he was prone to forget since he'd once lived in this house.

As soon as Meagan opened the door, she hugged him tight, obviously relieved to have him there. "I'm so glad you came, Daddy... I didn't know what to do."

"It's all right, sweetheart. It wasn't any problem." So, he lied. He had the feeling Hallie wasn't going to forget and forgive as easily this time, and he didn't blame her. He'd deal with whatever was bothering Mary Lynn and be on his way, hoping he could make amends to Hallie. "Where's your mother?" he asked Meagan.

"In the bedroom." She pointed toward it as if he needed directions. He didn't.

"Where's Kip?"

"I don't know. I haven't seen him since this morning. I...I don't think they're getting along."

"What about Kenny?"

"Asleep. He went to bed soon after you dropped him off."

Bed was exactly where Steve longed to be, and he didn't plan on cuddling up with a stuffed animal, either. He ran his hand through his hair and exhaled sharply. He was tired, impatient and in no condition to deal with one of Mary Lynn's moods.

He walked through the kitchen on the way to the master bedroom. Meagan had apparently made a peanut-butter-and-jelly sandwich for dinner; the peanut butter was still out and so was the jelly, along with an open loaf of bread.

"I didn't do that," she said, her gaze following his. "Kenny did."

"Have you had dinner?"

"Not yet," she said with a shrug. "I'm too worried about Mom."

"Hey, sweetie, I'm sure everything will work out. You eat something now and I'll go talk to your mom." He left Meagan rummaging in the refrigerator and hurried to the bedroom. He knocked once, then entered.

Mary Lynn was lying facedown on the bed, sobbing steadily. She raised her head to see who it was. When she saw him, she cried out, flung herself from the bed and ran into his arms.

"I'm so glad you came," she wailed. "Oh, Steve, I don't know what to do." In all the years he'd been married to Mary Lynn he'd never seen her this distraught. Meagan was right to be concerned.

He wrapped his arms around her and they both sat on the edge of the bed. "What's wrong?"

Her crying subsided to soft sniffles. "I...I'm such a fool. Oh, Steve, how could I have been so incredibly stupid?"

"You're not stupid," he assured her, gently rubbing her back. "Now tell me what's upsetting you so much."

"It's Kip—he lied to me."

Steve forced himself to relax. He was concerned about his children, and the effect Kip's lie, whatever it was, might have on them.

"I learned he's been married twice before—he didn't tell me about his second wife. I found out by accident. I...I opened some mail. From his ex—his *second* ex. He has a little girl by that marriage. She's barely two years old."

Steve continued patting her back. Okay, Kip had been married one time more than Mary Lynn realized, but she made it sound like the end of the world. "I'm sure this is a shock, but—"

"That's not all," she cut him off. "There's something else..."

Steve's shirt was damp with her tears. She lifted her eyes to his and bit her lower lip, as if to gauge how much she should say. "You can tell me anything, Mary Lynn, you know that."

"I...I'm afraid I might be in trouble with the law."

"The *law?*"

"I married a man...who's already married."

It took a moment for the meaning of her words to sink in. "You mean to say Kip never divorced his second wife?"

"No, he didn't. I talked to her myself, and she told me. I didn't want to believe her, and when I asked Kip he was so convincing. He said she was a shrew and a bitch who'd say or do anything she could to ruin our happiness."

"Maybe she *is* lying."

Mary Lynn shook her head violently. "I asked Kip if I could see his divorce decree and he couldn't find it, and then...then I had a friend—you remember Kelly, don't you?—check at the courthouse for me. There's nothing there. Nothing." Her shoulders shook with the force of her tears.

"Did you ask Kip about that?"

"Yes. He...he was furious I'd gone behind his back and had Kelly check the court records. He tried to tell me he'd gotten a divorce in Vegas. I said if that was true, he should be able to produce the documents and...he couldn't."

"Oh, Mary Lynn, I'm sorry."

"We had a terrible argument and he walked out. I don't think he'll be back—I'm not even sure I want him back. Oh, Steve, how am I ever going to face my friends? What will I tell my family? I feel like such a fool."

"When did you find all this out?"

"I talked to Kelly Friday afternoon, but Kip was away at a sales conference and I hadn't had a chance to hear his side of it. It's been eating away at me all weekend...you can't *know* how dreadful this week has been. He...he hadn't mentioned the second marriage, but I assumed he was divorced until Linda told me otherwise. Then Kip arrived and we had this terrible fight—and then he...he drove off in a huff."

"He'll be back," Steve said, looking toward the closet—formerly his closet—filled with Kip's clothes.

His ex-wife gazed up at him with wide appealing eyes. "You'd never have done anything like this to me. You were always a good husband."

If that was the case, he wondered why she'd been so quick to divorce him. He continued to hold her because that was what she seemed to need. Really, there was nothing else he could do. Nothing he could say.

Kneeling on the bed, Mary Lynn placed her arms around his neck and pressed her head to his shoulder. "Hold me, Steve, please, for just a little longer."

His ex-wife had never been a clinging violet. "Everything will work out," he reassured her, repeating the words he'd said to Meagan. "Kip will be back and you two can sort all this out. You loved him enough to marry him, didn't you?"

"I...I've been so foolish."

He wanted to agree with her, but resisted the impulse.

Mary Lynn lay back down, and the pressure of her arms still circling his neck pulled him down with her. "Make love to me, Steve. I need you."

He groaned. Not with desire, but with anger and frustration. She could have had him anytime, anyplace, a few months earlier. Instead, she'd left him high and dry and turned her loving attention to Kip. Now she was back. He'd gone through several of the longest and most sexually frustrating months of his life, and in the space of a single day he had two women wanting him. If it wasn't so ironic, he might have laughed.

"I don't think that's such a good idea," he said gently, trying not to distress her any more than she already was.

Mary Lynn raised her head from the pillow and kissed him, using every bit of knowledge, every advantage, that their years of marriage had taught her.

Steve broke off the kiss.

"No, Mary Lynn," he said sternly. "It isn't going to work for us any longer. You're feeling low and miserable. You don't really want me."

"I do, Steve. I want you so much." She squirmed and bucked beneath him, grinding her pelvis against his. "Don't reject me now. Please. Not when I feel like the whole world's caved in on me."

It wasn't him she wanted, Steve recognized, but the security his love had always offered her.

"Come on, Mary Lynn, you're involved with someone else." He nearly made the mistake of saying she was *married* to someone else when in all likelihood, she wasn't.

Steve struggled to a sitting position. She sobbed louder and clung to him, refusing to release him. "Lie down with me. Please. Is that so much to ask? I can't even remember the last time I slept."

He let her direct him downward, back onto the bed. She snuggled close, still sniffling. Steve kept his arm around her, thinking she'd soon drift off to sleep. The minute she did, he'd slip away.

"I don't know why I ever fell for Kip," she said, apparently needing to talk.

"He seems all right," Steve muttered.

"He's deceitful and stubborn," Mary Lynn countered.

Steve didn't feel obliged to list Kip's good points; besides, he didn't know the man. But as long as Kip was a decent stepfather, Steve didn't really care.

"I don't think he'll be back," Mary Lynn said bleakly.

Now Steve understood: *This* was what truly bothered her. "He'll need to pack his clothes, won't he?" he asked. "You can talk to him then."

She raised herself up on one elbow and reached for a tissue to blow her nose. "I don't know. He might have someone else come for his things. I told him I never wanted to see him again, and I don't think he'll want to see me, either. I really don't.''

"Let's not borrow trouble."

"How could Kip *do* this to me?" she asked, sounding more and more like a frightened little girl.

"Shh." Steve cradled her head against his shoulder. "Go to sleep." The sooner she did, the sooner he'd be free to leave. It wasn't Mary Lynn he wanted to hold, but Hallie. Although his ex-wife was in his arms, the woman he loved was in his thoughts. Her rose-petal-littered bed, the promise of her smile. The joy he felt just thinking about Hallie made him impatient to return to her.

"I'm so tired."

So was he, Steve realized with a yawn. After spending a whole night in one huge tent with ten Cub Scouts, he was exhausted. The nine-year-olds had been up and down until well after two. Steve was convinced he didn't get more than a couple of hours' sleep, if that. His son had already crashed.

Mary Lynn sobbed quietly.

"Everything will work out," he whispered again. "Everything does sooner or later." He wouldn't have believed it a few months ago, but he did now. Mary Lynn's decision to file for divorce had drastically changed the course of his life. For a time, a long time, he felt it had all been a terrible mistake. His pride, his ego, his sense of who and what he was had suffered one hell of a beating. It'd taken damn near a year to fight his way back, to rise above the shock and the rejection.

A year, and things hadn't seemed to get any better. And then he'd learned Mary Lynn was dating Kip. That had hurt, and it'd hurt even more when she remarried.

But her marriage, above anything else, had helped him face the truth. It was over for them.

He loved her, yes; a part of him always would. His being with her now was evidence of the depth of his feeling for her. She was the mother of his children, his first love—but their marriage was over. Dead and buried.

Accepting that had probably taken much longer than it should have, but he'd felt like he was fighting for his family, for the dream of what it could have been. He didn't blame Mary Lynn for the failure of their marriage, nor did he accept full responsibility himself. Despite his best efforts to keep his family intact, the divorce had happened and he couldn't turn back the clock.

Steve loved Hallie now. He wasn't sure about leaping into another marriage, but he knew her well enough to realize she wouldn't take anything less. The two of them could discuss that later.

Mary Lynn released a long wobbly sigh. Her shoulders trembled and her grip about him tightened, as though she feared he was about to leave her.

He would eventually, but only after she fell asleep. He battled back his own fatigue and decided to rest his eyes. But only for a minute. One minute.

The next thing he knew, Kenny was standing over him. "Dad?"

Steve's eyes flew open.

"What are you doing here?" Kenny whispered. "Where's Kip?"

Steve glanced to the other side of the bed to discover Mary Lynn curled up with a loose blanket tucked around her shoulders.

"I can't find my shoes," Kenny said, again in a whisper. "Are you and Mom getting back together?"

"Your shoes?" Steve sat up and tried to focus on his wristwatch. "What time is it?"

"Six."

"In the morning?"

Kenny nodded, and Steve cursed under his breath and bolted off the bed. He was going to have one hell of a time explaining this to Hallie.

Thirty-One

Goodbye, My Heart

Hallie didn't think she'd ever spent such a miserable night. Every hour or so she leapt out of bed, convinced she'd heard Steve's car. Not until after three did she finally acknowledge that he wasn't coming. That he'd spent the night with Mary Lynn.

His ex-wife had claimed she needed him and he'd rushed to her side, deserting Hallie. It didn't take a rocket scientist to realize this wasn't going to change. If she and Steve were to become involved, she'd better accept his feelings for the other woman now. But it stuck like a fish bone in her throat. Hallie doubted she could ever swallow Mary Lynn's presence in her life.

After three o'clock she didn't get out of bed whenever she thought she heard a car, but she didn't sleep, either. She tried. Heaven knew, she tried, and as the clock ticked on and the minutes rolled by, she fumed. The remaining hours of the night were spent tossing and turning. And trembling. She trembled like someone who'd almost made one of the biggest mistakes of her life.

At five she gave up the effort, threw aside the sheets and got up. She showered, changed into her work clothes and brewed herself a pot of coffee. She was going to need it.

Sitting at her kitchen table, she wrote in her journal, spilling out her grief and anger, when a loud knock sounded at her front door. She didn't need anyone to tell her it was Steve.

It amazed her how calm she was. Whatever emotion was left in her had burned itself out during the endless night.

Steve's eyes widened with what appeared to be surprise when he saw her. "You're up. I wasn't sure if I'd get you out of bed or not."

It was all too apparent that he'd recently come from one, Hallie noted.

"Hallie, I'm so sorry." He held out his hand in a gesture of hope, a request for understanding. "You have every reason to be furious, but if you'll let me explain—"

"I'm not angry," she said, interrupting him.

"You're not?" He paused and sniffed the air. "Is that coffee? Damn, I could use a cup."

"Help yourself." She motioned toward the kitchen.

He walked past her and took down a mug from her cupboard. After he'd finished pouring, he turned and leaned back against the counter. His eyes held hers. "I can imagine what you're thinking."

"I doubt that." She folded her arms and stood on the other side of the room, distancing herself from him physically and emotionally.

"Mary Lynn found out some distressing news about Kip," Steve went on. "I've never seen her this distraught."

"And so you spent the night with her." Hallie could see no need for them to tiptoe around the obvious.

"You slept with her." He'd practically admitted as much.

"No!" He said it with such vehemence that for one tiny instant she almost believed him.

"Yes, I slept with her," he corrected, "but I didn't *sleep* with her." He stopped abruptly and shook his head in unmistakable anger. "All right, we were in the same bed, but—"

"Please, spare me the details." Her stomach was already in knots, and she wasn't up to listening to a lengthy explanation, however plausible it might sound. He'd spent the night with his ex-wife. The reasons didn't matter. He'd been with Mary Lynn and not her, and damn it all, that hurt.

"It isn't as bad as it looks," Steve said, his gaze holding hers and refusing to let go.

"Perhaps not," she said, forcing a smile. She wasn't sure how well she'd succeeded. "But as far as I'm concerned, we were given a reprieve from making a major mistake."

"Mistake?" His echo was a demand for an explanation.

She sipped her coffee and prayed she could pull this off. "Yeah. You've heard what they say about friends and lovers—how sex ruins friendship. It wouldn't work with us, Steve. You know me too well, and—"

"Why wouldn't it work?" His eyes narrowed. She saw that his hands tightened around the coffee mug until his knuckles paled with the strength of his grip.

"You love Mary Lynn. You've never tried to hide that from me—"

"I love *you*."

It didn't slip her notice that he made no attempt to deny his feelings for his ex-wife. "I know," she said with an air of frivolity. "I love you, too. That's the way it is between friends. Good friends."

"We're more than friends," he declared.

Maintaining her forced smile had become impossible. "Perhaps at one point we might have been, but not now."

Steve slammed the mug down on the counter, and coffee sloshed over the rim, spilling onto the floor. "Are you telling me you don't want me?" His eyes dared her to contradict him.

Hallie had never been a good liar. "Don't misunderstand me, Steve. I'm grateful to Mary Lynn. She saved us from progressing into an area that would have been a disaster for us both."

"The hell she did."

"I can see the writing on the wall. You love her—"

"I was married to her for a long time. I can't turn feelings off like a faucet. She was frantic and frightened. All I did was hold her! If you want to crucify me for that, then be done with it."

"I know how you feel about Mary Lynn." Hallie countered his anger with a calm serenity. "She was your first love, your high-school sweetheart, your former wife. It's only natural that she'd continue to have a special place in your heart."

His eyes pierced hers. "I love you."

A lump formed in her throat. How convincing he sounded, how sincere and forthright. "But it's clear now that Mary Lynn comes first in your thoughts...and in your heart."

"If you'd give me a chance—"

She spoke quickly, not allowing him to finish. "She'll *always* be first with you, Steve—no matter what's happening between us."

"What was I supposed to do?" he shouted. "Meagan phoned, not knowing what to do. She's just a kid. She didn't know how to help her mother. Mary Lynn was hysterical."

Hallie's point exactly. "And so you hurried to her side." It was hard not to suspect Mary Lynn of manipulating him—and hard not to resent Steve for buying it. She bit the corner of her lip at the deep rush of anger. She loved Steve and Meagan and Kenny, and hated the emotion that surfaced whenever Mary Lynn's name was mentioned. Hallie had never seen herself as jealous and petty, but that was how she felt, how she acted.

It made her uncomfortable with herself. Hallie couldn't deal with the negative feelings his first marriage brought out in her. "It won't work, Steve," she insisted. "I'm just as sorry as you are, but it isn't meant to be."

"Why the hell not?"

"I want a husband, not—"

He interrupted her. "So that's what this is all about."

She ignored his comment and finished, "—an ex-husband."

That stopped him. His head reared back as if to assimilate what she'd said. "An ex-husband? What do you mean?"

"I only plan to marry once in my life—"

"You know that saying about the best-laid plans. I didn't even want that stupid divorce. It was Mary Lynn who was unhappy, Mary Lynn who claimed she'd missed out on life because she'd never lived on her own, never attended college, never made love with other men." His words became more heated, more angry. When he stopped, the silence seemed louder than his outburst.

Hallie waited before she spoke again, letting the silence surround them both. "I saw the look in your eyes when I mentioned marriage, Steve. You've been badly burned. I understand that, and I know why the thought of marrying again isn't exactly appealing."

He stood tight-lipped and Hallie was grateful he didn't deny his feelings.

"I guess what I'm trying to say, obviously not very well, is that I want a man who'll make a wholehearted commitment to me. A man—"

"Who'll come to you without a load of emotional garbage from his divorce and two emotionally needy kids."

She hesitated, and then because this seemed the easiest way to put an end to it, she nodded.

"Fine." He opened and closed his fist. "Be warned, this Mr. Perfect you're looking for may not exist. Let me know when you're ready for a real man and not some ideal." Without a further glance, he marched past her and out the front door.

Hallie tried to pretend it didn't matter. That they could still be friends, still rely on each other. Her hope was that if they couldn't be lovers, at least they could salvage the friendship. She had to admit that, to their credit, they both tried. And yet...they didn't succeed.

She'd met Steve on her way to work the morning after their confrontation. When she'd recovered from the unexpected encounter, she'd smiled cheerfully. "Beautiful morning, isn't it?"

"Lovely," he'd answered, making the one word

sound anything but. Then he'd climbed in his truck and promptly driven away.

Hallie had sat in her car, hands gripping the steering wheel as she battled wave upon wave of sadness.

She didn't see Steve again until Thursday. Her week had been limping along as well as could be expected and then—wham, she ran into Steve at the local grocery. They chatted, but the camaraderie was gone. Their conversation was forced, their enthusiasm false. Afterward, it seemed to her that the hole in her heart had grown larger, more ragged. It would always be like this, she realized. Seeing him would always be a reminder of what might have been. And she was reasonably certain from Steve's reactions that he felt the same way.

Something had to be done.

Friday afternoon, Meagan and Kenny stopped by her place. Apparently Steve wasn't home from work yet. "Hi, Hallie," the girl said, coming in and collapsing onto the sofa. Kenny helped himself to the television remote control.

"You two look like you're ready to go back to school," Hallie remarked. Both seemed bored, uninterested, lacking in energy. Meagan was half on and half off the sofa, and Kenny flipped through television channels as if he were counting them, instead of watching them.

"Mom and Kip made up," Meagan told her.

Hallie was pleased to hear it, particularly for the children's sake. She sat down on the sofa between them. "I have something to tell you both."

"What?" The kids perked up immediately.

"I bet you're marrying Dad," Kenny said, and stuck out his tongue at his sister.

"No."

"Hasn't Dad asked you yet?" This came from Meagan, and she sounded disappointed. "Don't worry, he will."

"No." Hallie folded her hands together. "I listed my condo with a real-estate agent." At their blank look she continued, "It's up for sale."

"Are you moving in with Dad?"

"No—I'm moving." It had been a difficult decision, one she'd debated all week. Then, when she'd almost made up her mind, she'd talked it over with a friend in real estate—the same one who'd found her this condo. Gabby convinced her the market was right to sell. That cinched it for Hallie.

This horrible tension between Steve and her wasn't going away. It would only get more awkward, and their friendship would become more and more forced. If she was ever going to find a man to marry, it wouldn't be while she lived next door to the man she already loved.

Nor was Hallie sure she could keep her feelings about his ex-wife to herself. It would hurt too damn much to watch him run to Mary Lynn every time the woman had a problem. Every time she felt like yanking the leash. It was useless to fight a losing battle.

"You're moving?" Meagan asked, her voice filled with shock.

"Eventually. Not right away. I have to sell my place first."

"But why?" Kenny wailed.

She ruffled his hair.

This was the question she wasn't sure she could answer. Hallie could think of no way to explain that she was leaving in order to protect her heart. She was still struggling with a response when Kenny asked another question. "Does Dad know?"

"Not yet." Hallie hadn't gathered the courage to tell Steve. Nor had she wanted a For Sale sign posted in her front yard.

"When are you moving?" This time the question was Meagan's.

"I don't know, but it probably won't be soon. It'll take several months to sell and a couple more to handle all the paperwork. I'll be around for a long time yet." She would miss Steve's children, almost as much as she'd miss him. "It doesn't mean you won't see me again." She could tell that neither one believed her, but she meant what she said. She'd come to care deeply for Meagan and Kenny and would make every effort to keep them in her life.

"It won't be the same around here with you gone," Kenny said morosely.

They didn't get a chance to finish the conversation. Steve arrived home as she was trying to reassure the kids; with quick goodbyes, they rushed out the door to join their father. Just as she suspected, it didn't take them long to deliver her news. He was pounding at her front door a minute later.

"Is it true?" he demanded brusquely when she opened the door.

She nodded. "Yes. I put my place on the market."

His eyes widened momentarily and then a slow sad smile touched his mouth. "I guess you were right, after all." He retreated a couple of steps, backing away from her.

"I generally am," she said, hoping humor would help. "How am I right this time?"

"What you said about the two of us. It'd never work. You recognized that before I did."

His words felt like a slap in the face. Hallie had no response, and even if she had, she doubted she could have spoken right then. Her heart actually hurt.

He buried his hands in his pockets. "I wish you well, Hallie McCarthy."

"You, too, Steve Marris." Her voice sounded weak and almost unrecognizable to her own ears.

He nodded once, then turned and walked away.

Thirty-Two

Wide Awake And Dreaming

September 7

I can't believe this summer is almost over.

I was reading over my goal planner and it struck me that here it is, nine months into the year, and I don't have even a single prospect for a husband. What's sad is that I don't care anymore. I suspect this is my ego making excuses for me.

Again and again I'm reminded of what happened with Donnalee. Sanford seemed wonderful, perfect for her. I can still hear some of her so-called friends when they learned she'd broken the engagement. But she was right, because now I'd say I've never seen her happier (or me more miserable). It was a painful time for Donnalee, but in the end she found the man she can love for the rest of her life. A man who shares her vision of the future. If she'd married Sanford, every time she saw a mother and child, she would've longed for a child of her own. In time that desire would almost certainly have destroyed their relationship.

I feel like I'm doing the same thing with Steve. Saving myself a lot of unnecessary grief. He loves Mary Lynn, and he's never bothered to claim otherwise. I don't have a chance competing against his first love.

Damn, this is so hard, especially right now when we see each other practically every day.

The most embarrassing thing happened yesterday afternoon. I was standing in line at the bank—not one of my favorite pastimes—and out of the blue, for no reason I can determine, tears appeared in my eyes and I just couldn't make them go away. I was mortified. I thought at first it might have something to do with missing my dad, but I don't think so. I do miss him—not a day passes when he doesn't come to mind for one reason or another—but I believe I've adjusted to his death. So has Mom. My gut feeling is these tears have more to do with Steve. It isn't easy to stop loving someone—which gives me a bit of insight into his continued involvement with his first wife.

It'll be better once I've moved. I was so surprised and grateful when my condo sold. Gabby had told me it could take as long as six months. I was in shock when I received a respectable offer the first week it was listed. I'm anxious to leave. Anxious to get on with my life. The deal should close in another week, now that the new owner's financing is approved.

I guess I can last another week living next

door to Steve. What worries me more is standing next to him at Donnalee's wedding in Oc-
tober. I'm her maid of honor and Steve is best
man. I just pray I don't repeat the scene from
the bank.

A trickle of sweat rolled down Donnalee's bared abdomen as she sat in the rocking chair in front of Todd's
summer home. A-frame cabins didn't traditionally have
large front porches, but he'd added one several years
before, building it himself. Donnalee loved sitting there
in the afternoon shade, looking out over the water. Often she relaxed with a good book while Todd fished or
worked about the property.

She wore shorts, and hoping it would cool her off,
she'd unfastened her blouse and tied the loose ends
together. Closing her eyes, she draped one leg over the
side arm of the rocker, dangling her bare foot.

No one from the office would recognize her. Not
without an expensive business suit and makeup. Not
with her midriff exposed and her hair in pigtails.

Donnalee was happy, happier than she'd been since
she was a child. Happy because she was deeply in love.

Hard as it was to believe, their wedding was less
than a month away. Todd had wanted her to move in
with him, and in reality, she might as well be living at
his place now, but she continued to hang on to her own
apartment. Every weekend they spent here, at the lake.

As a lazy afternoon breeze blew off the water, she
continued to rock slowly back and forth. She dreamed
of the future, the years to come, the family they would
have.

Donnalee was immeasurably grateful to Hallie. It

was because of her friend that she'd found Todd. But thinking about Hallie made her frown. Donnalee was worried about her. Worried about Steve, too. What a pair they were, both headstrong and stubborn.

She heard the porch creak and opened her eyes to find Todd approaching. She smiled and held her hand out to him. How good he looked, so tanned and handsome, so strong in mind and body. Often just seeing him produced a physical ache in her. One that was even deeper than sexual need—although they'd done their share of expressing *that,* too. The ache she experienced went beyond physical longing. It was a heartfelt sense of joy.

Todd clasped her hand in his and raised it to his lips. "You frowned just now. Are you worried about something?" He claimed the rocker next to hers, still holding her hand.

"I was thinking about Hallie."

Todd didn't respond right away. "I'd like to shake those two."

"So would I," Donnalee said. Although she didn't say so, her sympathies were with Hallie, but she'd heard both sides—and she knew her friend well enough to recognize that Hallie was equally at fault.

"Steve's been in a foul mood for weeks," Todd grumbled. "I had the audacity to suggest he patch things up with Hallie and he damn near bit my head off. That's not like Steve." Todd paused. "He apologized later, and we went out for a beer. The sad part is, he loves Hallie. He told me so himself."

This was news to Donnalee. "If he loves her, then why's he letting her move? I don't know that Hallie would admit it, but I think she was waiting for him to ask her not to go."

"He wouldn't."

"Why not?" Donnalee wanted to understand why two people who so obviously loved each other would allow this to happen.

"Well, Mary Lynn manipulated him for years. He's had enough of it. Steve refuses to play those games anymore."

"But Hallie's not like that! And no one knows it better than Steve."

"Another reason—he doesn't want a woman who'll walk out on him at the first sign of a disagreement. If Hallie loves him as much as you think, she should've been willing to work out whatever was wrong."

"That's not how Hallie sees it. She believes Steve will always put Mary Lynn's needs above hers. She decided long ago that if she got married she wanted a man who's as committed to the relationship as she is. Hallie couldn't see Steve committing himself to her alone. I don't blame her, after the way he's behaved."

"Just because he went to help Mary Lynn doesn't mean he doesn't love Hallie."

"You know, I don't think Steve was keen on marrying Hallie."

Now it was Todd's turn to frown. "Did she tell you that?"

"Yes...sort of." She sighed. "And now Hallie hasn't mentioned Steve in some time. I hate to pry, but I can see she's miserable. She's deluded herself into thinking this move will be a solution."

"Everything else aside, isn't that running away from him, instead of settling all this?" Todd asked.

"No." The force of Donnalee's feelings drove her out of the rocking chair and to the porch steps, where she sank down, arms resting on her knees. "She doesn't know what else to do. She's in love with Steve, but she's afraid."

"Afraid of what?"

"Steve's feelings for Mary Lynn, and her own for him. She's afraid she's always going to play second fiddle. You have to admit Steve's given her plenty of reason to assume so."

"Mary Lynn's remarried."

"Does that change Steve's feelings for her?"

"I don't know," Todd said reluctantly. "I'd like to think so, but who's to say?"

"Steve?" Donnalee suggested.

"All I can tell you is that he's grieving for Hallie as much as he ever grieved over the end of his marriage."

Donnalee felt an overpowering sadness for Hallie and Steve. "We can't ever let this happen to us," she said, emotion thickening her voice.

"We won't," Todd promised. He moved from the rocker to sit next to her on the step and placed his arm around her shoulders.

"They won't be able to avoid each other at the wedding." She twisted about and leaned against him, absorbing his strength.

"I'd like to think we might be responsible for getting them back together," he murmured into her hair.

"It would be fitting, since it's because of them that *we're* together."

Todd's hand reached inside the opening of her blouse. His fingertips slid close to her breast.

"Todd," she whispered in warning, "you're flirting with temptation."

"Oh, I'm more than flirting with it, Donnalee."

She smiled at him. They slept together every night

and joked that they'd be all worn out before the honeymoon. "Will it always be this good with us?" she asked in a whisper.

Todd smiled, as if giving serious consideration to her question. "I certainly hope so. Sometimes after we've made love, I have to stop and pinch myself to believe I've found you."

She shut her eyes and bit her lip when his hand closed firmly around her bare breast. Her body quickly responded; every part of her seemed to release a collective sigh. Taking advantage of her weakness for him, Todd quickly eased his hand between her thighs.

"I went a hell of a long time without a woman in my life and never gave it a thought. But I don't know that I can last ten minutes longer without making love to you." His voice was rough with need.

She moaned stiffly and rolled her head back. "I haven't made the bed yet."

"Good, then we won't need to worry about messing it up."

"Don't you think we should use a bit more restraint?" she asked halfheartedly.

"No." He unfastened the zipper on his jeans. "You're driving me crazy," he said huskily in her ear. He had her blouse completely open now and was molding her breasts with his hands. His kisses left her breathless, his tongue probing her lips and seeking entry.

Donnalee was grateful the property was secluded, seeing that they couldn't keep their hands off each other. She suspected that in time this powerful need of theirs would wane, but it hadn't happened yet and showed no signs of doing so anytime soon.

Todd urged her toward the cabin.

Looping her arms around his neck, Donnalee whispered in his ear. "It's such a beautiful sunny afternoon. Are you *sure* you want to go inside?"

"I'm sure." Without giving her time to argue, he hoisted her over his shoulder and advanced into the cabin.

Donnalee couldn't help laughing, the happiness spilling out of her. "Put me down this instant."

"I have every intention of doing so." He carried her directly into the bedroom and set her on the mattress.

Donnalee smiled up at Todd and was humbled by the love she saw in him. She could search the rest of her life and never find a man she would love more. Slowly she raised her arms to him in open invitation.

"Oh, Todd. I love you so much." Her words were closer to a sigh.

Todd groaned and joined her on the bed, kissing her with a passion that left her head spinning and her thoughts incoherent.

Their lovemaking was wild, wanton and wonderful. Exhausted, they napped afterward. Donnalee awoke to find Todd gently cradling her in his arms.

He kissed the side of her neck. "You're thoughtful again."

"I wish we could do something for Hallie and Steve," she whispered. "I'm tossing her my bridal bouquet," she went on.

"You think that'll help, do you?"

She could hear the smile in Todd's voice. "It certainly won't hurt."

"Is she dating again?" he asked unexpectedly.

"No. What about Steve?"

Todd's shoulders shook with amusement. "You're kidding, right?"

"No. He dates, doesn't he?"

"No. Hallie was the exception."

"She often is the exception," Donnalee murmured, wishing with all her heart that her best friend would experience the kind of happiness she'd found with Todd.

Thirty-Three

The Wedding

Panting and cursing, Hallie dragged the last box out of the bedroom and into the living room. She'd forgotten how much she hated moving, and this time was the most difficult yet. Physically and emotionally exhausted, she slumped onto the sofa. All she had to do now was wait for the movers.

All she had to do now was say goodbye.

It was the task she dreaded most. She knew she was going to miss Steve; she missed him already. She'd taken their friendship for granted and during the past few weeks without him—teasing her, helping her, laughing with her—the world had become a bleak, lonely place.

In an effort to ease the ache in her heart, she'd often stood at her kitchen window and gazed longingly toward his condo. Did he think of her as often as she thought of him? Did he stare out at her place, too? Did he wonder if he'd ever stop feeling so lost and lonely, the way she did?

Moving was supposed to be the answer, the only one she could come up with.

Out of sight, out of mind.

Would it be true?

Unable to stop herself, she glanced through the window at Steve's place. One last time. Just her luck to fall in love with a man who had bowling shoes for brains! She wasn't sure if that thought made her want to laugh or cry—or both.

Out of the corner of her eye, she saw a flash of color; the moving van had arrived. She opened her front door and secured the screen in the open position. The only thing left to do was step aside and let the brawny young men get to work.

Hallie did that, hurrying outside and out of their way. She shuffled aimlessly through the bright leaves that carpeted the lawn. She'd been there for barely a minute when Kenny appeared. He took one look at the movers and charged full speed toward Hallie, arms wide open.

She caught the boy in a hug. Kenny wrapped his thin arms around her neck and held on tight. "Do you *have* to move, Hallie?" he pleaded.

"Yes," she said, hoping he couldn't hear the tears in her voice. "I've got an apartment now." With her condo selling so quickly, she hadn't bought a new place yet. Nothing suited her. She found fault with every home she viewed, exasperating even someone as tolerant as Gabby, her real-estate agent and friend. Time had run out, and Hallie was forced to rent a place, for the next few months, at least, until she came across something she was interested in buying.

"Hallie?" Meagan raced across the yard and threw her arms around Hallie, too. "You're moving already?"

"Looks that way." No one was amused by her feeble joke, least of all herself.

"I don't want you to go," Kenny said, squeezing her neck harder.

Hallie hugged the boy, fighting back the emotion, wanting this to be over quickly because she wasn't sure she could bear much more. After a few moments she loosened Kenny's arms from around her neck. Straightening, she put an arm around his shoulder and held him close to her side. Meagan didn't seem to want to let go of her, either.

"We'll never see you again, will we?" Meagan's question was softly spoken.

"Of course you will!"

"When?" the girl demanded, challenging Hallie to give her a time and a place. "Where?"

"Whenever you want. Wherever you want. Just say the word and I'll find a way to be there." Hallie meant that. No matter how painful it was, she wouldn't abandon Meagan and Kenny. "Here," she said, handing them each a folded piece of paper. "This is my new address and phone number. I'll be on Federal Way—it's not too far. You can call me anytime, and visit, too."

Meagan read the information, but it didn't appear to satisfy her. "It won't be the same."

Hallie couldn't argue with that. "No, it won't be the same."

In what seemed like only minutes, the movers had everything she owned loaded in their truck. She checked the condo one last time to be sure they hadn't missed anything, Meagan and Kenny trailing along behind her. When she'd finished, Hallie discovered Steve standing outside.

They stared at each other, she on the top step and he on the grass.

"Meagan and Kenny are with me," she said, thinking he'd come looking for his children.

"I know. I thought I'd come and tell you goodbye myself."

"Oh." She couldn't think of a single sensible comment. As it was, she had to restrain herself from running into his arms. She ached for him, for his comfort. Her throat hurt from the effort it cost to hold back her tears. Her whole body shook with suppressed longing.

This was hell, she decided. Saying goodbye to Steve and his children, walking away, not knowing if she'd see him again after Donnalee and Todd's wedding. Hoping, wishing, praying things could be different—and knowing they couldn't.

"We're ready now, miss," one of the movers shouted from the cab of the truck.

Hallie briefly turned her attention from Steve. "I'll be right there."

"Don't worry, lady," the second man shouted back. "We're getting paid by the hour. Take as long as you need." The two men laughed.

Steve's hands were buried deep in his pants pockets. "You'd better go."

She nodded. Kenny and Meagan crowded around her.

"Hallie says we can come visit her new place anytime. Can we Dad?"

His gaze continued to hold hers. "If it's okay with Hallie."

"I'd like that, Steve. I'm going to miss...all of you." Her original intention had been to say only the children's names, but that would have been a lie. She'd miss him more. She'd mourn him, yearn for him, cry over him.

"Goodbye, Hallie."

"Goodbye, Steve."

While she still had the courage, she deliberately turned her back to him and locked the front door. Then she dropped a kiss on each child's head and raced past Steve to her car.

The dress Donnalee had chosen for Hallie to wear as maid of honor was one of the most beautiful she'd ever owned. It was simple and elegant, a pale rose that did wonders for her skin. She felt beautiful in it. And thin. Every time she studied her reflection, all she could think of was Steve's reaction when he saw her. But then, thinking about Steve had become something of a pasttime. No, an obsession. Every night she went to bed thinking about him; every morning she woke up to those same thoughts of him.

"He'll go out of his mind," Donnalee whispered.

It took Hallie a moment to realize her best friend was talking about Todd when he saw his wife-to-be in her wedding dress.

"Yes, he will," Hallie confirmed.

The wedding itself was going to be a brief simple ceremony, with only Steve and Hallie as attendants. The guests were family and a few select friends. Not so for the reception; Donnalee and Todd had built strong friendships through the years and wanted to invite as many of their friends as possible to share in their joy. There would be dinner, dancing, drinks.

Hallie hadn't seen Steve in two weeks. Fourteen days. That didn't seem so long, but it felt like fourteen years. She'd eagerly looked forward to the wedding...and yet she'd dreaded it more each day.

She longed to see him, yet was afraid to see him.

She was afraid of reviving, strengthening, her love for Steve, afraid of suffering the loneliness, the sense of loss all over again. She wasn't sure she could go through it a second time.

Her gaze automatically sought him out as the four of them crowded around Pastor Channing in the small chapel. Steve's eyes met hers, and with effort she managed to offer him a smile. One that wasn't returned. She quickly looked away.

The ceremony, short though it was, moved Hallie to tears. Donnalee and Todd gazed at each other, wrapped up in their love. For Hallie, their happiness was almost painful to see, and yet she was thrilled for her friends.

Steve stood there stiffly throughout the ceremony. Other than those first few moments, he completely ignored her. When they all signed the wedding certificate, Hallie's hand trembled. Steve showed no sign of emotion, his signature strong and bold.

Donnalee and Todd had hired a vintage 1928 Ford to drive them from the church to the reception at a nearby hotel.

Once they'd climbed into the car amid clapping and cheers, Meagan hurried to Hallie's side. "Hallie, Hallie!" She clamped her arms around Hallie's waist. "You look so pretty. Doesn't she, Dad?" she called to Steve, who was standing a few feet away.

"Lovely," he responded, and lowered his mask long enough to let his appreciation show in his eyes.

His brief admiring look greatly boosted Hallie's sagging spirits.

"Dad's new neighbors moved in and they don't have kids." This disgruntled remark came from Kenny. The boy wore an obviously new suit, complete with tie.

Hallie would wager it had taken a good deal of talking and bribing before Kenny agreed to the outfit.

"The new neighbors are okay," Meagan said.

Hallie had met the young couple and thought they were extremely nice. "I'm sure they'll have children soon enough."

"What bothers the kids most is that the new neighbors aren't you," Steve explained with a shrug. "But that's life. People come and people go. They'll adjust, just like I have." He seemed to be going out of his way to tell her he didn't miss her, didn't need her. That whatever he'd felt for her was gone.

"We all miss you, Hallie," Meagan said, as if to counter her father's cruel words. "It doesn't seem right without you there."

It didn't feel right to her, either, but she certainly couldn't say so.

The hotel where the reception was being held was filled with guests by the time they arrived. Applause broke out when Donnalee and Todd stepped inside the gaily decorated room. Hallie stood in the reception line between Donnalee and her parents. Todd stood next to Steve, and Steve next to Todd's mother and father.

Hallie gave up counting the number of hands she shook and the number of names she heard. Remembering everyone was a lost cause, so she just smiled and shook hands.

The reception line was followed by dinner. Hallie and Steve were assigned to the head table with Donnalee and Todd. She found him staring at her once, and she smiled, hoping to lessen the tension between them. She wasn't sure if it was the baked salmon or the champagne that went with it, but Steve finally began to relax. She did, too.

Once the staff had removed the dishes and the wedding cake was served, the music started. Donnalee and Todd danced the first dance, holding each other close. As was tradition, Steve escorted Hallie onto the floor next, but from the loose way he held her, she might as well have been his sister.

They'd never danced together before. What amazed her was how coordinated their movements were, almost as if they'd been partners for years. Almost as if her body sensed and followed his body's movements.

When the music ended, she thought she heard Steve sigh with relief.

"Come on, Steve, it wasn't so bad, was it?"

He stared at her blankly.

"Dancing with me," she elaborated.

He reached for a fresh glass of champagne. "Bad enough."

"I didn't step on your toes, did I?"

"No," he muttered, "just my heart."

"What about *my* heart?" she asked, angered by his response.

"I must say it looks mighty fine in that dress you're wearing. Let me guess who picked it out. Donnalee, right?" He didn't wait for her to answer. "The woman's too smart for her own good."

"What's that supposed to mean?"

"It means it's time for me to shut up and sit down before I make an even bigger ass of myself." He strode off the dance floor.

Hallie wasn't about to let him stop now, so she ran after him. If he realized she was right behind him, he didn't show it. Steve sat down at the table where Meagan and Kenny awaited him. A balding middle-aged man, Todd's uncle by marriage if Hallie remembered correctly, caught her by the arm.

"How come a pretty little gal like you doesn't have a dance partner?" He slid his arm securely about her waist and Hallie could see that Todd's uncle had had a few drinks too many.

"I'm so sorry, Harry," she said. "I've already promised this dance to my friend."

"Your friend?"

Hallie winked at Kenny and held out her hand. "I believe you wanted this dance?"

Kenny leapt to his feet and, taking her hand, led Hallie toward the dance floor. The music was fast-paced and lighthearted. Kenny solemnly clenched her hands in his as they stepped onto the polished oak floor.

"Dad needs another bowling partner," Kenny announced. "I told him he should ask you."

"Really?" Hallie didn't know how to respond.

"He said you wouldn't be interested."

"He did?"

"Are you?" Kenny pressed.

"I...I'm not sure."

"Is it 'cause you have a new boyfriend?"

Hallie smiled and shook her head. "No."

Kenny was silent for a couple of minutes. "Did you know Kip's back?"

"Yes—Meagan told me." Although Hallie wasn't sure of the details.

"He's divorced. Mom thought he might be a bigmist, but he's not."

"I'm glad to hear that." Hallie could appreciate the worry Mary Lynn had suffered while that mess got itself sorted out. It explained, too, what the big crisis had been when Steve disappeared overnight. Not for the first time, she felt guilty of overreaction that miserable Monday morning.

"I asked Dad if he was going to marry again. You wanna know what he said?"

"No."

Kenny acted as if he hadn't heard her. "He said that if he couldn't marry you, there wasn't anyone else he was interested in. He decided to join a men's bowling league this year."

Hallie wasn't sure of the significance of the men's bowling league, but she did understand the first part of what Kenny had told her. Her heart felt weak with excitement.

"Excuse me." She heard Steve's familiar voice behind her. "I'd like to cut in."

"Sure, Dad." Kenny beamed his father a huge smile and walked off the dance floor.

Thirty-Four

The Wedding Bouquet

Steve couldn't figure out what had prompted him to ask Hallie to dance. One thing was sure: the minute she walked into his embrace he was sorry he'd asked her. Her body, all soft and feminine, gently gliding into his arms, was the purest form of torture he'd ever experienced.

Steve closed his eyes. This was heaven. No, it was hell. He didn't want to feel the things he did for this woman, but had found himself incapable of *not* feeling them. Of forgetting. She haunted his dreams, and seemingly dissatisfied with that, she haunted every waking minute, as well.

As luck would have it, the music was slow and sultry. He noticed that neither of them felt compelled to speak. Steve suspected he couldn't have gotten a word out, even if he'd known what to say. Hallie in his arms again was enough. It felt incredibly good—too damn good. He scowled. She was the one who'd slammed the door in his face. She was the one who'd put her house on the market and moved. Talk about cutting her losses! With little more than a backward glance, she'd cast him out of her life. Well, a man had his pride, and although it had been mighty cold comfort, he wasn't crawling back to her. No, siree. Not him.

Nor was he interested in a woman who hightailed it out at the first sign of trouble. What irked him most was that their entire argument had centered on Mary Lynn. She'd called him in great relief a few days after her panic attack and told him Kip *had* gotten the divorce and had shown her the papers to prove it. While he was pleased Mary Lynn wasn't involved with a bigamist, her news had come too late to help him. He'd already lost Hallie.

The music ended and they parted, and both of their own accord moved off the dance floor and in different directions, Steve to his table where the kids were waiting, and Hallie to another. Over the next couple of hours Steve noticed that Hallie danced with a number of other partners. He stopped counting how many after six. When he couldn't stand to watch any longer, he turned his back to the dance floor. He had another glass of champagne, danced with Meagan and then with someone's great-aunt.

"Aren't you going to dance with Hallie again?" Kenny asked.

"No." He downed the last of his champagne in one big gulp, then snared a fresh glass from a passing waiter. He drank enough to dull the ache in his heart and increase the one in his groin. That he'd never gone to bed with Hallie was a blessing in disguise. He wanted her even now. He couldn't, wouldn't, lie to himself about that. But he feared that if they *had* made love, he'd never have found the strength to let her walk out of his life.

"Did you ask her to be your bowling partner?" Meagan demanded.

Steve shook his head. He could tell he was a big disappointment to his children. They loved Hallie. Well, they weren't alone, but a man had his limits.

"Hallie's not dating anyone," Kenny told him. "I asked her."

"Let's talk about something else, all right?"

"Mom's remarried," Meagan reminded him, tugging at his sleeve.

His daughter's assessment caught him off guard. He didn't need anyone to remind him that Mary Lynn was out of his life. It was Hallie he wanted, Hallie he longed for. Hallie who owned his heart.

Without questioning the right or wrong of it, he set the champagne glass aside and strolled across the room to where she was standing. The music had started again. Another slow ballad.

Wordlessly he offered her his hand. She hesitated before giving him hers. Then he led the way to the dance floor.

"We already danced," she whispered, sounding nervous. "Twice."

"I know. The first two times were for appearance's sake. This time it's for me." He brought her close, close enough to feel her breasts against his chest. Close enough to tell her without words the powerful effect she had on him.

She held herself stiff and unyielding. "For you? I don't understand."

"You seem to forget I was denied the pleasure of making love to you."

Her chin shot up to a lofty angle. "Not for lack of opportunity."

"I'll admit the fault was my own."

This seemed to appease her. "It seems this may well be my last chance," he said.

"You're not making any sense. Maybe we should stop now."

"Not on your life." He moistened the side of her neck with the tip of his tongue and was gratified to feel reaction ripple through her.

"Steve…I don't think this is a good idea." Her protest was weak. He saw she'd closed her eyes and seemed to have trouble holding up her head.

While his options were limited, especially with his children looking on, Steve didn't let the mere fact that two hundred people were watching stand in his way. His imagination would work just fine. With his mouth close to her ear, he told her in scintillating detail how he'd planned to love her. How he'd dreamed of it every night since, thought of little else but having her in his bed—and in his life.

While their bodies swayed gently to the music, he held her mesmerized with a whispered account of how he'd intended to satiate their need for each other. Sparing nothing, he told her all they'd missed, all that their pride had cost them.

He didn't know that his words were having the desired effect until he heard her soft gasp against his throat.

The music ended, but they didn't leave the dance floor. Didn't move out of each other's embrace. His arms tightened as he realized that if he lost Hallie this time, he'd forever regret it.

He'd assumed, he'd hoped, that the music would start again. It didn't. Instead, there was an announcement that Donnalee was about to throw the bridal bouquet.

Hallie eased herself out of Steve's arms, keeping her gaze lowered.

Steve glanced over his shoulder to discover that a group of eager young women had gathered around Donnalee, jockeying for position.

Donnalee stood on tiptoe. "Hallie, where are you?"

"I...have to go."

"So I see," he muttered, more than a little disgruntled.

She moved away from him, joining the entourage crowding the bride. Hallie made her way to the back and raised her arms. Once she saw her best friend, Donnalee turned and blithely tossed the bouquet over her shoulder.

It seemed to Steve that she aimed for Hallie, but it wasn't Hallie who captured the prize. A girl, hardly older than Meagan, leapt a good three feet off the ground and grabbed the bouquet in midair. Grumbles and murmurs followed as the teenager displayed the prize, waving it exuberantly over her head. Steve smiled at her display of joy, but when he went to look for Hallie again, he discovered she was gone.

Gone.

The best Steve could figure, she'd disappeared with Donnalee, who had changed out of her wedding dress and into a pretty pink suit before leaving with Todd for the airport.

She'd be back, he reassured himself. He could be patient; considering how long he'd waited already, a few extra minutes wouldn't hurt.

Hallie never did return to the reception.

Defeated, Steve sat with Meagan and Kenny. It was for the best, he tried to convince himself. It was over.

That was the way she wanted it. From this point on, there'd be no need to see each other again.

Steve didn't believe any of it.

As soon as he could leave without seeming impolite, Steve took his kids home. They both seemed tired and out of sorts, and his own mood wasn't much better. But despite his misgivings about being with Hallie again, he'd enjoyed the wedding. He'd certainly enjoyed dancing with her.

Today had brought back all the memories and all the hopes, the recollections of what could have been. Todd's happiness pleased him and at the same time made him conscious of his own loneliness. It also emboldened him. Maybe it wasn't too late for him and Hallie....

"I'm going to bed," Kenny said as soon as they got home. He'd already removed the suit coat and was working on the tie.

"I am, too," Meagan chimed, yanking off her party shoes.

'I'm going out,' Steve announced.

Meagan and Kenny stopped what they were doing and stared.

"Where are you going?"

The decision made, Steve didn't hesitate. "To talk to Hallie."

Kenny inserted two fingers in his mouth and let out a whistle loud enough to shatter crystal. Then he and Meagan exchanged high tens, slapping hands with their arms raised above their heads.

"Go for it, Dad."

"Yeah!" Kenny had finally managed to pull off his tie, and now he twirled it around like a New Year's streamer. "We want you to marry her."

"A lot has to be decided before we talk about marriage." Unsure how this meeting would go, Steve didn't want to build up his children's expectations.

"I knew she was the one for you ages ago," Meagan said, sounding very much like the teenager she was soon to become. It wouldn't be long now before she was convinced she was far wiser than any of the adults in her life.

"I said so first," Kenny argued.

"No, *I* did," Meagan returned with an air of superiority. "I told you I thought Hallie would be a good wife for Dad the very first time we met her. Remember?"

Whether or not he did, Kenny wasn't about to admit it.

"I don't know how long I'll be," Steve said.

"Take your time," Meagan told him.

"All the time you need," his son added.

Steve hurried out to his car, and as he started the engine, he saw Meagan and Kenny standing in the window, watching him. He waved and they excitedly waved back.

On the short drive to Federal Way, Steve mulled over his approach. After a quick stop at the grocery, he pulled into the guest parking lot at her new complex. It took him another ten minutes to find her apartment. After checking the number against the one listed on the folded sheet of notebook paper, he stepped onto the porch. If the lights were any indication, she was home.

His head was spinning, his skin was clammy, and his heart was dangling precariously from his sleeve when he pushed her doorbell. The door opened and his carefully thought-out greeting stuck in his throat.

A man answered. "Yes?" He was tall and young, too young for Hallie.

"I must have the wrong number." Frowning, Steve glanced down at his paper a second time, wondering if he'd copied the information incorrectly.

"Are you looking for Hallie McCarthy?"

Steve's face shot up. "Yes."

"Then come on in. She's in the bedroom with the baby."

Steve realized he was frowning again.

"I'm Jason, Julie's husband."

"Ah, yes." As Steve told him who he was and the two exchanged handshakes, Steve remembered that Julie was Hallie's little sister. Baby Ellen's mother. Come to think of it, Hallie owed him major bucks for his help in getting the baby to sleep that night last spring.

"Julie and I are on our way to Hawaii, and we're spending the night with Hallie before we catch a flight in the morning."

"I see," Steve muttered. His timing couldn't have been worse. "Perhaps I should talk to Hallie later." Not knowing what else to do with the bouquet of yellow roses he'd bought, he set them on top of the television.

He was halfway to the parking lot when he heard Hallie shout his name. He turned, shoulders squared, back rigid.

"If you walk away from me now, Steve Marris, there'll be hell to pay."

Hallie stood there, arms akimbo. "Is there a reason you brought me flowers?"

"Yes," he said, playing it cool. "It's a wedding bouquet. You were cheated back there and I wanted to give you another chance to catch it."

"Are you going to provide the groom to go with those flowers?" she asked, not missing a beat.

"That all depends," he called back. It seemed silly to be standing half a football field apart shouting at each other. He took several steps in her direction. She did likewise. They stopped with about five feet still between them.

"Why are you here?" she asked softly, her beautiful eyes pleading with him to say what she wanted to hear. "And if you tell me it's because you need a bowling partner, you go straight to jail."

"If I told you I loved you, would that get me past Go so I can collect my two hundred dollars?"

"It's a step in the right direction."

He grinned.

"Why do you love me?" she asked.

"Why?" Of all the things he'd expected her to say, this wasn't it. He rubbed his hand along the back of his neck, giving her a puzzled look. "No one told me there'd be a test."

"Is it so difficult?"

"No." But he had to get the answer right; he didn't want there to be any room for doubt.

"Because of Meagan and Kenny?"

"No." He smiled as he said it. "Do you want me to count the ways?"

"It might help."

"I love you, Hallie, for who you are. For the way you love my children. For the way your eyes light up when you're excited. I love the crazy way you throw a bowling ball and still manage to knock down pins. I think you bake the best chocolate-chip cookies I've ever tasted."

"What about my chicken dinner?"

"It's wonderful, and so are you."

It seemed to him that her eyes were especially bright. He said, "You're zany and stubborn and strong-willed and wonderful. I'm crazy about you."

"How crazy?"

"Crazy enough to know I'm going to love you the rest of my life—and to know you're the best friend I'm ever going to find. Crazy enough to ask you to marry me."

"Marry you?"

He nodded. "That's why I brought a bridal bouquet."

"Bingo."

Steve laughed out loud. "Wrong game. All I want is to get past Go, collect what's due me and spend the rest of my life making love to you."

Hurrying forward, Hallie stumbled into his arms. He caught her and lifted her from the pavement, his arms tight around her waist. If he didn't kiss her soon, he'd go mad.

As if reading his thoughts, her mouth haphazardly searched for his. The kiss was hungry, even rough, a kiss without subtlety or gentleness. It took several more such kisses to appease the pent-up longing. Then, and only then, was he capable of truly appreciating the woman in his arms. He set her back down on the pavement and his hands were in her hair. Her ragged breath was warm against his skin. He inhaled her clean distinctive scent.

"That was the lowest, dirtiest trick anyone ever played on me," she told him, her hands clasped behind his neck.

"What was?"

"Making love to me on the dance floor. Do you have a clue what you were doing to me?"

"I was experiencing the same thing myself. Do you forgive me?"

She nodded, but her thoughts seemed a thousand miles away. "We're going to be married, and if you so much as *think* of sleeping with Mary Lynn again, I'll claw your eyes out."

He lowered his head enough so she'd see and hear the truth in his words. "I didn't sleep with her."

"Fine. If you ever lie down in the same bed with her, then."

"Agreed."

"It's all or nothing with me, Steve Marris."

"Hey, I wasn't the one who packed up and moved out at the first sign of trouble."

Hallie shook her head as if she regretted that. "I was trying to protect myself. I love you too much to lose you, and hell, I didn't know my condo was going to sell that fast."

"Lose me?"

"To Mary Lynn."

"Not hardly. It's true I didn't want the divorce, but it happened and there's no way to go back now. Mary Lynn has apparently found what she wants, and she's welcome to it. By the same token, I've found you."

"I...I didn't think you wanted to marry me."

"I don't take that kind of commitment lightly, Hallie. It's all or nothing with me, too."

She cupped his jaw and spread a dozen kisses over his face, her aim less than perfect; nevertheless, they had the desired effect—as she discovered when he pulled her close against him.

Suddenly she raised her eyes to his. He saw they'd gone dark and serious. "What about children?"

He'd given fair consideration to that question himself. Hallie wanted a family, and he wanted to be the one to father her children. "I got pretty good at the diapering business. I imagine I can dust off those skills for a new baby."

She let out a small happy cry.

"Right now I'm far more interested in making that baby," he said with a lascivious wink.

Pure happiness radiated from her entire being. Giggling, Hallie tossed back her head. "Me, too. Oh, Steve, I love you—and I want you so much—but..." She glanced over her shoulder. "We have to go to your place. My sister and her husband are in town for the night."

He groaned in frustration. "I've got Meagan and Kenny."

Hallie banged her forehead repeatedly against his shoulder.

"Can you believe it?" he said. "We're finally ready to make love and we can't find anyplace to do it."

Snuggling in his arms, Hallie kissed the underside of his jaw. "Let's be patient. We've got an entire lifetime."

Steve closed his eyes and wondered if a single lifetime was long enough to love Hallie properly—in bed and out of it.

Then again, he'd soon find out.

Epilogue

January 1—two years later

Unlike the past few years, I won't take time to be poetic and inspired. I'm a married woman now, and much too tired and happy. Steve is thrilled that Travis decided to make his debut a week early—for the simple reason that we can deduct him on our income tax! For my part, I could have used an extra week's sleep.

Our baby is so beautiful. Steve made me promise I wouldn't say that. Baby boys aren't supposed to be beautiful, but the only other word that suits him is *perfect*. Steve's delighted to have another son to share guy things with. He's such a wonderful, natural father, but, of course, I knew that!

Every time I remember the afternoon I went into labor, I start to laugh. Steve was so calm about everything. He'd assured me again and again that he knew what to do, that I didn't have a thing to worry about. He got so involved in the breathing techniques, he had everyone in his bowling league trained. He must have read ten books and quoted them so often, it was all I could do to listen.

Finally it happened. D-day (*D* for delivery). I'd been to the doctor the day before and he'd assured me labor could start at any time. Steve had his beeper with him. Meagan and Kenny had theirs, too. I think everyone was thoroughly disappointed that they were all at the house when my water broke. They'd been looking forward to getting beeped!

Then my levelheaded, oh-so-prepared husband lost it. When he saw me in pain, when he realized his new child was about to be born, he couldn't remember a thing. I wasn't much help. What surprised me was the intensity of the labor pains. I'd read and heard a lot about labor, but this wasn't like anything I'd anticipated. It hurt, right away. No gradual increase for me. Travis wanted to make his debut as quickly as possible.

With the first contraction—which was like a kick in the stomach—I doubled over and groaned. Steve immediately started barking orders like a drill sergeant. He had Meagan, Kenny and my suitcase in the car and was halfway down the driveway before he realized he'd forgotten something. Me. That flustered him even more, and he ran a stop sign. Meagan was shouting at him and Kenny, whose job it was to time the contractions, miscounted and said they were only thirty seconds apart. Convinced he'd never make it to the hospital in time, Steve pulled over to the side of the road and announced he'd have to deliver the baby himself. Before I could persuade him otherwise, he'd slapped on a pair of latex gloves and donned a surgical gown. Where he got it I'll never know.

Meagan took one look at me and rolled her eyes. Thank heaven she remained sane during all of this! By the time we arrived at the hospital, I was at the wheel. Kenny was in the back seat with his father, fanning him with the instructions for an emergency delivery. Meagan was in the front with me, and the two of us panted together.

All's well that ends well, as they say. Things moved quickly once we got to the hospital, and the birth was textbook perfect. Travis was born five hours later, and it was a contest to see who cried loudest, father or son.

Meagan and Kenny are thrilled with their little brother. Kenny's so pleased to have another boy in the family, and Meagan has to fight her father for the privilege of changing the baby's diaper!

I love being a mother. The other morning as I held Travis to my breast I felt tears in my eyes at the sheer wonder and joy of this little one in my arms. To think he's actually a part of me and Steve, that he came from my body. I thought about Dad, too. I'm sorry he wasn't here to welcome his first grandson. He'd be so proud to know we named Travis after him. Travis Douglas is a pretty big name for such a little boy.

I feel whole now, complete. The emotional void that opened up in me after Dad died doesn't seem as deep anymore. I have Steve now, and our family.

Two years ago when I first decided I wanted a husband and family, I had no idea how far this adventure would take me. But I'm actually glad I delayed it, because otherwise I wouldn't be married to Steve and I wouldn't be a step-mom to Meagan and Kenny—and we wouldn't have Travis. I can't imagine what my life would be like without them.

I sat down this morning with a cup of Seattle's finest coffee—brought to me by my husband—and my goal planner. Just as I do every January 1. It didn't take me long to realize that my goals have shifted from my business to my home life. For now, anyway.

And that's just fine. This matter of marriage—and motherhood—couldn't have worked out better!